What Reviewers Say About Bold Strokes' Authors

Kim Baldwin

"Her…crisply written action scenes, juxtaposition of plotlines, and smart dialogue make this a story the reader will absolutely enjoy and long remember." – **Arlene Germain**, book reviewer for the *Lambda Book Report* and the *Midwest Book Review*

Rose Beecham

"…a mystery writer with a delightful sense of humor, as well as an eye for an interesting array of characters…" – *MegaScene*

"…her characters seem fully capable of walking away from the particulars of whodunit and engaging the reader in other aspects of their lives." – *Lambda Book Report*

"…creates believable characters in compelling situations, with enough humor to provide effective counterpoint to the work of detecting." – *Bay Area Reporter*

Jane Fletcher

"…a natural gift for rich storytelling and world-building…one of the best fantasy writers at work today." – **Jean Stewart**, author of the *Isis* series

Radclyffe

"Powerful characters, engrossing plot, and intelligent writing…" – **Cameron Abbott,** author of *To the Edge* and *An Inexpressible State of Grace*

"…well-honed storytelling skills…solid prose and sure-handedness of the narrative…" – **Elizabeth Flynn**, *Lambda Book Report*

"…well-plotted…lovely romance...I couldn't turn the pages fast enough!" – **Ann Bannon**, author of *The Beebo Brinker Chronicles.*

"…a consummate artist in crafting classic romance fiction…her numerous best selling works exemplify the splendor and power of Sapphic passion…" – **Yvette Murray, PhD**, *Reader's Raves*

Justice Served

by

RADCLY*f*FE

2005

JUSTICE SERVED

ISBN 1-933110-15-5

This Trade Paperback Original Is Published By
Bold Strokes Books, Inc.,
Philadelphia, Pa, USA

First Edition: June 2005, Bold Strokes Books, Inc.

Credits
Editors: Stacia Seaman and Ruth Sternglantz
Production Design: Stacia Seaman
Cover Photos: Lee Ligon
Cover Design By Sheri (GRAPHICARTIST2020@HOTMAIL.COM)

By the Author

Romances

Safe Harbor
Beyond the Breakwater
Innocent Hearts
Love's Melody Lost
Love's Tender Warriors
Tomorrow's Promise
Passion's Bright Fury
Love's Masquerade
shadowland
Fated Love
Distant Shores, Silent Thunder

Honor Series

Above All, Honor
Honor Bound
Love & Honor
Honor Guards

Justice Series

A Matter of Trust (prequel)
Shield of Justice
In Pursuit of Justice
Justice in the Shadows
Justice Served

Change Of Pace: *Erotic Interludes*
(A Short Story Collection)

Acknowledgments

With each Justice entry I write, I say, "That's it. I'm done with this series." It's difficult to write on many levels, but each time I begin a new story in the series, the characters spring to life and I lose myself in their journey.

My beta readers sustain me through the long weeks of uncertainty as each tale unfolds and I question if I will ever be able to do the story justice. They never let me down, providing insight, encouragement, suggestions, and critiques with tender care. I count on them to keep me from going astray. Thank you Athos, Diane, Denise, Eva, Jane, JB, Paula, Robyn, and Shelley.

In addition, I'd like to extend my appreciation to all the members of the Radlist for constancy and inspiration, to Ruth Sternglantz and Stacia Seaman for fine editorial input, and to Linda Hill, for her vision and commitment to lesbian fiction.

Lee has never complained about the sacrifices she's made to help me realize a dream. For that, I am ever grateful. *Amo te.*

Radclyffe 2005

Dedication

For Lee
For Taking a Chance

Chapter One

Monday

I don't think the doctor wants you going up and down stairs yet," warned the small blond in the skintight black Capri slacks, white ribbed tank top, and open-toed stack heels. October was around the corner, but Sandy Sullivan rarely wore more than the bare essentials.

"Have to try," Officer Dellon Mitchell grunted. Grimacing with the effort, she swung her injured left leg free of the crutch as she maneuvered up the first stair in the hospital stairwell. "You live on the third floor, remember?"

"We can stay at your place, Dell. *You* have an elevator and a doorman, *remember*?" Hands on hips, Sandy stepped back to allow the young, dark-haired police officer to set her crutches onto the next stair, but stayed close enough to catch her should Mitchell lose her balance and topple over. Considering that Mitchell was a head taller and twenty pounds of muscle heavier, Sandy might have trouble breaking her fall, but she was not about to let anything else happen to her new lover.

"I don't want to lie around in my apartment." Sweating, Mitchell paused long enough to brush her forearm across her forehead. The shock of jet-black hair promptly tumbled back into her eyes. Her bad leg felt like it weighed fifty pounds, and she couldn't believe how much her arms were shaking. She didn't want Sandy to see that or she had a feeling she would be forcibly dragged back to bed. Even if Sandy *was* half her size, when she was fired up, she was unstoppable. "I want to be able to get back to work."

Mitchell also didn't want to point out that it would be better for both of them if they remained visible on the streets in Sandy's neighborhood, a part of town known for its small-time hustlers, corner drug dealers, and prostitutes. Mitchell had just begun an undercover assignment, and Sandy was supposed to be her girlfriend. The fact that the cover story had suddenly become the truth complicated issues, but they still needed to maintain appearances.

"What's the matter? Are you afraid you'll get a bad reputation if you have a hooker in your swanky apartment?" Sandy's tone was less accusatory than anxious as she watched Mitchell, still in her hospital gown. The young cop was as pasty white as she had been the night before, her dark blue eyes clouded with pain that she thought Sandy couldn't see. "Getting soft, rookie? I didn't think you cared what your *doorman* thinks."

"I don't," Mitchell said through gritted teeth. "Especially about you. But I care about people tying me *or* you to the action the other night."

Thirty-six hours before, Mitchell had been stabbed while apprehending several key suspects in an Internet pornography ring. Those arrests had climaxed weeks of work by an unusual team of Philadelphia police officers and civilian consultants led by Mitchell's mentor and role model, Detective Sgt. Rebecca Frye. Mitchell wanted back on that team more than she'd ever wanted anything in her life, except the young woman who peered at her anxiously with a frown on her pale, worried face. And the fastest way to get back on the team was to get back on her feet. "If I didn't blow my cover already, I don't want to now."

"Screw your cover. You're shaking, Dell."

"I'm okay."

"No, you're not." Sandy moved closer and wrapped her arm around Mitchell's waist. "You're just as stubborn and blockheaded as a certain *other* cop I've met. But you don't have to be like Frye all the time."

"It's not about Frye." Mitchell allowed herself to lean against Sandy while she caught her breath and swiped futilely at the sweat now beaded on her entire face. "I'm just not used to these crutches."

"Yeah. And it doesn't have anything to do with the fact that you just got operated on yesterday morning and lost a couple of buckets of blood before that, either." Sandy snorted in disgust. "Jesus, cops are such a pain in the ass."

"Are you going to bitch at me the *whole* time I'm laid up?" Mitchell feigned distress, but she was grinning. She leaned back against the wall, angling her body to take the weight off her leg while making room for Sandy to snuggle up against her.

"I don't know," Sandy replied, wrapping her arms around Mitchell's waist before kissing her neck. They'd been lovers for less than a week, and Sandy couldn't look at her without getting wet. "It depends on how long it takes you to get better. If it takes *too* long, I could get very cranky."

"You think I won't be able to take care of business?" Mitchell dipped her head, brought her mouth to Sandy's, and ran her tongue lightly over the surface of Sandy's bottom lip. Sandy moaned softly, and Mitchell's heart rate skyrocketed. *Oh man, now I* will *fall down.* With the heat of Sandy's body warming her all the way through, she didn't care a bit if they ended up in a heap on the floor. As she flicked the tip of her tongue over the inside of Sandy's lip, she snaked a hand beneath the back of Sandy's tank top. She could practically span the entire width of her girlfriend's small waist with one hand. "God, you feel good," she muttered.

"I don't think this activity is on the prescribed list of treatments for stab wounds," a voice on the verge of laughter announced from behind them.

Mitchell, sliding her arm protectively around Sandy's shoulders, jerked her head up. Her gaze met the laughing brown eyes of her surgeon, Ali Torveau. Mitchell blushed.

"Uh…morning."

"Good," Sandy grumbled, lifting her chin in Dr. Torveau's direction. "Maybe Dell will listen to *you*." Carefully, she disentangled herself from her girlfriend and moved away. "She won't admit she's about to keel over."

"Sandy," Mitchell complained with a sigh.

"It's true, Dell."

Torveau leaned against the wall in the stairwell and folded her arms across her chest, her eyes narrowing as she watched Mitchell maneuver down to the landing. "How do you feel?"

When Mitchell hesitated, Ali added, "And don't try to snow me."

"Uh…"

"That bad, huh?" Ali pushed away from the wall and eased over to Mitchell. Casually, she slipped her hand under Mitchell's elbow. "Come on. Let's go back to your room and have a look."

Once Mitchell was back in bed, Ali collected disposable gloves and dressings from a cart in the hallway and prepared to change the dressing on Mitchell's left thigh. She glanced sideways at Sandy, who was standing by the head of the bed, her hand on the police officer's shoulder. "You okay with this?"

"I've probably seen worse."

Ali merely nodded. There was something in the young woman's eyes that spoke of hard truth. A minute later, she had the bandage open and perused the row of sutures that extended for ten inches from the top of Mitchell's midthigh down the inner surface. Carefully, she probed along both sides of the incision, then straightened. "The wound's nice and clean. Let's see how the artery is doing." When she finished palpating the pulses in Mitchell's foot, she nodded with evident satisfaction. "Everything is in working order."

"See. I knew that." Mitchell's voice was breathy with relief.

Sandy snorted again.

"However, your blood count this morning was lousy. If you were any older, I'd transfuse you. But I'd rather not unless it becomes a problem." As she spoke, the surgeon rewrapped Mitchell's thigh. "You feel crappy because you're weak, and you're not used to that."

"When will I feel better?" Unconsciously, Mitchell had reached out for Sandy's hand, and now she entwined her fingers with Sandy's much smaller ones. The strength in Sandy's grasp was comforting, and she held on tightly.

"It will probably take several months for your counts to come back up to normal, but you should start feeling better day by day." Ali smiled. "It just takes a little patience."

"Oh yeah, she's got *lots* of that." Although her tone was laced with sarcasm, Sandy regarded Mitchell tenderly.

"It seems to be an occupational trait," Ali replied. "If you've got someplace to stay where you won't have to do too much walking, you can go today."

"Okay! Yeah, we can make that work." Mitchell looked to her girlfriend for confirmation. "Right, San?"

Sandy sighed. "Yeah, yeah, rookie. If that's what you want."

The truth was, Sandy wanted Mitchell out of the hospital every bit as much as Mitchell wanted to go. The place scared her under the best of circumstances, and seeing her normally strong and capable lover weak and in pain was scaring her even more.

Softly, she stroked Mitchell's cheek. "We'll figure something out, baby."

❖

Dr. Catherine Rawlings pushed a stack of file folders aside and reached for her phone. "Yes, Joyce?"

"Rebecca's here," her secretary announced, adding without needing to be asked, "and you've got thirty minutes before your first appointment."

"Thanks. Tell her to come in."

Catherine waited behind her desk for the simple pleasure of watching her lover cross the room. They had met in this room not quite half a year before, when Detective Sgt. Rebecca Frye had been in the midst of a harrowing serial-murder investigation. They had begun their joint involvement in the case as polite adversaries and ended as passionate lovers. As if the whirlwind onslaught of unexpected love had not been enough, Rebecca had nearly died from a gunshot wound, and both she and Catherine were still recovering, physically and emotionally. Even had she not nearly lost Rebecca, Catherine doubted that the pleasure of seeing her for the first time after they'd been apart would have been any less. Rebecca, more than any woman she had ever known, moved her in the deepest reaches of her being. She smiled as the door opened and her tall blond lover, slender in her trademark tailored dark suit and coolly beautiful, entered her office.

"Hey," Rebecca said as she walked around the side of Catherine's desk and leaned down to kiss her. "Got a few minutes?"

"Mmm. On your way to see Dellon?" Catherine replied.

"That too." With an uncharacteristically self-conscious expression, Rebecca suddenly stepped back and slid her hands into the pockets of her trousers. "But I wanted to talk to you first. I…have some news."

"Oh?" Regarding her with concern, Catherine rose, walked around her desk, and slid an arm around her lover's waist. "Did something happen at your ungodly-early morning briefing with Captain Henry?"

"A lot," Rebecca conceded. "We worked out a compromise to keep the team together so that we can finish hunting down the leak in the department *and* have a shot at breaking this prostitution network, or whatever the hell it is, wide open at the same time."

"That's what you wanted, isn't it?" Catherine kept her voice neutral, a practice that was second nature to her from her many years of practicing psychiatry. She was still adjusting to the fact that her lover's profession carried with it the daily risk of injury or even death. Balancing the desire to support Rebecca in her work while dealing with her own fears and uncertainty was a constant challenge. Nevertheless, it was a struggle she kept to herself, knowing that Rebecca was a cop to her core. "To keep the team together?"

"Oh yeah. Absolutely." Rebecca curled an arm around Catherine's shoulder and rested her cheek against Catherine's thick auburn hair. "We're close to putting all the pieces together—who's been leaking confidential information and altering sensitive police files, who fingered Jimmy Hogan and Jeff Cruz for assassination, what's going on with the girls in the skin videos and the sex clubs, and how it all ties into organized crime. If we just have a little more time, we can break it."

It was impossible to miss the undercurrent of excitement and determination in her lover's voice. But Catherine, sensitive to nuance and inflection, heard something else there as well—reservation and frustration. Being next in line for the chairmanship of the Department of Psychiatry, she was no stranger to politics. "You said *compromise.* What did you have to give *him*?"

"It's not what I had to give," Rebecca grumbled. "It's what I had to *take*."

"Come sit down and tell me," Catherine murmured, drawing Rebecca toward the sofa opposite her desk. When they were settled side by side, she turned and rested her fingers on Rebecca's thigh. "So?"

"Avery Clark." Rebecca named the Department of Justice agent with obvious displeasure.

"He's back in the picture?" Catherine exclaimed with surprise. Avery Clark had been the federal government's liaison with Rebecca's team during the initial phases of their investigation into a widespread Internet pornography ring. However, when the joint task force had successfully made a key arrest, Clark had asserted jurisdictional primacy and cut Rebecca and her colleagues out of the information loop. Catherine couldn't imagine Rebecca or any of the other members of the team willingly working with Clark again.

"Oh yeah, he's back. And how." Rebecca blew out an exasperated breath. "No Clark, no team."

"Ah, so no choice." Catherine squeezed Rebecca's thigh sympathetically. "Sorry. But you'll find a way to make it work."

"Probably, but I don't know how I'm going to convince Sloan of it."

JT Sloan was the civilian computer consultant and a past DOJ agent herself whose history with the government was still shrouded in mystery. Whatever the unhappy association had been, Sloan's animosity toward the agency had grown exponentially when her lover Michael had been nearly killed in an assassination attempt. Sloan had been the intended target and, nearly wild with grief and guilt, she had attributed the tragedy in large part to Clark's withholding of critical information from the team.

"Sloan won't be a problem if you present it to her correctly."

Rebecca raised an eyebrow. "Oh? Your suggestion, Doctor?"

Catherine smiled softly. "Darling, what is the most important thing in the world to Sloan?"

"Michael," Rebecca answered immediately.

"Yes. Sloan wants to find the person who hurt her lover, but even more than that, she doesn't want to hurt Michael any further. You and I both know that the safest place for Sloan is on your team, not running around by herself. And Michael knows it too."

"That doesn't seem fair," Rebecca said, frowning. "Using Michael against Sloan."

"I love how honorable you are, but there's nothing *dishonorable* about this." Catherine leaned forward to brush her mouth over Rebecca's. "You're not using Michael. You're just offering Sloan the solution that's best for everyone."

Rebecca sighed. "You're right, but I'll bet she doesn't see it that way."

"She will. Just give her a little time." Catherine rested her cheek against Rebecca's shoulder and wrapped an arm loosely around her waist. "So it will be the whole team together again. Sloan and Jason on the computers, you and Watts on the street, and Dellon? What about Dellon and Sandy?"

"It depends on how quickly Mitchell recovers and if there are any problems as a result of the stabbing. You know she's going to need to be cleared by psych now."

Catherine, a civilian psychiatric consultant to the police department, stiffened nearly imperceptibly. "Yes. It's departmental policy after an officer is injured in the line of duty."

"So that could really hang her up—the paperwork and everything."

"You're not suggesting that I facilitate getting her back to work prematurely, are you?" Catherine's tone was still mild, but the question was edged in steel.

"I know better than that," Rebecca answered evenly. She kissed Catherine's forehead. "I *want* her to see you. I told you that before she was even injured. She's got some problems with her temper, and it's going to get her into trouble. This might be the perfect opportunity to get that all sorted out."

Catherine tilted her head and regarded her lover intently. "I do believe you're becoming a fan of psychotherapy."

Rebecca blinked and then laughed. "Well, maybe a fan of a certain psychiatrist."

"Oh, aren't you clever," Catherine murmured as she kissed Rebecca's neck. Tightening her grip on Rebecca's waist, she moved her lips to the corner of her lover's mouth before remembering where they were and what time it was. With a faint groan, she drew away. "Now I remember why it's a bad idea for you to visit me in the middle of the day."

"Seems like a really good idea to me." Rebecca's voice was husky and low.

Catherine moved back even further. "*You* might be able to recover from a quickie and head right back to work, but I don't think that I can."

Rebecca grinned. "Wanna try?"

Laughing, Catherine rose and held out her hand to her lover. "Tell Dellon I said hello and that I'll be over later to see her."

Catherine was the only one who called Mitchell by her full name, and it always gave Rebecca pause. It was a little disquieting, knowing that her lover had a very private and singular relationship with one of her officers—a young officer whom she had taken under her wing and whose career she intended to guide. She knew that Catherine would never discuss the details of her therapeutic relationships with anyone, but nevertheless, now and then, she wondered just what Mitchell said to Catherine in the quiet intimacy of their hours together.

"I will," Rebecca said, before adding, "Mitchell's being promoted. She's going to get her detective's shield."

"Rebecca, that's wonderful! Did you have something to do with that?"

Rebecca shook her head. "Absolutely not. Mitchell earned it, on the last operation and on this one. She's been an important part of the team, and she handled herself well under difficult circumstances."

"I'm so happy for her. It will mean so much to her."

"Yeah." Rebecca hesitated. "So am I."

"What?" Catherine asked, not following.

"Being promoted. Detective lieutenant."

Catherine stared. "And you're just telling me now? Rebecca! And you said *yes*?"

The possibility of Rebecca being promoted had been something the two of them had discussed before. Catherine had been in favor of it, secretly hoping that a more supervisory position would keep Rebecca off the streets and further away from potential harm—precisely why Rebecca had resisted.

Rebecca nodded.

"What part of this are you *not* telling me?"

"I more or less had to accept in order to keep the team together. And in exchange, I get to head the High Profile Crimes Unit within the division."

"I see," Catherine said slowly. "So in this case, a promotion doesn't mean a desk job."

Silently, Rebecca shook her head, watching Catherine intently.

Catherine walked behind her desk, sat down, and folded her hands in the middle of her blotter. After a few more seconds of silence, she said, "Congratulations. I'm very proud of you. And I'm glad you aren't being forced into a position where you would be unhappy."

"But you're not happy, are you?" Rebecca asked quietly.

"I *am* happy. I'm happy for you." Catherine lifted one hand and smiled. "I just need to rearrange my thinking a little bit."

Rebecca glanced at her watch. "We only have a few more minutes."

"That's my line, darling."

"Catherine," Rebecca said intently, moving around the side of the desk and leaning down over her lover. "I love you."

Catherine reached up and stroked Rebecca's cheek. "Go to work, Detective. Everything is all right."

"You're sure?"

Of one thing, Catherine was certain. She needed Rebecca more than she needed air, and Rebecca needed a clear mind to do the work she did safely. Whatever misgivings or disappointments she might have, she would not burden Rebecca with them now. "Of course I'm sure. I love you. Call me later?"

Rebecca kissed her swiftly. "You bet. I'll even bring home dinner."

"I'll hold you to that," Catherine called as the door closed behind her lover. Then she leaned back in her chair and closed her eyes. She too needed to be focused for the work she did, and she resolutely forced down the nagging kernel of fear beginning to grow in her depths.

Chapter Two

Rebecca discovered Detective William Watts waiting for her in the crowded main lobby of University Hospital. He slouched against the admissions counter chatting up the receptionist, who was laughing at something he had said. Rebecca mentally shook her head, wondering what it was about the large, often crude cop that some people found so appealing. She knew that Catherine, whose judgment she considered impeccable, liked him. When the out-of-shape, interminably shabby fifty-year-old detective had been assigned to work with her after the murder of her longtime partner, Jeff Cruz, she had resisted vehemently. Jeff had been her friend as well as her partner, and no one could take his place on or off the job. Plus, Watts had a reputation for being a slacker.

Although seemingly totally engrossed in his conversation, Watts greeted Rebecca without looking away from the young woman on the other side of the desk. "How's it hangin', Loo?"

Rebecca gave a start. *How's it hanging.* Jeff's greeting.

"Better than yours," Rebecca heard herself say, just as she had countless times to Jeff.

"Yeah," he sighed as he straightened, then swiveled to face her. "I don't doubt it."

She didn't reply but merely continued wending through the crowd toward the elevators at the rear of the lobby, Watts trailing behind. She'd been paired with Watts almost as long as she had known Catherine, and during those tumultuous months she'd learned that her initial impression of the detective had been wrong. Beneath his façade of insouciance, Watts was a sharp and thorough cop. He was also trustworthy and solid under pressure. Without her knowing it, and certainly without her *intending* it, he had become her partner. And she still wasn't sure how she felt about that.

"How long do you figure until we can get the team up and running again?" he asked as they stepped into the elevator.

"Today."

He grunted but said nothing.

Rebecca waited until they reached the fifth floor and exited, out of earshot of the other passengers, before elaborating. "As soon as we see how Mitchell is doing, we'll head over to Sloan's place and have a strategy meeting."

"She's going to be pissed about Avery."

"Uh-huh."

"What if she won't play ball?"

"She will." Rebecca pushed open the door to room 503 and stopped so abruptly that Watts nearly climbed up her back. "Christ. I don't see this."

"What?" Watts snapped, craning his neck to peer around Rebecca. "Whoa. *I'm* seein' it. Hey, move over so I can get a better look."

Sandy lay in Mitchell's hospital bed curled against the officer's right side, her head on Mitchell's shoulder and a hand on Mitchell's stomach under her police-issue T-shirt. Mitchell, the sheets askew and the tops of her lean thighs bare below white briefs, had apparently been dozing with her cheek pillowed against the top of Sandy's head. Now she blinked sluggishly in Rebecca's direction. "Hey."

"We'll be back in a minute," Rebecca grated. "Get yourselves together." Then she backed from the room, forcing Watts out into the hall as the door swung shut.

He emitted a long, low whistle. "Looks like the kid is taking her undercover gig as that little hooker's *boy*friend to heart—can't say as the work looks too hard to take, either. Man, what I wouldn't give for *that* assign—"

"Let it go, Watts."

He shrugged. "Hey, I always say never pass up a tasty morsel if it's free."

"Sandy's my CI," Rebecca said with an edge to her voice, "and she put her life on the line the other night. Show her some respect."

"Yeah, she did," Watts said with a sigh. He hunched his back, hooked his thumbs over his belt, and rocked on his heels while contemplating the closed door. "I'm just a little peeved that the only ones getting any action around here are the women." In a barely audible undertone, he muttered, "With the *other* women."

"Pay attention," Rebecca said with a perfectly straight face. "Maybe you'll learn something. You never know, even *you* might get lucky."

Watts stood flat-footed, his mouth open, staring at his lieutenant's back as she rapped once sharply on the door and then shouldered through. It was the first time she'd ever joked with him about anything remotely personal. With a happy little laugh, he hustled after her.

"So the doc says I can go home today," Mitchell announced, propped up in bed now with the sheet pulled to her waist and Sandy perched on a chair within arm's reach.

"That's great." Rebecca leaned both hands on the footboard of the bed, a frown forming between her eyes. "Where are you going?"

"Uh, Sandy's, we figure. I'm supposed to have a place in the same building…I mean, I *do* have a place there." Mitchell thought of the tiny studio apartment she'd rented down the hall from Sandy's. It was empty save for a bare mattress in the middle of the living-room floor, and she'd never slept there. She'd just assumed that staying with Sandy meant *in* Sandy's apartment. Realizing that maybe she'd jumped the gun, Mitchell cut her eyes to her girlfriend.

"I already told the super that Dell and I kinda have a thing going," Sandy said with a dismissive shrug. "And we kinda made it a point to be seen around the neighborhood this week. It will look natural for her to stay with me."

"It's important that people not know about your injury," Rebecca pointed out. "It's not likely that anyone will associate you with what happened with the sting, but we don't want to take any chances."

Mitchell's eyes brightened and excitement rippled in her voice. "So I'm going back undercover?"

"Let's say it's a possibility," Rebecca equivocated. She wasn't certain how soon Mitchell would be streetworthy, and she had a feeling that the investigation was going to move quickly. The data Sloan and her associate Jason McBride had gathered on the Internet sex video subscribers had led to dozens of arrests in the last two days. The people behind the prostitution and pornography operations had to be getting nervous.

"You can't even walk yet, Dell," Sandy objected quietly.

"Just a couple of days," Mitchell said, her eyes riveted to Rebecca. "Dr. Torveau said I'd be good in just a few days."

Sandy jerked upright in her chair, a flush rising in her cheeks. "She did not—"

Rebecca held up a hand to forestall the storm. "There's no point arguing about it now. When I have the plan mapped out, I'll let you know *if* you have a part." The truth was she needed both Mitchell *and* Sandy on the streets, but she wasn't about to send a young, inexperienced officer—who was also less than 100 percent emotionally and physically fit—into danger. "There'll be some paperwork to take care of before you can get back to duty, Mitchell."

Mitchell dropped her head back against the pillow with a groan. "Oh man. Not the shrink again." Then, as if realizing what she had said and to whom, she hastily added, "I mean, Dr. Rawling's terrific, but—"

"It's SOP, Detective," Rebecca said, "so just suck it up and get it done."

"Yes, ma'am, but until—" Mitchell faltered, her jaw working but no sounds emitting. She swallowed hard. "I'm sorry? What did you say?"

Rebecca grinned and Watts guffawed.

"Congratulations, Mitchell," Rebecca pronounced. "You've earned yourself a provisional promotion. Detective One."

"For real?" Without thinking, Mitchell held out her hand to Sandy, who took it while edging closer to the bed.

"You'll need to take the exam next time it's offered to satisfy all the requirements, but yes, it's for real." Rebecca didn't try to hide her pleasure. "Well done."

"Yeah, nice going, kid," Watts chimed in. He gestured toward Rebecca with his chin. "The Loo here deserves some congrats too."

"Lieutenant?" Mitchell echoed, before grinning broadly. "That's great!"

"Thanks," Rebecca said quietly.

"And the team is staying together?" Mitchell asked anxiously.

Being laid up made her worry that the investigation would move on without her—something she fervently did not want to happen.

"Let's say we're restructuring." Rebecca went on to describe the High Profile Crimes Unit in general terms, leaving out the political machinations behind the scenes. "So, *Detective*, bottom line is that you're on medical leave until cleared by both Dr. Torveau and the department. Then we'll talk about assignments."

"Oh man," Mitchell whispered. "Detective." Her eyes tracked from Rebecca to Watts and then to Sandy. "What do you think?"

Sandy's expression was unreadable as she quietly said, "I think you'll be a bigger pain in the ass now than ever."

Mitchell grinned. "Yeah. Most likely."

The room was very quiet after Rebecca and Watts left. Sandy still sat beside the bed. Her small hand, the nails tipped in a red so dark it might have been blood, rested motionless on the white sheets next to Mitchell's thigh. Mitchell hooked her index finger around Sandy's thumb and shook gently. "You mad?"

"No. Why?"

Mitchell eased the rest of her fingers over the top of Sandy's hand and closed them. Sandy did not return the pressure. "Before they showed up, you seemed pretty warm and cuddly. It's kinda cold in here now."

"You know, Dell, I have to do sex pretty much twenty-four hours a day. Sometimes I'm just not in the mood, okay?"

A muscle in Mitchell's jaw twitched, but she kept her hand on Sandy's. "That's a fucked-up thing to say to me."

Sandy slowly turned her head and met Mitchell's eyes. The sharp retort died on her tongue when she saw the undisguised pain in the deep blue eyes. She closed her own and took a long, wavering breath before opening them again. "I'm sorry."

"Okay," Mitchell said quietly.

"I want you all the time," Sandy murmured.

"Same here." Mitchell lifted Sandy's hand to her cheek and rubbed it against her skin. "You pissed off about the promotion?"

Sandy shook her head.

"About me staying with you?"

"No."

"Come on, honey. Just tell me."

The silence dragged on so long that Mitchell couldn't stand it. "Sandy?"

"It's the undercover thing."

Mitchell's brows furrowed. "I thought you liked Mitch," she said, referring to her undercover persona. She bit the tip of Sandy's index finger playfully. "*He* likes you."

"It's not Mitch. You *know* what Mitch does to me." Sandy swiveled on her chair, gripping Mitchell's hand hard. "In case you haven't noticed, since all this started, somebody popped Frye's partner in broad daylight, and then somebody else tried to run down Sloan and almost took out her girlfriend instead. *You* got knifed two days ago and just about bled to death. These guys aren't fucking fooling. You go poking around down at the clubs, and the next time that blade is going to be in your chest."

"Jeez, Sandy. I'm a cop." Mitchell's tone was clearly incredulous. "I can handle myself. *You're* the one who's likely to get into trouble, being Frye's confidential informant. If anybody ought to quit, it's you."

Sandy snorted. "Look, *rookie*. I've been managing on the streets a lot longer than you've been a cop. I know my way around."

"Oh yeah, sure you—" Mitchell broke off as a knock sounded at the door. "Yeah?"

The door swung open, and Sloan took one step into the room. "Safe to come in? Or should I wait until you're done throwing things?"

"I oughtta go," Sandy said, leaping up as she released Mitchell's hand.

"Hey," Mitchell protested. She rolled over and made a grab for Sandy's hand, then caught her breath and groaned as pain lanced through her leg. "Oh, ow, fuck. Ow."

"Dell!" Sandy grasped Mitchell's shoulders and pushed her gently back to the pillows. "Lay down, you blockhead."

"Don't go," Mitchell gasped.

"Okay, okay. Jeez." Sandy stroked Mitchell's cheek. "I'll stay already."

Sloan cleared her throat. "You two squared away now?"

"Yeah," they answered in unison.

"Good." She tilted her chin at Mitchell. "How're you doing?"

"Not too bad," Mitchell said, fighting to keep her breath even. Her leg throbbed as if someone had kicked her, more than once. She took in the circles under Sloan's normally vibrant violet eyes and the sallow tint to her skin. Now that she was paying attention, Sloan, dressed in her usual faded jeans and tight white T-shirt, looked thinner than Mitchell remembered. "You?"

Sloan lifted a shoulder. "Jason and I have been working around the clock extracting data from the computers we confiscated in the raid the other night. We've got a dozen sources of potential subscribers to sift through—chat-room transcripts, e-mail distribution lists, on-line bulletin boards. We're drowning in data." Despite her obvious fatigue, she exuded excitement.

"You know," Mitchell said, suddenly energized. "I could work on that until my leg's better. I helped Jason with the initial data analysis, and I set up some of the traces."

"It's an idea," Sloan replied hesitantly. She had considered suggesting it herself, but had resisted trying to recruit one of Frye's people for her own private investigation out of respect for the homicide detective. But if Mitchell was otherwise unoccupied… "Look, why don't we see how you're feeling in a few days—"

Mitchell pushed up on the pillows, shaking her head vehemently. "I'm okay. They're going to let me out of here today. I could start tomorrow."

"There's just one little problem," Sandy interjected with the barest hint of sarcasm.

"What?" Mitchell asked, turning to her girlfriend.

"You can't walk, let alone drive or ride the bike."

"By tomorrow, I'll—"

"Stay at our place," Sloan interjected. "We've got plenty of room, and all you have to do is ride the elevator one floor."

"Yeah? That would be grea—" Mitchell halted, carefully not looking in Sandy's direction. "Thanks, but I'll be fine at Sandy's."

"Both of you." Sloan grinned at Sandy. "*I* don't plan to keep an eye on her, and somebody should. You'd be doing me a favor if you hung out at our place for the next few days and made sure she doesn't get into trouble."

"What do you say?" Mitchell gave Sandy a pleading look.

"I'm not going to sit around there all day, you know," Sandy said flatly. "I've got things to do too."

"I know. No problem." Mitchell's eyes were alight with anticipation. "So that's a yes?"

Sandy turned to Sloan, trying unsuccessfully to mask her grateful expression. "Sure. Why not."

Chapter Three

Just as Sloan settled behind the wheel of her new gunmetal gray Porsche Carrera GT, her cell phone rang. She peeled out of the parking space and accelerated down the exit ramp before hitting the speaker button on her phone.

"Sloan."

"It's Frye."

Sloan shoved bills at the bored high school student in the glass-enclosed booth and then gunned the 5.7L V10 engine, just missing the slowly rising toll arm as she sped beneath it and onto one of the narrow one-way streets behind the hospital. "What's up?"

"Can you meet me at Police Plaza *now*?"

"Why?" Sloan's hand tightened on the wheel. A trip to the heart of police bureaucracy was the last thing she wanted to do. Just being inside any law enforcement complex brought back memories she didn't care to revisit.

"I'd like you to have a talk with my captain."

"Is this an official request?"

"Not exactly."

Sloan pushed the Carrera east toward downtown, having intended to return to her office/residence in a renovated four-story factory building in Old City. With a slight detour, she could be at Police Plaza in ten minutes. It was a tangent, however, that held far more than a few moments of lost time in the balance. She had promised herself seven years before that she would never again voluntarily associate with organized law enforcement on any level.

"It's important, Sloan."

Rebecca might be a friend, but she was still a cop. That wasn't something Rebecca Frye ever stopped being. Some part of this request *was* official, and that's exactly what Sloan wanted none of. She could do a lot of things on her own to discover who had orchestrated the hit-and-run assault that had almost killed Michael. She was confident that, in time, she would have a name. She was equally confident that she could do what needed to be done for justice to be served, with her own hand and with a clear conscience. She didn't need official sanction; she needed retribution. The silence grew. The purr of the huge engine and the steady throb of barely leashed power echoed the animal hunger for vengeance that raged in her depths.

"Sloan?"

"Yeah." Sloan eased her grip on the wheel, downshifted, and turned left toward North Philadelphia. "Be there in five."

Rebecca stood waiting for her on the other side of the security booths in the main lobby, and Sloan followed her silently toward the elevators.

"There've been some developments since the last time we talked," Rebecca said as they waited for the elevator doors to open.

"Problem with the arrests?" Sloan asked, suddenly concerned that some legal loophole had popped up to taint the evidence that she and Jason had gathered from the bust the previous weekend. Electronic evidence and computer forensics were still something akin to black magic to most law enforcement agents, who preferred to base their cases on court-tested modes of proof such as fingerprints and eyewitness identification.

Rebecca shook her head. "No. They're all solid. The two of you did a great job." Once on the third floor, Rebecca led the way down the hall. "In fact, that's why you're here."

The nerve center of the detective bureau was a huge, brightly lit room filled with the sounds of ringing phones and rumbling male voices. Sloan glimpsed only one woman, against the far wall, her voice lost in the cacophony. Picking her way along a narrow pathway created by a dozen or so haphazardly placed desks, she felt the eyes of everyone in the room on her back. All too aware of the rapid pounding of her heart and the knot of anxiety in the pit of her stomach, she waited beside Rebecca, who rapped on the door of a glass-enclosed office. The last time she'd been in a police station, she'd been wearing handcuffs. She fought the urge to reach over and rub her left wrist where a faint scar still remained. They'd tossed her none too gently into the backseat of a patrol car, and she'd fallen so that the weight of her body had pinned her arms to the seat. The pressure on the too-tight cuffs had torn her flesh.

"The captain has a proposition for you."

"Look, Frye," Sloan began urgently, "I don't think—"

"Just hear him out." Rebecca pushed the door open and said, "This is Captain John Henry. Sir, JT Sloan."

Sloan had no choice but to enter the small room, made smaller by the two chairs in front of the desk and a bank of file cabinets along one wall. The big man behind the paper-covered desk rose and extended his hand.

"I thought it was about time we met, Ms. Sloan," Henry said in his rich basso profundo.

"Just Sloan," Sloan replied automatically as she took his hand. "Captain."

Henry pointed at one of the chairs and Sloan sat, crossing her blue jeans–clad legs with a nonchalance she did not feel. She rested her hands on her knees with her fingers loose, despite the fact that she wanted to ball them into fists. Tension thrummed through her limbs like current along a high-voltage line.

Rebecca sat silently beside Sloan.

"I won't even pretend to understand what it is that you do, Ms.… uh, Sloan," Henry said, sitting erect in his chair, his hands clasped on the desk. As usual, his white shirt was wrinkle free and buttoned to the top, where his tie lay neatly knotted. He had rolled each cuff up precisely once. His eyes, intent on Sloan's face, were brown, a shade darker than his skin, and sharp with intelligence. "But I appreciate the fact that you played a critical part in Detective Frye's investigation. I also understand that there's more work to be done."

"At this point, Captain, your electronic surveillance unit should be able to follow up on most of the information we uncovered." Sloan knew that probably wasn't true, but it was the polite thing to say.

"You're right," Captain Henry said, nodding thoughtfully. "At least, you *would* be, if we *had* an electronic surveillance unit. But we don't."

Despite the fact that, in the last few years, all branches of government and industry had stressed computer security, local law enforcement agencies lagged far behind in developing electronic surveillance units, mostly because they lacked personnel with the necessary skills. Sloan said nothing.

"The mayor and the chief and the head of City Council are very grateful that you and Detective Lieutenant Frye were able to uncover this pornography ring." Captain Henry's expression remained neutral, but the barest undercurrent of sarcasm edged his tone. "They were also, however, deeply embarrassed by the fact that such a thing existed in our city. They want to be sure something like this doesn't happen again."

Sloan took a quick look at Rebecca. *Detective lieutenant, huh? I guess a lot* has *happened in the last twenty-four hours.* Frye stared straight ahead, her expression completely unreadable. Sloan was momentarily irritated, wishing that Frye had given her a heads-up as to what the hell this meeting was all about, because she still didn't have any idea. Then her mind focused on what Henry was saying, although she couldn't really believe what she was hearing.

"...been authorized to hire a civilian consultant to set up the unit. We'd like you to do it."

"I'm not available, but I can recommend several well-qualified security experts who could handle the job," Sloan said immediately.

"City Hall wants to see immediate action on this," Henry countered evenly. "You're already cleared. Security screening on the others would take too long."

Sloan couldn't help but laugh—a short, humorless sound. "Obviously, your system *does* need help. *I* wouldn't pass a decent security screen."

"You've already demonstrated your considerable abilities, and Lieutenant Frye vouches for you personally." Henry's expression never changed. "In addition to that, you've already been cleared at the highest level."

"Highest level?"

"Agent Clark from the Justice Department."

"Clark," Sloan whispered.

"While overseeing the development of the ESU," Henry continued smoothly, "you'll be assigned to Lieutenant Frye's unit."

Sloan was still trying to absorb the fact that Clark had vouched for her. He should know that her arrest and subsequent dismissal from the

Justice Department disqualified her from a position such as this. The fact that he had paved the way made the entire offer suspect.

"I need to think about it."

Henry stood. "Of course." He extended his hand. When Sloan took it, he squeezed gently. "Just remember, we have two dead police officers whose murderer is unaccounted for, an unsolved attempted vehicular homicide—I believe you're familiar with that incident—and"—he glanced at Rebecca—"a mole somewhere with direct access to our personnel and case files. The identities of those individuals is probably somewhere in here." He rested his hand on his computer. "I'd like you to find them, if you can."

Sloan stared at the blank computer monitor, but what she saw was Michael lying in the street in front of their building, her face pale, her body battered and bruised, a maroon river streaming from beneath her head. Her hands closed into fists.

"Oh," Sloan murmured softly, "I can."

Michael Lassiter stared at the computer screen, willing her eyes to focus. A dull throb reverberated at the base of her skull, impeding her ability to concentrate. Queasiness simmered in the pit of her stomach. With effort, she settled her trembling fingers on the keyboard and began a memo to the division heads of Innova Design Consultants, the company she had founded with her ex-husband and now headed. Fifteen minutes later, she had completed one paragraph, and her head threatened to explode. Sporadic flashes of light streaked across her field of vision, and the queasiness had swelled to a surging tide of nausea. She closed her eyes, hoping to fight down the sickness.

"Michael?" Sloan crossed the loft in long strides, her face creased with concern. She knelt by Michael's chair while cupping her hand at the base of Michael's neck. "Baby?"

Comforted by the cool touch of her lover's fingers, Michael leaned into Sloan's caress. "Aren't you supposed to be working?"

"Missed you," Sloan murmured, her eyes riveted to Michael's pale face. "What are you doing?"

"Trying to get a little work done myself."

Sloan struggled not to let her apprehension show. Michael looked so frail, and her obvious pain knifed Sloan's heart. "Rushing things a little, aren't you?" She lifted Michael's hand and brushed a kiss over her knuckles. "Ali said you should take it easy for a few weeks. Not to expect too much."

Michael turned her head, resting her cheek in Sloan's palm. "I didn't think that reading my e-mail qualified as a major endeavor."

"Why don't you lie down for a little while." Sloan slid her hand beneath Michael's elbow. "Come on, I'll walk you into the bedroom."

"Is there something you're not telling me?" Michael asked, remaining motionless, searching Sloan's face. "Something about what happened to me?"

"No." Sloan crouched again until their eyes were at the same level. She held Michael's gaze as she lightly stroked her cheek. "No. You had a really bad concussion. Remember Ali said it might be a few weeks before the symptoms cleared up? Headaches especially. It's probably just too soon to work at the computer."

"Sloan," Michael said fervently, "that's where I do most of my work. I'm a design consultant."

"I know, baby, I know." The edge of anxiety in Michael's voice was unmistakable, and Sloan ached to reassure her. "But you've only been out of the hospital a week. This is normal."

"I hate this." Michael wrapped her arms around Sloan's neck and leaned into her, resting her cheek on Sloan's shoulder. "I hate feeling so weak, and I hate feeling useless. And I hate being apart from you most of all."

"Oh no, baby. No." Sloan rose slowly, enfolding Michael in her arms, and kissed her forehead, then her lips. "You're getting better, and that's the most important thing to me. Lying with you at night, holding you, waking up with you beside me. That's everything."

Michael pressed against her, needing her solid strength. "Not quite everything."

Sloan's pulse skyrocketed as Michael's breath caressed her neck and the soft curves of Michael's body melded to her own. The rush of arousal was entirely beyond her control, and she tried valiantly not to let her desire show. They had made love briefly several days before, despite Sloan's protests. Michael had seemed to need the connection, and Sloan could refuse her nothing. But despite her body's acute response to her lover's nearness, sex was the last thing on Sloan's mind. All she wanted was for Michael to be well. "No, definitely not everything, but those other things can wait."

"No choice." Michael sighed, brushing her lips over Sloan's. "Damn—I'm sorry. I need to lie down." She mustered a smile. "Then I want you to tell me what you've been doing since last night."

Once they were settled in the bedroom, Michael curled against Sloan's side with her head on her lover's shoulder. While Sloan recounted the details of the meeting at Police Plaza, Michael listened without comment, her arm curved around Sloan's waist.

"So you agreed?" Michael asked when Sloan fell silent.

"More or less," Sloan said. "I agreed to submit a preliminary assessment of the status of their electronic retrieval and analysis capabilities, along with my recommendations for developing a state-of-the-art electronic surveillance unit. Probably once they see my bill, that will be the end of it."

Michael laughed gently. "Why *did* you agree? You don't need the work, and I can't imagine that they'll be able to pay your going rate."

Sloan shrugged but said nothing. Her continued silence triggered every one of Michael's alarms, but the persistent throbbing in her head made it hard for her to think clearly. She was aware only of a sense of unease, and her frustrating inability to process it made her headache even worse. She sighed.

"I can't figure this out on my own, love," Michael said quietly. "Please tell me."

"Developing the ESU is a straightforward job. It'll be a little frustrating due to the antiquated equipment and bureaucratic roadblocks that are sure to exist, but all in all, it might be fun."

"And?"

Sloan pressed her lips to Michael's temple and rubbed her hand in gentle circles over the center of Michael's back. "And I'll have access to every computer in the system. Somewhere in there is the answer that we've all been looking for."

"You mean…" Michael began hesitantly. Frowning, she tried desperately to sort out the fragments of memory and shattered connections in her still-traumatized brain. "…who killed Rebecca's partner?"

Sloan nodded.

"And who...hurt me?"

"Yes."

"And then what will you do?"

Sloan knew the answer that Michael wanted. She knew the answer but hesitated, because she couldn't lie to her. "I don't know."

Michael raised her head, ignoring the surge of pain, to look into Sloan's eyes. "You promised me you would tell Rebecca. I remember that. You promised."

"I did," Sloan whispered. She closed her eyes and pressed her face into the soft fragrance of Michael's hair. Her voice barely registered a whisper. "It's just that…I want to hurt someone for hurting you."

"I know." Michael stroked Sloan's cheek, then threaded her fingers into Sloan's hair. She raised her mouth to Sloan's and kissed her gently. "I won't ask you to keep your promise, because I know that you will."

Sloan let the comfort of Michael's kiss soothe her troubled soul, wondering if she would be able to keep her lover's trust.

Chapter Four

Sloan jerked awake to the ringing of the bedside phone. Cursing silently, she tried to reach it without shifting Michael's head from her shoulder, hoping not to rouse her.

"I'll get it," Michael whispered, rolling carefully toward the side of the bed. She retrieved the portable handset and passed it to Sloan before curling up against her lover's side again.

"Sloan," she said, her voice thick with the remnants of sleep. She couldn't believe she'd dropped off in the middle of the day. She rarely slept, day *or* night, when in the middle of a project. The investigation with Rebecca's team had been ongoing for several weeks, and her role in it had grown so steadily that she and Jason had put all their other contracts on hold. Now, when she was so close to a breakthrough—with finding Michael's assailant as the payoff—she could think of little else. Only her concern for Michael's well-being took precedence. "Uh-huh. Sure. That sounds fine."

"Problem?" Michael asked when Sloan hung up with a faint groan.

"No, just a meeting with Frye." Sloan kissed Michael's forehead and eased away. "But I'm going to have to go. I'm sorry. You should sleep a little longer."

Michael laughed. "Darling, all I do is sleep." She sat up slowly, then stood. "Let me walk you out."

Sloan took her hand as they left the bedroom. "You know, there's something I forgot to tell you. I invited Mitchell to stay here for a few days—until she's getting around a little bit better."

"I think that's a good idea. When is she coming?"

"Today sometime. Her girlfriend Sandy too."

"Well, we've got room."

"You don't mind?" Sloan stopped in front of the loft doors and curved an arm around Michael's waist, drawing her near. "Because if it's too much—"

"I don't plan on cooking and cleaning for them, darling," Michael chided gently. "It'll be fine. The company will be nice." She kissed Sloan lingeringly, cleaving to her as she did. When she drew away, she sighed contentedly. "God, you feel so good."

"You too," Sloan replied, her voice husky and low.

"My headache's gone." Michael cupped her hand behind Sloan's neck and kissed her again.

"Oh, baby," Sloan gasped. "I have to go. Frye is going to be here any minute."

"You go ahead." Michael smiled, her eyes liquid with desire. "I'll be here later."

"I know," Sloan murmured, drawing a finger along the edge of Michael's jaw and over her mouth. "And knowing that is the best thing in my life."

In the conference room on the third floor of Sloan's building, Rebecca helped herself to a cup of coffee. The rest of the huge space was partitioned into various work areas crammed with computers and a vast array of electronic equipment, some of which was not yet available on the open market. At the sound of footsteps at her back, she turned and greeted Sloan. "Sorry for the short notice."

Wordlessly, Sloan shrugged and headed straight for the coffeepot. She poured a cup, took a long sip, and lounging against the counter, regarded Rebecca inquiringly. "No problem. Something come up?"

"Clark arrived for a meeting with Henry, and I decided I needed to be unavailable."

"What's that bastard doing back in the picture?"

"I don't know." Rebecca looked past Sloan to the door and nodded to the handsome blond man who stood on the threshold. His expensive, meticulously tailored shirt and pants contrasted distinctly to Sloan's casual attire, but the shadows beneath his deep blue eyes mirrored hers. "Hi, Jase. How's it going?"

Jason McBride, Sloan's associate at Sloan Security, smiled tiredly.

"It feels like moving a mountain with a tablespoon, there's so much data to sift through."

"You should take a break before Sarah comes and drags you out of here," Sloan suggested, referring to her best friend and Jason's live-in lover. "Go home, get some sleep."

"Yeah, like you, I suppose," Jason remarked with friendly sarcasm.

"*I* just woke up."

Clearly surprised, Jason sank into one of the chairs at the conference table. "So miracles really *do* happen."

Laughing, Sloan joined him.

Jason looked to Rebecca. "What's happening on your end?"

"A few noteworthy bits, but let's wait for Watts. He'll be here any minute."

Right on cue, a subdued pinging emanated from a speaker in the far corner of the room. All three heads turned toward the bank of security monitors lined up along the wall. The first screen showed an image projected from the video camera above the street-level door. Watts stood on the top step, frowning up at the camera. Before Sloan could buzz him in, he turned his back to the building, as if looking back down the street.

"Hey," Jason said as another figure materialized. "That's Mitchell!"

"I'd better go give them a hand," Sloan said, punching in a number sequence on a keypad to release the security locks on the street-level door.

"Stay put," Rebecca interjected. "I'll go."

As soon as they were alone, Jason queried Sloan. "Why the meeting?"

"It looks like the team is back in business," Sloan said.

"Really? Good, because we could use some help tracking down the rest of the video-porn subscribers. And anything else we find along the way."

Sloan said nothing.

"What?"

"You might have to handle that alone."

Jason frowned. "Why?"

"I'm going to be tied up with another job."

"You're kidding." Jason stared, clearly confused. "What could be more important than delivering the coup de grâce to this smut ring?"

"You know what, Jason," Sloan replied softly.

"We've got a line into their organization now, Sloan," Jason pointed out. "We'll nail down the porn distributors, and one of them is going to roll. Then we'll be able to pinpoint Michael's assailant or at least find out who gave the order."

"Starting tomorrow," Sloan said with evident satisfaction, "I'm going to have access to everything I need to figure out who is responsible." At his look of puzzlement, she went on, "I agreed to help develop an electronic surveillance unit for the police department. I'm now an official civilian consultant."

"You're kidding." The sound of voices from just outside the door prevented him from elaborating further on his disbelief. He turned, and a smile lit his handsome features. "Dell? Hey. How are you?"

"Great." Mitchell, seated in a wheelchair with Sandy at the helm, grinned back. "The doc said I can't weight-bear until tomorrow. But then I'll be mobile."

"Crutches," Sandy muttered. "Freakin' crutches, Dell."

"Excellent," Jason said. "Hi, Sandy."

"Hi," Sandy replied as she helped Mitchell move from the wheelchair to a seat at the table.

Rebecca sat down on Mitchell's right, with Watts on her opposite side. Once Sandy joined them, Rebecca began. "Okay. Everyone's here, so let's get up to speed. As of this morning, we are now officially the High Profile Crimes Unit." She looked around the table. "Jason, you and Sloan will have official status as civilian consultants. Sloan's going to be doing some work directly from police headquarters, but you'll still be based here. In fact," she regarded Sloan now, "I'd like to base the entire unit here if at all possible. I don't trust the security at headquarters."

"That's fine with me," Sloan said. "Jason and Mitchell can set up a secure databank to handle the necessary documentation. We'll store everything using the Justice Department encryption protocol, so we should have no problem with the records being admissible in court."

"Handy," Watts observed. "You just *happening* to have that program."

"I learned everything I know from Uncle Sam." Sloan grinned. "Just your tax dollars at work."

"Uh-huh, right."

"Jason," Rebecca's voice rose above the friendly bantering. "Where are you with the data analysis?"

"In addition to the guys running the video relay stations that we've already identified, we could potentially track down about three hundred subscribers just in the greater metropolitan area alone. How hard do you want to go after them?"

"How long would it take?"

Jason waggled his hand. "We have to backtrack through credit card accounts, Internet aliases, multiple e-mail addresses, servers—the whole works. With just Dell and me working it, probably a few weeks."

"In all likelihood," Sloan interjected, "these are the end users. The guys who don't know anything about the structure of the organization and who just want to get off to porn. For our purposes, the return might not be worth the effort."

Rebecca's gaze was distant as she considered options. "These guys are perverts, and some of them are probably active pedophiles. They need to be investigated."

"No question," Sloan agreed. "But do *we* need to be investigating them?"

"What's the chance that we'll pull a name out of those computers that will lead us to our mole?"

"Not an impossibility," Jason mused. "Most of the porn makers and distributors got into the business because they like the product. Maybe that's what hooked our insider too, but we can't count on it."

"For the time being," Rebecca said, "you and Mitchell keep at it. At least until Mitchell is ready for street duty."

At that, Mitchell sat up straighter, her body nearly quivering with anticipation. "Am I going back undercover?"

From the corner of her eye, Rebecca saw Sandy stiffen. "We've disrupted part of the porn ring, but I think it's pretty clear that they're using prostitutes as models. Some local street girls, but others whom we haven't been able to identify. They're not in our system—so who are they? I want to know who they are and how they're being recruited. So far, the sex clubs are our best leads." She glanced from Mitchell to Jason. "And Jasmine and Mitch have an in there, so I want them to work it."

Jason's mouth curved into a smile that was pure Jasmine. When he spoke, his voice took on a honeyed texture, although nothing else in his posture changed. "What fun."

"Jasmine needs to talk to the drag kings and tell them Mitch was in a motorcycle accident. It will explain his leg *and* his absence."

"Not a problem. The boys have a show tonight, and Jasmine can drop around."

During the conversation, Watts shifted in his chair, the ponderous creaking underscoring his uneasy expression. "*Mitch* rushing out of Ziggie's right before that bust the other night might raise some suspicions."

"No one knows I was at the factory during the arrests," Mitchell pointed out hurriedly. "I can always say I got a call from my girlfriend busting my balls"—she glanced apologetically at Sandy—"because I was out late clubbing, and I crashed the bike speeding to get home."

Watts nodded. "Yeah, that might play." He regarded Mitchell steadily. "And you *did* manage to get in places none of us could."

"Well, *Mitch* did," Mitchell replied with just a hint of self-satisfaction.

"Oh yeah—the guy with the plastic pole," Watts grumbled. "He's a wonder, all right."

"Okay," Rebecca said, nodding to Mitchell. "As soon as you're cleared medically and by…the department, I want you to reconnect with the kings and start working the clubs at night. Concentrate on Ziggie's."

"Yes, ma'am."

"Sloan, you've got the department computers. Anything new on the identity of the inside man?"

Sloan shook her head. "Nothing beyond what we knew this weekend. There are two ADAs who had access to the warrants and who could've tipped someone off to the details of the computer investigations: Margaret Campbell and George Beecher."

"Let's sit down with their profiles tomorrow and look for something that's off," Rebecca said. "Make sure their jackets are complete—criminal records search, education and financial summaries, job evals—all of it."

"Done."

"Watts and I will arrange surveillance on both of them. It'll be tricky, because they're likely to be suspicious after the arrests this weekend. They'll be looking for something out of the ordinary." She glanced at Watts. "You and I should be the ones sitting on them, at least in the beginning."

He pursed his lips. "Can't do it 24-7."

"Agreed, but I think it's safe to assume they're not likely to have contact with anyone during the day. So we'll start with night tails."

"You're the boss."

"During the day, Watts," Rebecca went on pointedly, "I want you to go back over everything you can find in Jimmy Hogan's files. If Avery Clark is back in the picture, and Jimmy Hogan was one of his undercover agents, then the Justice Department thinks there's still something here to find. And I think whatever that is, it's what got Jimmy…and Jeff…killed." Her eyes were a flat, hard blue, as impenetrable as the surface of a bottomless well. "And I know that Avery Clark is not going to tell us. He's hoping to wait in the wings again while we dig out the information he's interested in. But this time, we aren't handing it over."

Her remark prompted a chorus of *damn rights* and a single, harsh *no fucking way* from Watts.

"Anything else?" Rebecca asked, looking around the table. When no one spoke, she bumped her fist lightly on the table top. "Right, then. Let's do it."

As the team dispersed, Rebecca approached Sandy. "Got a minute?"

"Not really." Sandy indicated Mitchell, who was pale and shaking, with a tilt of her chin. "I think the rookie oughtta be in bed."

"I'll take her upstairs and get her settled," Jason offered.

Sandy looked as if she wanted to refuse, but she finally shrugged. "Whatever."

"Let's go for a walk," Rebecca said, leading the way to the elevator.

They rode down in silence with Watts. Once outside, she and Sandy headed toward the waterfront while Watts walked west after mumbling goodbye.

"Cold?" Rebecca asked.

Sandy shook her head, although she wore only a short, tight red vinyl jacket that did not close across her small breasts. Her nipples stood out starkly under the nearly sheer top.

"You look cold."

"I'm not." Sandy's voice held the barest edge of annoyance. She shot Rebecca a look out of the corner of her eye. "Okay, maybe I am a little."

Rebecca hooked her fingers beneath Sandy's elbow and tugged her into a coffee shop on Front Street. They navigated the narrow path between the counter and a single row of tables until they reached the last table in the rear. On the way, Rebecca held up two fingers and asked for coffee. A minute later they sat with steaming cups cradled between their palms.

"I need you to find Trudy," Rebecca said, referring to the young dancer-cum-prostitute who had been with Sandy in the porn studio the night of the arrests. "We haven't been able to find her since she left the ER the other night."

"Can you blame her?" Sandy said bitterly. "First she ends up going down on that pig for the camera, and then she gets caught in the middle of your raid. Watts drags her off to the hospital, where some doctor takes her clothes away and pokes and scrapes her everywhere." Sandy sipped her coffee, apparently oblivious to the scalding heat against her lips. "What do you expect?"

"I expect she's laying low, but that won't last long. She's going to need money." Rebecca stared into Sandy's eyes. "She's going to do what she's always done to get it, which means hook or pose. Either way, she's going to expose herself to danger."

Sandy laughed, a short mirthless sound. "You mean more so than usual?"

"I *mean* that if anyone knew she was going to be at the shoot that night, they might suspect her of tipping us off." Rebecca didn't add that if anyone knew that Trudy had been meeting *Sandy* to bring her to the porn shoot, she could be in danger too. She knew from the look in Sandy's eyes that she'd made the connection. "I want to find out what else she knows—"

"What?" Sandy snapped. "Before someone dumps her in an alley?"

"And," Rebecca went on with no change in expression, "see if I can get her into a program or shelter somewhere."

Sandy looked as if she were going to retort, but stared down into her coffee instead. After a long moment of silence, she looked up into Rebecca's face. "I'll ask around. She wasn't that hard to find the first time."

Rebecca nodded.

"Dell's not ready for the street. The doctor said she was going to be weak because of losing blood and stuff."

Still Rebecca said nothing.

"She wants to fucking be just like you." Sandy's eyes flashed. "Tough, like nothing ever hurts and nothing could ever hurt her."

"She's a cop, Sandy." Rebecca spoke quietly, her tone even and mild. "You're going to have to accept that about her if you're going to be with her."

Her words took them both by surprise, and they blinked simultaneously.

"Christ," Rebecca muttered, realizing that she'd had almost the same conversation with Mitchell about Sandy just days before. It was crazy, the two of them together. But for some reason, she couldn't bring herself to split them up. There were things that she could do, including threatening Mitchell's career, to force them apart, but she hadn't done that. When she considered it, as she did in this moment, Catherine's face came into view—disappointment and sorrow in her eyes. "Look, I don't want to know about you two. Keep your personal stuff personal, and just let Mitchell do her job."

"I'm not going to let her get her head blown off," Sandy said vehemently.

Rebecca leaned forward over the table, her hands not quite touching Sandy's, their faces inches apart. "If you want her to be safe, then don't make her crazy. She has to go out the door every day knowing that you'll be there when she comes back. If you can't give her that, then let her go now."

Sandy's eyes widened. "Jesus. Who are you?"

Wordlessly, Rebecca held Sandy's searching gaze.

"I heard Dell say that sometimes an older cop takes a rookie under their wing and helps them out. It's some kind of special big-deal relationship. *Rabbi*, she said. Is that what you are now?"

"Something like that."

"So you're sending her out there with nothing but her dick in her hand?"

Rebecca had to work to suppress a smile, just imagining how Mitchell would respond to this conversation. "She'll have backup. Most of the time, Jasmine will be with her." She held out a hand before Sandy could protest. "*And* she's a natural. She's one of the best undercover cops I've ever seen."

"Can I say you said that?"

"*No.*"

Sandy grinned. "Man, she'd like to know you think that. But I don't plan on telling her. She'd be impossible."

"Good. You hungry?"

"Yeah."

Rebecca waved a waitress over and ordered two burgers with fries and Cokes. While they waited, she said, "I don't want you hooking."

"I'm not going there again," Sandy said flatly. "I can't work the streets and not hook. That'll get me killed faster than anything."

"You'll just have to fake it."

Sandy laughed. "Fake blowing some guy in an alley? You think he might notice if I don't do anything except stare at his hard-on?"

"I don't want you *doing* anybody in alleys or backseats of cars or three-dollar rooms in ten-dollar flophouses. If you run into someone you know, tell them you just finished with a trick. Since you don't have a pimp, nobody's keeping score."

"I'll be careful."

"You're out of business, Sandy." Rebecca's tone held absolutely no room for negotiation. "I'll see that you get money on a regular basis."

Sandy cocked her head and regarded Rebecca thoughtfully. "You've changed. There's something inside of you now besides just business. How come?"

Rebecca was silent, but she stumbled over the memory of Catherine's scent enveloping her in the dark. And she knew.

Chapter Five

Catherine smiled at the assistant who sat guarding the door to Hazel Holcomb's inner sanctum.

"Hi, Stef, is she around?"

The slender African American woman shook her head. "Not to anyone but you."

"That busy, huh?" Catherine smiled. "Never mind, then. I'll catch her before the five o'clock management conference."

"No, you'd better see her now if you really want to talk to her. No guarantee she'll even make it to the conference. Budget's due."

The way Stef said *budget* made it sound as if she were speaking of a virulent pathogen capable of destroying nations.

"I promise I'll only stay a minute."

The assistant waved her toward the partially open door to the chief of psychiatry's private office and returned her attention to the computer screen on her desk. Catherine murmured her thanks and, tapping lightly on the door to announce her presence, stepped into Hazel's office.

"Oh, thank goodness, you've come to rescue me." Hazel, a vigorous sixty-year-old with short salt-and-pepper hair and a piercing gaze, slipped off her reading glasses and let them dangle on the braided cord around her neck. Indicating a chair in front of her desk with a quick gesture, she leaned back and sighed. "Most of the time I forget why I didn't want to be an administrator. This week, I remember quite clearly."

Catherine regarded the mountain of paperwork covering every available surface of Hazel's desk and grimaced sympathetically. "It looks awful."

"It's worse."

"I'm sorry. I'd volunteer to help but the thought terrifies me."

Hazel snorted. "It would probably be good practice for you. You're going to be doing it yourself one day soon."

"I'm not at all certain I want the job," Catherine said immediately, "and what's more, you're going to be here for a long time to come."

"There are days I wonder about that," Hazel said with uncharacteristic solemnity. "There seem to be more and more of them when it just isn't fun anymore."

"Those are the times we have to remember to separate the work from the bullshit."

Hazel blinked, then laughed with genuine pleasure. "You're right. And I'm sorry. You came to talk about something, and I ended up telling you my troubles."

"It seems only fair, since I'm always burdening you with mine."

"Nonsense. We're friends, and that's what friends do."

Since Hazel was regarding her expectantly, Catherine got right to the point. "I need advice, of course. It's about a former patient whom I expect to be treating again. Since the last time I saw her in therapy, I've gotten somewhat personally involved with her. What's more, Rebecca is involved with her too."

"How do you know she'll be returning?" Hazel asked astutely.

"She's a police officer, and she's sustained an on-duty injury. She'll need to be cleared psychologically before she returns to duty. Since she's seen me before, I expect she'll return."

"And you've gotten to know her outside of therapy, I take it."

Catherine nodded. "It's complicated." She laughed at her own understatement. "Of course it's complicated, or I wouldn't be here. She's an officer assigned to Rebecca's team, and I've worked with the team as a consultant fairly closely for the last month or so. The officer and I have worked together in that capacity."

"So it was still a professional relationship, essentially."

"Yes, and this particular individual is extraordinarily respectful of boundaries. She's very much like Rebecca." Catherine smiled, thinking of Dellon's quick temper and Rebecca's cool, tight control. "Although they're as different as night and day."

"You're fond of her, aren't you?"

Slightly taken aback, Catherine hesitated, considering the early-morning call she'd received from Rebecca just a few days before telling her that Dellon had been seriously injured and was on her way to the hospital. She remembered her swift relief that it hadn't been her lover who had been hurt, followed immediately by her concern for a young woman she had come to know and like. "I *do* like her. But I like many of my patients."

"I agree. If you didn't, I'd worry about that." Hazel lifted a mug and sipped, then made a face. "Cold tea. Almost as bad as cold coffee." She leaned forward, punched in several numbers on her phone, and asked Stef if she would mind bringing two cups of tea. "So you'll be seeing her in a somewhat limited capacity—short-term, focused on her recent injury. Correct?"

"Yes. Usually these things are resolved in three to five sessions." Catherine waited while Hazel got up to take the tea from her assistant. "Thank you," Catherine said, taking a mug from Hazel. "But sometimes other things come out, and I end up seeing the individual for long-term therapy."

"And that's where you think problems might arise?"

"Potentially." Catherine blew on the surface of the hot liquid and sipped. "Not necessarily. It's just there are more confounding factors in this particular relationship than I'm used to dealing with, and I wanted to talk it out with you. I don't want to transfer her in the midst of emerging issues."

"I take it you haven't been personally—socially—involved in any way."

"No, Rebecca wouldn't have that kind of a relationship with anyone she worked with, particularly a subordinate. Nor would I."

"I think the very fact that you're talking about it means you'll be particularly sensitive to boundary issues. I wouldn't worry about it." Hazel rested her mug on the corner of her desk. "So, how are things with you and the detective sergeant?"

"The detective sergeant is now a detective lieutenant. She just told me earlier today."

"That's wonderful, isn't it?"

"It is. I think." Catherine shook her head. "It's not what I thought it would be. I just assumed her promotion would mean she'd be doing mostly administrative work. Instead, they've given her command of some special unit to investigate high-profile crimes. That doesn't sound an awful lot safer than what she's been doing."

"Her job still worries you," Hazel observed matter-of-factly.

Just as honestly, Catherine answered. "Yes. It does. She goes to work every morning to a job where someone might try to kill her. I freely admit, I'm not well-adjusted to it."

Hazel smiled. "You sound a little angry. That's better than depressed, which was how you sounded the last time we talked about it."

Catherine huffed out a breath. "I suppose I'm moving toward acceptance, but I don't think it's ever going to be easy."

"I can't imagine that it ever could be. Are you happy with her?"

"Oh God, yes," Catherine replied instantly. "I…" She blushed. "I'm madly in love with her."

"Wonderful."

"We've talked about living together."

"That's news."

"I'm ready," Catherine said. "But I'm not sure that Rebecca is. Rather, I'm not sure that Rebecca *thinks* she is."

"She's afraid to disappoint you."

Catherine jerked, startled. "How did you know?"

"A better question is, how did you *not* know?"

"Oh," Catherine muttered with obvious frustration. "I hate it when we get to this point in these conversations." She took a breath and let it out slowly. "I did know. I *do* know. I just want her to realize that I'm different from the other women she's been with."

"I imagine she knows that," Hazel said gently. "What she doesn't realize is that *she's* different with *you* than she's been with anyone else. When she can see that, she'll trust herself with you."

"I'm having some sort of territorial reaction, aren't I?" Catherine gave a rueful laugh. "I can't believe I'm jealous of women I've never even met."

"Perfectly natural."

"Relationships certainly do bring our hidden fears rushing to the surface, don't they?"

"Being in love definitely does." Hazel stood and moved around her desk toward Catherine. When Catherine rose, Hazel put a friendly arm around her shoulders and together they walked toward the door. "You sound like you have a very firm hold on everything that's happening, both with your young police officer and your new lover. Trust your judgment. I always have."

"Thank you. I'm going to trust *your* judgment on this, because sometimes where Rebecca is concerned, I have no perspective at all." Catherine returned Hazel's hug and, feeling lighter of heart, left to face the rest of her day, looking forward to her evening with her lover.

"Come on, honey, get into bed with me."

Sandy folded her arms across her chest and regarded Dell suspiciously from the doorway. "What did you take?"

"Whatever Jason gave me." Mitchell pointed to several prescription vials on the bedside table. "He said I was supposed to take them."

"Whatever it was, it made you high."

"Nuh-uh. *You* do that." Mitchell patted the bed beside her and grinned. "If you cuddle up with me, I'll take a nap like I'm supposed to."

"You're going to want to fool around."

"Nah. I won't."

"You're lying, Dell."

"Maybe." Mitchell held out her hand. "Come on, honey. Please?"

"Just for a few minutes." Sandy slipped out of her sandals as she walked to the bed and, with practiced efficiency, shed her top and skirt as well and arrived at the bedside nude. "What?"

"You're so hot." Mitchell's voice was hoarse, her eyes huge as her gaze drifted down Sandy's figure. "Stand right there."

"What are you doing? You know we can't, not with your leg the way it is."

"Shh. I'm just looking."

"Then how come it feels like you're touching?"

"Must be 'cause I want to so much."

Sandy's hips gave a small involuntary jerk. "Shut up, Dell. There's no way we can do anything."

"Every time I see you, it's like…wow."

"Well, you're done lookin', rookie." Sandy lifted the sheets and slid into bed, pulling the covers to her shoulders. She turned on her side and propped her head in one hand, resting the other on Mitchell's abdomen. "Close your eyes and go to sleep."

"How come you covered up?"

"You know why. You turn me on bad when you look at me the way you just did."

"Yeah?" Mitchell leaned over, nudged the sheet aside with her chin, and kissed Sandy's breast just above her nipple. "So are you now?"

"Uh-huh." Sandy arched her back and drew her tense nipple across Mitchell's lips. "Kiss me there."

With a quiet moan, Mitchell closed her mouth on Sandy's small breast and sucked. When Sandy's fingers trembled in her hair, holding her head closer, she used her teeth. When Sandy's breathing caught, stuttered to a stop, and then picked up again, rapid and shallow, Mitchell teased her fingers up and down the center of Sandy's abdomen, making the muscles jump and twitch.

"You like that?" Mitchell beat her tongue back and forth across the tip of Sandy's nipple. "Baby?"

"Yesss." Sandy fisted her hand in Mitchell's hair and pulled. "Stop. Dell, stop."

Trembling, Mitchell laid her cheek in the hollow between Sandy's breasts, fighting to contain the wild urge to taste her everywhere. The tips of her fingers rested just at the edge of the silken strands between Sandy's thighs, and she struggled not to slide her fingers lower into the thick wet heat that she knew awaited her. Sandy's heart raced beneath her ear like a frantic rabbit running from a fox. Fearful that she'd gone too far too fast and forced Sandy into a place that wasn't pleasure, but pain, Mitchell asked gently, "Did I do something you didn't like?"

Sandy made a strangled sound, half sob, half laugh. "Sometimes… when you're touching me…it feels so good that I get confused."

"Confused?" Mitchell didn't move, didn't change the inflection or tone of her voice. She listened with all her heart, wanting nothing more than to understand what this one woman needed from her.

"When your mouth is on me like that…I can't tell where you are, but I can feel you everywhere inside of me…touching me in places I know you can't be touching me. I feel like I'm going to break, Dell. And I don't know what will happen if I do."

"I won't let you," Mitchell promised fervently. "I'll be right here. I'll hold you."

Sandy inched down on the bed until her face was even with Mitchell's. She looked into Mitchell's eyes. "I believe you. I do. But…

no one's ever made me feel what you do." She laughed harshly. "God, I never wanted anyone to make me feel *anything* when they touched me."

"I love you."

"Even knowing…what I am?"

"What *are* you, Sandy?" Mitchell's lips were almost touching Sandy's. She stroked Sandy's hips very gently with just the tips of her fingers.

"You know, Dell. I trade sex for money."

"When was the last time?"

"You don't want to know these things."

"Yes," Mitchell said quietly, but firmly. "I do."

"A week or so ago. A couple of car jobs down on Arch."

Mitchell never stopped her gentle caresses. "Before you signed on with Frye as her CI?"

Sandy nodded. "She told me it was part of the deal…that I don't hook."

"And that's the reason you stopped?"

This time, Sandy shook her head in the negative. "It wasn't for Frye."

"Why then?"

"I don't know," Sandy whispered. "After that psycho murdered Anne Marie, I quit everything except the quick stuff. Too much can happen when you're alone in a room with a guy."

Mitchell blinked. "That was months ago."

"Yeah."

"Maybe you're done with it?"

"Are you asking?"

"Not yet." Mitchell moved her hand from Sandy's hips to her belly and continued her soft caresses. "But I can't think about anyone else touching you."

"Don't think about it. Please." Sandy traced her fingers over the arch of Mitchell's cheekbone and down along the angle of her jaw. She very gently rested her fingers against Mitchell's mouth. "No one touches me except you."

"Someday," Mitchell whispered, "I'm going to have to ask."

"Dell," Sandy said softly. "I won't lie to you."

"I don't want you to."

"Then don't ask about what you don't want to know, okay?"

"For now." Mitchell kissed Sandy gently. "Can I look at you some more now?"

Sandy's laugh was shaky. "No sex."

"No promises."

"Dell," Sandy whispered, covering the hand that stroked her abdomen with her own. Looking into Mitchell's eyes, she guided Mitchell's hand lower between her thighs. "You see?"

"Oh, baby, you are so beautiful." Mitchell had a hard time getting air into her lungs, and the fever in her belly burned bright. "You have to let me make you come."

"You think…I'll say…no?" Sandy's hips undulated gently to the sweet, slow rhythm of Mitchell's fingers sliding over her ready flesh. Her lids flickered, and her eyes lost focus. With a small cry, she rested her forehead against Dell's, shivering all over. In a voice barely a whisper, she said, "Do it harder, baby."

"Not yet," Mitchell choked, fighting not to hurry. "I love the way you feel. I want it to last forever. Don't come yet."

Sandy's hand tightened on Mitchell's forearm, her fingers spasming erratically as her hips surged into Mitchell's palm. "Can't. Can't stop."

Mitchell held her breath, intent on capturing every sigh as Sandy climbed toward her climax. She stroked harder, faster, knowing it was too late to do anything but bring Sandy the release her body screamed for. At the first rolling tremor, she filled her, and the sudden pressure drove her over.

"Oh, Dell," Sandy sobbed. "Good…so good…so good."

Mitchell stayed inside her long after the contractions ended and Sandy curled against her, moaning quietly. Even so intimately joined, Mitchell ached to be closer. "I love you."

"If I touch you," Sandy said, her voice lazy with pleasure, "will you promise not to move?"

Mitchell laughed. "Sure."

"I mean it, rookie. If you so much as twitch, I'll stop. I'm not going to risk hurting your leg just so you can get off."

"I'm a cop. I have perfect control."

"Oh yeah? Let's see about that."

Mitchell held out longer than she thought she could, and when she finally broke under the tender torture of Sandy's hands, Sandy held her tightly and kept her safe. Just as Mitchell knew she would.

Chapter Six

"Oops, sorry." Sandy stumbled to a stop just inside the kitchen alcove, staring at the woman across the room and wondering how to disappear. The loft was so quiet she'd thought she and Dell were the only ones there. *Glad I put clothes on.*

Michael turned from the stove with a half smile and an inquiring expression. "Hi. I'm Michael."

"Oh, so you're Sloan's…" Sandy hesitated, because *girlfriend* didn't seem to suit the classy woman who managed to look Cosmo-beautiful even barefoot and wearing nothing but a black silk robe.

"Yes, I'm Sloan's, all right," Michael answered with a laugh. "And I guess you're Sandy?"

"Yeah. Look, I didn't mean to bother you. I'll just—"

"I was about to make some tea. Would you like some?"

Tea. Although what she'd been in the mood for was a beer, Sandy nodded. Trying not to be too obvious, she studied Michael in the dim glow of the overhead track lights. The woman looked very pale and unsteady on her feet. Sandy knew what had happened to her, but until that moment, she'd never appreciated how serious the injury had been. "You should probably sit down. I can do the tea, if you tell me where the stuff is."

"I've been trying to become more self-sufficient," Michael said, smiling wanly.

"Why?" Sandy asked as she padded over to the stove, suddenly conscious of how she must look. She'd pulled on Mitchell's jeans and T-shirt, and both hung loosely from her smaller frame. Barefoot, too, she was a head shorter than Michael.

"I hate being sick, and I'm tired of Sloan taking care of me." Michael leaned against the marble counter. "The tea is in that box over there."

"Sloan probably doesn't mind," Sandy said, as she studied the rows of tea bags neatly lined up in the slotted wooden case. She didn't recognize any of the names.

"I mind. And she's got enough things to worry about without me adding to it."

Catching the obvious note of frustration in the other woman's voice, Sandy glanced over her shoulder at Michael. "It hasn't been all that long, right? Since you got out of the hospital?"

"About a week." Michael pushed a hand through her shoulder-length blond hair. "God, it feels like forever. I just can't seem to…think clearly."

"That happens when you've been knocked around. It'll get better."

Michael's eyes moved to the pink scar on Sandy's forehead. "It's not fun, though, until it does, is it?"

"Nope. So…are some of these, like…special?" She tilted her chin toward the box. "Peppermint? Sleepy Time?"

"I'm not much on the flavored ones, myself. Would you rather have something else? There's soda or…" She hesitated, starting to assess Sandy's age before realizing that was foolish. Whatever the girl's chronological age, it had no bearing on who she was. "…beer or wine."

"Tea's fine." Sandy dangled two bags by their strings, swinging them gently. "How about English Breakfast? That sounds pretty straight."

"Perfect." Michael finally relented and sat at the breakfast bar while Sandy assembled the tea. "Thanks."

"Sure," Sandy replied as she settled on an adjacent stool. "This place is really neat. It's just like Sloan's place downstairs—all open except for the partitions."

"Are you working with Sloan?" Michael frowned. "I'm sorry. I'm still not remembering everything. You're not a police officer too, are you?"

Sandy snorted. "Oh man, no way."

"Computer security?"

"I, uh…help Frye out sometimes."

"Oh. How's Officer Mitchell doing?"

"Too much," Sandy complained. "She can't wait to get back to work."

"That seems to be some kind of occupational requirement." Michael smiled as if at some secret thought. "I'm glad you two decided to stay here until her leg heals a bit and she's getting around more easily."

"That was really nice of you. Thanks." Sandy sipped her tea, surprised to find that she liked it. "At least this way, Dell can work with Jason till she's better. That really matters to her…being part of the team."

"It's quite a crew, isn't it," Michael said with obvious fondness. "Sometimes I know that Sloan would rather be on her own, but I feel better that she's working with the others. I like to think they keep each other safe."

"Yeah." Sandy thought of Frye, and of how that night in the warehouse, with the guy between her legs—pinning her down—she'd trusted that Frye would come. Somehow in the last few weeks, she'd learned to count on Dell and Frye and the others, and when it wasn't scaring her, it felt good. "Yeah, I think you're right."

"Hey, honey," Mitchell said lazily. "Whatcha got for me?"

"Tea," Sandy replied, setting the mug on the bedside table. She switched on the lamp and examined the plastic prescription vials. "Jeez, strong stuff." She opened one, shook out a pill, and extended it to Mitchell. "Here, take this."

"Tea? How 'bout a beer?"

Sandy shook her head. "Nuh-uh. Not with this stuff—it'll knock you on your ass." She pursed her lips. "Although maybe that's not so bad."

Mitchell laughed and reached for the tea. "I'll take it tonight, just for you. But that's it. I can't think when I'm on this."

"Aw, you're so good." Sandy leaned down and kissed her. "Maybe you'll get a reward later."

"Going somewhere?" Mitchell demanded. She caught Sandy's hand and prevented her from moving away. "It's late, San. Come back to bed."

"I told you I wasn't going to be hanging around here all the time," Sandy replied, extracting her fingers from Mitchell's grip. "I have a life, y'know. I have things to do."

Mitchell pushed herself up in the bed and shoved the tea and the pill onto the bedside table. "What *things*? What can't wait until tomorrow morning?"

"I need clothes." Sandy indicated the borrowed jeans and T-shirt she still wore.

"So you can get them in the morning. You're not gonna wear anything to bed, are you?" Mitchell grinned.

"Jeez, what *is* it with you? Didn't we just take care of things for you?" Despite her words, Sandy's tone had softened. She brushed her fingers through Mitchell's hair. "No more for you tonight. You need to get some rest."

"Okay. So come to bed, and I will."

Sandy backed up a step. "I'll be back later, Dell."

"What are you doing, Sandy?" Mitchell's eyes were dark, her voice urgent. "Are you working? Is that it? Because if you need money—"

"If I do, I'm not taking it from you," Sandy snapped. "Not now, not ever. So just forget it."

"Wait!" Mitchell called as Sandy spun around and started from the room. She flung the covers off and swung her legs over the edge of the bed. The pain hit instantly. "*Fuck.*"

Inside a heartbeat, Sandy was back at her side. "*Idiot.* You're such a fucking idiot." Gently, she helped Mitchell lift her legs back to the bed and lie down. "What are you trying to do? Break something open?"

"You're making me crazy," Mitchell groaned. A wave of nausea followed the pain, and she closed her eyes, fighting the urge to vomit.

You're making me crazy.

Sandy stared, Frye's words echoing in her mind. *If you want her to be safe, then don't make her crazy. She has to go out the door every day knowing that you'll be there when she comes back. If you can't give her that, then let her go now.*

"Here," Sandy said softly, offering the tea and the pain medication again. "You need this. Take it, Dell."

Weakly, Mitchell complied, then closed her eyes again. When she felt the gentle weight of Sandy's body settle on the mattress next to her, she lifted her arm and made room for Sandy against her side. She leaned her cheek against her lover's. "You mad?"

"No. Just…" Sandy feathered a kiss over the edge of Mitchell's jaw. "You gotta give me a little space, Dell. I'm not used to answering to anyone."

"I know. I'm sorry."

"Fuck," Sandy muttered, inching closer. With a sigh, she nuzzled her face against Mitchell's neck. "It's okay. It's even…sorta nice, when I think about it."

Mitchell stroked Sandy's bare arm, then kissed her. "I'm not used to being with anyone either. I just love you so much…"

"Don't start with that now," Sandy warned, her voice husky. "I gotta go. I'm not fooling."

"Okay."

"I'm coming back, Dell. I promise. I'll be right here when you wake up." Sandy smoothed her hand down the center of Mitchell's chest and rose up enough to kiss her firmly on the mouth.

Mitchell closed her fingers around the back of Sandy's neck, holding her into the kiss long enough to taste her, deep inside. Then she let her go. "See you soon."

Catherine awakened to the sound of quiet movement in the dark. Far from being frightening, the experience was becoming not only welcome, but soothing. It meant that Rebecca was home, safe. The clock by the bedside read 3:38. Not many months ago, Rebecca would have patrolled the streets until the sun came up.

"You're early," Catherine murmured as she lifted the sheets and slid over to make room.

Sighing, Rebecca settled next to her and drew her close. "Sorry. I tried to be quiet."

"You were, but you don't need to be. I like to wake up when you come home." Catherine curved her leg over Rebecca's thighs, and the touch of her lover's skin stirred her as always. "Is everything all right?"

"Yeah." Rebecca slid her hand under Catherine's hair and alternated between stroking the back of her neck and weaving the thick, soft strands through her fingers. "I spent most of the last six hours watching George Beecher hit on women in fern bars."

Catherine laughed. "I don't think they call them that anymore, darling."

"Well, whatever they call the places where swinging singles go to hook up, that's where I was. Jesus, what a life."

"He's still one of your two prime candidates as the Mob's inside man in the department?" Even as she asked, Catherine shook her head. "I can't believe I'm even saying this. It seems impossible." Then she remembered the night that she'd raced from Sloan's building to find Michael lying in the street unconscious and knew that it was all far too real. "God, an assistant district attorney."

"Better than a cop," Rebecca pronounced.

"Yes."

"I trust Sloan's information. We have to run with the names she's given us until we come up with something more solid."

"So you're going to…what? Follow him around every night?"

Rebecca shrugged. "Once we get the first bit of hard evidence, I can justify twenty-four-hour surveillance to Henry. Until then, yeah, it'll be just me. Watts is taking the woman."

Catherine was silent, struggling to assimilate the reality of her lover's work. That it was a valuable service, she did not doubt. That it was essential to the structure of the society in which she lived, she did not doubt. She respected Rebecca's skill and was proud of her dedication. And she hated every minute, day or night, that Rebecca squared off, face-to-face, with evil.

"I see," Catherine finally said, because regardless of how she felt, Rebecca would do what needed to be done.

"It's not dangerous," Rebecca said as if reading Catherine's thoughts. "Only deadly boring."

"I don't mind you being bored now and then," Catherine murmured, smoothing her palm over the center of Rebecca's chest. The tips of her fingers brushed the ridge of scar tissue at the upper border of her lover's left breast, and she faltered, the tactile sensation triggering the memory of the bullet impacting Rebecca's chest.

"It won't happen again," Rebecca murmured, gathering Catherine's fingers and lifting them to her lips. She kissed each fingertip, then the palm. When Catherine moaned softly in appreciation, the sound struck home hard. Suddenly, every cell vibrated, and the need to join exploded in the very heart of her. "Catherine."

The word was a benediction in the darkness.

"Yes," Catherine answered the unspoken.

Rebecca arched her back and angled her hips until Catherine was beneath her and her hands framed Catherine's face. "Don't worry."

"I don't." Catherine kissed her, a gentle brush of lips, then a deeper caress of tongue against tongue. "Not much."

"You lie very badly, Dr. Rawlings." Rebecca drew Catherine's lower lip between her teeth and nibbled gently before easing her mouth over the crest of her lover's chin and down her throat. As she worked her lips along the smooth skin, Catherine tilted her head back, exposing the fragile structures to Rebecca's teeth. The trust in that simple gesture drove the breath from Rebecca's chest, and as need ripped through her, she skimmed a hand between Catherine's thighs. Finding her lover wet, she teased a finger between her lips and over her firm clitoris, sliding through Catherine's desire with tantalizing slowness.

Gasping, Catherine dug her fingers into Rebecca's back and lifted her hips, seeking more of the enticing touch. "You're so good at that."

"What?" Rebecca rubbed her cheek over Catherine's breast and captured a nipple with her lips. She toyed with the hard nub, flicking it with her tongue as she echoed the rhythm with her fingers. "Oh." Flick. "You mean…" Tug. "This?"

"Yes. Oh God." Catherine nearly screamed as her body stiffened. She drove her face into Rebecca's neck and, in a voice almost too strangled to be heard, pleaded, "Inside. Make me come…deep."

Rebecca pushed herself up on one arm as she buried herself in Catherine's yielding depths. She pushed steadily, gasping as tissue slick with passion enveloped her, claiming her even as she laid claim.

"Oh Christ," Rebecca whispered. "I love you." She leaned back to bring Catherine up to face her, her arm thrusting steadily between Catherine's thighs.

"I can't…" Catherine gasped for air. "Can't wait much longer."

Rebecca's thumb found Catherine's rigid clitoris, and she stroked firmly. "I don't want you to wait. I want you to come all over me, right now."

"Oh, I am. I am." Catherine shivered, then froze as a cry tore from her throat. As her climax crested, she dropped her head to Rebecca's shoulder and sucked hard on the thick muscle.

The unexpected sensation lanced through Rebecca's chest and belly, igniting the nerve endings that already danced on the edge of explosion. "Touch me. Catherine, God, touch me."

Still coming, Catherine skimmed her hand down Rebecca's tensed abdomen and between her legs, closing unerringly around her clitoris. Beyond thought, she tugged at Rebecca with the same staccato rhythm that pulsed through her body, harder than she might have had she been aware of her actions.

"Oh," Rebecca shouted, shocked into orgasm. "Oh yeah…oh."

As they clung to one another in the final moments of release, their cries mingled and eventually dwindled to faint moans and soft whimpers. Rebecca carried Catherine with her down onto the bed, cradling her against her chest. Catherine groped for the sheet and pulled it over them.

"I don't know how you do that," Catherine murmured, her voice thick with the vestiges of passion. "Know just what I need, just when I need it."

"Just lucky, I guess," Rebecca said seriously. She stroked Catherine's hair. "I feel so damn lucky to have you."

"What we have," Catherine said. "It's precious."

"I know." Rebecca sighed. "I'm trying to deserve it. I know I probably don—"

Catherine pressed her fingers to Rebecca's mouth. "Shh. That's not what I meant." She pressed a kiss to the scar that marked Rebecca's heart. "I want you more than anything else in my life—more than safety, more than certainty, more than promises. Just you, here with me like this, every night. When you can, give me that."

"I will," Rebecca whispered. *When I'm sure I won't disappoint you, I will.*

Chapter Seven

Tuesday

Hey, it's about time you showed up." Jason greeted Mitchell with an affectionate smile and rolled an office chair in her direction. "Park it there, and let's get to work."

Gingerly, Mitchell leaned her crutches against a bench, eased into the chair, and propelled herself across the hardwood floor with her good leg to Jason's side. "Man, it feels good to get down here."

"How'd you escape?"

"Sandy got in late. She's still asleep. I think Michael's napping too."

"Well, let's just see how much we can get done before Sandy hauls your ass back upstairs."

"I'm a lot better," Mitchell protested.

"Don't tell me—tell her. She's the one riding herd on you."

Mitchell grinned. "Where's everyone else?"

"Rebecca called earlier. She and Watts have to be in court for some other case and will be by later. Sloan is at Police Plaza with the detectives she's training for the new Electronic Surveillance Unit." He shook his head. "They have no *clue* what they're in for."

"You know, six weeks ago I would've done anything to get assigned to that unit."

"So what changed your mind?" Jason pushed a stack of computer printouts toward her. "I bet Rebecca could get you assigned if you wanted. It wouldn't hurt for us to have another inside computer technician."

"Uh-uh. I've got other things to do now." Mitchell shuffled the papers. "Are these the hits on the porn subscribers?"

"Yep. We need to start putting names to accounts." Jason brought up a spreadsheet on the monitor. "This is how I've broken down the data so far."

"Okay. Split it up and I'll get going."

"So," Jason said, transferring files, "you like the undercover thing, huh?"

"Yeah," Mitchell said absently as she scanned the figures scrolling on her screen.

"And Mitch. You like Mitch too."

Slowly, Mitchell swiveled to face Jason. "You know I do."

"And you're still okay with it?"

If it had been anyone other than Jason, she might not have answered. But Jason was the one person, other than Sandy, whom she trusted to understand. "It feels good. Like, just another part of me."

Jason nodded, his eyes on her face. Waiting.

"And, well, Sandy likes it too."

"That's handy."

Mitchell grinned. "And *I* like that she likes it."

"Even better." Jason appeared to be weighing his words. "Sometimes it can get confusing."

"Are you ever confused?" Mitchell asked softly.

"No," Jason replied just as softly. "Never about what I feel, only about what others might think."

"I already know what the only people who matter to me think."

Jason looked as if he wanted to ask more, but he merely nodded. "The boys were asking after Mitch last night. I told them he was laid up for a few days because of the motorcycle accident. They want to visit."

Mitchell blinked. "Here?"

"I told them he was staying with some friends. It would probably be good for your cover if they saw you and Sandy together."

"What about all the security and stuff in the building? Don't you think that'll make them curious?"

"They won't ever see this floor, because we'll program the elevator to go right to the loft. All they're going to see is the garage and Sloan and Michael's apartment."

"What about the camera over the door? Most people don't have one of those."

Jason grinned. "We have a custom light fixture that screws over it for just such times as these."

"Okay then. When?"

"Jasmine has a show tonight. The kings will probably be there. You up for it afterward?"

"Sure." Mitchell wondered, however, if Sandy would be ready for Mitch to get back to work.

Watts, carrying a Styrofoam cup brimming with mud-colored coffee, ambled down the hall leaving a trail of splashes on the scuffed tile floor in his wake. He leaned against the door frame of a large room that resembled the vice squad room with its haphazard arrangement of desks and mismatched chairs—but there were ten times as many computers here. Sipping his coffee absently, he regarded the two men in shirtsleeves and baggy chinos—the kind of nerdy guys who got their asses kicked in high school—as they listened with rapt attention to Sloan. She was half turned away from him, one hip hiked up on a desk, as she pointed to something on a monitor that Watts couldn't see. He had assumed that she'd be bored to tears setting up whatever it was the city wanted her to do, but to his surprise, she seemed to be into whatever she was saying. Even from where he was standing, he could sense her energy. He pushed away from the doorway and strolled in to join the group.

"How's it going?" he asked.

"Just getting organized," Sloan replied, easing off the desk. "You guys go ahead and get the network hardwired. I'll be back."

When she indicated the hallway with a tilt of her head, Watts nodded and preceded her out. Once there, he said, "I'd have brought you coffee, but this stuff doesn't qualify."

"Thanks anyway. I know better than to ingest anything around here."

"I see you got stuck with the pocket-protector twins." Watts snorted. "Hard to believe they're detectives."

Sloan suppressed a smile. "They're eager."

"So you're really going to set up this electronic spy thing?"

"That's what they're paying me to do." Sloan grinned. "Although if I only gave them what they're actually paying me for, they *might* be able to manage interdepartmental data retrieval in a decade or so."

"Nothing but the best when you work for the city."

"Yeah, I noticed that." Sloan glanced into the room where the two detectives were absorbed in sorting out a tangle of cables. She lowered her voice. "But once I get the various networks connected, I'll be able to browse any database I choose. I already *know* someone on the inside has been hacking data from the crime lab and the detective bureau's files. With unlimited access, I can trace him back to the source computer, not just the department."

"How long?" Watts asked eagerly.

"If I had Jason and Mitchell here, maybe a week, but there's no way to do that without someone getting suspicious." Sloan lifted a shoulder. "Working by myself—I don't know. I could get lucky, or it could take me a few weeks."

"How long if you sleep once in a while?"

Sloan's mouth tightened. "I have a wife, Watts. I don't need another one."

Watts smirked. "How about a boyfriend?"

"How about you finish your coffee break somewhere else and let me get to work."

"I was hoping you could do me a favor."

"What?"

"I need to look at some files that don't exist."

"Yeah?" Sloan's eyes brightened. "And where might these nonexistent files be located?"

"Well—I figure one of three places. Captain Henry, Avery Clark, or buried in the narco records."

"You want to know what Jimmy Hogan was doing for the Justice Department that got him killed."

Watts nodded.

"It's not Henry," Sloan said with certainty. "When the initial evidence pointed to him as being the mole, I went through every byte of data in his system. He never had anything to do with Hogan's undercover assignment and never got a single report from him. That all went to narco, because Hogan was presumably their boy." Her expression hardened. "Of course, no one knew he was *really* Justice's plant and working for Clark. So it's possible he never filed any kind of substantive report with the PPD but just passed everything he got on to the feds."

"Maybe. But Hogan must've been feeding *some* tidbits to Jeff

Cruz, or else why would Jeff have been with him down on the docks the day they were shot?" Watts slid a crumpled pack of cigarettes from his jacket pocket and shook one out. He lit it with a scratched and dented Zippo and took a deep drag. "Hogan either thought Jeff knew something, or he decided to cut Jeff and the Loo in on his investigation."

"Hogan was supposed to be undercover investigating the drug arm of Zamora's operation. Frye and Cruz didn't have anything to do with drugs." Sloan followed the trail of smoke from Watts's cigarette as it curled indolently toward the ceiling. "You're gonna set off the smoke alarms."

"Nah. None of them work."

"No," Sloan mused, her mind still occupied with the elusive connection between Jimmy Hogan, a federal agent working undercover as a narcotics detective working undercover as a small-time drug dealer, and Jeff Cruz, a detective in the Special Crimes Unit who dealt primarily with sex crimes. The obvious tie-in was that all of those criminal endeavors were part of the organized crime network. "Too loose."

"Huh? What? The smoke detectors?"

"The association."

Watts squinted through the fumes. "You wanna give me a hint here?"

"It has to be something more specific than just the fact that the Zamora organization was behind the crimes that both Hogan and Cruz were investigating. Something links the drugs and the sex."

"It always comes down to the same thing," Watts noted sourly. "Puss—uh, girls. It's gotta be the prostitution."

"That makes sense, since Clark showed up and put us all on the trail of the Internet pornographers." She jammed her hands in her pockets and started pacing. "There have to be reports from Hogan to Clark. If he wrote them on a computer or e-mailed them, I can find them."

"You work on that," Watts dropped the butt and crushed it under the toe of his scuffed wingtip, "and I'll drop around to narco and see if I can get anything out of the guys Hogan was *supposedly* reporting to. If I can get you a name, you'll have another thread to pull."

"Fine. I'll be here turning the Wonder Boys into cybersleuths for a while yet."

"Yeah. Don't forget their red capes. Meanwhile, I'll do some real detecting." Laughing to himself, Watts sauntered off, a happy man with a mission.

❖

"Mmm." Sandy purred and stretched as a warm mouth slowly deposited gentle kisses down the back of her neck and between her shoulder blades. Without opening her eyes, face still buried in the pillow, she reached behind her and felt for the familiar form. Finding it, she smoothed a hand over the subtle curve of hip. "I'm sleeping, Dell."

"Go ahead," Mitchell whispered, continuing her tactile journey down the center of her lover's back. She swirled the tip of her tongue in the hollow at the base of Sandy's spine as she caressed her fingers up the inside of Sandy's leg, stopping to stroke the buttery-soft skin high on the inside of her thighs. "I'm fine here by myself."

Sandy shifted, drawing up one knee, opening herself to her lover's quest. "Yeah? Then how come you're touching me instead of yourself?"

"'Cause you're sexier." Emphasizing her words, Mitchell traced a fingertip ever so lightly along the lacy border of Sandy's labia, coating the delicate tissue with the moisture that rose beneath her touch. Her voice was husky when she murmured, "See?"

"I'm too tired for sex," Sandy groused, but her hips lifted in silent invitation.

"I'm just petting you. You don't need to wake up." Mitchell eased onto her right side, taking care not to put any weight on her injured leg, and cupped Sandy's sex in her palm. Still squeezing gently, she followed the curve of Sandy's ear with her lips until she reached the fleshy lobe. Sucking the plump flesh in and out between her lips, she pressed the pad of her finger to the tip of Sandy's clitoris.

"Too late," Sandy gasped. "Everything just woke up."

Mitchell chuckled. "I noticed." She rocked the stiff prominence of Sandy's decidedly aroused clitoris, her stomach tightening as Sandy whimpered. "Oh man, me too."

"What?" Sandy pushed back into Mitchell's hand, rotating her hips, working herself against the teasing fingers. "What, baby?"

"*Wide* awake."

"Too bad." Sandy's breath came in short, shallow bursts. "You started it. You finish me first."

"Say please," Mitchell taunted, pulling her fingers away from the spot where she knew Sandy wanted her, at the same time dragging her teeth down the side of Sandy's neck. Sandy shivered and moaned.

"If you fuck with me now you'll pay, rookie," Sandy warned, pushing her hips into Mitchell's crotch. "I swear…you'll be sorry."

"I'll risk it."

"Come on, baby. Don't tease. I wanna come."

"Bad?"

"Touch me and see." Sandy's breath caught as Mitchell dipped inside her, then out again. "Do that…again…I'll come for you."

Mitchell's stomach tightened, her clitoris twitching, but she ignored the painful pleasure. She pressed her thumb firmly to the tight circle of muscle between Sandy's buttocks while sliding her fingers over the slick, swollen labia. Sandy bucked as if jolted with an electric current.

"Dell…" Sandy's voice shook. "I don't know…if…"

"It's okay," Mitchell soothed. "I won't if you don't want me to."

"I…just…easy." Sandy fisted the sheets, her legs tensing. "Talk to me…talk to me while you make me come."

"That's it, honey," Mitchell whispered, her mouth against Sandy's ear as she carefully massaged the sensitive ring. "That's all I'm going to do this time, just make you feel good." When Sandy began to push back against her, Mitchell held pressure with her thumb while sliding her fingers in and out of her lover's warm depths. "That's right. Take me all the way in, honey."

"More," Sandy gasped.

Despite the urgent thrust of Sandy's hips, Mitchell held back, fearful of going too far too fast. Instead, she worked her free hand beneath Sandy's body and caught her clitoris in her fingers.

Sandy made a faint, high keening sound, and Mitchell squeezed harder.

"*Coming.* Dell…Dell…"

Eyes closed, Mitchell pressed her forehead to Sandy's back and worked her lover with both hands, squeezing and stroking and filling her to overflowing. Mitchell's arms trembled and her hips thrust erratically in time to her lover's as Sandy climaxed with a choked cry. Releasing a pent-up breath, Mitchell smiled and relaxed against Sandy's side.

Long moments later, Sandy muttered, "You fall asleep?"

"Uh-uh."

"Did you come?"

"Uh-uh."

"Wanna?"

Carefully, Mitchell rolled over onto her back and Sandy followed, curling up in the curve of her body. "I think I'm pretty good. Sometimes when you come, it feels like I did too."

"You think you'll get tired of it?"

"Tired of what?" Mitchell snugged her cheek against the top of Sandy's head while making aimless patterns over Sandy's shoulder with her fingertips. She'd never felt so peaceful in her life.

"You know…the sex thing."

When Mitchell didn't reply, Sandy stiffened. "Never mind. It's dumb."

"Sandy," Mitchell murmured, tightening her hold before Sandy could move away. "I want to make love with you for the rest of my life."

"Jeez, rookie." Sandy forced a laugh, struggling to hide her shock. "I just meant…that's not why I…you don't have to say—"

"I know," Mitchell interrupted. "I'm just telling you the way I feel."

"I don't think we oughtta talk about this. Because it's just too crazy."

"Okay," Mitchell replied easily. "We don't have to talk about it now." She lifted her head and kissed Sandy soundly on the mouth. "But I meant it."

"You just don't quit, do you," Sandy complained. But her eyes were soft with longing and desire.

"Not where you're concerned," Mitchell whispered. She caught Sandy's hand and drew the small fingers down the center of her abdomen and between her legs, where she held them cupped against her. "And I'm wide awake now, honey."

Chapter Eight

Rebecca piloted the Corvette through the narrow one-way streets of South Philadelphia. Watts, hunched in the passenger seat beside her, was for once mercifully silent. Turning left onto Delaware Avenue, the wide four-lane highway that ran along the waterfront, she drove north until she reached the parking lot adjacent to the Maritime Museum. She parked alongside the huge wooden pilings, interconnected by rusted links of chain, that formed the only barrier between someone standing on the blacktop and the roiling brown water of the Delaware River twenty feet below.

Wordlessly, she switched off the engine and slid out. A moment later, Watts joined her at the edge of the pier. Directly below them, a fifteen-foot-square wooden dock rocked on the water, matching the rhythm of the ebb and flow of the currents. The chalk outlines of the two bodies that had lain there six months before had been washed away by the waves and the rain in the intervening months. But Rebecca could still see, with photographic clarity, exactly how her partner Jeff Cruz and the undercover narcotics detective, Jimmy Hogan, had looked. Right down to the small, neat, matching holes in the backs of their heads. Her hands closed into fists.

"Loo?" Watts asked carefully.

"We should have something by now, Watts." Rebecca's tone was pensive, her expression brooding. "We've been taking bites out of the Zamora operation all summer—even made a few busts, grabbed a few headlines." She snorted derisively. "But we can't get a handle on who killed two of our own." She turned her head, gave Watts a hard stare. "What the fuck are we missing?"

"Well, you know, we figure it was a contract hit, right? Untraceable."

Rebecca stared back at the water. "We might never get the

triggerman. But whoever gave the order is right here." She let her gaze follow the river south, then half turned and swept the city skyline. "Jimmy and Jeff—one of them was getting close to something big. Something *so* big it made killing two cops an acceptable risk."

"This pornography ring," Watts offered. "Shutting that down has got to be taking a chunk out of Zamora's income. Maybe Hogan got wind of it through his drug connections and wanted to clue you and Cruz in. And maybe that's what got them killed."

"How long do you think it will be before this network is up and running again? Or one just like it?"

Watts shrugged as he fingered a cigarette from his pocket. "Half a year, maybe. The equipment doesn't cost much, there's always plenty of perverts, and a new crop of girls hits the streets every day."

Rebecca nodded. "You know it. I know it. So does Zamora. Why take the chance of bringing the full attention of the PPD down on your head for six months' income?" She shook her head. "Just doesn't play."

"Maybe Jimmy got wind of a big drug shipment. An eighteen-wheeler full of blow is definitely worth a couple of bodies."

"Agreed." Absently, Rebecca leaned forward with both hands braced on the wooden piling in an attempt to stretch the tight muscles in her chest. Between the surgical incisions and the damage from the gunshot wound, the left side of her chest was constantly in spasm. It didn't help, and she pushed off with an irritated shake of her head. "Except I have to believe that Jimmy would've told someone in narco about it and not us. We're sex crimes, not drugs."

"Yeah, can't argue." Watts flicked the butt into the river. "Something in the middle. It always comes back to that."

"The currency of flesh."

"Huh?"

Rebecca regarded Watts solemnly. "Sex. It sells, it pays, it's the common denominator that runs through every branch of Zamora's organization. We have to concentrate on the girls."

"Yeah," Watts spat in frustration. "But what *about* them? Most of them have no pasts we can trace, no permanent address, and no interest in helping us. It's like they're right there in front of us and invisible at the same time."

"Exactly. We need to start creating some solid profiles. Facts, not fantasies."

Watts snorted. "Should be a snap. And just where do you plan on starting?"

"Ziggie's."

❖

"Honey?"

"Yeah?" Sandy replied, leaning into the closet as she sorted through the clothes in a faded floral brocade suitcase she'd brought from her apartment.

"I'm gonna need your help a little later on tonight, so can you plan on being back here around midnight? I mean, if you're going out?"

Slowly, Sandy pivoted, a white satin thong dangling from her fingers. "I was thinking of wearing this. What do you think?"

"I think it's really sexy," Mitchell said, trying to keep the bite from her voice. *I think if you're going out, you shouldn't be wearing anything like that. Why would you need to?*

"Yeah," Sandy mused as she closed her fingers around the slip of material. "Me too. *And* since I was planning on staying here and watching videos with you and Michael, I thought you could think about it while you're eating popcorn."

"You like to tease me, don't you?" Mitchell rolled to the edge of the bed and levered herself upright with her crutches in one adroit move.

"Slick," Sandy observed, holding out one arm with her palm extended. "Just stay right over there, supercop. And yes, I like to tease you. It makes your eyes get this dark, dark hungry blue color. You complaining?"

"Nope." Ignoring Sandy's directive, Mitchell closed the distance between them until she was inches from her lover. Then she angled the crutches against the wall and placed both hands on Sandy's waist for balance. "But you know what happens if you tease the animals." She lowered her head and nipped at Sandy's neck. "You get bitten."

Sandy slapped a hand against Mitchell's chest. "No teeth. No lips either. I told Michael we'd hang out with her tonight. She's ordering pizza and everything. I don't want to be horny the whole time."

Mitchell snaked her arm further around Sandy's waist and nuzzled her neck. "Give me five minutes. I promise to make you happy."

"All I have to do is push," Sandy murmured seductively, her mouth against Mitchell's ear. "And you'll fall on your ass."

"I don't mind if you're on top. Makes me hot." Mitchell chuckled when Sandy bit her earlobe. Hard. "Okay. Okay."

"What's happening later, anyways?"

"Jasmine is bringing the kings around. I want to gear up."

Gently but firmly, Sandy pushed Mitchell away. "You're not going out with them tonight."

"No. Uh-uh. They just want to see how Mitch is doing."

"Okay." Sandy's tone was doubtful.

"I'm going to see Dr. Rawlings tomorrow afternoon," Mitchell informed her quietly. "I need to get cleared so I can go back to work, San."

"You're still on crutches."

"I have that appointment with Dr. Torveau in the morning, too, remember? You're coming, right?"

"I said I was."

"So," Mitchell said nonchalantly, "maybe I can get a cane."

Sandy sat on the side of the bed, her arms braced on either side of her body as she leaned back and regarded Mitchell suspiciously. "Promise you don't go back to work until you're a hundred percent."

Mitchell fidgeted.

"Dell."

"I was sort of planning on going to the club this weekend. I should be okay by then."

"Are you going to ride your bike?"

Mitchell raised a shoulder. "Probably."

"Then Dr. Torveau has to say it's okay."

"Oh Christ, come on, Sandy—"

"Promise."

Carefully, Mitchell shuffled to the bedside and eased down next to Sandy, keeping her left leg out straight. She put her arm around the smaller woman. "I promise."

Sandy settled against Mitchell, both arms around her waist and her head on Mitchell's shoulder. "Then I'll help Mitch get ready tonight."

"Thanks."

"Under one condition."

Mitchell sighed. "Okay."

Sandy raised her head and peered at Mitchell curiously. "Okay? Just like that?"

"I'm going to say yes eventually."

Laughing, Sandy nipped at Mitchell's chin, then kissed the tiny red spot. "You're pretty smart for a cop."

"Yeah." Mitchell kissed her. "So what did I just agree to?"

Sandy smoothed her hand down the front of Mitchell's T-shirt, danced over her fly, and cupped her between the legs. "Mitch wears his working gear."

Oh yeah. Too busy kissing Sandy again, Mitchell didn't answer.

"How's it going?" Sloan brushed her hands over Michael's shoulders as she leaned down to kiss her neck.

"Mmm." Michael tilted her head back against Sloan's chest and closed her eyes as strong fingers massaged the tight muscles along her spine. "A little better than yesterday. I can actually read for ten or fifteen minutes at a time without getting a headache."

"That's great, baby." Carefully, Sloan swiveled the office chair around so that Michael faced her, then knelt before her. With a thumb, she traced the smudges beneath the sapphire eyes that were still dimmed with pain. "Tired?"

Michael covered Sloan's hand with hers and rubbed her cheek against Sloan's palm. "Yes. But that's better too."

"Good."

"How was *your* day?" Michael combed her fingers through Sloan's hair, then rested her hand against the side of Sloan's neck. "You look a little…harried."

Sloan gave a crooked grin. "I'd forgotten just exactly how much I hate working in a bureaucracy. It takes three times as long to do anything. And the equipment…I don't know how they can keep track of parking tickets with the system they have, let alone collate data on criminals." She laughed. "It's a challenge."

"Did they give you some help?"

"A couple of fairly decent guys." Sloan thought of the two detective threes who'd been pulled from burglary to form the core of the ESU. Two guys who'd been selected because they'd once upon a time taken a computer course. But their inexperience bothered her less than her new official status as the civilian head of the unit. The ESU might be tucked away in the corner, but news would travel fast. She forced a smile, determined to concentrate on Michael and forget about what she couldn't control for a few hours. "I've missed you."

"I love you." Michael caressed Sloan's cheek. "You know, not talking about it won't help."

Sloan frowned. "I'm sorry?"

"There's something you're not telling me."

"You're definitely getting better. You're back to reading my mind."

"I may have forgotten some things, darling, but I remember everything about you." Michael leaned down and kissed Sloan lingeringly, a gentle but possessive kiss. "You don't hide things from me. And even when you try to avoid telling me what you think I'm not ready to hear, it shows."

"It's nothing you need to be concerned about."

"Is it something to do with you?" Michael asked mildly.

"Not exactly. Maybe."

"Then it has to do with me."

With a sigh, Sloan inched closer and pillowed her head against Michael's breasts. Michael in turn stroked the back of her neck. Finally, Sloan mumbled, "It's the visibility. If there's anyone the least bit suspicious that we might be trying to track them down, my presence at Police Plaza is going to tip them off. They could start to cover their tracks. Computer tracks, that is. I'm working against the clock."

"They know who you are, don't they."

"Probably."

"They know that you can find them."

Sloan nodded wordlessly.

"And you think," Michael said haltingly, "you think my accident wasn't an accident. That someone was trying to hurt *you* and I was just in the way."

"We don't know that," Sloan said quickly.

"But that's what you think."

"Michael—"

"So it follows...*God,* I wish I could think clearly. It follows, doesn't it...if they see you at police headquarters working on the computer system, they might feel even more threatened." Michael's fingers trembled against the back of Sloan's neck. "And they might want to...be more...*thorough* than the first time."

"It's not going to happen." Sloan leaned back and framed Michael's face in her hands, her thumbs gently caressing the curve of her lover's jaw. "Baby, there's nothing for you to worry about."

"Promise me you'll be careful."

"Always."

"Can you stay here tonight instead of going back to work? Sandy picked up some videos, and I'm going to order pizza."

Sloan thought about the work she had planned to do in the office downstairs, reviewing the data that Jason and Mitchell had collected in the last few days and running some traces herself. She thought about the long hours she had been away from home since the case had started to break the weekend before, and how often Michael had been alone. By the time she came to bed it was often almost morning, and she frequently rose after only an hour or two of sleep and went back to work. With guilty eyes, she noted the circles under her lover's eyes, the pale cast of her skin, and the whisper of hollows beneath her cheekbones. Michael might be out of danger, but she was far from well.

"Comedy or drama?"

"Actually, I think she got *Night of the Living Dead* and every one of the sequels."

"I'm in." Sloan rose and guided Michael to her feet, pulling her into a loose embrace. She buried her face in Michael's fragrant hair, relaxing into the welcoming curves of her lover's body. For the first time all day, she felt calm. "Pizza?"

"Extra cheese."

"Maybe I'll just forget about working tonight. After the movies, we can escape and go to bed early."

Michael guided Sloan's mouth to hers, whispering against her lips, "I'd like that."

Chapter Nine

"It won't work, Mitch." Sandy stood with a hand on her cocked hip, studying Mitch through narrowed eyes as he finished buttoning his fly. His dark hair was slicked back, with just a single thick wave slashing across his broad forehead, his chest and stomach were flat beneath the tight stretch of his black T-shirt, and his narrow hips seemed tight and powerful beneath the faded black jeans.

He looked up, surprised and worried. "What's wrong?" He ran a hand over his chest. "Is the Ace too bulky? Does it show through my shirt?"

Sandy shook her head. "No, it looks good."

"Not enough shading?" He traced along his jaw where Sandy had expertly accentuated the already strong lines with the subtle application of makeup.

Another negative head shake.

"So what—?"

"It's not your *face.*" Sandy smiled faintly at Mitch's obvious expression of distress and twined her arms around his neck. With her body tight to his and her mouth against his ear, she whispered, "I can tell you have a hard-on."

Mitch laughed, a combination of embarrassment and pride. He pulled her closer to his groin, his hands spread across her lower back. The pressure of her body against the fullness in his jeans sent the blood thundering to his belly. "You told me that's what you wanted, right? The working gear?"

"Yes," Sandy admitted, rolling her hips over him lazily. "But Michael might get up. And I don't want her to see you like this."

"Why?" Mitch searched her face, frowning. "Are you embarrassed?"

Sandy bumped him sharply, groin to groin, making him gasp in surprise. "No," she said, as if speaking to a five-year-old. "I just don't want any other woman but me checking out your equipment."

"Sandy," Mitch complained, distracted by the subtle insistence of her hips moving against him. "It's always gonna show some. And even if Michael sees, she isn't going to be interest—"

"You don't *know* that," Sandy whispered as she slid a hand between their bellies and cupped the rigid length of him. "You look so hot." She squeezed, massaging him rhythmically. "And this is mine, baby."

Mitch was losing focus, every sense concentrated on the exquisite pressure against the turgid tissue beneath the cock in Sandy's hand. His stomach spasmed, and his legs shook. "Sandy. *Honey.* You gotta cut that out."

With a hand between his legs and one around his shoulders, Sandy walked him back against the dresser, until she had him pinned with the weight of her body fused to his. She pumped him faster and watched his eyes glaze. "You like it, baby?"

"Oh…jeez…honey…" Mitch trembled and groaned. "You're gonna get me off like that."

"I could," Sandy said sweetly, stilling her hand as she kissed his mouth. Still leaning into him, she stroked her tongue inside his mouth until he quivered the way he did when he was getting ready to come. Then she eased away. "But I'm not going to, not right now."

Mitch braced an arm along the edge of the dresser for support, his chest heaving. "What are you doing to me? Honey, what are you doing?"

She stroked his cheek. Kissed him again. Pumped his cock one more time with her hand. Eased farther away. "I want you to remember where this belongs. Now go change into something that's not gonna make every girl within a mile want to fuck you."

"If I move right now, I might come."

"Are you hard, baby?"

"Oh yeah."

She nipped his chin gently. "Good. Save it." Forcing herself to back completely away, when what she wanted to do was unbutton his jeans and pull him down on top of her and *into* her, she said, "I'm going to get dressed."

Smiling a satisfied smile, Sandy pretended she didn't hear him whimper as she turned her back and stripped off her top.

❖

"Darling?" Michael massaged Sloan's back as she lay with her head pillowed against Michael's breast.

"Mmm?"

"I think there's a party going on in the other room."

"Mmm."

"Are you awake, or are you just humoring me by pretending to be listening?"

"Mmm-hmm."

Michael gently extricated herself from her lover's grasp and sat up in bed. "I think I hear Sarah's voice."

Sloan rolled onto her back and lazily opened her eyes. "How come I'm wasted and you're wide awake?"

"Because you did all the work," Michael murmured, stroking Sloan's cheek. "In fact, as I recall, you were having one of those butch attacks and wouldn't let me do anything." Her fingers hesitated, then began their slow caress again. "Are you afraid to let me get too excited?"

Sloan stiffened. "No. You had an orgasm, right?"

"Yes," Michael agreed gently. "A very sweet, very tender, very *quiet* orgasm. And when I wanted to touch you, you—"

"Baby," Sloan interrupted, "I just couldn't wait. I just…lost it there."

"I know, and I love it when you're like that. When all you have to do is lie on top of me and come in my arms." Michael leaned over to look directly into her lover's eyes. "But tell me that you weren't trying to keep me from exerting myself."

"Ali said—"

"Ali *said* we could have sex," Michael said firmly. "She didn't say we could only have sex if I stayed very still and let you tend to me. That's not the way we make love." She kissed Sloan to take the edge off her tone. "I happen to like to make you scream."

"Jesus," Sloan groaned, her body twitching. "You know how crazy you make me. And just being next to you—"

"Is wonderful, yes. But it's not everything that I want." Michael glided her hand down the center of Sloan's chest, over her stomach, and between her legs. She closed her fingers and watched Sloan's eyes grow hazy. "I want you like this." Never taking her eyes from Sloan's face, she slid into her, pressing her palm hard against Sloan's clitoris, still swollen from her recent orgasm. "I want to make you come *my* way, *my* time."

Sloan's chest jerked with spastic breaths, her hands trembling on the sheets. "Please. Michael, please, I love you so much."

"I know, my darling," Michael whispered, beginning to thrust. "I know."

Sandy sat on one end of a leather sofa across from the matching one where Jasmine, in tight black satin slacks and a deep burgundy, scoop-neck top, lounged beside a redhead in a pale green oxford shirt and chinos. Sandy watched the two of them with curiosity, trying to figure out the score. Every time the really cute redhead—Sarah, she said her name was—spoke to Jasmine, she rested her hand lightly on Jasmine's knee. Jason had *said* he liked girls the first time he'd helped Mitch get dressed. Sandy had made it pretty clear then that Mitch was off-limits, and Jason had said that wasn't a problem because he was involved. As for Jasmine, Sandy wasn't so sure. Jasmine flirted with the drag kings, so maybe *Jasmine* liked boys. And *Mitch* was a guy.

"Whatcha thinking, honey?" Mitch murmured, sliding an arm around Sandy's waist as he settled a hip on the arm of the couch for support. He'd been using one crutch to get around, and he propped that against the back.

Sandy leaned into his body and tilted her head up to see his face. "Jasmine's really hot, isn't she."

Mitch grinned. "Sizzlin'."

"Phil," Sandy whispered, indicating the small, hard-bodied drag king with the hint of five o'clock shadow, tight blue jeans that announced in no uncertain terms that he was a guy, and short-sleeved, retro striped shirt, "has the major hots for her."

"As long as it's her and not you," Mitch growled as he dipped his head and kissed her behind her left ear. "All those guys are horny. I thought their tongues were gonna fall out when they first saw you."

"They were just being guys," Sandy said offhandedly. "At least they looked at my face before my tits."

Mitch laughed softly. "It's a tough choice."

"You better think so." Sandy dropped a quick kiss on his neck. "Is everything going okay?"

"Yeah, they all seem cool."

"No questions about why you're here?"

Mitch shook his head. "Jasmine already took care of that. They know she's friends with Sloan and Michael, and that's how I knew them. They offered to let me stay here for a few days until my leg's better because of the elevator."

"Good." Sandy hooked an arm around his leg, absently stroking the inside of his thigh, still watching Phil talking to Jasmine. The young drag king's bright eyes were fixed on Jasmine's face, and although Sandy couldn't hear the conversation, the tone of Phil's voice telegraphed his excitement. He had it bad, that was plain to see. "Does Jasmine turn *you* on?"

"What?"

"You heard."

"No," Mitch said quickly.

Sandy gave him a look. "Something wrong with your hormones?"

He leaned down, pulling her close against his side as he bent his head to hers. "She's gorgeous. And sexy. And the only woman who gets me hot, even a little, is you."

"You know," Sandy whispered, rubbing her mouth on the edge of his jaw, "you really learn fast."

"Honey, it's the truth." Mitch smoothed a hand down her bare arm. She wore red satin slacks that nearly matched Jasmine's and a lacy white bit of nothing on top that showed off her small, firm breasts to mouth-watering advantage. "Besides, you think I have energy for anyone else after what you do to me?"

Before Sandy could reply, a voice from across the room caught their attention.

"Can anybody come to this party?" Sloan asked, her hand in Michael's.

Immediately, the three drag kings who made up the core of the Front Street Kings Drag Troupe jumped to their feet, their eyes fixed on

Michael. With her hair down, in a faded gray workout T-shirt of Sloan's and loose cotton pants, she was as naturally beautiful as a woman could be. Despite the lingering hints of trauma that shadowed her face, her eyes were clear and warm as she smiled at her unexpected guests.

"Hello, I'm Michael." She held out her hand to the nearest king, Ken Dewar, who took her hand.

"Ma'am," Ken murmured, and brushed his lips over her knuckles with courtly grace. "I've seen you at the club with Sloan, but she's never introduced us." He lifted bedroom eyes to hers, the corner of his mouth raised in a rakish smile. "Probably wise."

Michael laughed, delighted at his charm. "So very nice to meet you. And I shall certainly take Sloan to task for not introducing us sooner."

Ken tossed a grin to Sloan, who merely growled good-naturedly, before indicating his companions with a sweep of his arm. "These two outstanding fellows are Phil E. Pride and Dino."

"Gentlemen," Michael replied, offering her hand to each in turn. "I take it you all have everything you need? Food? Something to drink?"

"We're great," Dino said with just a hint of South Philly in his voice, hoisting his bottle of Black & Tan. "Jasmine took care of us."

"Thank you," Michael said as she leaned down to kiss Jasmine's cheek. "Hello, Sarah."

"Hi." Sarah stood, sliding an arm around Michael's waist. "You look terrific."

"You're a true friend to lie about that. Thanks." Michael's gaze went to Sloan, who stood talking to Ken with an arm draped over his shoulder in friendly companionship. "I *feel* wonderful, though."

Sarah laughed. "Can't imagine why. Sloan looks pretty contented too."

Michael blushed and shushed her. "Quiet. We have guests."

"I don't think the boys would be shocked."

"Maybe not. But I'd prefer not to make an announcement."

"Fair enough." Sarah cast an eye toward the sofa where Phil had taken her place next to Jasmine. "I see my girlfriend has another admirer. Sometimes I wonder why I let her out of the house alone."

Michael followed her gaze and smiled. "You're not really worried, are you? I mean, it all gets a bit confusing to me still, but Phil does *know* that Jasmine is, well, more than Jasmine."

"Oh, sure. Phil knows Jasmine is a transvestite, just like Jasmine knows that Sloan is a lesbian and that Phil is a drag king. But that doesn't stop Jasmine from teasing Sloan, or Phil from lusting after a sexy woman like Jasmine. Sometimes one reality just gives way to another, don't you think?"

"Well," Michael mused, "I know that Sloan finds Jasmine attractive and that it confuses her at times."

Sarah tilted her head thoughtfully. "But you don't? Find Jasmine attractive, I mean. And you're a lesbian."

"Well, I think *you're* very attractive, and I love you as a friend, but…well—"

"I don't have a starring role in your fantasies?"

"Actually, no one does except Sloan. But that's just me. Sloan," Michael murmured, watching her lover grinning at something Sandy had just said, "is put together differently. She has a different kind of On button than I do."

"And you're not bothered by that?" Sarah's tone was curious, not censuring.

"I can hardly be upset with her for something she can't help." Michael met Sarah's eyes. "I trust her to put our relationship first before casual attractions."

"I guess we're pretty much in the same place, then. Jasmine is more a good friend than a lover, although now and then…" Sarah shrugged. "We cross lines."

"Really? I've wondered."

"Well, there are times when I'm watching Jasmine get ready to go out or up onstage performing, that I get this overwhelming desire to just…ravish her." Sarah laughed self-consciously. "And then, when I do, right in the middle of it all…guess what I find."

"I think I have a pretty good idea." Michael laughed as well and returned Sarah's hug. "I think sometimes we just have to accept things the way they are, even if they're not the way we think they will be. That seems to be the case more often than not around here."

"Mmm. Especially tonight." Sarah leaned near so as not to be overheard. "Mitch is certainly a surprise. The other guys look terrific, and I've known them all long enough that I don't think of them as anything other than guys, but Mitch…Mitch is the most natural-looking drag king I've ever seen."

"If I didn't know," Michael agreed, "I'd bet any amount of money that he's Dell's brother. The resemblance is there in exactly the same way it often is between brother and sister—similar features, but no confusion as to who is male and who is female."

"Fascinating, isn't it. His girlfriend is keeping a close eye on him too. She's a little cutie."

"Sandy." Michael smiled fondly. "She's very sweet and very capable. I also have the feeling that there's very little of life that she hasn't experienced."

"So, do you know what's going on?"

Struck by the serious tone in Sarah's voice, Michael felt a wave of apprehension. "What do you mean?"

"I just thought Sloan might have said something. Jason has been working nonstop since the end of last week, and I know they're close to wrapping up this big case. And Jasmine is somehow involved."

"And she hasn't said?"

"Oh, as much as she ever does. *I'm just facilitating things down at the club, sweetie. Don't worry, I wouldn't ruin my manicure doing anything dangerous.*"

"Why is it that Sloan says very much the same thing—minus the manicure, of course."

"Because we're just girls, and they're all big, tough superheroes?" Sarah's voice held a hint of exasperation mingled with affection. "Even Jasmine."

Michael sighed. "I can see that Sloan and I are going to have another talk."

"Uh-oh. Did I just get her into trouble?"

"Oh," Michael said softly, "she'll survive. After all, she's a big, tough superhero."

At the sound of Michael's laughter, Sloan tuned out the conversation with Ken and half turned in her lover's direction. It had been too long since she'd heard Michael's voice free from pain, and her heart tightened at the lilting sound. Michael stood arm in arm with Sarah, and the two were obviously sharing a private joke. At that instant, Michael met her eyes, and Sloan nearly staggered at the impact of her lover's gaze. It was as if Michael reached across the distance between them and caressed her. It was always that way. No one ever touched her the way Michael did.

"She's...ah…incredible," Ken remarked as if reading Sloan's thoughts.

"Yeah."

"The first time I saw the two of you at one of the shows, I figured it must be a mistake. You couldn't have gotten that lucky."

"Still can't believe it myself."

"So—it's nice of you to help Mitch out."

Slowly, Sloan searched Ken's eyes, appreciating the unspoken question. "He got pretty banged up."

"So Jasmine said. I remember him tearing out of the club that night. Funny, I thought I saw his girlfriend there earlier too. Of course, it could've been someone else, but she's so hot, she's hard to forget."

Sloan regarded Sandy, who still sat within the circle of Mitch's arms, chatting now with Dino. "I don't know every girl Mitch is seeing."

"He did mention he wasn't married," Ken said. "But if you ask me, she's got him by the roots. And he doesn't look like he minds."

Before Sloan could formulate an answer to that, Ken continued, "I've known Jasmine a long time. All the Kings have. Whatever she's into, we're there. Just so you know."

"Thanks. I appreciate that. Before you leave, I want to give you a couple of numbers to call. Just in case...you ever need to."

"That would be fine. Now," Ken said with a slow smile, "I'm going to go invite the very beautiful Michael to one of our shows. Front-row seats, this time. Courtesy of the Front Street Kings."

"You guys are dangerous," Sloan complained.

Ken raised a brow and shrugged insouciantly. "We have to maintain our reputations."

Sloan watched him walk away, appreciating that they had gained another ally in the underground warfare to come.

Chapter Ten

Wednesday

"Well, hello," Catherine said with a smile. "You look much better than the last time I saw you."

Mitchell hooked her cane over the arm of the chair in front of Catherine's desk and settled into it, keeping her left leg straight as she did. "Thanks. I *feel* a lot better too."

"How's the leg?"

"Pretty much healed. The stitches stay in for another week, but," she indicated the cane with a tilt of her chin, "no more crutches."

"Wonderful." Catherine eased back in her chair and crossed her legs. As was her habit on the days she saw clients, she'd dressed conservatively in a two-piece taupe brushed-silk suit and low heels. Mitchell's file, unopened, was centered on her desk blotter. "Are you still at Sloan and Michael's?"

"Probably for another day. Then I'm going back to my… apartment."

"The one in Sandy's building?"

"Uh-huh."

"Does that mean that you're going back to work as well?"

Mitchell shifted in the chair and studied the knees of her black chinos, which she'd worn with a white, open-collared oxford shirt and black loafers for her day of doctor's visits. "Well, I can't go back to work until I'm cleared by you."

"What about Dr. Torveau?" Catherine asked, showing no reaction to the subtle evasion. "Has she released you to work?"

"Not in so many words," Mitchell admitted. "She said I could do anything I wanted except ride my motorcycle and lift weights."

"Anything? That's excellent."

Mitchell brightened and sat up straighter.

"Do you think she meant physically subduing a suspect?" Catherine's tone was mild, her eyes kind.

"She didn't mention that, exactly."

"But you did talk with her about the kinds of things you need to be able to do in the line of duty, right?"

"I told her about most of it." Mitchell's voice was pitched low.

Catherine said nothing.

Mitchell sighed. "Actually, I told her about working with Jason on the computer traces."

"Rather sedentary."

"I didn't *say* I had a desk job…" Mitchell raised her eyes to Catherine's. "Not in so many words."

Catherine nodded.

"But I might have let her *think* it was…mostly…a desk job."

"Why did you let her think that, do you think?"

"Because I want to get back to work." Mitchell forcefully enunciated each word, as if the importance of what she was saying couldn't be overemphasized.

"I know you do. But why tomorrow and not a week from tomorrow?"

"Because this is my big chance, and I don't want to miss it."

"Big chance. Tracking down the rest of the Internet pornographers?"

Mitchell shook her head impatiently. "No. I mean, that's *part* of it. But that's not…that's not what I'm going to be doing." She leaned forward, her hands loosely fisted. "I'm going to be working undercover. That's a big deal for a detective. Especially a rookie detective like me. I'm going to be going after the intel that could *break* this case. Not just the pornographers, but maybe the whole prostitution ring. It's big, and the lieutenant is putting me right in the middle of it."

It's big and it's dangerous and you can't wait. Catherine had worked with police officers long before she'd fallen in love with one, and she'd rarely seen one who didn't live for the excitement. Rebecca, she believed, thrived on the hunt, and although that drive was instinctual, her deeper motivations were philosophical. Rebecca sought justice. She wondered what Dellon searched for. "Why is it good?"

"Are you kidding me? This is a chance to really *do* something. To put away some of the scum who use girls like they're disposable—to be wadded up and tossed in the toilet after they've come in th..." Mitchell colored and looked away. After a second, she said quietly, "Sorry."

"For what, Dellon?" Catherine asked just as quietly.

"Look, it's my job. This is an important case, and I want to do my job."

Catherine considered the unanswered question and then decided to let it pass for the moment. She'd learned in their previous sessions that Dellon often revealed more in what she didn't say than in anything she might if pressured. And the young detective was pale and shaking, a vivid reminder that she had been out of the hospital less than a week. "I know how much the job means to you. But you understand my concern for your safety."

Mitchell nodded. "If I get Dr. Torveau to sign off for me to resume active duty—*real* active duty—will you clear me to go back too?"

"Dr. Torveau and I are interested in slightly different things, Dellon." Catherine smiled. "Are you having any problems sleeping?"

"Not when I get the chance."

Catherine looked puzzled. "I don't follow."

"I just meant...well...Sandy's staying with me at Michael and Sloan's. So, sometimes I don't get to sleep until...late."

"How are things between the two of you?"

"They're..." Mitchell colored. "More or less...fantastic."

Catherine laughed. "May I infer then that your lack of sleep and your new relationship are related?"

"Pretty much. Yeah."

"Congratulations."

Mitchell finally grinned. "Thanks."

"No nightmares?"

"What?" Mitchell grew very still, pressing her palms to her thighs. "No."

Catherine was familiar with the posture. She'd seen it when Dellon had first been referred to her following a temporary suspension from duty after a physical altercation with a suspect. Some might have interpreted her body language as defensive, but Catherine recognized it now as protective. Her question had triggered something in the young woman with the potential to hurt.

"Have you found fragments of the episode breaking into your

consciousness at odd moments? Memories surfacing and taking you unawares?"

"No," Mitchell said, her voice suddenly rough. "It wasn't like that."

"Like what, Dellon?" Catherine asked softly.

"Like what nightmares are made of." Mitchell gazed at Catherine, but she was seeing the past.

"Tell me about the other time." Catherine's invitation was gentle, her voice soothing. But there was strength in her tone, as if whatever was coming would not be too much for her to hear.

Mitchell blinked and shook herself, as if she had just surfaced from the bottom of a murky pond into bright daylight. She smiled crookedly. "Tired. I guess I'm a little out of it."

"You were going to tell me about the nightmares."

"There's nothing to tell," Mitchell said briskly. "I don't have nightmares."

"Anymore?" Again, the question was gentle.

Mitchell's eyes blazed, a combination of pain and defiance. "That's right, not anymore."

Catherine waited, but Dellon remained silent. The clock behind Dellon revealed they were almost out of time. "When do you see Dr. Torveau again?"

"Not until the beginning of next week—for the suture removal."

"You're not ready for duty, Dellon."

Mitchell's jaw set hard, her chin jutting forward as the muscles tightened. "How long?"

"I really can't say. Certainly not before Dr. Torveau reevaluates you in light of what you are likely to be doing in any kind of street situation. Let's talk tomorrow."

"Tomorrow?"

Catherine laughed. "You want to get out of here and back to work, don't you?"

"Almost more than anything."

"Then I'll see you tomorrow."

Catherine watched the young detective carefully rise and make her way with a determined gait to the door. Despite her best efforts, she couldn't hide her limp. And Catherine now knew that in addition to the knife wound, there was some former trauma, some other pain, that had once plagued her. And whatever that old pain was, it had the potential to rise up again and cause destruction if not purged once and for all.

Rebecca grimaced as the pager on her belt vibrated. She was twenty feet from the front door to Catherine's office building and had hoped to catch Catherine between patients for an early dinner or a quick cup of coffee. Spending the major portion of the last two nights tailing George Beecher had meant that she'd seen little of her lover in the past half week, other than a few murmured words when she'd slipped into bed in the middle of the night.

In previous relationships, days, sometimes weeks, had passed without meaningful contact with her lover when she'd been in the midst of a case. Her excuse had always been that she had to work when the trail was hot, because once the case grew cold, she had little chance of breaking it. But in truth, she'd always been most comfortable alone in the night, chasing evil or, if that pursuit failed, chasing away her own demons with a drink. Even after she'd given up the bottle, she hadn't been able to give up the obsessive need to work until she had nothing left inside but the ashes of fury and frustration.

Now, she had another need.

She needed the touch of Catherine's hand to settle her, the sound of Catherine's voice to soothe her, and the press of Catherine's body in the night to replenish her.

She was a better cop now, a better woman, because of Catherine.

Her pager vibrated again. Swearing, she pulled it from her belt and read the number. Exchanging the beeper for her cell phone, she pressed two on the speed dial.

"What?" she said by way of greeting.

"I might have something," Watts replied, eschewing social niceties as well.

"Something break with Campbell?" Rebecca was beginning to feel that Margaret Campbell, the ADA who had financed her way through law school by stripping, was the Mob connection and leak in the law enforcement system. Because George Beecher appeared to be nothing more than a rich guy who spent his non–working hours chasing women.

"No. She's as boring as the sports teams in this town. She goes right home after work and stays there. Oh—once she went out to the drugstore, but she didn't buy anything exciting. Cold medicine."

"Okay, I got the picture. So why are you calling me?" Rebecca glanced at her watch. It was just before six and she knew that Catherine started her evening hours at seven. If they were going to have any chance to see one another, it needed to be soon.

"I found a couple of faxes Jimmy Hogan had stored in his locker. Somebody had cleaned out his stuff and tossed everything that didn't look official into a cardboard box. Including some paperwork."

"Wait a minute. No one claimed Hogan's personal items?"

"Nope."

"And you were down in storage going through them?"

"Yeah."

"Good thinking, Watts," Rebecca muttered.

"What was that?" he asked, his tone suggesting he'd heard clearly.

"Nothing. Go ahead."

"Like I said…"

Rebecca heard the click of metal on metal, then his long intake of breath as he drew on his cigarette.

"…there were some unfiled papers, and three of them were faxes from Port Authority. Shipping schedules for the two months right before he was killed."

"Shipping schedules." Rebecca rubbed the bridge of her nose, digesting this new piece of information. "What do you think? Stolen cars? Drugs?"

"Can't tell. We'll have to try to figure out which ships he was checking on. Maybe get a look at their bills of lading."

"Christ. That's a million hours of paperwork."

"Maybe not."

Rebecca waited, and when he said nothing, finally complained, "Come on, Watts. I've got better things to do tonight than reading your twisted mind."

Watts laughed. "All three faxes came from the same person. A supervisor at Port Authority. Maybe…uh, here it is…*C. Reiser* has some idea what Jimmy was after."

"First thing in the morning, let's go find out."

"Any chance we can get together at Sloan's first? Her coffee beats the hell out of that crap at the station house."

"Seven thirty. Tell the others."

"You got it, Loo."

"And Watts—nice work."

"What was that?"

Rebecca hung up.

Mitchell hummed to herself as she waited for the elevator in the ground-floor garage of Sloan's building. Sandy should be home by now, and maybe no one else would be. Jason, she knew, would be deep in the data traces on the third floor, Sloan was most likely still at Police Plaza, and Michael had gone with Sarah for a late-afternoon doctor's appointment. Which meant that she and Sandy would be alone. Not that being alone was a prerequisite for making love, but it sure made things more fun when you didn't have to worry about making noise. And somehow, Sandy always got her to make noise.

Grinning at the memories and the images of things to come, she used her key to program the double-wide converted industrial elevator to the private fourth-floor residence. When the doors slid silently open directly into the living room, she stepped out, calling, "Honey? Hey, San? Your baby's home and ready to rumble."

"Dell," Sandy said quietly from the direction of the kitchen.

One-handedly loosening her belt and stripping it off with a snap that cracked like a bullwhip, Mitchell turned in the direction of her girlfriend's voice. "Hey, sexy, I—"

The first thing she saw was the uniform. For some reason, it still stirred her to see it, the gleaming silver bars, the crisp creases in the deep green material, the row of duty medals and ribbons. The United States Army. The dreams of her childhood. Her eyes followed upward, over the neatly buttoned jacket, to the face framed by dark hair, only an inch or two longer than her own and with a touch of curl that hers never had. The blue eyes were hers, though. As was the rest of the face.

Mitchell's gaze jumped to Sandy, whose face was pale, her eyes dark pools of questions and hurt. *I would've told you, honey, but she's part of the past. And the past is dead. Buried.*

"Hello, Dellon." The voice, modulated and oddly devoid of emotion, drew Mitchell's attention from her lover.

"Erica." Mitchell whispered the name as she stared at the face that was the mirror image of her own.

Chapter Eleven

Rebecca!" Catherine tossed aside the insurance form she had been in the midst of completing and hurried around her desk to greet her lover.

"Hi," Rebecca replied hastily. "I know you don't have much time, but—"

Catherine stopped her words with a kiss. Settling her palms against Rebecca's shoulders, she leaned into her, savoring the taste of her after a day apart. Then she drew back with a smile and a sigh. "I have almost an hour. It's so good to see you."

Rebecca skimmed an arm around Catherine's waist. "I still can't believe how much I miss you, even when I see you every day."

"Darling," Catherine chided gently, "*seeing* me for five minutes in the middle of the night when we're both too tired to even talk hardly counts." She touched her fingers to Rebecca's cheek, then kissed her softly again. "It's been a long week. I've missed you too."

A quicksilver flash of concern flickered in Rebecca's eyes and then quickly died. But not before Catherine had seen it.

"I know how hard you're working," Catherine said. "I know how important this case is. I understand."

"Do you?" Rebecca asked, almost to herself, thinking of how many women she had lost because of her obsession with work. *Not Catherine. God, please not Catherine.*

"I *do*." Catherine wrapped both arms around Rebecca's waist and tightened her hold. "You look exhausted. What else is bothering you?"

"Nothing—I'm fine."

"Rebecca." Catherine drew out the word. *I can hear the evasion in your voice.*

"It's just...hell...I don't know how...I need you to know that just because I'm not home..." Rebecca raked a hand through her hair.

"Christ, I don't even know how to tell you how important you are to me."

"Oh, Rebecca," Catherine murmured, "you're here. That's how you tell me." She took her lover's hand and led her to the sofa that sat against the wall opposite her desk. Curling into one corner, she drew Rebecca against her with an arm around her lover's shoulders. "Just to have these few moments together makes all the difference."

"It does." With a sigh, Rebecca pillowed her cheek against Catherine's shoulder. "I just have to be with you and something inside me settles." She tilted her head enough to meet Catherine's eyes. "Some days, I'm not sure how I would keep going without you."

"Oh, Rebecca," Catherine murmured, gently stroking Rebecca's face as she pressed a kiss to her forehead. "I love so many things about you. Your strength, your conviction, your need to right the wrongs in a world where those things don't seem to matter to many people any longer." Unconsciously, as she spoke, she caressed Rebecca's back, urging Rebecca to relax against the curve of her body. "But more than anything, I love being important to you. I love knowing that my loving you makes a difference in your life."

"I don't know how I held on until you, Catherine." Rebecca closed her eyes and let peace take her. In Catherine's arms, she relinquished the memories of so many nights when loneliness of the spirit and desolation of the heart had scoured her, leaving her hollow. Of the years filled with alcohol-induced numbness and meaningless encounters with women whose names she could not remember. "I love you."

"I love you."

Catherine sensed Rebecca drift away and held her fiercely.

"I was happy with my life, before you," Catherine whispered, stroking Rebecca's hair. "I had everything I wanted—my career, good friends, satisfying interests." She rested her chin against the top of Rebecca's head and reveled in the sharp, clean scent of her. "You brought me to the fire, Rebecca. You brought me to the passion. Oh, darling, you are my life."

In the still room, Catherine watched the rest of the hour pass, listening to her lover's quiet breathing, guarding her as she slept. Providing this one woman refuge, creating for her a place to rest, a place to heal, brought Catherine the fulfillment she hadn't known she'd needed.

"Darling," Catherine finally murmured.

"Hmm?" There had been a time when Rebecca would have snapped into immediate consciousness at the slightest sound, already reaching for her gun. But now, she lingered on the edge of waking, reluctant to relinquish the safety of her lover's embrace.

"It's time," Catherine announced gently.

"I know." Rebecca eased away but kept one arm around Catherine's waist. "I had intended to ask you out to dinner at Chucksteak Charlie's."

"Oh, I can't believe we missed that!"

Rebecca grinned. "Sorry."

"This was much better." Catherine leaned forward and kissed Rebecca softly. "Thank you."

"For what?"

"For letting me love you."

Rebecca gave a short, incredulous laugh. "Letting you? Jesus, like I have a choice."

Catherine smiled. "Good. Remember that."

"Always." With a sigh, Rebecca stood and stretched, rubbing one hand briskly over her face. "I'll probably be late again tonight."

"Be careful." Rising, Catherine threaded an arm around Rebecca's waist to walk her to the door. "I'll see you when you get…home."

Home.

The word lingered in the air between them as Catherine searched Rebecca's face. *When will you let it really be our home? In your heart, and mine?* She knew the question must show in her eyes, because a shadow passed through Rebecca's. She waited and watched Rebecca struggle with that final barrier, knowing that tonight would not be the night that it fell.

"I'll see you later," Rebecca said at last, sweeping her fingertips over Catherine's cheek.

"Yes." Catherine kissed her one more time and stepped away. "Be safe, darling."

Mitchell dragged her eyes away from her twin and strode directly to Sandy. In a low voice, her back to Erica, she asked, "You okay?"

"I guess." Sandy's gaze flickered from her lover's face to that of the woman who watched them intently from across the room, her expression devoid of emotion. Except cold calculation. "Jesus, Dell. What the fuck?"

"I can explain." A frantic edge of desperation underlay Mitchell's voice. She caught Sandy's wrist in her hand, expecting her to pull away, but the flinch at her touch cut even deeper than withdrawal. "Sandy. *Please.* Just give me a chance to find out what's going on."

"That would be good, don't you think?" Sandy's voice was flat, her eyes empty. "I'd sort of like to know that myself." She couldn't seem to keep her eyes off the other woman. "Jason must've thought she was you, because he keyed the elevator automatically. He was probably so busy with his head up some computer he just glanced at the monitor."

"She's my sister."

"Well, *duh.*" Sandy grabbed Mitchell's waistband and yanked her a few more steps back until they were almost in the kitchen alcove. In a low voice taut with nerves, she said, "She's been here almost an hour and hasn't said word one. Except to ask if *Officer Mitchell* resided at this address. Oh, and to introduce herself as Lieutenant Mitchell. Fuck, she's like a zombie in a slick uniform."

"That's her normal attitude."

"You could've warned me she was coming!"

"I didn't *know.*"

"Then how about mentioning a carbon-copy sister running around?" Sandy glanced at Erica again. "She's watching me like I'm going to lift your wallet." She shivered. "God, she looks just like you."

"No, she doesn't," Mitchell said, her voice brittle and tight.

"When she walked in, I thought at first…" Sandy shook her head. "I'm glad I kept my clothes on."

Mitchell laughed quietly, the first glimmer of hope returning to her heart. Sandy seemed more freaked than pissed. "I'm telling you, I didn't know she was coming. I don't know why she's here. I have to talk to her."

"Yeah, you do." Suddenly serious, Sandy extricated her arm from Mitchell's grip. "I'm gonna take off."

"No," Mitchell said, more loudly than she intended.

"*Yes,* Dell," Sandy said stiffly. "Whatever's going on here, it's… family stuff."

"You're the only one who matters to me." There was something verging on panic now in Mitchell's voice. "Please. Please don't leave me."

Sandy's eyes narrowed as she stared at her lover. "Is she going to do something to you? Hurt you somehow?"

"No," Mitchell said with a shaky laugh. "No. I just…I just don't want to lose you."

"Lose me. Lose me *how*, Dell?"

Mitchell couldn't breathe. Sweat trickled from her hair down her neck. Her stomach threatened to heave. "Don't let them chase you away."

"*Them?* Who?"

"The people who say we're wrong." Mitchell's voice was barely a whisper, and her face was ashen. Her eyes, normally so clear, were unfocused, clouded with past torment.

"*Dell.*"

Mitchell twitched and blinked. She focused on Sandy's face, relieved to see the temper in Sandy's eyes. "Yeah?"

"You know what I said before?" Sandy asked, placing her palm along the edge of Mitchell's jaw. "About you being pretty smart for a cop?"

"Yeah?" Mitchell trembled, holding her breath.

"I take it back." Sandy traced her fingers tenderly down Mitchell's neck and rested her open hand against her chest, caressing her softly. "I'll see you later, rookie."

"Sandy."

There was an interminable moment of silence, or so it seemed to Mitchell. *Please. Please I need you.*

"I promise, Dell," Sandy whispered.

Mitchell didn't move until she heard the faint whisk of the elevator doors open, then close, and the distant whir of the motor taking Sandy away. She waited another twenty seconds, steeling herself, searching for anger to be her strength. Then she turned and faced her twin.

"What are you doing here?"

"Who's the girl?"

"I asked you first."

"The hospital needed some kind of insurance information, and they didn't have a current telephone number. At least not one you answered. Apparently they got your emergency contact information from an old form on file at the police department. It took *me* a few calls, but I finally got someone who'd said you'd been detailed here recently." She surveyed the loft. "I take it they didn't mean *here,* precisely. Interesting setup."

Mitchell ignored the unspoken request for an explanation. It wasn't she who needed to explain. "Why did you come?"

"I'm your sister, Dellon."

"And that's supposed to mean something?"

Erica's eyes, the same deep blue as Mitchell's, sparked with ire. "I'm not the one who relinquished my commission. I'm not the one who walked away. *I'm* not the one who left everything—and *everyone*—behind."

"Like I had some kind of choice?"

"You *had* a choice. You had a choice before you ever got into bed with—"

"That's enough." Mitchell didn't raise her voice, but it whipped through the air between them like a hand striking flesh. "You should leave."

Erica's body was rigid, her shoulders back, her arms straight at her sides. She looked like a recruiting poster, clear-eyed and righteous with purpose. "Damn you." Her voice was surprisingly soft, nearly plaintive. "Do you know how much it hurt me to lose you?"

"I know." There was no sympathy in Mitchell's voice, only bitterness. They had shared the same womb, the same birthday, the same hopes and dreams. They'd been closer than lovers. She'd bled from the loss as if from an amputated limb, until her heart had run dry.

"That girl…she can't be more than sixteen. You can't seriously be—"

"Leave it alone, Erica."

"Have you lost your mind, Dellon?" Erica finally broke form and approached Mitchell, stopping a few feet away. They did not touch. "You threw away one career. Now you're willing to risk another for someone like that?"

"Someone like that," Mitchell said very slowly. Her entire body quivered; the hairs on her arms stood up from the tension wiring her skin. She was afraid if she moved, she'd burst into flames and never be able to contain the rage. "Oh—you mean not shallow and fickle?"

"Robin I could almost understand," Erica spat, "but her? She's nothing like…us."

"No, she's nothing like us." Mitchell's voice was dangerously soft. Her hands cramped from the effort to keep them at her sides. She wanted to break things. "She's nothing like Robin, either, is she? And we both know how virtuous and honest Robin was."

"She made the right decision. You should have too."

Mitchell's head snapped up and she had to step back, back from the wrath left unrequited for so long. "I chose an honest life."

"You *threw away* your life!" Erica laughed, a hollow sound. "God, you always were so damned idealistic."

Mitchell's eyes traveled over the pristine uniform, the symbol of all that she had once believed to be good and honorable. She thought about Sandy, a young woman who fought seemingly insurmountable odds just to survive, and who should have been hardened and jaded by the struggle. Sandy's hands, Sandy's heart—so tender. She thought of the sweet acceptance she had discovered in Sandy's arms and met her sister's furious gaze. "It's not idealistic when it's real."

"What?"

"Never mind." Remembering Sandy's touch, Mitchell felt an inexplicable calm lick at the flames of her fury. "You wouldn't understand."

Chapter Twelve

Dee Flanagan did not look up from her microscope at the sound of approaching footsteps in the empty lab. It was well after hours; even her lover—a senior crime scene investigation technician—had left for the day. Maggie had gone home to prepare supper, another meal like so many that, more often than not, Dee would miss while caught up in analyzing some tantalizing bit of evidence.

"We're closed," the CSI chief growled. "Try back after 7:30 tomorrow morning."

"Sorry to bother you, Chief," Sloan said mildly as she slid a single sheet of paper onto the granite counter next to Dee's right hand. "I just wanted to talk to you about this report."

Slowly, Dee straightened, granting Sloan a sideways glance. She fixed her gaze on Sloan's chest. "What's with the shiny new ID?"

Grimacing, Sloan fingered the laminated badge clipped to the pocket of her faded blue work shirt. "Civilian consultant. Pretty special, huh?"

Dee merely grunted. "You know, it took Frye close to ten years before I let her walk around in here unsupervised."

Sloan rocked casually back and forth on her boot heels, her thumbs hooked over the front pockets of her jeans. She was a few inches taller and a good twenty pounds heavier than Flanagan, but it didn't feel that way when the wiry CSI chief had her hackles up. "But *Frye* taught me the rules. Don't touch anything."

"Apparently she forgot the one about not interrupting me when I'm processing evidence." Dee was not smiling.

"Actually, she didn't. And I wouldn't have, if I didn't think this was something you'd be interested in."

Dee squinted, assessing Sloan, who met her eye to eye. Then she nodded once, apparently liking the unflinching determination in Sloan's expression. "All right. What's this all about?"

"The results of a tox screen on the body that was tossed in a dumpster behind Methodist Hospital last night."

Dee's posture shifted subtly, like a dog on point catching the scent of its prey. "That report isn't finished yet. I haven't sent it out."

Sloan tipped her head toward the page on the counter. "Interesting reading."

Her gaze still on Sloan, Dee picked up the sheet and quickly scanned it. A muscle along her jaw bunched, and a sound close to a growl reverberated in her chest. When her eyes rose to Sloan's again, there was a challenge in their blue depths. Most people would have stepped back, but Sloan did not. "Where did you get this?"

"From your computer."

Automatically, Dee shot a look over her shoulder at her office. The door was closed, just as she had left it. The lights were out. "Want to tell me how you got past me?"

"I didn't. I got it from a computer upstairs on the third floor, through the network."

"Let's go talk." Without waiting for a response, Dee led the way between the lab benches to her office. She opened the door and flicked on the light, illuminating a small room made even more claustrophobic by the piles of journals, file folders, specimen containers, and evidence bags piled on every available surface. Her desk, an old-fashioned wooden affair covered with scratches and dents, was surprisingly orderly despite the stacks of paperwork. Waving in the direction of a stool, Dee said, "Have a seat. Then explain."

As she shifted manila folders and a plaster model of a shoeprint from the nearest backless stool, Sloan said, "I have sysop privileges."

"Meaning you can snoop around." Dee tilted back in the wooden captain's chair, her hands hanging loosely over the arms. To a casual observer she would have appeared relaxed, except for the piercing focus in her eyes. It was the calm readiness of a sniper lying utterly still but ready to deliver death in an instant.

"Essentially, yes. I'm familiar with your system, of course, because I worked down here a week or so ago. But then, I was trying to get *into* the main system. Today, I reversed the process."

"Why?"

Sloan shrugged. "Curiosity. Plus, your department is the epicenter of evidence for the entire police department. The autopsy reports, the trace analyses, the tox screens, ballistics—everything the detectives rely upon to make a case passes through here. If I wanted to influence the outcome of an investigation, this is where I'd start."

"And you pilfered that report from my hard drive."

"I did. Yes."

Dee didn't move a muscle, but her voice had dropped dangerously low. "You should've asked."

Sloan's voice was steady, her expression unperturbed. "I don't have to. That's the point. I own the system now."

The two women stared at one another until, finally, Dee smiled. "Now I know why you play on Frye's team. But I'd bet you don't play unless you want to."

"Ordinarily, you'd be right." Sloan lifted a shoulder. "Right now, I'm Frye's."

"I'm impressed. So—what's your point, besides that?"

Sloan grinned. "Can I tell Frye you said that? About being impressed?"

"I'll deny it."

"Thought you might."

"Do I have a problem down here?" The humor had fled from Dee's eyes, leaving them glacially cold.

"You do. Since I was already looking around, I discovered that I'm not the only one who's accessed your computer with sysop privileges. Except, of course, that shouldn't be *possible*, because until today, the network wasn't set up to allow that."

"Meaning what?"

"Meaning you've been hacked. And by someone who's good at it." Sloan leaned forward, her elbows on her knees, her hands clasped. There was an edge of excitement, verging on respect, in her voice. "My guess is someone sent a Phatbot—"

"A factbot?"

"No—Phatbot." Sloan spelled it, then continued, "a form of Trojan horse—a bit of malicious code that's tacked onto something that appears harmless. An e-mail, a doc file, an image. The kinds of things that you open and review dozens of times every day."

"I know what they are—but what exactly do they *do?*"

Sloan raised her hands and let them fall. "Just about anything the intruder wants. If a computer is infected, a remote attacker will have access to all the files and programs. They can copy data, alter data, insert data. Pretty much have the run of the house."

"Jesus Christ," Dee said in a strangled whisper.

"When you and I talked about this before, all I could do at the time was patch a quick fix onto your system. Beef up your firewalls. Now, with unrestricted access to the network, I can do something *real* about it."

"I need to protect the evidence." Dee bolted up so quickly that the chair spun back against the wall. "Christ." She leaned forward on her desk and fixed Sloan with a fierce stare. "You need to fix this *now*."

"I will. What we're going to do is follow the bread crumbs back to the source. The advantage I have now that I didn't have a week ago is that I've eliminated a number of potential sources and narrowed down the field of possible suspects. I'm going to insert a bit of code of my own into your operating system and see if we can't catch the mole in our trap."

"Is there some way for you to tell if something has been…tampered with?"

Sloan grinned. "You know what they say in this business—it's almost impossible to commit the perfect crime."

The instant Sandy stepped off the elevator into the darkened loft, she sensed her in the shadows. Waiting.

"Dell?"

"Here."

Navigating to the hollow echo of Dell's voice, Sandy circumvented the furniture in the dark until she reached the sofa in front of the floor-to-ceiling windows that overlooked the Delaware River. Even now, well into the night, lights flickered on the water, ships gliding in and out of the Port of Philadelphia. Dell was hunched in one corner of the broad leather sofa, her injured leg propped on the coffee table. Sandy kicked off her silver, stack-heeled shoes—the ones that matched her shiny, short, patent leather skirt and silver bustier—and curled up beside Mitchell with her legs tucked beneath her. Sandy's breasts pressed against Mitchell's right arm as she reached between Mitchell's thighs to mold her palm to the inside of Mitchell's leg—high up, but not touching her crotch.

"Where's the evil twin?"

Mitchell laughed, a short, sharp-edged laugh slivered with pain. "Gone."

"Gone where?"

"Don't know. Probably back to DC."

"She lives there?"

"Stationed there."

Sandy stroked the inside of Mitchell's leg rhythmically. "Isn't that the same thing?"

"Not really. A duty station never really feels like home, no matter how long you're there." Mitchell shrugged. "Maybe it's knowing that you might be deployed elsewhere at any time. You don't want to get too settled."

"Sounds like foster care," Sandy said dryly.

Slowly, Mitchell swiveled her head and looked directly at her girlfriend for the first time. The moonlight reflecting off the leather and silver made her sparkle. "Is that how it was for you?"

"Yeah."

Mitchell smoothed her fingers down Sandy's arm and caught the hand between her thighs, covering it with her own. "How long were you—you know, in the system?"

"Look, Dell—"

"How long?" Mitchell asked gently.

"Ten years. Until I was fifteen, and then…I split."

Three years on the streets. Not many girls survived that long—not without becoming addicts or victims of violence and disease.

"You're never going back there again," Mitchell said with lethal conviction, her fingers tightening unconsciously around Sandy's small hand.

"Where, baby?" Sandy's voice was gentle, soothing.

"The fucking streets."

"I work there."

"You been working tonight?"

Sandy grew very still, and her hand stopped moving against

Mitchell's thigh. "Remember we said no questions you don't want to know the answer to."

"You're all dressed up for work." Mitchell gave another stilted laugh. "And you know what? I think you look so sexy like that. Jesus."

"Why is that bad?"

"Because I think about…them looking at you, and it makes me crazy." Mitchell groaned, nearly a sob. "I don't want anyone else touching you."

"What do you want me to do, Dell? Starve because you've got a thing about my body?"

Mitchell jerked as if she'd been slapped. "A *thing* for your body? Yeah, that's it. That's all I want from you." When she braced an arm on the sofa and pushed up, struggling to stand on her weak leg, Sandy tugged on the back of her jeans and pulled her back down.

"Look, I'm *sorry*." Sandy huffed out a breath. "I don't know what to do. I don't…I don't *want* anybody to touch me except you."

The tension ebbed from Mitchell's body in one blessed rush. "I love you."

"That won't get me breakfast, Dell." Sandy's voice was soft as she spoke.

"Then let *me* buy you breakfast."

"I'm not talking about just breakfast."

Mitchell wrapped an arm around Sandy's shoulders and held her tightly, pressing her lips to the top of Sandy's head. "Neither am I."

"I don't think we better talk about this anymore right now."

"Making you nervous?"

"Big time."

"I'm not going to give up, you know," Mitchell murmured.

"You mean it?" Sandy tried but couldn't keep the tremor of need from her voice.

"Oh yeah, I mean it."

"Okay."

"Okay?"

"Okay, you can bug me about the life…if you want to. Just…not all the time."

"Where did you go tonight?"

"Nowhere special." Sandy tugged Mitchell's T-shirt from her

jeans and slid her hand beneath, playing her fingertips along the curve of Mitchell's ribs. "Just around."

"San. Don't blow me off, okay?"

"I checked out a few places on the strip. Then down on Delaware at the Blue Diamond."

"The Blue Diamond?" Mitchell's voice hardened. "Jesus. That's one of Zamora's places. What were you doing there?"

"Looking for Trudy."

"For Frye." The way Mitchell said it, it wasn't a question.

"Maybe."

Agitated, Mitchell rubbed her hand up and down Sandy's bare arm. "You gotta be careful, honey. People are going to be on edge because of the bust. Looking for something that's off. Don't go asking around for her right now."

"You think I'm *dumb*, Dell? You think I made it this long without you by being stupid?" Sandy pulled away. "Jesus. Sometimes you are just as bad as a guy."

"Whoa. What's that supposed to mean?"

"It's supposed to mean just because we're fucking I don't need you to take care of me."

"What if I want to?"

"Not if you're going to be a pain in the ass about everything."

"What if I want you to take care of me?"

Sandy caught her breath. "Do you?"

"Sometimes, yeah, I think I do."

"Fuck, Dell." Sandy settled back against her, seeking the warmth of her skin with her fingers again. "I...you know...I love you too, rookie."

"I missed you while you were gone tonight."

Sandy kissed Mitchell's shoulder, then rested her cheek on the spot. "Why did your sister come today?"

"I don't know. She said it was because...she wanted to make sure I was okay."

"How come you don't sound like you believe her?"

"Because she doesn't care if I'm okay."

"How do you know?" Sandy stroked Mitchell's stomach, dipping her fingers beneath the waistband of her jeans where they rode low over her hips.

Unconsciously, Mitchell lifted her hips into the touch. "She stopped caring two years ago."

"What did she do?"

"She followed the rules," Mitchell murmured softly, reaching for the button on her jeans.

"Dell, baby, what…"

"I don't want to talk right now," Mitchell said, pushing Sandy's hand deeper into her jeans. She closed her eyes, wanting only the solace of Sandy's touch. "Please, honey."

"Shh," Sandy crooned, stroking tenderly as Mitchell gave a small cry. "It's okay, baby. Everything is going to be okay."

Chapter Thirteen

Thursday

At 7:20, Rebecca settled in her usual place at the conference table in Sloan's office, struggling to ignore the faint headache building behind her eyes. She hadn't had more than a few hours' sleep a night in over a week, but it wasn't the lack of rest that was wearing on her. It was the case. There was something she was missing, *had* been missing since the day she'd looked down on Jeff's and Jimmy's bodies, and, whatever it was, it still eluded her. The investigation had splintered in too many directions too quickly. From the very beginning, her focus had been fragmented. Jeff had been killed in the midst of a madman's serial-murder spree, and she hadn't been able to pursue her partner's killer while hunting a maniac. She'd had to keep working, and she had been able to do little more than bury her shock and pain over Jeff's death.

Then she'd been shot, nearly died, and had fallen in love, all in the course of a few weeks.

As soon as she returned to duty—*too* soon by all accounts—the "desk job" she'd been assigned to led to a morass of underground criminal activity ranging from Internet pornography to child prostitution. And now she had to ferret out the mole in the police department who had very likely orchestrated the murder attempt on Sloan, crack the prostitution ring that had supplied the young girls for the porn videos, and discover why two cops had been executed. Still too many threads with nothing to connect them.

She sighed, leaned her head back, and closed her eyes.

"Rough night?" Sloan asked.

"A few of them." Rebecca might not have admitted that to anyone but Sloan, but in many ways they were equals on the job. Whatever Sloan had done for the government in her past life, Rebecca had no doubt that she'd been the team leader, not one of the troops. Rolling her head on the chair back, she surveyed Sloan's rumpled shirt and pasty complexion. "You look a little ragged yourself."

Grunting in agreement, Sloan slumped across from Rebecca with her own cup of coffee cradled between her hands. "Just got home."

"Were you at Police Plaza all night?"

Sipping her coffee, Sloan nodded.

Rebecca sat up straighter. "Anything?"

"I know who it is."

Rebecca was suddenly very much awake, flashing back to the last time Sloan had thought she'd discovered the person behind the murder attempt that had nearly killed Michael. Sloan had come close to taking matters into her own hands. "Why didn't you call me?"

"Just put the pieces together."

"And?"

Sloan met Rebecca's gaze head-on. "No one's dead yet."

"Good," Rebecca said gruffly, the tension in her chest dissipating. "Am I going to like this?"

"Like I thought, it's not a cop."

"What isn't?" Watts asked, as he lumbered into the room and made straight for the coffeepot.

"You'll find out in a minute," Rebecca informed him. "Let's wait until everyone's here, and then we'll bring the team up to speed."

Grunting assent, Watts shuffled toward the table with his coffee in one hand and two doughnuts in the other. "Who sets all this stuff up, anyhow?"

From the doorway, Jason replied, "I do."

"You'll make somebody a great wife," Watts mumbled around a mouthful of jelly and dough.

"I already have the wardrobe."

Watts sputtered and choked, inspiring Sloan to pound him on the back as she laughed. He was still wheezing when Mitchell arrived, walking slowly but without her cane.

"How's the leg, Detective?" Rebecca asked as she rose to refill her coffee. She lifted a cup in Mitchell's direction and scrutinized her.

"It's fine, Lieutenant. Thank you." Mitchell did her best to hide the limp as she moved as quickly as she could to the counter next to Rebecca. "I can get that, ma'am. But thanks."

Rebecca raised a brow. "I thought we dispensed with the formalities a while back."

"Yes, ma'am…Lieutenant." Mitchell took the offered cup of coffee.

"Good to see you up and around."

"I should be ready for full duty anytime now."

"I want it in writing. From Torveau and…" Rebecca shot a look over her shoulder toward the others gathered at the table and lowered her voice. "Whoever else you're seeing."

"Dr. Rawlings." Mitchell held Rebecca's gaze, searching for a reaction.

Rebecca merely nodded. "Good enough. Now, let's get this meeting started."

Mitchell maneuvered into a seat next to Jason as Rebecca returned to the head of the table and said, "So, where do we stand? Watts?"

Watts gulped down the last of his second doughnut and cleared his throat. "The stakeouts have pretty much been a bust. Neither Campbell or Beecher has done anything even a little bit suspicious. Considering our lack of manpower, I say we can that detail."

"We'll come back to that in a minute. Anything else?"

"Charlie Horton and Trish Marks's homicide investigation into Hogan and Cruz's murders went nowhere. For all practical purposes, they've pretty much cold-cased the files. I got nothing from talking to the guys in narco about what Jimmy was into—nothing that we didn't get from the first round of interviews, anyhow. If someone there was running him, no one knew who it was. More likely, he was reporting directly to the feds and giving everyone else just enough to avoid suspicion."

"I'll take another run at Clark myself," Rebecca said stonily. "If he's holding something back now, then he'd better have a very good reason for it."

Watts muttered a disparaging observation about Clark's lineage, then continued, "The only other thing I got was the possible lead at Port Authority."

"Go ahead and fill in the others," Rebecca advised.

Watts recounted his trip to the property room, his discovery of a few of Hogan's unfiled papers, and the undercover detective's interest in activity at the Port of Philadelphia. "We're gonna take a run down there today to check things out."

Rebecca studied Sloan, who had a faint frown line between her brows. "What do you think?"

"I suppose it's possible that Hogan tripped onto something illegal on the docks that got him killed. Stolen cars coming in by boat, a drug shipment, wholesale-container thefts—there's a lot of merchandise moving on those docks every day. It's not that difficult to divert a tractor-trailer full of electronics or other pricey commodities to a warehouse somewhere. One 'misplaced' shipment among hundreds every day is going to take a while to catch anyone's attention."

"That's what we think too," Rebecca said. "At least it's a plausible explanation for why someone would be willing to risk killing two cops. Protecting an operation as lucrative as that could be worth it."

"It won't be all that easy to prove," Jason remarked. "Tracking those shipments is going to be time-consuming."

Rebecca gave a feral grin. "I figure there has to be a way to do it by computer."

Both Sloan's and Jason's eyes sparkled. In unison they said, "Maybe."

"Let's get a feel for the situation down there, and then we'll put some pressure on Port Authority to let us have a look into their system."

Watts snorted. "That could take some doing. Port Authority cops aren't always the most cooperative."

That was, Rebecca knew, an unfortunate fact. More often than not, law enforcement agencies were not terribly forthcoming when it came to sharing intelligence. Sometimes not even about sharing basic operational information. What it came down to was that everyone protected their own turf in an attempt to ensure the longevity of their own positions. "We'll be…insistent."

That idea seemed to please Watts, because he grinned and crossed his hands over his belly, a contented man. Rebecca nodded in Sloan's direction. "Go ahead."

Sloan gave no sign of tension, other than her fists clenched around the coffee mug, as she spoke in a level, quiet tone. "The network connecting the various departments at Police Plaza and City Hall is lousy with worms and viruses. Someone has been monitoring almost everything that goes on down there…I can't say exactly for how long… but more than a year."

"That takes sophisticated computer know-how," Mitchell said.

"You're right. And I doubt that anyone inside the system could do it. I haven't seen any sign of that level of internal expertise. I'd say the job was probably shipped out to a hacker who programmed the malicious code on a laptop and then handed that off to someone who worked inside. *They* carried the laptop into the building, connected it to the network, and let the beasts loose."

"The Mob has the resources to pull off something like that," Jason observed.

"They do. On the other hand," Sloan said as she kept her eyes on Rebecca, "so do the feds. It's hard to know who your enemies are anymore."

"Can you find out who's behind it?"

"Not directly," Sloan admitted. "If the programs were encrypted off-site and delivered from a remote location via laptop, the hacker is essentially untraceable."

Watts groaned.

"But I *can* trackback to the internal source of the contamination."

"To whoever logged in to the network and injected the virus into the system," Mitchell said.

"Right." Sloan sipped her coffee, careful to keep the tremor from her hand. "George Beecher. The ADA."

"Son of a bitch," Watts whispered. He suddenly sat up straighter, his palms flat on the tabletop, his attention riveted to Rebecca. "Can we pick up the slimy little bastard? I'd like to get him alone in a room."

"Sloan?" Rebecca countered. "Is there enough for a warrant?"

Sloan shook her head. "Right now, all I can do is show that his computer was the source point for the intrusion. His attorneys would simply argue that that kind of evidence is circumstantial. Anyone could've logged on to his computer when he wasn't around and uploaded the malicious code."

"Are *we* even sure it's him?" Rebecca asked, all too aware that Sloan was barely able to be objective, given the situation. She wasn't surprised when Sloan stiffened, her eyes growing cool.

"I've now tracked two intrusions from two different network

points—Captain Henry's office and the forensics lab—back to him. Give me enough time, I'll find you a dozen."

"It still doesn't prove that he *personally* is responsible."

"Then maybe we should pay him a visit," Sloan said flatly. "And…ask."

Mitchell shifted subtly in her seat, then said, "What we need is corroborative evidence. Maybe Jason and I can find some connection in Beecher's personal data that will strengthen our case." She gave Jason a questioning look. "What if we really hit him hard—dig down another layer. If it's him, we'll find hidden bank accounts somewhere. Real estate transactions. Stocks. Unaccounted-for expenditures. Something."

"We can phish him too," Jason thought aloud. "See if we can get him to bite on a fake request for credit card information from one of the Internet video porn sites. If nothing else, we can squeeze him with that."

"Do it," Rebecca said. "Today."

"Yes, ma'am," Mitchell said, her voice tight with anticipation.

"I've got street sources looking for other girls who've been hired for the porn shoots," Rebecca went on. "We'll show his picture around. Maybe he likes to sample the merchandise."

Mitchell stared straight ahead, her posture rigid. Rebecca saw the reaction but noted with satisfaction that this time Mitchell kept her temper in check. It took effort, and Rebecca gave her points for it.

"Watts and I," Rebecca finished, "will ride down to the docks today and see if we can get a line on what Hogan was chasing down there. Tonight, we'll take shifts watching Beecher. Sooner or later he'll misstep." Rebecca rose, indicating the meeting was over. Turning to Sloan, she said quietly, "Let's take a walk."

Wordlessly, Sloan followed her to the elevator. Once inside, Rebecca leaned a shoulder against the wall and slid her hands into her trouser pockets. "Are you going to be able to handle this Beecher situation?"

The elevator doors glided open, and they walked across the garage to the street door. Sloan hit the exit bar with her hip, and the two of them stepped out into bright, cold October sunshine.

"It depends on what happens, I guess," Sloan finally replied.

"That's not the answer I was looking for."

Sloan angled her head and smiled at Rebecca humorlessly. "What did you expect me to say? That it would be all right with me if he goes free or cuts a deal? Even if we *can* find enough evidence to nail him?" She wore only an oxford shirt and jeans with no jacket, but the wind did not seem to bother her. "If he walks, you'd best look the other way."

"You know I won't."

"Then I'll just make sure there's nothing for you to see."

"Make sure there's nothing for me to even *think* about." Rebecca stopped walking and put her hand on Sloan's shoulder. They very rarely touched, and it wasn't a comforting or even a particularly friendly gesture. But it was an honest one. She squeezed slowly and turned Sloan to face her in the middle of the sidewalk. "I know what you're feeling."

"I know that you do," Sloan said, not resisting the hand that restrained her. "But when someone threatened *your* lover, you blew his heart out."

"I'm a cop. I had no choice."

"We'll never know that for sure, will we?"

"You know, if you go after this guy on your own, Michael will know."

For the first time, anger flared in Sloan's eyes. "You don't talk to Michael about this."

"I won't have to, Sloan." Rebecca's tone was level and mild. "She'll *know.* Because...they always do. The women who love us."

Sloan stood very still, her gaze unwavering. Then, her muscles eased and a genuine smile appeared. "Fuck. They do, don't they."

"Yep." Rebecca dropped her hand and rolled her shoulders, relaxing as she watched Sloan reach a decision. "I promise you this. If it's him, we'll get him. We'll get him now, or tomorrow, or next month. But he won't get away with it. You have my word."

"All right." Sloan shivered. "So are you done with the interrogation, Lieutenant? Because I'm freezing my ass off out here."

Laughing, Rebecca gripped Sloan's shoulder, in camaraderie this time, as they turned to head back. Sloan would keep her word, for Michael.

Chapter Fourteen

Rebecca drove south on Delaware Avenue deep into South Philadelphia. The Walt Whitman Bridge to New Jersey loomed overhead—a huge blue spiderweb, the shadows of vehicles traversing the central span like so many prey struggling to escape. Rush hour was nearly over, and it took less than ten minutes to reach the main gates of the Port of Philadelphia. Rebecca slowed and extended her ID out the window at the security booth, a four-by-four-foot kiosk with a wooden gate and a single, bored-looking Port Authority officer inside.

He ignored them for a full thirty seconds before leaning out and squinting at Rebecca's badge. "Yeah?"

"Philadelphia police. We're looking for Officer…Reiser."

"That would be Captain Reiser. Building C, all the way in the back. The captain know you're coming?"

"No. It's a social call."

The grizzled officer eyed Rebecca laconically. "Uh-huh. Sure." Taking his time, he half turned back into the tiny booth, pushed a button that powered the motor to raise the barrier arm, and gave Rebecca a perfunctory nod. "Have a nice day."

Rebecca proceeded into the complex as Watts muttered, "You have a nice fucking day too. Moron."

"How do you think we should play this?" Rebecca asked, maneuvering cautiously between rows of gigantic containers that had been off-loaded from ships that morning and awaited transport to the adjoining railroad yard. There they would be stacked on flatbed cars and shipped up and down the East Coast. The workday was in full swing on the docks, and a multitude of orange forklifts, their front-loaders raised and extended, scurried about like so many ants in a hill. Rebecca began to wish she had driven a department vehicle and not her 'Vette. The last thing she wanted was for one of these teamsters to spear the side of her car with a forklift or—worse yet—dump a couple of tons of metal on top of it.

"Well, we could go for typecasting," Watts suggested helpfully. "You could be the bad cop, and I'll be the good cop."

Rebecca flicked him a glance, and he looked back, perfectly straight-faced. She grinned. "What's your *next* idea."

"Why not tell this guy we're just following up on the homicide investigation because Horton and Marks ran out of steam. Since Jeff was one of ours, that would make sense."

"Yeah. And we just came across these notes and are tying off loose ends. That plays." Rebecca pulled into a space in a small employee lot in front of an eight-foot chain-link fence that ran parallel to the water as far as the eye could see in both directions. Beyond it, sheet-metal-covered warehouses as big as airplane hangars lined the waterfront. "Guess we go on foot from here."

"Christ, it looks like it's a mile away." Watts lit a cigarette the instant he stepped from the car.

"At least you'll get some exercise."

"Yeah, yeah."

Rebecca watched as a decktop crane on an enormous cargo ship pivoted over the water with a container as big as a Cape Cod cottage swinging from its massive arm. With surprising precision, the operator lowered the loaded storage crate onto the dock at the end of a row of a dozen others exactly like it.

"It's amazing how they can keep track of anything here. All these cargo ships, hundreds of containers." Rebecca shook her head. "What a perfect way to smuggle contraband."

"Special delivery, right to your door," Watts agreed.

Pointing to one of half a dozen identical buildings distinguished only by six-foot red letters painted on the front of each one, Rebecca said, "This way."

After they stopped a harried dockworker to ask where the office was, they were directed to a side door leading into the warehouse. Once inside, they followed an unadorned corridor lit by bare fluorescent tubes dangling on chains toward the interior of the building. Just before the passageway opened into a cavernous space filled with pallets of boxes and more containers, they found the office. The door was open, and Rebecca and Watts stepped inside.

The top half of one wall of the twenty-by-twenty-foot room was glass, affording anyone inside a view of the interior of the warehouse beyond. File cabinets lined the opposite wall, a metal desk sat in the center of the room, and a small TV stand in one corner held a water-stained coffee machine. A single monitor displaying a view of the dock immediately in front of the building was mounted high in one corner opposite the desk. An African American woman in a spotless uniform sat behind the desk.

She studied them with an expression of curious interest. "Can I help you two?"

"Captain Reiser?" Rebecca asked.

"That's right."

"I'm Detective Lieutenant Rebecca Frye, and this is Detective Watts. PPD."

Reiser pushed back her chair and stood in one fluid motion, extending her hand. "Detectives," she said, as she shook each of their hands in turn. Indicating a stack of metal chairs along one wall, she said ruefully, "Grab yourself a seat."

"Thank you, we're fine," Rebecca said.

Seated again, Reiser nodded. "Same question. How can I help you two?"

"We wanted to ask you some questions about Detective Jimmy Hogan."

Reiser's expression didn't change. "Doesn't ring a bell."

"Somebody put a bullet in his head down here about six months ago," Watts said conversationally.

"Ah, yes. Him and another police officer. I'm sorry."

"We thought you might be able to tell us what he was doing down here." Rebecca's tone was casual. Friendly. But her ice blue eyes were sharply appraising.

"Is there some reason you think I might know?" Reiser replied, her expression equally relaxed and her deep chocolate eyes just as intent as she scrutinized Rebecca.

"Watts," Rebecca said softly.

Watts reached into his rumpled tweed jacket and extracted three creased sheets of paper. Wordlessly, he leaned forward and deposited them in the center of Captain Reiser's desk.

After only an instant's hesitation, the Port Authority captain picked up the pages and scanned each one in turn. Then she read them again. Finally, she placed them back in the same position that Watts had deposited them. "He called on the phone. Said he was working with the Harbor Patrol and that they were trying to track ships suspected of illegally dumping waste after they'd left port. Garbage mostly, sometimes industrial items." Frowning, she swiveled her chair and stared through the glass partition into the dimly lit, crowded warehouse beyond. "I think he had a list of ships—he wanted their schedules, port-of-origin information, and manifests."

Rebecca felt a spark of excitement. Hogan *had* been on to something down here. Almost certainly something involving cargo, since the Harbor Patrol story was completely fabricated. While technically a division of the PPD, the men and women who policed the waterways were much more closely tied to the Port Authority than to the city police. There was very little overlap in assignments.

"Any reason you didn't report this before?" Watts questioned, his voice rough with irritation.

Reiser met his gaze steadily. "I didn't make the connection. I remember the call now that you show me the list, because at the time I thought it was an unusual request. Usually the Harbor Patrol is more interested in *civilian* waterway violations, not commercial." She frowned. "I recall pulling some of the manifests. But, for some reason, the name *Hogan* doesn't ring a bell." She shook her head. "No—I think I would have put it together when those two cops were gunned down. So maybe it wasn't him."

"Your name's in those reports, Captain."

"Yes. I see that." She still seemed more curious than alarmed. "What's this all about?"

Rebecca studied the other woman. Reiser looked to be in her late thirties or early forties, tall and solidly built. Her attitude was one of quiet confidence, and Rebecca didn't get the sense that she was hiding anything from them or was even particularly concerned about their visit. Rebecca made a decision. "We think something Hogan stumbled onto down here got him killed."

Immediately, Reiser sat forward, her hands clasped on the desk, her face severely intent. "What kind of *thing*?"

Rebecca shook her head. "We don't know. We were hoping that you would."

"Maybe the three of us should take a walk." Without waiting for their answer, she stood and pulled a black wool overcoat from an aluminum coat stand in the corner. Shrugging into it, she eyed Watts's sport coat and Rebecca's silk blazer. "You two are going to freeze out there. The wind off the water is going to make it feel like twenty degrees."

"We'll be fine," Rebecca assured her. Watts just grunted.

"Good enough."

Watts and Rebecca followed Reiser as she led them from the office, through the warehouse, and out the rear to a loading dock. She hadn't exaggerated. A brisk wind blew off the water, whipping their clothes and penetrating to skin with the ease of a knife blade. A cargo ship blocked their view of the river as it rode low in the water, laden with containers stacked ten high on the deck.

"Three thousand ships load and off-load at the Port of Philadelphia every year." Reiser shouted to be heard above the wind. "We handle more than one quarter of the entire North Atlantic District's annual tonnage, making us the fourth-largest port in the U.S. for imported merchandise."

As she spoke, another container swung out from the deck of the ship on the end of the crane arm toward a waiting truck. Reiser pointed up at the crane.

"That's a three-hundred-seventy-five-ton container crane—one of the largest in use anywhere. We handle bulk merchandise, containers, automobiles, perishable goods—a broader range of imports than almost any other U.S. port." She hunched her shoulders inside her heavy regulation coat. "Four hundred and twenty-five trucking companies pick up and transport out of here on a regular basis."

She led them back under the shelter of the warehouse eaves. "Do a few crates fall off the back of a truck now and then? Probably. We have a central computer system with a staff of ten who do nothing but cross-check bills of lading, ports of origin, and destinations against incoming and outgoing manifests. Do we check each barrel, crate, and container? No. They've been cleared by Customs at the point of origin, and U.S. Customs agents do visual inspections upon arrival."

"We're not suggesting any of your people are at fault, Captain," Rebecca interjected.

Reiser scanned the area. They were surrounded by dockworkers, but no one paid them any attention. "The majority of personnel you see are civilians—longshoremen, teamsters, truckers. They don't work for or answer to me."

"Who *do* they work for?" Watts questioned.

"The unions." Reiser held Watts's gaze. "Supposedly."

"Huh." Watts looked as if he smelled something unpleasant. "And we know who *they* answer to."

Rebecca made no comment, watching Reiser, attempting to decipher just how much the captain really knew of organized crime's presence on the waterfront. Or how much of what she knew she would share. But she clearly had not wanted to have this conversation in plain sight of the workers in the warehouse. *So there's something she suspects, at least.*

"I don't know what your man found, Lieutenant," Reiser said empathically, finally turning to Rebecca. "If anything. I'm not saying there's nothing to find. What I *am* saying is if there's anything *big* to find, we would know."

"So if *someone* swipes a load of goods bigger than an armload, you'll know about it," Watts summarized.

Reiser smiled fleetingly. "Well, let's say bigger than a truckload. Obviously, vehicles are checked upon exiting the compound, but off the record, I wouldn't swear that a case here or there doesn't end up in someone's backseat."

"I doubt that something like that would have interested Jimmy Hogan," Rebecca said. "What about drugs?"

"Imports from South America make up a large percentage of the traffic here. Again, the merchandise is checked at the point of origin, and Customs clears it here. Is there a bag of cocaine tucked into a crate of coffee somewhere? Possibly, but large scale? Doubtful."

"But not impossible," Watts said.

"No," Reiser agreed. "Not impossible."

"Is there anything about the particular information that Hogan requested that raises a flag for you?" Rebecca asked.

"Not offhand, but why don't you leave me copies of those requests, and I'll look them over again. If something clicks, I'll call you."

"Good enough. Appreciate it, Captain." Rebecca extended her hand, and they shook.

Five minutes later, Rebecca slowed for the same taciturn guard at the security post, who waved them through with barely a glance.

"You think she's straight?" Watts asked.

"I do," Rebecca replied immediately. "What's your take?"

"She's careful, but something was bothering her. Because nobody *likes* to freeze their balls off for no good reason."

"Yeah, that little trip outside had to be because she didn't want anyone seeing her cozying up to us."

"Well, she didn't tell us much."

Rebecca was silent for a full minute. "She seemed pretty certain that something big wouldn't get by her—or her people."

"I think there's a hell of a lot of stuff moving in and out of that port every day, and I don't care how many computer jockeys they've got watching it—stuff has to disappear."

"I agree. But why would Jimmy Hogan care?"

"Could be Zamora is moving stolen merchandise through there. Maybe using the proceeds to underwrite his drug operation. Jimmy could've gotten wind of it, started poking around." Watts drummed his heavy fingers on the dash. "That tends to make people suspicious."

Rebecca nodded, slowing for a light at the turn onto I-95. "So how does Jeff come into it?"

"Cruz and Hogan were tight, right? From the academy? And Jimmy passed Jeff intel before when he wasn't going to act on it himself." Watts shifted and tried to stretch his legs in the narrow space beneath the Corvette's dash. "Jimmy couldn't afford to be involved in any kind of bust that involved Zamora, because it would blow his cover."

"It still comes back to Jimmy, and what he knew." Rebecca sighed. "We need to get as close to Zamora's organization as we can."

"Well, we've got two ways in already." Watt's tone suggested that he wasn't all that happy about the fact. "Our boy Mitch and his cute little squeeze."

Mitchell and Sandy. Rebecca suppressed another sigh. *A wet-behind-the-ears detective and a smart-mouthed streetwalker. Wonderful.*

Chapter Fifteen

Sandy emerged from the bedroom, sleepy-eyed and fuzzy-headed in pink satin bikinis and one of Mitchell's T-shirts. Shuffling through the quiet loft toward the kitchen, she yawned and stretched, baring a long expanse of hip and belly. The quiet voice from across the room made her jump.

"Good morning," Michael said.

"Jesus," Sandy blurted, pivoting in Michael's direction. The other woman sat on a tall stool at the angled draftsman's table next to a computer console bearing two widescreen monitors. "Man. I didn't think anyone was here."

"I just came home an hour ago." Michael smiled ruefully. "I knew that Sloan would be working late, so I stayed at Sarah's last night. Jason brought me back early this morning. I'm sorry. Did I scare you?"

"Uh-uh," Sandy replied, still breathless. "Sorry. I didn't mean to bother you." She started to backpedal toward the guest room, but Michael shook her head.

"You're not bothering me. I was just thinking of taking a break. Tea?"

Sandy made a face but managed to stifle a groan. "Uh, I think it better be coffee this morning."

"Late night?" Michael asked conversationally, her smile friendly.

"Yeah, sort of." Sandy thought of Dell, and how upset she'd been after the visit from her sister, and of what she had seemed to need so desperately from Sandy. Sandy had made love to her for hours, Dell reaching for her again and again in the night, until they'd both collapsed from exhaustion. Dell had slept with her head nestled to Sandy's breast, their arms and legs entwined. Sandy had never before experienced sex as healing, and knowing that she had given her lover something that no one else could made her feel powerful and nearly overcome with awe.

"Working?"

Sandy jumped, the question resounding in the air. "No. Not last night."

Michael slid from the stool and crossed the loft to Sandy's side. "How about that coffee? I think there are some scones left from yesterday. Interested?"

"Sure." Sandy paused a beat, then asked hurriedly, "Do you and Sloan talk about…everything?"

Struck by the serious note in Sandy's voice, Michael halted. "I think so. Sometimes, it takes one of us longer to say what we need to than it should, but eventually we get there. Why?"

"So, did Sloan tell you what I do?"

"Do? Oh! You mean for work?"

"Uh-huh." Despite feeling very vulnerable, standing half naked in front of a woman so privileged and sophisticated that Sandy doubted she'd ever even *seen* the strip at night, Sandy kept her head up and her eyes on Michael's.

"No, she hasn't." Michael's voice held a note of curiosity.

"I'm a prostitute."

"That's something Sloan would consider yours to tell," Michael said gently, her expression holding no trace of censure. She touched Sandy's arm fleetingly, then turned toward the kitchen. "Coffee?"

"Oh yeah. Bad." Sandy padded after her, barefoot. Funny, how getting the truth out in the open made her feel better. It mattered what Michael thought—because she liked her, and she knew that Dell did too. But mostly it felt good not to hide.

Michael crossed to the counter along the wall and assembled the makings for French-press coffee. As she worked, she said, "Is it something you decide? Or just something that happens?"

Sandy settled on a stool at the breakfast bar opposite Michael and hooked her toes over one of the wooden rungs. "A little of both, I guess. After a while, you run out of choices. Or at least…choices that won't kill you pretty fast."

"Is that how it was for you?" Michael poured boiling water into the coffeepot, set the kettle carefully back on the burner, and turned, her hips resting along the edge of the tiled counter.

If there had been the slightest hint of condescension or even pity in Michael's tone, Sandy might not have answered. But what she heard, besides gentle interest, was a subtle sense of caring that what Sandy had to say mattered. Even Dell had not asked. Sandy smiled. "Dell and me…we're pretty into each other, you know?"

Michael nodded, containing a smile. She was glad for the fact that the loft, despite its open design, had well-insulated, private sleeping quarters, because even with the distance between their bedrooms, now and then she heard an ecstatic cry or a desperate groan. "Every time I've seen you two together, I've had the sense that she was crazy about you."

Sandy's face lit up. "Yeah? You think?"

"Oh yeah," Michael said with a grin.

"She's never asked me why I do it."

The seeming non sequitur did not disturb Michael. She reached for the strainer for the French press and pushed the coffee grounds to the bottom of the pot. As she poured steaming, rich coffee into two mugs, she said, "She's probably waiting for you to tell her."

"*You* asked."

Michael crossed to the breakfast island and handed Sandy the coffee. Edging onto the adjacent stool, she blew on the steam wafting from her mug. "I'm not in love with you."

Sandy sipped the coffee and considered Michael's words. "That changes things, doesn't it."

"Being in love?"

"Uh-huh."

"Oh, yes. It changes everything."

"The only thing I had that was worth anything was my body." Sandy said it matter-of-factly, without rancor. "I could've traded it for drugs and a place to flop—being stoned would've made some things a lot easier…well, at least, I wouldn't have known if they were bad or not." She laughed hollowly. "But I decided I'd rather have the money and maybe a life."

"It looks like you made the right choice." Michael leaned past Sandy for a basket of scones and drew it near. She indicated the pastries to Sandy. "Hungry?"

"Yeah." Sandy helped herself. "Dell doesn't like it."

"I imagine," Michael said quietly. "It must be very dangerous, isn't it?"

Sandy shrugged. "Maybe, if you're not careful. I'm careful." She sighed. "But I haven't really been working for a while."

"You quit?"

"I don't know about that," Sandy said hastily. "I mean, I have to make money, so I'm not sure I *quit* quit. But…it really bothers her. And…I know what happens sooner or later to everyone in the life."

"Does she know?"

Sandy shook her head.

"How come you haven't told her?"

"Because what if I go back?" Sandy broke off a piece of the scone and nibbled on it. "She'll be…disappointed."

Michael placed her coffee cup carefully on the breakfast bar. She leaned forward, curling her fingers around Sandy's forearm, stroking softly. "She loves you. She won't stop."

Eyes clouded by fears she couldn't voice, Sandy finally said hesitantly, "You know, tomorrow is the ceremony for her promotion thing. It's kind of a big deal."

"Mmm. I know. Are you going?"

Sandy shrugged. "She asked me to."

"Well?"

Sandy squirmed and looked past Michael at nothing in particular. "I dunno."

"What's stopping you?" Michael persisted, keeping her hand lightly on Sandy's arm.

"I won't fit in." She blew out an irritated breath. "You think I can go there and everyone won't know I'm a whore? Jesus, like that should matter to me."

"That's not who you are," Michael said firmly, never raising her voice. "You're not defined by what you've had to do to survive. Nor by the mistakes that you may have made."

Sandy narrowed her eyes at the note of fierce intensity in Michael's cultured tones. She knew that appearances rarely told the whole story; some of the most violent johns were well-dressed, well-spoken men. Michael seemed like the most together woman Sandy had ever met, but Sandy could still hear the pain in her voice. Something or someone had hurt her badly once.

"I don't have anything to wear."

Michael laughed. "Well, that's something we can easily fix."

"Yeah?"

"Yeah." Michael stood and slipped her hand into Sandy's, giving her a tug. When Sandy stepped to the floor, Michael wrapped an arm around her waist. "Let's go shopping."

"You don't say anything unless I ask for your report," Rebecca said with finality.

Sloan snarled.

"Or you don't sit in."

"Okay, okay," Sloan muttered. "Jesus."

Watts, looking pleased, said nothing as the three of them walked through the detective squad room toward Captain Henry's office.

Sloan eyed him dangerously. "You have something to say?"

His grin broadening, Watts held up his hands in surrender. "Not me."

The fact that Rebecca pushed open the door to Henry's office forestalled Sloan's retort. Sloan looked past her to the men in the room and stiffened. Henry sat in his customary place behind his broad desk. Avery Clark, clad in the federal agent's requisite uniform of dark suit, pale blue shirt, and rep tie, leaned against the file cabinets a few feet from Henry's desk with his arms crossed over his chest. His gaze flickered over each of the new arrivals as they entered the room, his expression registering nothing.

"Have a seat," Henry said, indicating the mismatched, armless chairs fronting his desk.

Rebecca and Watts complied, but Sloan moved to the wall opposite Clark and rested an elbow on top of a small watercooler. From there, she could look directly at Clark, which she did. She'd learned long ago never to give field advantage to an adversary, and she wasn't at all convinced that Clark was on their team.

"You've had some developments in the case, Lieutenant?" Henry asked of Rebecca.

"In one aspect of the case, yes, sir. We believe we've identified the source of the leak in the department. We also think the same individual was involved in the attempt on Sloan's life."

Henry's eyes glinted. "Let's hear it."

"Sloan?" Rebecca requested.

Still leaning against the watercooler, Sloan reviewed their investigation, starting with the premise that only those people who'd had advance knowledge of the plan to trap one of the midlevel Internet porn distributors could have fingered her for execution. She described the process by which they'd eliminated the suspects, conveniently leaving out the fact that Henry had been one of them.

"A few days ago, I found several computer traces that led back to Beecher as the likely source of the network intrusions. In all likelihood, someone is accessing his computer regularly from a remote location and using it as the portal into the entire law enforcement system. Your files are open books."

Looking as if he had been carved from stone, Henry angled his body toward Clark. "We'll need to go right to the district attorney, seeing that Beecher's one of hers. This is going to be very messy."

"Computer evidence alone often isn't enough to convince a DA to bring charges." Clark spoke softly, his posture relaxed. He didn't look at Sloan when he spoke but directed his comments to Henry as if they were alone in the room.

Sloan stiffened and took a step forward. "How did I know you—"

"Sir," Rebecca interjected, cutting off Sloan in midsentence, "we're in the process of gathering further documentation of Beecher's involvement in the Internet pornography operation."

Watts cast her a sidelong glance, but said nothing.

"We only wanted to bring you up to speed on these developments in case things move quickly and we need a warrant." Glancing at Clark and then back to Henry, she added, "Appreciating, sir, that this situation could be…delicate."

Everyone in the room knew that only Clark was immune from the politics of this situation and that Henry was likely to be the messenger first in line to be shot.

"And *I* appreciate your concern, Lieutenant," Henry said dryly. He turned to Sloan. "How solid is your evidence?"

"Rock," Sloan said flatly.

"Good." Henry nodded as if pleased before addressing Rebecca. "I'll give you the weekend to put together a package I can take to—"

"I'm not so sure we want to take Beecher out of the picture," Clark interjected quietly.

"Why aren't I surprised," Sloan snapped.

"I'm not saying *not* to take him," Clark said. "But for now, he's our best chance of discovering who's really behind this. He's obviously not working solo."

"So we bring him in and sweat him," Watts suggested. "A guy like that, not used to rough handling? Verbally…I mean," he said with a sly smile. "And he'll tell us everything he knows."

"You're probably right, detective." Clark spoke with the merest hint of condescension. "But what about what he doesn't know? Once we have him, whoever is running him will start covering their tracks. If we somehow lose that connection, all we have is a dirty ADA. Small fry."

"Who was involved in a murder attempt that was almost successful," Sloan said through gritted teeth. "Beecher needs to go down for that."

"That and a lot more, Sloan." Clark finally met her gaze squarely, and for the first time, his voice had lost its friendly edge too. "Have you forgotten how it works?"

Sloan quivered with the effort to contain her temper. "You know I haven't."

"Then make the case and set your personal issues aside."

"My *personal issues* are still struggling to recover from the hit-and-run." Sloan's voice was ice.

When Sloan took another step in Clark's direction, Rebecca bolted up, blocking Sloan's path. "That's exactly what we plan to do, Captain. Nail this down tight. We've got Mr. McBride, our other computer consultant, and Detective Mitchell working on additional evidence tying Beecher to the pornography operation. Watts and I have been tailing him, but we could use some extra help on that."

"Done. I'll assign twenty-four-hour coverage."

"We'll need photos," Clark said, his tone calm and even again.

For the first time, Henry looked annoyed. "We do know how to run surveillance in Philadelphia, Agent Clark."

Clark merely smiled. "Of course."

"What else have you got cooking, Lieutenant?" Henry asked.

Rebecca lifted her shoulder. "We're exploring a number of avenues, sir."

A flicker of amusement crossed Henry's face and was quickly gone. "Then I'll expect you to keep me apprised of your progress along those lines."

"Of course," Rebecca replied. With a nod to Clark, she moved toward the door, Sloan and Watts close behind. Once outside, with the door firmly closed behind them, she muttered, "Let's get out of here."

"I'll be in the ESU," Sloan snapped and strode away.

Watts looked after her and grunted. "She's gonna snap Clark in two someday."

"We need to see she doesn't," Rebecca said quietly.

"Us and whose army?"

"She'll hold," Rebecca said, hoping that she was right.

Chapter Sixteen

"You look like you're walking more easily," Catherine observed as Mitchell crossed the room to her customary seat in the chair opposite Catherine's desk. "How's the leg doing?"

"It's fine. Almost good as new."

Even had she not been trained to hear the unspoken words and decipher the subtle signals that people telegraphed without meaning to, Catherine would have been hard-pressed to miss Mitchell's distress. The normally strong planes of her face were hollow and drawn, her vibrant deep blue eyes shadowed and dull. Even the timbre of her voice rang with pain.

"You'll be seeing Dr. Torveau for another evaluation tomorrow?"

Mitchell nodded, almost too weary to speak. She drew a breath and forced herself to deal with the one issue that really mattered. "I need the paperwork filled out for the lieutenant. About my duty status."

"Yes, I know." Catherine pushed her chair back a few inches from her desk and crossed her legs, relaxed but attentive. With a gentle smile, she asked, "I take it you're ready to return?"

"Definitely. I'm going stir-crazy."

"But you've been keeping busy, correct? Working with Jason?"

Again, Mitchell signaled assent with a twitch of her shoulder.

"Dellon," Catherine said quietly. "Want to tell me what's going on?"

Mitchell considered her options, which were few—that is, in addition to the truth. Denial, lying, or evasion. She contemplated those choices. Perhaps if it had been the first time she'd been in this situation with Catherine Rawlings, she wouldn't even have hesitated. She would have said "nothing." Things had changed, and she hadn't even noticed. It was harder for her to keep what bothered her inside. It was harder for her to keep people on the outside. Part of that was a result of the support she had gotten the first time she'd been forced into therapy with Catherine. Despite her initial discomfort and anger at her powerlessness, she'd found understanding and an unexpected surcease from pain when she'd shared her feelings.

And then there was Sandy.

Sandy, who had managed to step over, circumnavigate, or simply crash through every barrier she'd imposed, with a single sharp word or tender glance. Last night—last night all she'd wanted was for Sandy to keep touching her, because with Sandy inside her, there was no room for anything else. Mitchell took a shuddering breath.

"I was forced to resign my commission in the Army."

Although the revelation was completely unexpected, Catherine's expression indicated only compassionate interest and none of her surprise. "Forced. So it wasn't voluntary?"

"In theory, I had a choice. It was simple—take an honorable discharge or be court-martialed." Mitchell laughed hollowly and shook her head. "Some choice."

"What were the circumstances?"

Mitchell rubbed her face vigorously with both hands and then dropped her arms back to the armrests, her fingers limp. "I assaulted a superior officer."

"Male or female?"

"A man."

"Assaulted how?"

"I punched him. Hard enough to put him in the hospital overnight."

"Tell me how *that* came about." Catherine had seen Mitchell with Rebecca and knew how deeply ingrained her respect for hierarchical authority was. Whatever had prompted her to break rank in such an excessive fashion must have been extreme.

"He was trying to…he forced himself…on a woman."

"You stopped a rape?" Catherine asked incredulously. "And for that, you were threatened with court-martial?"

"It wasn't a rape…yet. He was just…" Mitchell swallowed, the memory still so clear. Her stomach churned with rage and revulsion, just as it had that night. "He was just touching her." *He had his hands on her breasts, his mouth on her neck. He was pressing himself into her.*

"Against her will?"

Mitchell nodded.

"Then I don't…I'm sorry. I don't understand," Catherine said intently. "Why were *you* at fault?"

"She was my lover."

Oh, Dellon. Catherine rose and walked around the desk to the chair beside Mitchell's. She did not touch her, but angled in the seat so that she could look directly into Mitchell's face. "Tell me about her."

Laughing, Michael stepped out of the elevator, her arms filled with packages. Sandy followed close behind, saying, "I can't believe the look on her face when you told her I was your girlfriend."

"Well," Michael said, still irritated by the saleswoman's superior attitude, "she was so clearly trying to eavesdrop on our conversation, I just thought I'd help her out."

"You were great…" Sandy trailed off as she noticed the woman standing across the room by the windows. "Hey, Sloan."

"Hi, Sandy."

Surprised, Michael deposited the spoils of their trip on the sofa and went to her lover. "Darling? I didn't expect to see you this afternoon."

Sloan smiled and kissed Michael's cheek. "Missed you last night."

Michael brushed her fingers through Sloan's hair, studying her lover's eyes. "Did you get any sleep at all?"

"A few hours."

From across the room, Sandy called, "I'm gonna unpack these and then take off for a while. I have some errands to run for Dell."

"Don't put them where she might see them," Michael said. "Use the closet down the hall."

Sandy grinned. "Gotcha."

Once alone, Michael twined her arms around Sloan's waist and settled against her. "Tired?"

"No." Sloan smoothed her hands up and down Michael's back, loving the feel of silk sliding over even softer skin, reveling in the warmth beneath her fingertips. When she'd left Henry's office and gone back to the ESU, she'd thought she'd be able to work. Thought the work would quench the anger, as it had so often in the past, but this time was different. She couldn't concentrate. All she'd been able to think about had been Michael—almost dying, and the horrible void that had filled her heart and mind for those few terrible hours. Unconsciously, she tightened her hold on the woman in her arms.

Michael leaned back enough to look into Sloan's eyes. There was turmoil in their depths. "What is it?"

Sloan rested her forehead against Michael's. "Nothing. I love you."

"What did you do this morning?" When no answer was forthcoming, Michael stroked the back of Sloan's neck and kissed her gently. "Sloan?"

"Just a briefing with Rebecca and some of the hotshots in the department."

"Problems?"

Sloan shook her head.

"Progress, then?"

"Some." Sloan stiffened as she thought about what she had learned. "I know who hurt you. At least who set it up."

Michael gasped. "How?"

"I tracked him through the computer system at Police Plaza."

"You know his name?"

"Yes."

"A police officer?"

"An ADA. He's probably Mob connected—I don't know how just yet."

"Has he been arrested?"

"No." The bitterness in Sloan's voice lay heavy in the air.

Michael cupped her fingers along the sharp angle of Sloan's jaw, sensitive to the tight muscles quivering beneath the smooth, pale skin. Now she understood why Sloan had come home in the middle of the day, in the middle of a big case. Something she would ordinarily never do. She was in pain. "You know what I'd like?"

"What?" Sloan's voice was husky, her hands terribly gentle as they rested in the soft curve above Michael's hips.

"I'd like to go to a movie, and then out somewhere for dinner, and then come home and spend the rest of the night in your arms." Her fingers trembled faintly as she traced their tips over Sloan's mouth. "Can we do that?"

Sloan buried her hands in Michael's soft golden hair before lowering her mouth to Michael's. After she'd filled her mind with the touch and taste of her lover, she whispered, "Yes. Always for you, yes."

Catherine stepped from her car and turned at the sound of her name. Smiling, she leaned a hip against the fender and watched Rebecca coming toward her, a pizza box balanced in one hand. Under the streetlights, Rebecca's blond hair glinted. Her blazer swung open, revealing the long line of her chest and hips. Catherine's heart skipped a beat, and she felt the familiar tingling that always accompanied the first sight of her lover.

"How did you know I'd be home now?" Catherine asked as Rebecca drew near.

"I'm a detective." At the sight of Catherine's raised brow, Rebecca grinned. "I called Joyce, and she told me when you'd be finished."

"Mmm. Good thinking." Catherine wrapped her arm around Rebecca's waist as they strolled down the sidewalk side by side. "You need to start wearing an overcoat, darling."

Rebecca kissed Catherine's cheek. "Why? Is it going to snow?"

"It feels cold enough to."

"I'm fine."

"Is there some rule about police officers not wearing coats?"

"I don't like them. Too confining."

You think it will get in the way of you reaching your gun, don't you? Catherine had noticed that whenever they walked together, Rebecca took the street side, as if shielding her. She was also very aware that no matter where they were, Rebecca constantly scanned the surroundings, looking for something or someone out of place. It wasn't a question of Rebecca always working, it was simply that Rebecca was always a cop. And in that regard, there was no middle ground. "If you won't wear an overcoat, then you need to switch to wool blazers. The silk is not heavy enough for this time of year."

Rebecca laughed. "If that will make you happy, I will. Except they're still in storage from last winter. It might be a week or so before I have time to retrieve them."

"Give me the tickets, and I'll pick them up for you."

"You don't have to," Rebecca said as they climbed the stairs to Catherine's brownstone.

"I want to. That's all a part of our being together."

Inside, Catherine shed her coat and briefcase as Rebecca took the pizza into the kitchen. A moment later, Catherine joined her. She made an appreciative sound as Rebecca opened a bottle of cabernet and filled a glass for her.

"This is wonderful," Catherine sighed after her first sip of the dark wine.

With a contented groan, Rebecca leaned her hips against the counter, arms outstretched on either side, her fingers curled around the edge, enjoying Catherine's pleasure. "Better than wonderful."

Appreciating the way the fine, pale linen stretched across Rebecca's chest, Catherine nodded. "It's the first night you've been home for dinner all week. We should celebrate."

Rebecca patted the pizza box. "That's what I thought too."

Catherine took another swallow of wine and set the glass on the small butcher block next to the stove. Then she stepped up to Rebecca and placed her hands on the counter inside of Rebecca's, trapping her lover between her arms. "I wasn't thinking about food."

With Catherine pressed along her length, Rebecca remained motionless, content for Catherine to lead. "Not hungry?"

"Well," Catherine murmured as she slid her hands over Rebecca's back, "I am, but I was thinking of pizza for the *second* course."

"I like cold pizza." Rebecca tilted her head back, offering her throat. She growled softly as Catherine's teeth caught at her skin. When she raised her hands from the counter to embrace her lover, Catherine grasped her wrists.

"No. Keep them right where they were." Firmly, Catherine guided Rebecca's hands back to the curved edge of the counter. Then, as she kept Rebecca pinned with the force of her pelvis between Rebecca's thighs, she kissed her. Slowly at first, the tip of her tongue tracing the juncture of lips and moist inner recesses. Then a little harder, a little deeper, until their tongues danced in teasing counterpoint. While she savored Rebecca's mouth, she slipped her hand between them and unbuttoned Rebecca's shirt.

"Catherine," Rebecca whispered at the first touch of fingertips against her breast. With her hands clenched around the edge of the counter, she braced her arms for support. The muscles in her legs trembled as Catherine kissed her, one warm palm kneading her breast, a thumb flicking at her nipple.

"Mmm," Catherine moaned as she broke the kiss and dragged her fingernails down the center of Rebecca's abdomen to her belt. As she deftly slid the leather free of the clasp, she whispered, "So much better than pizza."

"You make me feel so good," Rebecca gasped. "You make me forget…everything, except us." Her head swam as Catherine's fingers dipped inside her trousers and found her ready. "When you touch me…" The exquisite pressure left her breathless.

"What?" Catherine's voice was deep, husky with desire as she kissed the corner of Rebecca's mouth, her jaw, her neck—one hand inside Rebecca's shirt, caressing her breasts, the other stroking rhythmically between her legs. "What happens, darling? What?"

Rebecca's vision wavered as her stomach tightened, her thighs turning to jelly. Her breath came in short pants, and a sound somewhere between a plea and a prayer tore from her throat. "You make me whole."

"We make…*oh God*…" Caught unawares by a sudden surge of heat that raced along the inside of her legs and up her spine, Catherine shuddered. Eyes nearly closed, she rested her forehead against Rebecca's and slipped inside her, never breaking the rhythm of her strokes, only moving deeper, taking more of her. Taking all of her. As she felt Rebecca spasm around her fingers, she whispered, "We make each other whole."

Long moments later, when Rebecca could speak, she whispered, "I love when you do that to me."

Sated by her lover's pleasure, Catherine nestled her head on Rebecca's shoulder, arms loosely clasping her waist. Eyes closed, she drifted without thought, only knowing that she was happy. "Mmm. Do what?"

"Just take me, like I'm yours."

Catherine raised her head, her eyes still hazy with arousal. "You *are* mine."

Rebecca grinned weakly, finding it difficult to control her body, which still felt boneless. "Yeah. I know. But when you have your way with me, I *really* know."

"Stick around, detective," Catherine murmured, nipping at Rebecca's chin. "It gets better."

"I don't see how it could," Rebecca replied, suddenly serious. She filled her hands with Catherine's hair, holding her head as she took her mouth with fierce intensity. She kissed her, suddenly desperate for the taste of her. When she felt Catherine tremble against her body, she moved her mouth to Catherine's ear. "I'm not going anywhere."

Catherine wanted to ask for her promise, but instead, she found Rebecca's hand and guided her lover's sensitive fingers underneath the edge of her skirt, along the path her pleasure had streamed earlier, and to the center of her desire. Pressing Rebecca's fingers through the slick heat, into the waiting heart of her, she had no need for words.

Chapter Seventeen

Sandy stood by the bedside, watching Mitchell sleep. An open book lay on her chest, the edges of the pages crumpled against her bare breast. Lamplight shone in her face, and she didn't budge even when Sandy leaned down and kissed her lightly. Moving carefully, Sandy stripped and lifted the sheet to slide in next to the slumbering woman. As she reached to turn off the light, Mitchell stirred.

"Hey, honey," Mitchell murmured, turning on her side, knocking the book to the floor in the process.

"Hi, baby." Sandy snuggled close, edging her thigh between Mitchell's. "Go back to sleep."

"Mmm, in a minute." With a contented sigh, Mitchell nuzzled Sandy's neck, inhaling her scent. "Missed you."

"You and Jason were so into your spy stuff when I left, I wasn't even sure you heard me say goodbye."

Mitchell chuckled and wrapped an arm around Sandy's waist. "I heard you." She kissed the tender spot below Sandy's ear. "Everything okay?"

Sandy rubbed her palm back and forth across Mitchell's chest, finally trailing her fingers over the inner curve of one small, firm breast. "Yeah."

"You're home earlier than usual. S'good."

"Uh-huh." Sandy debated sharing the news that she'd run into a girl at the Blue Diamond who'd seen Trudy in the club the night before, asking some of her old friends for a place to crash. After a few more stops in a few more strip joints, Sandy had finally scored a phone number to get a message to Trudy. It wasn't *Trudy's* telephone number, of course. It was a link in a phone-message tree that the street girls often used to thwart their pimps when they were planning to cut out on them or if they just wanted privacy. Rather than risk having their cell phones confiscated and their messages intercepted, they passed messages from one to the other through a convoluted set of phone relays. Eventually a message would reach its intended recipient, and a callback number or time for a meeting would wend its way back up the tree to whoever had initiated the contact.

Sandy *had* gotten a return message—with the time and place for a meeting with Trudy the following night. She wasn't certain their getting together would come to anything, because she didn't know if the girl had any more information about the video porn ring than she'd already revealed. Still, it was a place to start, and Sandy could at least try to talk Trudy into contacting her if she learned anything new or if she had another offer to do a porn shoot. No way was one police raid going to shut down that kind of business for good. Anything selling sex was impossible to kill.

In the end, she decided that only Frye should know, because that was what the detective was paying her for. She didn't like keeping anything from Dell, but she didn't want to get her into trouble, either. And, she admitted to herself, the less Dell knew about these activities, the better. She'd only worry. Or get protective. And even though Sandy liked the way it felt to have Dell care about her that way, the downside was having Dell get all bent out of shape about it. So she kept silent about the details.

"You okay about tomorrow?" Sandy asked instead, stroking the back of Mitchell's neck.

"About the promotion ceremony?" Mitchell nuzzled Sandy's nipple until it hardened, then flicked at it with her tongue. "Yeah. You're comin', right?"

Sandy directed Mitchell's mouth back to her breast. "Uh-huh."

"Good," Mitchell mumbled before devoting herself to sucking Sandy's nipple to rigid attention.

"Mmm, that's nice," Sandy sighed, closing her eyes and savoring the heat that washed through her as Mitchell teased. "Did you hear from your sister today?"

Mitchell stiffened, but kept her mouth to Sandy's breast. "No."

"Does she know about tomorrow?"

"Don't see how." Mitchell rolled over onto her back.

In the silence that followed, Sandy leaned up on an elbow and settled her palm on Mitchell's abdomen. The muscles beneath her fingers felt like wood. "What did she do to you?"

"Nothing. She was only here an hour or so yesterday."

"I don't mean *yesterday*, Dell," Sandy said impatiently. "I mean before. Whenever."

"Look, Sandy, honey—"

"It's like a splinter, Dell. You gotta pull it out, no matter how much it hurts."

Mitchell laughed—a short, hard sound. "Jesus. First in therapy, now in bed. I can't get away from old history."

"You did, though, right?" Sandy smoothed her hand in slow circles, not the way she did when she wanted to get Dell hot, but the way she gentled her after she'd already made her come. Coaxing the clenched muscles to relax, Sandy continued softly, "Get away from it, I mean. All this time that you haven't seen her—you've been keeping all of this stuff deep down inside somewhere."

"How do you know that?" Mitchell rasped, her throat thick with the effort of keeping a lid on her emotions. Seeing Erica had been so hard, and then talking to Dr. Rawlings about Robin had hurt so much, and *now*…now, Sandy's tenderness was crumbling the last of her defenses to dust.

"I can feel it. When I hold you. When you hold me. When we make love." Sandy shifted until she was lying on top of Mitchell, her narrow hips between Mitchell's thighs, supporting herself on her elbows so that she could see her lover's face in the moonlight that angled over the top of the sleeping partition. "You don't have to tell me. But I want you to. It makes *me* feel…better…to tell you things."

Mitchell wrapped both arms around Sandy's waist and pulled her down into a tight embrace. With her face buried in the curve of Sandy's neck, she haltingly surrendered her secrets.

"Rebecca, darling," Catherine murmured. "Phone."

Rebecca was already awake and leaning over her, fumbling on the bedside table for the handset. Clearing her throat, she said sharply, "Frye…Where?...Be there in fifteen. Do me a favor and roust Watts for me too." She paused to listen, sliding from beneath the covers and automatically tucking them along the curves of Catherine's body. "And, Frankel, keep this quiet. I don't want to see anything about this in the morning papers. Yeah, well, do the best you can."

Catherine sat up and switched on the bedside lamp. A check of the alarm clock told her it was close to 4:00 a.m. "What is it?"

"Trouble," Rebecca grumbled on her way to the bathroom.

"Four a.m. calls always are," Catherine whispered. She followed her lover into the bathroom and pulled her robe from behind the door. Slipping into it, she leaned against the vanity and observed Rebecca's sleek form shimmer behind the glass shower doors. Raising her voice to be heard above the water, she asked, "Can you tell me?"

After twisting the hot water knob to off and enduring fifteen vicious seconds of cold water beating on her head, Rebecca stepped from the shower and took the offered towel. "Thanks." Rubbing down briskly, she said, "That was one of the night Ds. He called in a homicide, and Captain Henry told him to call me. Details are sparse, but if Henry's putting me in the middle of someone else's case, it can't be good."

"That's it?" Catherine leaned against the bathroom door and watched Rebecca efficiently assemble her battle gear. Dark suit, pale shirt, thin black leather belt, shoulder harness, handcuffs, bifold leather wallet with its shiny gold badge declaring to all the world just who Rebecca Frye was.

"For now." Rebecca halted abruptly in the midst of dressing and leaned to kiss Catherine's cheek. "I'll let you know when I know."

Catherine stepped into Rebecca's arms and kissed her mouth. "If you don't get home before morning, call me. I have a break at noon."

Rebecca took the time to hold her lover for an extra twenty seconds that in the past she would never have spent. Holding Catherine, savoring her warmth and remembering the sound of her climaxing just hours before, Rebecca murmured, "I'll call just as soon as I can. I love you."

"Be careful, darling. I love you too."

Catherine went back to bed, retrieved a book from a stack on the bedside table, and tried to read. It was always hard to sleep when Rebecca worked at night, and now that she was wondering what new challenge her lover was about to face, it was impossible.

❖

"Don't touch anything yet," Dee Flanagan ordered automatically and, since she was addressing Rebecca, needlessly. Rebecca always waited until given the go-ahead before slipping on gloves and examining anything at a crime scene. At least, at one of *Flanagan's* crime scenes.

"Just give me the word," Rebecca replied as she always did, even though Flanagan routinely made a point of telling *her* first when she released the scene.

Rebecca hunkered down next to Watts. Their shoulders and thighs touched as they stared into the open driver's side of a BMW sports coupe. A white male, thirty to forty years of age, was slumped behind the wheel, very dead. "Is the ID for certain now?"

"Yeah."

"Fuck."

"You got that right."

"Time of death?" Rebecca questioned.

"Flanagan hasn't graced us with her opinion yet."

Rebecca nodded, silently assessing the body. The victim was casually dressed in chinos and a polo shirt. His topcoat was unbuttoned, as if he had been sitting in the car with the heater running—waiting for someone, perhaps. Or holding a conversation. No sign of a struggle. No sign of a weapon.

"There's blood and such on the driver's door," Watts said quietly. "The window's down a couple of inches, so maybe he was here awhile."

"Looks like one shot. Exit wound on the left temple." Rebecca studied the two-inch crater between the corner of the victim's left eye and ear. The edges of the wound—a pastiche of skin, muscle, and bone—were exploded outward, indicating the shot had come from the opposite side. "Passenger?"

"Could be. Or else he met someone here who opened the passenger door, leaned into the car, and—bam."

Rebecca looked over her shoulder, scanning the empty parking lot between Market and Front Streets under the massive arch of the Ben Franklin Bridge. Under ordinary circumstances, the lot was shrouded in shadow, but the potholed surface now appeared eerily bright under the halogen glare of the portable crime scene unit lights. A bevy of black-and-whites were parked along the perimeter, the reds and blues from their light bars adding to the surreal glow. Yellow crime scene tape ringed the block-square asphalt field. "Desolate area under the best of circumstances. Had to be someone he knew to get him down here this time of night."

"Or someone he wasn't afraid of," Watts said.

"Or maybe someone he *was* afraid of. And couldn't refuse."

Watts grunted. "Can't wait to see what the surveillance team has to say about this."

Rebecca studied George Beecher, the man she had spent the previous three nights shadowing. She had been relieved of that burden after Captain Henry had assigned round-the-clock surveillance on him. Clearly, something had gone awry. "Anybody talk to them yet?"

Straightening slowly, stretching his back before casually adjusting his crotch, Watts shrugged. "Who the fuck knows." He looked around with a sour expression. "Between the brass and the press, it's a goddamned three-ring circus. I can't even tell who's in charge of the case."

"Wait until the DA hears about this. She's going to have someone's head." Rebecca searched the crowd for Flanagan. Right now, what she needed was hard data. And Flanagan was the only one who would have it.

Watts grunted. "Well, as long as it ain't ours."

"Don't bet on it."

"You know, Loo," Watts said with uncharacteristic hesitancy, "this place is three blocks from Sloan's."

Rebecca gave him a sharp look, but the fact hadn't escaped her. "You have a point?"

With his gaze fixed somewhere beyond Rebecca's left shoulder, he nodded. "I don't like coincidences."

"Neither do I."

"We got company."

The increasingly dyspeptic expression on her partner's face tipped Rebecca to the identity of the new arrival. Her own face expressionless, she turned to watch Avery Clark cross the parking lot toward them.

"Man, this guy gives me a giant pain in the balls," Watts muttered.

"Me too."

Watts chuckled and shifted his weight from foot to foot, as if expecting a punch—or getting ready to throw one. Rebecca doubted that he was aware of just how intimidating he looked—a bulky, hard-eyed, tough guy who could just as easily have been a thug as a cop. She hadn't the slightest inclination to rein him in.

"Well, Lieutenant, this is an unfortunate occurrence," Avery Clark observed, bending down to peer into the vehicle.

"I'd wager Mr. Beecher feels the same," Rebecca replied.

Clark straightened. "Yes, well, we have a bit of a problem, don't we?"

Rebecca said nothing, aware of Watts next to her, rocking back and forth like a rodeo bull ready to burst from his pen. Clark pretended not to notice.

"We've lost a suspect," Clark intoned as if it were news. "A high-profile suspect likely to give us credible intelligence concerning a major crime organization in this city. That does not look good."

"To who?" Watts asked abruptly, the words chopped out with the force of a blow.

Clark spared Watts a glance before locking eyes with Rebecca. "To anyone."

Rebecca took this to mean that some of the dirt from this fiasco was going to rub off on Clark, and he didn't like it. She didn't really care whether he liked it or not. What she *did* care about was that they'd had a briefing in Police Plaza less than twenty-four hours earlier where they'd discussed their suspicions regarding George Beecher, and now he was dead. He was undoubtedly their leak, and now it appeared as if he might not be the only one. He'd been neatly and swiftly eliminated before they could question him.

"We need to move quickly to freeze all of his accounts, get his computers from both his residence and his office, and start looking for connections," Rebecca said. "Because whoever eliminated him is burying their trail right now."

When she turned as if to leave, Clark nonchalantly stepped into her path. "I'm wondering if this hit might not be something a bit closer to home."

Beside her, Watts made a sound in the back of his throat that reminded Rebecca of an attack dog warning off an intruder. She said nothing, because she knew Clark's game. He was looking for information and hoping to goad her into providing it.

"Maybe this has nothing to do with anything…professional," he went on. "Maybe it's someone with a *personal* score to settle with Beecher."

Unfortunately, Rebecca knew what he was after and also what needed to be done to protect the integrity of her team. "I'll talk to her."

"I'll have one of my agents pick her up—"

Rebecca stepped forward so quickly that Clark took an involuntary step backward. With her face an inch from his, she shot out in a clipped, deadly voice, "You don't go near her. *I'll* question her. The report will be on Henry's desk by eight a.m. If you want to know what it says, read it there."

Clark blinked, a slow flush darkening his features. "I have jurisdiction—"

"You don't have dick," Rebecca interrupted. "This is a homicide. This is PPD business. The only reason you're standing here right now is because I'm trying to be cooperative. You touch any of my people and I'm not going to be so obliging in the future."

For a moment, they stood toe to toe in the unforgiving glare of the artificial lights, looking like two fighters in the middle of the ring waiting for the starting bell to sound. Waiting to throw the first punch. Then, Clark abruptly pivoted and strode rapidly away.

"So now we know who's *really* got the balls around here," Watts remarked appreciatively.

Rebecca flicked him a look of amused irritation. "Let's go talk to Sloan."

Chapter Eighteen

Michael surfaced slowly from deep sleep, roused by an annoying, repetitive beep. It took her a few seconds to recognize the sound as the alarm from one of the security sensors. She rolled over with a murmur of protest and extended one arm. "Sloan, darling…"

The bed beside her was empty. Sighing, she drew back the covers, reached automatically for her robe at the foot of the bed, and absently tied the sash around her waist as she walked down the hall. Beside the elevator doors, a panel slid open at the touch of a button to reveal a recessed cabinet holding a bank of security monitors. Squinting at the image on the screen above the blinking red light, she recognized Rebecca Frye standing on the small landing at the front entrance.

"Rebecca?" Michael asked after switching on the audio.

"Sorry to bother you, Michael, but we need to see Sloan."

"She's not here," Michael replied. "Maybe downstairs in the office."

"Can we come up?"

"Of course. I'm sorry. I'll buzz you in." Michael gave a small laugh. "I'm still half asleep."

"Sorry."

"No, no need to be. Come up. I'll put coffee on."

Two minutes later, Rebecca exited the elevator with Watts by her side. They stopped just inside the loft, waiting.

"Good morning," Michael said with a smile, emerging from the kitchen alcove. She indicated the leather sofas in the living room. "Would you like to sit down?"

"No, we're fine," Rebecca said out of habit.

"Coffee, then?"

Before Rebecca could answer, Watts jumped in. "That would be terrific. I can smell it from here."

"It'll just be another minute or so. Please, won't you sit down?"

Rebecca acquiesced, and they moved into the living room. Rebecca and Watts took opposite ends of a deep teal leather sofa while Michael settled on an ivory one across from them.

"Do you know where Sloan is?" Rebecca asked.

"No, I called downstairs while you were on your way up. No one answered, so I'm afraid I can't help you."

"It's pretty early," Rebecca said.

Michael laughed. "Sloan has no regard for time, especially when she's involved with a case. She keeps odd hours."

"But she *was* here earlier in the evening?"

"Oh, yes. We went out in the late afternoon and were back here by nine, I think. We…" Michael smiled faintly and blushed. "We went to bed early."

Watts shifted uneasily and made a point of gazing out the wall of windows toward the Delaware River. Barge traffic was already heavy on the river below.

"Would you happen to know about when you…got to sleep?"

Michael laughed softly. "I'm afraid I wasn't watching the clock, Lieutenant."

"No, of course not," Rebecca said evenly. "So you have no idea when she might have left?"

"I'm sorry, I don't. I seem to sleep very deeply once I finally nod off." Michael tilted her head, her expression quizzical. "Why don't you call her cell phone? Most of the time she forgets to turn it on, but since I've been…ill, she's very good about it."

"We will," Rebecca replied. At the moment, she wasn't actually interested in speaking to Sloan. What she wanted was to establish a timeline for Sloan's activities the previous evening. Hopefully, a timeline that would put her far away from the parking lot at Front and Market.

Rebecca waited until Michael had gone to the kitchen and returned with a tray holding coffee mugs, cream and sugar, and a small plate of muffins before continuing her questions. "Would you know if she made any phone calls last night from home?"

"No, I'm quite sure she didn't. We came in and went directly to bed."

Watts coughed and busied himself with his coffee.

"What about incoming calls? Did she perhaps receive a call and go out afterward?"

Michael frowned. "No. Nothing that I recall. What's going on? Is…she's all right, isn't she?" She sat forward, paling visibly. "You don't think she's hurt or in danger?"

"No," Rebecca said quickly. "Nothing like that."

"But *something*'s wrong. What's happened?"

Rebecca hadn't touched her coffee. She'd gotten little help from what Michael had given her, and that frustrated her. But the sudden change in Michael's appearance worried her even more. Michael was trembling, and there was something close to panic in her eyes. "Michael, I…"

The nearly inaudible swish of the elevator doors sliding open brought Michael to her feet, and the sudden change in position made her light-headed. She swayed unsteadily.

The first thing Sloan saw when she walked into her home was her lover, looking as if she was about to fall.

"Michael?" Sloan cried in alarm, reaching Michael's side in four long strides. "Baby, what's wrong?" She slid an arm around her lover's waist and eased her down on the sofa. She brushed her lips over Michael's forehead. "Hey. What happened? Did you get sick? Why didn't you call me?"

"It's all right, darling," Michael murmured, smiling weakly. "I'm fine. It's fine. I was asleep when Rebecca came. I'm just not quite awake yet."

"You're not hurt? Not sick or anything?" Sloan passed trembling fingers over Michael's cheek.

"No. I'm really all right." Michael stroked Sloan's arm, then covered Sloan's hand with her own, placing a fleeting kiss on the palm.

With one protective arm still around Michael, Sloan looked from Rebecca to Watts in confusion. "Then what are you doing here?"

Rebecca was about to answer when a voice called from the other side of the room, "Hey, what's going on?"

Sandy shuffled into view, Mitchell's T-shirt brushing her thighs mere inches below her panties. Mitchell was right behind her in a PPD T-shirt and boxers. "We heard voices. Problem?"

Watts took one look in Sandy's direction and immediately glanced away. "Jesus Christ. No one around here has any clothes on."

"What do *you* sleep in?" Sandy mumbled as she walked past him in the direction of the kitchen. "Ugh. No, never mind. Forget I asked."

"We needed to talk to you, so we thought we'd come by," Rebecca said to Sloan. "Where have you been?"

Mitchell and Sandy returned, each holding a cup of coffee. Sandy curled up on the sofa on Michael's left. Mitchell stood uncertainly midway between Sloan and Rebecca, who sat facing one another across the expanse of living room.

"What the fuck's going on?" Sloan said sharply.

"I need to know where you were tonight, from the time you left here until now." Rebecca's face was a blank, her voice still calm. But now, a core of steel crept into her tone.

"Same question goes. Why?"

"Just answer the question, Sloan," Watts urged in a surprisingly gentle voice.

Sloan jumped to her feet so rapidly that only Rebecca's quick reflexes prevented her from being taken off guard. She surged upright just as quickly, so that she and Sloan ended up only a few feet apart.

"Do you think I don't recognize an interrogation when I hear one?" Sloan's body vibrated with fury. "You have the fucking balls to come here in the middle of the night and question my *lover*?"

"Sloan," Michael said gently, standing as well. She placed her hand in the center of Sloan's back. "Darling, let Rebecca talk."

"She's done talking. She's leaving *now.*" Sloan took another step in Rebecca's direction, one hand raised as if to shove Rebecca aside.

"You don't want to do that, Sloan," Rebecca warned.

With surprising grace, Watts gained his feet and insinuated himself between them in one fluid motion. His face was an inch from Sloan's, his voice like granite. "You dumb fuck. If she hadn't stood up for you tonight, you'd be downtown in a locked room with Clark right now. So put your dick away and answer the questions. Then we can all get back to work."

Sloan stared into his eyes for a long moment. Whatever she saw in their hard, cold depths must have extinguished the blaze of fury consuming her reason, because the tension in her broad shoulders eased visibly. She took a long breath and shifted her gaze to Rebecca's. "Are you going to tell me what this is about?"

"No. I'm going to ask questions, and you're going to answer." Rebecca needed the interview to be by the book if it was to be credible to Avery Clark. She waited, wondering how far Sloan's tenuous trust would extend. Wondering, not for the first time, what had happened during those lost years in Sloan's past.

"I was here until just after two," Sloan stated in a flat, uninflected tone. "I woke up thinking about the computer traces that Jason and Mitchell have been running. I haven't had a chance to go over any of their data because I've been so busy at Police Plaza with the…other situation. So I decided to have a quick look at what they've got. I dressed and went downstairs."

"Is there any way to verify that?"

"No. Michael was asleep."

"What about a time stamp on the security cameras?"

Sloan shook her head. "The internal cameras are turned off when we're home."

Mitchell spoke up quietly. "There should be a record of when you logged on the system downstairs."

"Circumstantial," Sloan replied. "Doesn't prove it was me."

"It's corroboration," Rebecca said. "There are only a limited number of other people who it might've been." She scrutinized Michael, then Sandy and Mitchell. "The only real possibility is Mitchell."

"Dell was with me from one thirty on," Sandy said immediately.

"Did either of you hear Sloan leave?" Watts asked.

Mitchell shook her head. Sandy replied, "We were talking, and then we were…busy."

Watts snorted.

"So we wouldn't have noticed," Sandy added sweetly as Mitchell blushed.

Watts looked glum. "Perfect."

"All right." Rebecca made a notation in her notebook. "You were with Michael all night. Went to the offices just after two." She turned to Mitchell. "I want you to secure the computer logs. No one touches the system until you're done."

"Yes, ma'am," Mitchell said smartly. "I'll get dressed and get right on it."

When Sloan opened her mouth to protest, Michael said softly, "Let Rebecca help you, darling."

Sloan reached for Michael's hand, nodding silently.

"You weren't here when we arrived at four fifty-five," Rebecca stated. "There was no answer. Where were you?"

"I went for a walk after a couple of hours of scanning the data."

Rebecca stared at her, and Sloan held her gaze unflinchingly. Finally, Rebecca said, "At four in the morning?"

Sloan shrugged. "I was awake. I was restless. I went for a walk."

"I don't suppose you have any way of proving that?" Watts interjected.

"Not real…" Sloan slid her hand into the front pocket of her jeans and extracted a crumpled slip of white paper. "I bought a cup of coffee at the diner at Third and Market around ten minutes to five."

"Christ, she couldn't have been any closer to the scene and not tripped over one of us," Watts muttered.

Rebecca took the offered receipt, smoothed it out, and noted the time and date in her notebook. She then placed it carefully in the breast pocket of her shirt. "Is someone there going to remember you?"

"The waitress. Jenny. She knows me."

Watts looked skeptical. "She's a…what? Friend?"

Sloan gave him a withering look. "Acquaintance."

"There's nothing between the two of you that might bring her verification of your alibi into question?" Rebecca asked as discreetly as she could.

"No. Nothing. I've never even seen her outside of the diner."

"Good," Rebecca muttered.

"Look," Sloan said irritably. "I've told you where I was. Now tell me what's going on."

"George Beecher was murdered about three blocks from here sometime in the last six hours," Rebecca informed her, watching Sloan's face intently. As she had anticipated, Sloan's expression never changed, but her violet eyes darkened to nearly black. Rebecca was convinced she hadn't known.

"And you think I did it?" Sloan's voice was cool, her posture relaxed.

"No," Rebecca replied. "I don't."

"But Clark does," Sloan murmured, filling in the blanks.

"Darling, what is this all about?" Michael asked quietly. "Who is George Beecher?"

"No one."

"No one who someone thinks you might want to ki—" As if a sudden realization had struck, Michael faltered and looked from Sloan to Rebecca. "Is this the person who might have had something to do with my accident?"

"That's right." Rebecca was curious as to just how much Michael knew. Although she believed Sloan innocent, she was too much a cop not to examine all the evidence from every angle.

"Sloan would never have done anything to him," Michael said with absolute conviction.

"Why do you say that?" Rebecca asked.

"Because she promised me she wouldn't."

Watts laughed. "*That* will certainly go a long ways in court."

Michael turned solemn eyes to his. "If you don't understand why that matters, then you don't know Sloan very well, Detective Watts."

Watts blushed and actually ducked his head. "Sorry, ma'am."

At that moment, Mitchell returned in black chinos and a navy shirt. "I'll head downstairs, Lieutenant."

"Good," Rebecca said. "Watts, go with her and take Sloan. Make sure you document everything that Mitchell does." She turned to Sloan. "You don't touch anything down there. If there's even the possibility that you've altered the data, none of it will help us. All I want you to do is walk them through as much as you can remember of what you did and when."

Sloan nodded. "Okay." She kissed Michael, murmured something that none of the others could hear, and followed Mitchell and Watts to the elevator.

"I'm sorry to have upset you, Michael," Rebecca said.

Michael sank onto the sofa. "I understand."

Sandy leaned close. "You okay? How about I get some tea?"

"That would be lovely. Thank you," Michael replied gratefully, giving Sandy a small smile. Then, to Rebecca, she added, "Thank you for being so patient with her. I know you're trying to help her."

"I'm trying to do my job," Rebecca rejoined. "If I thought she were guilty, I would do the same."

"Yes, I know. And so does Sloan." Michael shook her head. "She'll realize you're on her side when she's feeling less threatened."

"Don't you mean pissed off?"

"Oh, that's part of it, to be sure. But it's coming from something far more serious. She was betrayed, Rebecca, by someone she loved. Abandoned by the system she believed in. Incarcerated by those she thought she could trust." Michael sighed. "She keeps expecting it to happen again."

"It won't," Rebecca said empathically. "You'll never betray her. And I won't let anyone make her a scapegoat. I promise that no one will touch her."

"You didn't say 'if she's innocent.'"

"I didn't need to."

"Thank you, Rebecca."

"I'd better go—I want to catch that waitress at the diner. And I really am sorry to have put you through this."

Michael shook her head. "No, you needn't apologize. Not when you're helping Sloan."

"Thanks." Rebecca turned and started for the elevator. She stopped as Sandy approached with two mugs of tea. "Anything?"

"Maybe."

"I'll call you later."

Sandy shrugged. "Yeah, sure."

When Rebecca left, Sandy returned to her spot on the sofa by Michael's side, tea in hand. "Maybe you should go back to bed."

"I can't. I want to be here when Sloan comes back upstairs."

"It could take a while." Sandy didn't add that if Sloan ended up downtown for questioning, it could take all day. "And you look kind of…tired."

"I'm all right. I don't do very well yet when I haven't had enough sleep, that's all." Michael sipped the tea absently, her attention fixed on the elevator doors, willing them to open and Sloan to appear. "I can't believe she has to go through this again."

"What d'you mean?"

"Proving her innocence." Michael closed her eyes, both hands clenched tightly around the mug on her lap. "God, it makes me so angry."

"Frye is a great cop. She'll figure this out."

"I hope so, because I can't stand to see her hurt like this."

"They're not so tough, are they," Sandy said. "They just kinda want you to think they are."

Michael took Sandy's hand, needing the comfort and the connection. "Sometimes I think the more tender the heart, the more easily it's broken."

"Yeah," Sandy whispered, remembering Dell's tears on her breast. "You got that right."

Chapter Nineteen

Friday

The elevator doors slid open a few minutes before 8:00 a.m. Mitchell exited, followed by Sloan. Mitchell headed directly down the hall toward the guest bedroom and disappeared. When Michael started to get up from the sofa, Sloan shook her head.

"No, stay there." Quickly, she crossed the width of the living room and settled beside Michael, extending an arm to pull Michael into the curve of her body. She kissed Michael's forehead and then leaned her head back with a sigh. "How do you feel?"

Michael nestled her cheek against Sloan's shoulder, one arm wrapped around her waist. "Tired. No headache. I'm all right." She lifted her chin to kiss the undersurface of Sloan's jaw. "What happened downstairs? Is everything…cleared up now?"

Lids partially closed, Sloan stared at the exposed pipes overhead, idly following the branching pathways as they disappeared into walls and behind the high ceiling. When she worked at the computer, her mind's eye saw the same pathways, highways of data, streaming within and between way stations in the network—a cyberuniverse as real to her as the concrete and stone that made up her physical world. "Mitchell's done dicking around inside my system. She got everything there is to get."

"Will it be enough?" Michael asked quietly.

"I don't know," Sloan admitted with a sigh. "It'll depend on what the crime scene unit turns up—time of death will make a big difference. Rebecca will know later today." She didn't add that even if the time of death placed her at home with Michael, she had only her lover's word as an alibi. Not exactly ironclad.

"It's ridiculous for anyone to think that you murdered that man."

Sloan laughed softly and kissed Michael's forehead again. "Baby, *everyone* knows I wanted that guy dead. And every cop—federal, state, or city—knows that the most likely suspect usually turns out to be the guilty party." She stroked Michael's arm, as much to comfort herself as her lover. "In this case, I'm the prime suspect. Christ," she muttered disdainfully, "even *I* can't blame Clark for going after me. I'd do the same in his shoes."

"No, you wouldn't," Michael said vehemently. "You wouldn't because you don't take the easy way out. You do what's right, not what's expedient."

"I'm not that noble, baby," Sloan murmured. She buried her face in Michael's hair, and some of her tension eased. Michael was the calm at the eye of her storm. She was the one fixed point in the swirling tide of Sloan's anger and pain. "It feels so good when you hold me."

With surprising strength, Michael rose, keeping her arm around Sloan's waist and drawing her upward. "Let's go back to bed. You haven't had any sleep, and I need very much to have you in my arms."

"Okay," Sloan whispered, wanting nothing more than to lay down her shields and shelter in the protective circle of Michael's embrace. "Yeah, I'd like that too."

"So, is everything okay now?" Sandy asked as she sat on the side of the bed watching Mitchell shed her clothes.

"I don't know. I don't think so." Mitchell balled up her shirt and threw it on the floor by Sandy's suitcase. "Man, this sucks." Shirtless, she stalked across the room and flopped on the bed next to Sandy. Legs dangling over the side, she ran her fingers down the center of Sandy's back. "I don't know how the lieutenant did it this morning. The way she went after Sloan, like she didn't even know her. I…fuck…I'm going to be a lousy detective."

Sandy turned, her eyes sparking with indignation. "That's *bullshit*. Frye's been doing it a long time. And besides," Sandy said dismissively, "Frye is ice. There's no one like her."

Mitchell thought back to the one time she and Rebecca had leveled with one another—when she'd confessed her love for Sandy, and Rebecca had admitted to the panic that had nearly crippled her when Catherine had been in danger. Mitchell had an inkling of the depth of emotion that Rebecca Frye never revealed and despaired that she would ever be able to control her own passions anywhere near as well. "She's the best. But she still has feelings."

"Yeah," Sandy admitted, "I know. But you still can't expect to be her, rookie. Not yet." She feathered her fingers through Mitchell's hair. "Besides, I like you a whole lot better than Frye."

"I kept praying I'd find something that would clear Sloan." Mitchell turned on her side and pulled Sandy down beside her. She kissed her on the mouth, then tilted her forehead to Sandy's with a weary sigh. "I don't think that's how I'm supposed to be feeling when I'm gathering evidence."

"Baby…" Sandy played her fingertips across Mitchell's lips, then drew them away and traced her tongue in their place before kissing her again. "You're supposed to feel the way you feel."

"How come *you* make me feel so good?"

"'Cause you're so easy."

Mitchell laughed, sliding her hand under Sandy's T-shirt. Sandy's skin was soft and warm, her breasts free beneath the loose cotton. Sweeping her fingertips rhythmically across Sandy's nipples, Mitchell asked softly, "Oh yeah?" She kept up the teasing strokes, intermittently squeezing the rapidly hardening nipples, watching Sandy's eyes cloud with pleasure. "Easy, huh?"

"Dell," Sandy murmured as she grasped Mitchell's wrist. "Stop that."

"You're kidding, right?" Mitchell eased over on top of Sandy, pressing one thigh hard and high between Sandy's legs. "You're hot. I can feel you right through my pants."

Sandy fisted both hands in Mitchell's hair and yanked her head up and away from her breast, where Mitchell had just settled her mouth. "You've got that thing. We have to get ready."

Redirecting her mouth toward the soft, warm, wonderful flesh, Mitchell muttered, "There's plenty of time." As if to drive her point home, she caught Sandy's nipple between her teeth at the same time as she slid her fingers beneath the edge of the pale blue wisp of material between Sandy's legs. She sucked the tight nipple into her mouth as she sank her fingers into Sandy's depths.

Sandy arched her back and screamed.

"That's it, baby, that's it. Oh, yeah, you feel so good." Mitchell was half out of her mind with the wild pleasure of possessing Sandy so completely and the indescribable comfort of just being inside her. When Sandy pumped upward into her palm and simultaneously lifted a knee into Mitchell's crotch, she felt herself unexpectedly teetering on the edge. "Oh fuck, I'm gonna come."

"Do it with me, baby," Sandy sobbed, hips thrashing with the first convulsive wave. "Oh, Dell…oh, here I come."

Mitchell squeezed her eyes tight and tried to keep her rhythm, but everything was tearing loose inside her. She was aching and soaring and crumbling all at once. Shuddering, she pressed her lips to Sandy's temple and whispered, "I love you."

Lost in sensation, Sandy could only cling to her desperately, unable to answer. Her body, open and undefended, spoke for her.

Catherine stood by the bureau in her bedroom, still in her robe. She'd showered an hour earlier but, since she'd taken the morning off from work, had not yet dressed. "There's coffee for you on the bedside table."

"Thanks."

Leaning her hips against the dresser, Catherine sipped from her own mug and studied her lover's carefully guarded face. Rebecca had said nothing since she'd walked in a half hour previously, placed her weapon on the top shelf of the closet, stripped off her clothes, and gone directly into the shower. Catherine supposed that cops had rules about this sort of thing—questions she should not ask, secrets she should not know. Like all rules, those dictums probably served a purpose. And like all absolutes, they often failed in the face of individual human circumstances. True or not, she did not care. What she cared about was the critical connection between herself and her lover. "Was it bad?"

"Typical homicide." Naked, Rebecca swallowed coffee, unmindful of the temperature.

Typical homicide. Well, that's something to ponder another day. Catherine placed her mug on the dresser. "Can you tell me why they called *you* out in the middle of the night? I thought lieutenants got special dispensation around that sort of thing."

Rebecca turned to face her.

"This is the part where I'm supposed to let you in, isn't it?"

Catherine smiled. "Am I being particularly unsubtle this morning, or are you just reading me frighteningly well?"

"Frighteningly?" Rebecca put down her coffee and circled the bed to Catherine. She put her arms around her and kissed her. "It's what you want, isn't it? For me to know what you need?"

"How long have you known *that*?"

"From the beginning." Rebecca reached between them and loosed the tie on Catherine's robe. With one hand she parted the silk fabric until their bodies touched, skin on skin. "I've just never been sure I could do it."

"You're not supposed to do it all by yourself," Catherine murmured. She placed her palm in the center of Rebecca's chest, then moved her fingers over the scars. It was a gesture that had become automatic, almost essential, as if she could physically connect to Rebecca's heart. "I'm supposed to help you by telling you. I want to know where you go when you leave here, what you do, what others do to you. I want to know what you feel, what hurts you, what makes you feel satisfied."

"You," Rebecca said thickly, her hands moving over Catherine's back, the curve of her hips, the soft weight of her breasts. "You make me satisfied. You make me happy." She brushed her mouth over Catherine's lips, a fleeting, nearly fragile, kiss. "You fill me up."

Catherine's body quickened as her heart soared. "When you say these things, when you touch me this way, all I want is to lie down with you and have you touch me everywhere."

"Sounds just right to me." Rebecca shifted a thigh between Catherine's legs and kissed her again. She gave a surprised grunt when Catherine pushed her gently away. "What?"

"Talk first."

Rebecca raised a brow. "That's blackmail."

Catherine nodded, feeling the heat in her face and the tight pebbling of her nipples, knowing that her excitement was apparent to her lover. Her words were breathy as her chest lifted unevenly, passion already rampant in her depths. "Besides, we have somewhere important to be."

With a look of regret, Rebecca kissed her once more and then stepped away. "I'll tell you while we dress."

"All right."

"The dead man's name is George Beecher."

As Rebecca outlined the facts, leaving out the brutal details, she and Catherine moved around one another opening drawers, slipping into clothes, adding their individual accoutrements—watch and earrings, gun and badge. By the time Rebecca related her visit to Sloan's loft, they were completely dressed. She turned from the mirror to face Catherine, tightening the knot in her tie. "Michael was shaken. Sloan was pissed. It wasn't pleasant."

Catherine had never seen Rebecca in her dress uniform before. The formal jacket and striped trousers, the gleaming buttons, the badge perfectly placed just above the spot the bullet had struck. She was beautiful. Catherine had mixed feelings about Rebecca's profession, especially having almost lost her to it. But in that moment, the only thing she felt was pride. "I'm sorry you had to question Sloan that way, but I'm glad it was you and no one else. I'm sure you'll straighten this out for her." She kissed her softly. "You look very handsome. I'm very proud of you."

"Thank you." Rebecca reached for Catherine's hand. "I need you by my side, you know. I…count on it."

"And I need you." Catherine took Rebecca's other hand and met her eyes. "Please won't you marry me?"

Rebecca took a deep breath and then the corner of her mouth lifted into a grin. "I don't want a big wedding."

"Absolutely not." Catherine laughed, her voice ringing with joy. "Just a few friends, and William, of course."

Rebecca made a choking sound. "Watts? No fucking way."

"Well, we have plenty of time to discuss that." Catherine kissed her again, a long, contented kiss that promised more. Then she linked her arm through Rebecca's. "Now let's go celebrate your promotion, Lieutenant."

"Oh man," Mitchell breathed, stopping in midmotion, her eyes huge.

"What?" Sandy said defensively.

"You look…" Mitchell swallowed, at a loss for words.

"Your mouth is open, Dell. You look dumb." Sandy flushed, pleased. The navy Dolce & Gabbana pants had wide legs and a flat front and sat low on her hips. An elegant silver pinstripe accented the tailored suit, and she wore the one-button, fitted jacket closed over just her silk bra, revealing the barest suggestion of cleavage. The Manolo Blahnik heels gave her several inches in height, and she liked the new perspective. Michael had said it was a sexy, low-key, professional look, acceptable for daytime. From the expression on Mitchell's face, she'd been right about the sexy part. When Mitchell took a step toward her, Sandy held out one arm, palm up. "Do *not* come near me. You'll mess me up."

"Honey, that outfit *screams* 'mess me up.'" Mitchell took another step. "Come on. Let me touch. Just one finger."

"Where?"

Mitchell reached out, her index finger extended. She dipped it into the hollow at the base of Sandy's neck, then slowly snaked down her chest to the vee where the jacket closed. Then she curled the tip under the edge of the lapel and along the top of Sandy's bra. In a husky voice, she whispered, "Just here."

Sandy slapped at Mitchell's hand and backed away. "Cut it out. You're making me horny. I can't be horny in this outfit."

Mitchell laughed. "Why not?"

"Because I think I'm just supposed to stand around pretending I'm too cool to get hot." She fingered Mitchell's uniform jacket. "Anyhow, look at you. I'm not making out with you in that getup."

"Why not?" Mitchell asked again, glancing down at her dress blues. Her shoes gleamed, the creases in her pants were so sharp-edged the material barely moved when she walked, and her uniform jacket fit her form without an errant fold. "You don't like it?"

"Baby," Sandy crooned, walking her fingers up the inside of Mitchell's thigh. She cupped her for a fleeting second, high between her legs, making her gasp, and then moved quickly out of reach. "I want you to fuck me blind."

"Oh man," Mitchell moaned, hurrying out of the room after her girlfriend. "I'm not gonna live through this."

Chapter Twenty

You gonna be okay?" Mitchell asked quietly as she and Sandy exited the elevator on the second floor of Police Plaza.

"Sure," Sandy said, her voice tight with bravado. The wide corridor was bustling with officers, some in uniform and others in street clothes, all looking harried and officious. Sandy's stomach curdled as she thought about the few times she had been inside a police station. None were pleasant memories. "Great. No problem."

Mitchell caught Sandy's hand and tugged her close to the wall, out of the stream of traffic. "Look, you don't have—"

"Jesus, rookie," Sandy snapped, snatching her hand away. "Are you crazy? Look where we are. Do you want everyone to know?"

"I don't *care* who knows." Mitchell grabbed Sandy's hand back. "If you're not comfortable here, you don't need to st—"

"Hello," a warm voice interrupted. "Quite a gathering, it seems."

Sandy looked from Dell to the newcomer. "Hi. Yeah, it's a big deal, huh?"

Catherine smiled. "Yes, it is. I'm looking forward to it. Hello, Dellon. Congratulations, by the way."

"Thanks," Mitchell said, coloring. She looked past Catherine. "Is the lieutenant here already?"

"Yes. She stopped downstairs to talk to Watts about something. She should be right up."

"Good."

The relief in Mitchell's voice was evident, and Sandy realized at that moment that her girlfriend was every bit as nervous as she was. Moving closer, she gave Mitchell's hip a tiny bump with hers. "You're gonna be fine. You look so hot."

Mitchell grinned. "I don't think anyone's going to care about that."

"I do."

"Sandy," Catherine asked, "would you mind sitting with me? I'd appreciate the company."

"Sure. Okay." Sandy smiled shyly. "I'd like that."

"Wonderful." Then, as if hearing her name, which would have been impossible in the midst of so much activity, Catherine turned toward the elevators. The doors slid open, and Rebecca stepped through with Watts close behind. "Let me just say goodbye to her, and then you and I can go in and find seats."

"She's cool," Sandy murmured as she glanced furtively up and down the hall. When no one seemed to be looking, she stretched up and quickly kissed Mitchell. "That's for luck."

Without glancing around, Mitchell leaned down and kissed Sandy back. "That's for love." Then she turned and walked down the hall toward Watts, who waited by the auditorium door.

Sandy watched her go, shaking her head, the kiss still tingling on her lips. In a voice too low for anyone else to hear, she whispered, "Blockhead."

"Hiya, Sandy," Rebecca said.

"Hey, Frye," Sandy replied, still watching her girlfriend. When she finally turned to look at Rebecca, she gave a small murmur of appreciation. "Huh. Nice look."

"I don't think that was the intention. It's good to see you. Good for Mitchell too."

Then she too walked away, leaving Sandy staring after her. "What *is* it with them today?"

"They're nervous," Catherine commented upon hearing the question as she rejoined Sandy. "They're much more comfortable *doing* than being the focus of attention."

"So that makes them get all sappy—being nervous?"

Catherine smiled. "I think it makes them a little bit vulnerable. I don't know about you, but I'm rather fond of sappy now and then."

Sandy laughed. "It's supposed to be a big secret, but Dell gets like that pretty much all the time."

"How wonderful for her that she can do that with you."

"You think?" Sandy asked, a hint of uncertainty in her voice. She didn't like to think too much about why Dell seemed to love her, fearing how much it would hurt if she stopped.

"I do." Catherine reached for Sandy's hand. "Shall we go in? I want to get seats up front so I can see everything."

"Okay, sure..." Sandy's voice trailed off. "Uh—you should go ahead. I'll be there in a minute."

Catherine followed Sandy's gaze questioningly. Then she gave a small start, amazed to see a woman approaching who looked exactly like Mitchell except for the fact that she wore a different uniform. "Well."

"You got that right," Sandy said, acid etching her tones. She took a step in the newcomer's direction. "And there's no fucking way she's going in that room with Dell today."

Before Catherine could even comment, Sandy was down the hall and in Erica's path.

"You shouldn't be here," Sandy asserted.

Erica regarded her in confusion. "What? Who…?" She hesitated. "Oh. Sandy, isn't it? I didn't recognize you."

Sandy snorted. "No, I'm sure you only saw what you expected to see. Whatever. Dell doesn't need you here today."

"I hardly think that's up to you to decide."

"You know what? It is." Even in heels, Sandy was inches shorter than Erica, but her eyes never wavered from the ice blue of the taller woman's. "You walked out on her once when she needed you to stand up for her. She doesn't need you now."

"You don't know anything about that."

Sandy's vision wavered as anger swept through her. She could still feel Dell's tears scalding her breast and the way that Dell, always so strong, had trembled in her arms. She heard the broken words uttered through a throat choked with grief.

Robin was a captain and a general's daughter. She was career Army, and I couldn't let her lose everything. So when she denied that we were lovers and said that I'd gone off on the guy for no reason, I didn't argue. They were willing to let me leave quietly, even gave me the honorable discharge, as long as I didn't make waves. They didn't want to know about us, and she wasn't willing to give up her future for me.

"Yes, I *do* know," Sandy grated. It was all she could do to keep her hands at her sides, because she wanted to smack the superior smirk off Erica Mitchell's face. "I know you let her be treated like a criminal when all she did was defend her lover." Sandy spat out the words.

"Her *lover* who didn't have the guts to stand up for her. And you didn't either."

"Dellon knew the rules."

To Sandy's astonishment, she heard pain in Erica's voice. But no amount of hurt would make up for the suffering she had witnessed in Dell. "Love isn't *about* rules. Love is just something that happens to you, and you don't have a choice. You take it, you hold on to it, or you lose everything that matters."

Erica stared at Sandy. "That's how you feel about her?"

"Yes." There was defiance and pride in Sandy's voice. She tilted her chin as if offering it for Erica's punch, a warrior ready to take a blow in the name of honor.

"I thought…" Erica shook her head. "I don't know what I thought."

Catherine stepped up to Sandy's side. "Is anything wrong?"

"No," Sandy said levelly. "She was just leaving."

"You must be Dellon's sister," Catherine said, extending her hand. "I'm Catherine Rawlings. My partner and Dellon work together."

"Ma'am," Erica said, shaking Catherine's hand. She looked uncertainly from Sandy to Catherine, obviously trying to discern their relationship. "I don't want to keep you from the ceremony."

"No, I don't want to be late," Catherine agreed. "My partner is being promoted as well." She rested a hand lightly on Sandy's shoulder. "Are you coming in?"

"I…" Erica shrugged. "I don't know."

Sandy looked up at Catherine. "I don't want anything to spoil this for Dell."

"I know. Neither do I. But you'll be there, and that's the most important thing." She gave Sandy's shoulder a squeeze. "But I think she might like it if her sister were there too."

"What if it throws her…seeing *her*?"

"It might, for a second or two." Catherine smiled. "But you know…she's got good reflexes."

Sandy laughed, then cast Erica a considering glance. "You be careful with her. You don't get another chance."

"Understood," Erica said quietly.

"Well, then," Catherine said quietly, including both Sandy and Erica in her gaze. "Why don't we go in?"

❖

Mitchell shouldered her way through the throng congregated in front of the stage. She kept losing sight of Sandy as people cut across her line of vision. Finally, she edged her way up to her girlfriend. "Hey, how're you doing?"

Sandy broke off her conversation with Catherine and smiled up at Mitchell. "Okay. I didn't know you were going to get a medal too."

"And well deserved," Catherine added. "Congratulations, Dellon. Now, I'm going to find Rebecca and try to steal her away for lunch somewhere."

After a quick look around, Sandy brushed her fingers over the medallion pinned above Mitchell's left breast. "It's nice."

Fleetingly, Mitchell caught Sandy's hand and squeezed. "Thanks. I'm glad you're here."

"Me too."

The closeness of the crowd made it easy for Mitchell to ease her thigh against Sandy's hip, and as she did, she steeled herself to greet the other woman present. After another few seconds' hesitation, she met her sister's eyes. "How did you know about this?"

"Your colleagues are very talkative. When I called the station earlier this week looking for information about you, I heard most of the story." Erica extended her hand. "Congratulations, Detective."

Mitchell swallowed and blinked against sudden tears. She forced the words through a sandpaper throat as she took her sister's hand. "Thanks."

Erica held Mitchell's hand in the silence that settled between them. Sandy wrapped an arm around Mitchell's waist and squeezed, murmuring, "You okay, baby?"

"Yeah," Mitchell replied softly, letting go of Erica's hand. She smiled at Sandy. "I'm okay. I'm great."

"I should go say something to Frye," Sandy said with obvious reluctance, her eyes flicking to Erica.

"Go ahead. Everything's fine," Mitchell urged, sounding more like herself. "Then how about we grab some takeout for lunch and go home."

"Okay, if you're sure." Sandy looked once more from Erica to Mitchell, then ventured into the crowd.

"So," Mitchell said. "What are you doing here?"

"You were being honored for bravery *and* promoted. It's a big deal."

"Yeah, and nothing I've done in the last year and a half has mattered to you, so why should this?" Mitchell tried to curb the bitterness in her voice, but failed. "Why did you come here at all this week?"

"Because I have to work at not thinking about you every day, and when I found out you were injured and in the hospital, I couldn't stop worrying. I just…had to come." Erica's shoulders sagged slightly and she inched closer, her eyes dark with pain. "I miss you. Damn it, Dell. I *miss* you."

"Nothing's changed…" Mitchell caught herself and grinned ruefully. "Actually, everything's changed. I know who I am. I *like* who I am. I love Sandy. What are you going to do with all of that, Erica?"

"I don't know." Her sister shook her head. "Sandy is…she's fierce, the way she…loves you."

Mitchell's eyes sparkled. "Yeah. She's pretty amazing."

Erica studied her, her expression puzzled. "And you're happy? She makes you happy?"

"Like you wouldn't believe."

Erica's gaze swept the room where small groups, composed mostly of men, continued to mill about, talking and laughing. The rumble of many voices drowned out neighboring conversations. Nevertheless, she lowered her voice. "That's not a problem, here?"

"Sometimes it can be," Mitchell acknowledged. "But I don't care. I can handle it."

"You always thought you could handle everything," Erica said with a mixture of affection and irritation.

"That's because I can."

Erica laughed, sounding very much like Mitchell. "You are so full of shit, Dell."

"Yeah. Like you're not." Mitchell reached out and fingered the row of ribbons on her sister's chest. "Looks like you've been busy racking up the points. You must be looking at a promotion yourself soon."

Erica blushed. "Maybe, I don't know."

"They're fast-tracking you, aren't they? The posting in DC? Grooming you for a command post somewhere soon."

"Probably," Erica admitted.

Mitchell was surprised to realize that she felt no animosity, no jealousy. With a start, she realized that she no longer wanted the life her sister was headed for. The life she had thought she wanted. Some of the anger she had nourished to shield herself from pain eased. "That's cool. That's good."

"I have to get back to the base," Erica said. "I wish we could talk."

"About what?"

"About…Robin. What happened."

Mitchell shook her head. "There's no point. It's over. We all made our choices back then. And we're all living with them now." She looked away, scanning the crowd, smiling as she spied Sandy heading their way. "Sometimes the choices we're forced to make take us to the place we wanted to be all along." She met her sister's eyes. "I'm happy, Erica."

"You ready to go?" Sandy asked as she reached Mitchell's side.

"Yep."

Sandy turned her attention to Erica. "If you're anything like Dell, and I guess you probably are, you're insane for pizza. We can order extra."

"Thanks," Erica said sincerely. "I need to catch a train." She held out her hand to Sandy. "It was very nice meeting you."

Sandy appeared thoughtful as she took Erica's hand. "It would probably be good if you came back for another visit."

"Thank you." Erica looked from Sandy into her sister's eyes. "I'd like that very much."

Mitchell and Sandy were silent as they watched Erica walk away. Then Sandy said, "Are you sure everything's okay?"

"Have I mentioned that I really like it when you take care of me?"

Sandy stood on tiptoe and spoke quietly, close to Mitchell's ear. "Yeah, but you're usually talking about sex when you do."

Mitchell laughed. "Well, then too."

"So what do you say we pick up some pizza, and I can take care of you some more."

"Oh yeah—love in the afternoon," Mitchell said, grasping Sandy's hand. "I think I just got lucky."

"Yeah, yeah, rookie. Don't get used to it."

"Too late." Tugging Sandy through the crowd, Mitchell finally knew that she was exactly where she wanted to be.

Chapter Twenty-One

This is such a nice treat, having you all to myself in the middle of the afternoon," Catherine said, leaning her head against Rebecca's shoulder.

Rebecca, in sweats and a T-shirt, her feet propped on the coffee table next to the empty deli containers, sighed. "I could get spoiled, that's for sure." She kissed Catherine lightly. "But I have to go back to work. Flanagan said she'd have something for me today on the shooting."

"I know, and I need to go in to the office and take care of billing before Joyce loses patience with me entirely." Catherine too had changed into a favorite pair of slacks and a pullover, and now she drew her legs onto the sofa to curl closer against Rebecca's side. "I really enjoyed the ceremony. I noticed *you* trying to slip away from the photo-op at the end."

"The department never passes up an opportunity for publicity," Rebecca said wryly. "Hardly my style."

"But you *are* newsworthy, darling." When Rebecca stiffened, Catherine laughed and hugged her. "This is the second time in less than a year that you've received a departmental commendation, you were just promoted, and you're without question the sexiest police officer in the city."

Rebecca tilted her head back to look into her lover's face. "About that last part…"

"We have to work," Catherine murmured, captured by the light dancing in Rebecca's eyes. Her body flushed hot, then she shivered. "But there's something about you in that uniform that's had me on edge since this morning."

"The uniform, huh?" Rebecca guided Catherine's hand beneath

her T-shirt, then pressed Catherine's palm to her stomach. "Will this outfit do?"

"Darling," Catherine whispered, sliding her hand up to cup Rebecca's breast. "You in absolutely *anything* does it for me."

Laughing, Rebecca pulled Catherine down on top of her. Work would always be there.

"You want that last piece of pizza?" Mitchell, propped up naked in bed, looked down at Sandy, whose head was cradled in her lap. The pizza box lay on the floor beside them where they'd placed it earlier so they could eat in bed. When Mitchell had indulged herself by licking off a few drops of sauce that had fallen on Sandy's breast, they'd gotten sidetracked. They'd made love, fast and hard, and then consumed the rest of the pizza in postcoital indolence.

Sandy nuzzled Mitchell's navel, then tugged at the skin around it with her teeth. "Nuh-uh."

"Jeez, San, cut that out. I don't have time to go again." Mitchell squirmed as Sandy bit harder. "Ouch. Come *on.* I've got that doctor's appointment, and Jason's been waiting all day for me to finish up some stuff."

"Say please," Sandy muttered, circling her tongue where her teeth had just been.

"Oh man," Mitchell sighed, her stomach quivering as her body went molten. "*Honey.*"

Sandy slid a hand beneath the sheet and up the inside of Mitchell's leg. "What do you say?"

"Please," Mitchell whispered.

"Good afternoon, *Lieutenant*," Flanagan said when Rebecca rapped on her open office door. "I hope you're not bringing your bulldog in here."

"Watts?" Rebecca grinned. "No, he's down at the docks following up on some paperwork with Port Authority."

"Good, because even when he *does* keep his hands in his pockets,

I don't trust him in my lab." Flanagan capped her pen and shuffled papers into a folder. "So, nice showing this morning."

"I didn't see you there," Rebecca said, surprised. Flanagan was not one to appear at departmental gatherings, official or otherwise. "Maggie make you go?"

Flanagan harrumphed as she stood. "Actually, no. I just put my head in for a minute. Saw you get the commendation. Congratulations."

"Well, thanks."

The two regarded one another from a few feet apart, then spoke at once.

"About the case…"

"So regarding the findings…"

With comfortable routine once more restored, they moved companionably into the laboratory where Flanagan led Rebecca to a workbench.

"Nothing new about COD. GSW at close range. From the trajectory, I put your shooter in the car with the victim, not just leaning in the door. That means considerable blowback—his, or *her*, clothes and body would have been grossly contaminated with the spray. No professional would get into another vehicle like that."

"I've got uniforms checking every dumpster, sewer drain, and alley in a three-block radius. But down there, in the middle of the night, with no one around, the shooter would have had ample opportunity to discard the weapon *and* their clothing somewhere we'd never find it." Rebecca shrugged. "And by now, any evidence that might have been *on* his body is gone."

"Probably dumped the clothes in the river."

"Yeah," Rebecca agreed. "The dive team is dragging in the immediate area, but with the currents…we'd have to get real lucky to find anything. How are we doing on time of death?"

"According to the surveillance team, Beecher dined at eight at a Thai place on Third." Flanagan leafed through several pages clipped inside a file folder that had been labeled with a case number, the initials *GB*, and the date. "Decomposition of the stomach contents puts TOD at three a.m., give or take an hour and a half."

"Can you narrow it down any more than that?" Rebecca asked, thinking that Mitchell's report had put Sloan squarely in front of her computers at 3:00 a.m. There was ample data to make a case that it couldn't have been anyone else using the computers. Neither Sandy nor Michael had the expertise. Mitchell did, but Sandy had stated unequivocally that Mitchell was with her from 1:30 on. Tapes from the exterior cameras had shown Sandy's arrival at 1:20, supporting that. The tapes also verified that no one else had entered the building until Rebecca's arrival. The only occupant who could have been logged on to the system at 3:00 a.m. was Sloan.

But a time of death of 4:30 a.m. was going to be a problem, because Sloan had logged off at 3:52 a.m. The crime scene was only three blocks from her building. She could easily have walked there and killed Beecher a few minutes after 4:00 a.m.

"You want a window of less than ninety minutes?" Flanagan snorted.

"Less than sixty."

Flanagan eyed her speculatively. "That critical?"

"Yes."

"Get one of your detectives to question the wait staff at the restaurant. I'll need as precise a time as possible for when he was actually served the meal. If you want a window that narrow, I need to know if we're talking eight thirty or nine. Without that, what I gave you is as good as you're going to get."

"I'll talk to them myself as soon as we're done. What else do you have?"

"Something personal going on here?" Flanagan asked. "You're pushing more than usual, even for you."

Used to keeping the facts of a case to herself, often not even sharing everything with Watts, Rebecca hesitated. Flanagan, however, was one of the few people in the department she trusted implicitly. "Clark has a suspect in mind whom I'd like to clear."

"Then the less I know, the better. I don't trust the feds not to claim collusion."

"No one in their right mind would believe that about this lab."

"Thanks," Flanagan said gruffly. "So, not much else to tell you." Then as if on an afterthought, she said, "Except about the bullet."

"You're kidding." Rebecca whistled softly. "You got a bullet? How? It was a through-and-through shot, the bullet went through the window of the driver's door, and the car was parked in the middle of nowhere."

"True. All true."

Rebecca followed as Flanagan moved down the aisle to the far end of the bench and lifted a section of wood that, on closer inspection, proved to be a round cut from a tree. Rebecca raised a questioning eyebrow.

Unable to suppress a grin, Flanagan picked up a thin metal probe and pointed out a neat, round hole punched into the bark that led into the interior of the section of wood. A bullet track. "Voilà."

"No way."

"This morning, Maggie and I took a crash-test dummy, sat him behind the wheel of Beecher's car in the position we assume he was in prior to death, and shot a hole through its head using the same trajectory as that found in the body." Flanagan pointed to the section of tree. "Then we aimed a laser beam through the hole in the dummy's cranium, out the open window of the car, and traced its path through the parking lot, across the street, and into this tree."

"Beautiful," Rebecca breathed in true awe.

Flanagan's expression grew serious. "The bullet's a match to a previous homicide, Rebecca."

Alerted to the unusual use of her first name, Rebecca tensed. "Okay."

"It's the same gun that killed Jeff and Jimmy."

"Son of a bitch." Rebecca's jaw clenched.

"The shooter probably didn't think we'd find the bullet, so he wasn't worried about a match. Or maybe he just doesn't care." Flanagan shrugged. "Some professionals get very attached to their weapons. Some just figure they're too clever to ever get caught. For whatever reason, he didn't ditch the gun after the first murders."

"Or he did, and someone else is using the gun this time," Rebecca pointed out.

"And how likely do you figure it is that Beecher, who is peripherally, at least, related to the first murders, was killed by a *different* shooter?"

"Not very likely," Rebecca said grimly. "We always assumed that Jeff and Jimmy were done by some out-of-town hit man. Looks like we were wrong. This has got to be local."

"Because of the timing?"

Rebecca nodded. "Whoever did this set it up very quickly. There wasn't enough time to bring someone in to do that hit."

"Find me a gun, and I'll tie these all together for you in a neat little package."

"This guy just made a big mistake," Rebecca said, almost to herself. "He just stuck his head out where we can see him."

"Look, Frye," Flanagan said carefully. "I know this guy shot Jeff, but…"

"There aren't any *buts* about this." Rebecca's expression was completely unreadable, but her eyes were molten pits of fury. "He pays."

Sloan absently reached for the phone on the desk beside her, still scrolling with the other hand. "Sloan."

"Got a minute?" Rebecca asked.

Her voice decidedly cool, Sloan replied, "Do I have a choice?"

"I've called the team together for seven at your place. I'd like to meet with you alone first."

"I was about to wrap things up here anyhow," Sloan conceded. She stretched her back and swiveled in the desk chair to survey the room. The two detectives assigned to the new unit had left for the day, and she found the solitude welcome. Boxes of computer equipment, tools, stacks of cartons filled with files—years of data to be sorted and input—surrounded her. Peaceful. "Where are you?"

"Downstairs. How about I buy you a drink at Barney's?"

The cop hangout was a ten-minute walk away. Sloan had never been there. "Sure."

It took Sloan less than that to get there, and when she did, she found Rebecca already seated at a booth in the back of a long, narrow, noisy, smoke-filled bar. So much for the No Smoking signs. Of course, with the room filled with cops, who was going to complain? She settled onto the cracked leather-covered bench across from Rebecca. "Frye."

"Thanks for coming," Rebecca said.

A waitress appeared, and Sloan ordered scotch on the rocks after Rebecca asked for a cup of coffee. Then Sloan waited.

"I just finished a briefing with Captain Henry and Clark," Rebecca said with a hint of disdain. "George Beecher was killed by the same shooter who took out Jimmy Hogan and Jeff Cruz. Also, Beecher was killed sometime before four a.m this morning, within the frame of your alibi."

"I suppose no one could come up with a good reason why I might have wanted to kill two cops I didn't know?"

"No one tried. You're clear regarding last night's shooting." Rebecca saw no point in adding that Clark had grilled her relentlessly about the evidence, but she'd had Flanagan's report in hand, and that was unimpeachable. No one questioned Dee Flanagan's conclusions.

"I suppose Clark was disappointed," Sloan said.

"What's he got in for you?"

"I'm not sure he has anything in for *me*, not personally." Sloan nodded her thanks to the waitress who passed her her drink. She took a swallow, then set the glass on the wooden tabletop. The scars of many years marred the surface, each with a tale to tell. "Federal agents don't look kindly on those of us who've left the fold. Especially when we leave under a cloud. It's in his nature not to trust me."

"Do you know why he's here?"

Sloan shook her head. "My guess is that your case bumps up against something the feds are interested in. I don't think it's a local Mob organization. I don't think it's Internet porn, either."

"No, neither do I. I don't think it's *ever* been about that. Clark put Jimmy Hogan undercover in the PPD because something was going on here that the feds were interested in. He wanted someone deep undercover—so deep that *we* didn't even know." Rebecca cursed under her breath. "That's probably what got Jimmy killed. And Jeff. Jimmy was essentially on his own, and he couldn't even ask us for backup. He was trying to feed Jeff information without revealing his identity, and the whole thing came apart in his face."

"Which means Jimmy was getting close to whatever it was Clark is after."

Rebecca nodded. "And I think we are too. Beecher's a piece of it, but I'm not sure where he fits."

"Someone probably thought he'd talk if you squeezed him. Cut a deal to save his own skin."

"Someone tightening up their ship. Snipping loose ends," Rebecca mused. "That plays." She took a sip of coffee, then winced. "Christ, this is awful. Jason has spoiled me."

"Why don't we go over to the office and wait for the rest of them,"

Sloan suggested. "May not be as good as Jason's, but I think I can manage to put together a passable pot of coffee."

"Good idea." Rebecca made no move to leave but instead leaned forward, her eyes fixed on Sloan's. "I'm sorry I upset Michael this morning. Is she all right?"

"She was sleeping when I left," Sloan said quietly. "But she's fine. Getting better every day."

"I'm glad."

Sloan took a breath, blew it out slowly. "I keep walking around thinking something's going to happen to her. That she'll end up back in the hospital. This morning…when I saw her like that…" She looked away, swallowed. "I got pretty hot with you. I'm sorry."

"Forget it. I'd've done the same if it had been Catherine."

"I appreciate you getting me off the hook with Clark so fast."

Rebecca stood. "Fuck Clark."

Sloan slid from the booth to join her. "If it's all the same to you, I'd rather not."

Chapter Twenty-Two

"Okay," Rebecca said, turning with coffee cup in hand and surveying the team, who had gathered at the conference table. "Let's start with Beecher."

She brought the others up to speed with the forensic evidence and the link between the previous homicides and the present one. It took a full minute for the murmured curses and general unrest to settle after she'd announced that whoever killed Jeff and Jimmy had also eliminated Beecher and was still eluding them. "So what else do we have?"

"I got a positive hit on Beecher's Visa card from an on-line porn relay station," Jason reported. "The same network we busted."

"Doesn't mean he knew anything about the actual operation," Watts pointed out.

"True, it's only an indirect link, but it's still a connection."

"On the other hand," Mitchell interjected, "it *does* prove he used it, and it's one more link in the chain tying him to organized crime." She glanced at Rebecca as if seeking confirmation. When Rebecca nodded, she continued, "And if you put this together with all the other evidence we have linking Beecher to criminal activity, it would only be a matter of time before we had something solid to charge him with."

"Which," Rebecca added, "made him a very bad security risk."

"Not anymore," Watts said.

"Precisely."

"Except no one could've known how much we had on him," Jason said reasonably.

"It would seem that way on the surface of things." Rebecca settled into her seat at the head of the table. "We've been careful not to circulate our reports." She queried Sloan with a raised eyebrow. "What are the chances that whoever was using Beecher's computer to access the law enforcement network would know you were onto him?"

"If they were good, which they are," Sloan answered, "they'd know I've been looking. Hell. They've known *all along* we were looking, because we reported it all to Henry before we knew how widespread a leak we really had." She grimaced and shook her head. "They may not know just how close I've gotten, but they have to know it's only a matter of time. It's impossible even for the best cracker to hide their tracks from someone just as good." Her smile was vulpine. "Or better."

"There's one more thing," Jason said. "I just got a hit on the deep-level financial search we ran on Beecher's accounts. Until eighteen months ago, he made sizable cash withdrawals from his personal account on a regular basis, extending back over a period of three years. Then they stopped."

"What's your take on that?" Rebecca asked, leaning forward with interest.

"I'd say he was being blackmailed."

"And then," Rebecca thought out loud, "someone thought he would be more useful as a source of *information*. Once they started using him to infiltrate the department, they stopped blackmailing him. Probably an incentive for him to cooperate. Any idea what they had on him?"

Jason shook his head. "Not yet, but I'm willing to bet it has something to do with his taste in young girls. Remember, he had a previous sexual assault charge that was dismissed."

"So someone knew about his...proclivities…and used it as leverage—first to blackmail him and then to set him up as their inside man."

"That's the way I see it," Jason said.

"When he became a liability, they cut their losses," Watts noted.

Rebecca turned to another page in her notebook. "I'm going to hand off Beecher's case to the homicide team that caught it. They can follow up on the routine leads and forensics. I'm having his personal and work computers brought here." She looked at Sloan. "That's yours."

Her eyes glinted. "Got it."

"Watts," Rebecca said, moving on. "Anything from Port Authority?"

"You mean other than a big, fat headache?"

Rebecca suppressed a smile.

Watts gave an eloquent grimace. "You know how many pieces of paper it takes to move a crate of overpriced fish eggs from some Commie factory on the Caspian Sea to America?"

"Are you telling me that Jimmy Hogan had developed an interest in caviar?"

"I don't know *what* the hell he was interested in," Watts said grumpily. "The only thing I know right now is that all three ships he asked about originated from the same port in Russia."

"Whoa," Mitchell said, unable to restrain her excitement. "That has to be something, right?"

"Damned if *I* know, kid. Carla…uh, Captain Reiser…says that 30 percent of the ships coming into this port start out somewhere over there. The big question is why *those* three ships."

"You need to track down everything about them," Rebecca said, making another notation in her pad. "Check the shipping companies, the cargo manifests, the origination and final destination points, the crew—anything that they might have in common. Jimmy picked up on something. We have to know what it was."

"Reiser is already on it. I'll have more information for you to feed into your computers in a day or so."

"Good," Rebecca said. "You run with that for now."

"No problem." Watts's tone suggested that he did not mind the assignment.

"Mitchell, what's your duty status?"

"Dr. Torveau cleared me today," Mitchell said, unconsciously sitting up straighter in her seat. "All I need is my psych clearance."

"I don't know, kid," Watts muttered. "You could wait a long time for that."

Mitchell grinned.

"Get it. I want Mitch and Jasmine back in the clubs. With Beecher dead and nothing solid from Port Authority, the only place to shake out a new lead is there." Rebecca folded her notebook and slid it into the inside pocket of her blazer. "My street sources are coming up empty. The bust at the video studio has sent people underground, and with the hit on Beecher, it's not safe for my CIs to do much digging. I don't want them calling attention to themselves."

No one at the table looked at Mitchell; everyone knew that Sandy was one of Rebecca's CIs. Mitchell pressed her palms hard into her thighs to prevent herself from curling her fingers into fists.

"Saturday night is always a big night at Ziggie's," Jason said into the void. "Mitch and Jasmine and the Kings could hit it tomorrow night. There ought to be enough after-hours activity that no one would notice us asking a few questions."

"Do it. It's time to *make* something happen."

"Just think about it," Mitchell heard Michael say as she stepped off the elevator.

"Yeah, okay," Sandy replied hesitantly.

"I mean it. You'd do fine." Michael turned to the sound of Mitchell approaching. "Hi, Dell. Is the meeting over?"

Mitchell nodded, looking curiously from Sandy to Michael. Sandy appeared uncomfortable, a distinctly unusual condition for her. Mitchell had seen her angry, stubborn, even hurt. But almost never uneasy. "What's up?"

Sandy popped up and hurried down the hall in the direction of the guest room. "Nothing."

"Something's going on," Mitchell insisted as she hustled to catch up.

"I think we should go home," Sandy said, walking directly to the closet and lifting out her suitcase.

"Me too." Mitchell sat on the side of the bed, her arms out to either side, watching Sandy pack. "I'm pretty much healed, and it's time for me to get back to work."

"Don't you have to see Cath—Dr. Rawlings too?"

"Yep—first thing tomorrow."

"Huh." Sandy folded one of Mitchell's white T-shirts and laid it next to a camisole in her suitcase.

"What's wrong?"

"Nothing."

"Then how come you won't look at me?" Mitchell frowned. "Did Michael say something to upset you?"

"No," Sandy snapped.

"Well, it's something," Mitchell persisted.

Sandy slammed the dresser drawer hard enough to knock over several bottles of perfume that stood on its top. She whirled in Mitchell's direction, her eyes glinting with irritation. "If I *wanted* you to know something, I'd tell you. So stop with the questions."

Mitchell blinked at the unanticipated assault. Then, in an extraordinarily quiet voice, she said, "I want to know what Michael said that bothered you. If you don't tell me, I'm going to go ask her."

"You can be a real pain in the ass, Dell. Once in a while you should just mind your own business." Despite her words, Sandy's voice had lost most of its edge.

"You *are* my business."

Sandy sighed and joined Mitchell on the bed, her thigh their only point of contact where it lightly touched Mitchell's. Staring straight ahead, she said in a subdued tone, "She offered me a job."

"Yeah?" Mitchell said, carefully hiding her surge of excitement. "How did that happen?"

"She had to drop some papers off at her office the other day when we went shopping for my new outfit. While we were there, she showed me around. Innova takes up the whole twentieth floor, and you can see everything—all the way to New Jersey—from up there."

"Cool."

"Yeah," Sandy said quietly. "You can tell everyone thought Michael was like…a queen or something. And she was nice to everybody."

"She's like that," Mitchell observed, her hand creeping across the space between them to grasp Sandy's. "She pays attention to everyone."

Sandy nodded silently.

"So?" Mitchell asked finally. "What about the job?"

"The guy who runs the supply room—you know, orders all the stuff that everyone needs, like paper and files and even cell phones—is leaving soon. Moving out of state. They want to train a replacement before he goes."

"So that's the job?"

"Yeah."

"What do you think?"

"I don't know. I've never done anything like that before." Sandy unconsciously squeezed Mitchell's hand. "What if I messed it all up?"

"Like how?"

"I don't know—ordered the wrong stuff. Or forgot to order something."

"Well, I suppose you'd just return the wrong stuff and order the right stuff." Mitchell shrugged. "I bet that happens a lot."

"There's computers."

Sandy said the word as if it were a life-threatening disease.

Mitchell couldn't help herself. She laughed.

"Shut up," Sandy snapped, slapping Mitchell's arm and trying desperately not to smile.

"Honey, look at what I do every day. You don't think maybe I could teach you what you needed to know?"

"I've never had a job. I don't how how to do it."

"Well," Mitchell said softly and kissed Sandy gently on the cheek. "We'll just have to teach you. There's nothing you can't do, San. I promise."

"I don't want to disappoint you."

Mitchell gaped. "You're kidding, right?" She tugged Sandy upright and framed her face with both hands. Leaning close, she said very distinctly, "I love you. If you want to try this job, then you should. You'll be great. If you don't want it, then forget it."

"But you'd like it if I did, wouldn't you?"

"It's too dangerous out there, doing what you're doing for Frye. I want you to stop. Job or not, I want you to stop." Mitchell kissed Sandy's forehead, then her mouth. "If you had another job, you'd feel better about quitting this one."

"I have some things to finish for Frye, Dell." Sandy drew away, anticipating Mitchell's protests.

"Look," Mitchell said, trying hard to contain both her temper and her fear. "Frye said just this afternoon that the heat is on around this whole Internet porn thing, and that it's too dangerous for the CIs. She's going to pull you anyway."

"Well, she hasn't yet." Sandy stood, thinking about her upcoming meeting with Trudy. She had to at least see her, warn her to keep her head down. She resumed packing, pretending not to hear Mitchell's teeth grinding.

"Honey," Mitchell said, "you have to trust me on this one. It's not safe ou—"

"*You* have to trust *me*." Sandy scooped up a pile of panties and dumped them into her suitcase. She closed the hasp and straightened. "I have a meeting tonight. It's important. I'm going."

"Then I'm coming with you."

"*No*," Sandy barked. "Jesus, Dell. I might as well put a big sign on my head that says *police informer*. Get a grip."

"I can't," Mitchell whispered. "I'll go crazy if something happens to you."

Sandy's features softened and she strode quickly to Mitchell, driving her fingers into Mitchell's hair, tilting her head back before kissing her soundly on the mouth. "Nothing's going to happen. It's just another night—business as usual." She stroked Mitchell's cheek. "Except I'm not doing any *business* anymore. And that's because of you."

Mitchell frowned, then her eyes darkened with understanding. "Nothing?"

Sandy shook her head.

"For how long?"

Sandy lifted a shoulder.

"Honey?"

"A while." Sandy didn't protest when Mitchell pulled her down into her lap. Rather, she threaded her arms around Mitchell's neck and rested her head against the curve of Mitchell's shoulder. "I got so I didn't want anyone near me except you."

"Oh man," Mitchell moaned, burying her face in Sandy's hair, her hand sliding under Sandy's top. "I gotta have you all the time."

"You already do," Sandy said with a shaky laugh.

Mitchell shook her head, the fingers of one hand splayed beneath the soft curve of Sandy's breast. "I don't mean that way. Well, I *do*, but I mean the other way too."

Sandy leaned back to look into Mitchell's face. "What are you talking about, rookie? You're sounding a little crazy."

"I *am* crazy. Totally." Mitchell's thumb brushed Sandy's nipple, and she smiled at the instant response. "I want to be with you all the time. I want us to live together."

Caught off guard, Sandy laughed harshly. "There's no fucking way I'm living in that fancy place you've got. I probably wouldn't even pass the security check."

"Fuck their security checks," Mitchell spat. "If that's where we wanted to live, that's where we'd live. But I don't want to live there either."

"You don't?" Sandy couldn't hide her curiosity. "Where then?"

"I was thinking maybe we can get a place around here somewhere or Queen Village. There's a lot going on down here—you know, with Jasmine and the Kings performing and everything." She traced a fingertip over Sandy's lips. "We can look for a place as soon as this case wraps up."

"I didn't say yes." Sandy licked the end of Mitchell's finger with the tip of her tongue, then nipped at it with her teeth.

"Yeah, I know." Mitchell eased her finger between Sandy's lips and into her mouth, closing her eyes partway as Sandy sucked on it. "But you will."

Chapter Twenty-Three

Saturday

The sensation began in the pit of her stomach—an ever-increasing pressure like the tight coiling of the spring mechanism in an old-fashioned clock. The muscles on the insides of her thighs quivered, her calves contracted, and her heels dug into the mattress as her hips lifted. She had stopped breathing, the moan dying in her throat. Searching desperately behind her with one arm, she found the smooth, curved edge of the headboard and clamped her fingers around it. She cupped the back of Rebecca's head in her palm and thrust her clitoris hard against Rebecca's mouth. In her mind, she was screaming, but only the barest groan escaped. Flames licked her skin and she flushed hot; an agony of raw nerves and raging blood beat between her thighs; hot lightning scorched the length of her spine. She summoned all her strength but managed only a whisper.

"I'm coming."

For a few seconds, minutes, hours, eternity, there was no thought, no awareness beyond the torrent of pleasure flooding the plains of her body, rolling through the fields of her mind, laying waste to reason, replenishing her spirit like a deluge in the desert. And then, mercifully, peace followed the cataclysm, and the tension left her body. Catherine drew in her first full breath in what felt like eons and expelled it on a long sigh.

"Oh my God. My ears are still ringing."

Rebecca grunted and rolled away, fumbling with one hand on the nightstand. She was still struggling to recover from her own orgasm, induced by a few swift tugs on her tumescent flesh when she felt Catherine approaching climax. "Fucking phone."

"Oh no," Catherine protested, running her hand down the center of Rebecca's bare back.

"Yeah. Frye."

Catherine knew the instant her lover slipped away and the detective took her place. Rebecca swung her legs to the side of the bed and sat up in one fluid motion. The muscles beneath Catherine's fingers tightened, as if preparing to surge into motion. The very air around Rebecca's body crackled with tension.

"What was she wearing?"

Rebecca's tone was sharp. Catherine did not need to see her face to envision the fierce focus in her ice blue eyes.

"No! Stay there. I'll get back to you as soon as I make a few calls."

Rebecca swore under her breath.

"All right. I'll pick you up in fifteen minutes."

As Rebecca closed the phone and stood, Catherine checked the clock. A little before six a.m. "What is it?"

"Sandy's missing."

Rebecca drove with one hand on the wheel, the other on her cell phone. Beside her, Mitchell sat rigid, her back so stiff it did not touch the seat. Her feet were planted flat on the floor, palms pressed to her thighs. Her splayed fingers were white.

"What exactly did she say when she left?" Rebecca asked.

"She'd set up a phone meet with Trudy. It was the first time they'd connected since the bust." Mitchell's voice was gravelly, her throat desert dry. She stared through the windshield at the familiar neighborhoods, registering nothing. There was an odd numbness in her chest and belly, as if she'd been gutted. There was no pain, only a vast emptiness, dark and endless. "She didn't say where."

"What's your best guess?"

In the silence that followed, Rebecca pushed her own sick fears deep down inside. She'd put Sandy out there. Never mind that Sandy knew the risks. In the end, she alone was responsible for anything that happened to her. Sandy—sharp-tongued, quick-witted, tough, vulnerable Sandy. She probably weighed all of a hundred pounds. Jesus Christ.

"Mitchell?"

"I don't know."

Rebecca slammed on the brakes, downshifted hard, and swerved to the curb. In the same motion, she turned in the seat and grabbed Mitchell's shoulder, forcing the younger woman to look at her. "She's out there, and we're going to find her. That's what we do. If anyone's hurt her, we'll take care of it. Now get your fucking head together, because I need you. And so does she."

Mitchell blinked. The fingers digging into her shoulder created small circles of pain, a welcome reminder that she was still capable of feeling. The sharp edges of Rebecca's words cut through the mist of desolation that clouded her mind. She was not helpless. Sandy was *not* gone.

"The…diner, maybe."

"No, too busy. Too many pimps who might see them." Rebecca inched closer, easing her viselike grip. "Come on, Mitchell. She's your girl. You know her. Someplace she trusts. Somewhere safe."

"Chen's. That's where we used to meet, back when we first started…going out." Mitchell shivered as the ice encasing her heart cracked. It hurt to feel her heart beat, but the pounding was a welcome ache. "South Str—"

"I *know* where it is," Rebecca snapped as she shifted back into her seat, her foot already jammed on the gas pedal. The Corvette peeled down Bainbridge, the engine screaming in the nearly empty Saturday-morning streets.

"Yes, I remember," Lilly Chen said. She'd answered their knock immediately, wrapped in a long robe, looking as if they hadn't just awakened her from a sound sleep. "With another girl. Last booth in the back. Two o'clock."

"Anything unusual happen?" Rebecca asked.

Lilly frowned. "I don't think so. They talked, they ate. We were busy. Friday nights are like that."

Rebecca sensed Mitchell growing restless beside her, but she kept her own posture and expression relaxed. Witnesses frequently didn't realize how much they truly knew, and if they felt pressured, they often forgot or fabricated. Neither was desirable, especially not now, when they had so little to go on. "Do you remember any customers acting strangely right about that time—say, leaving without finishing their meal?"

"There *was* one like that!" Lilly exclaimed, her eyes bright. "He ordered but didn't eat. Left too much money on the counter because the check wasn't ready."

"What time was this?" Mitchell asked calmly.

"Just after two, I think."

Mitchell's heart jumped into overdrive. "Did he talk to them?"

Lilly shook her head. "No. No one did, or at least I didn't see."

"What about your waitresses? Would they have noticed?" Rebecca asked.

"My children. They were working last night. I could wake them."

"No," Rebecca said, "not right now. We may want to talk to them later, if that's all right." Questioning the kids would take too long, and what they needed now was an idea of where Sandy might have gone. Finding out who might have gone after her could wait.

"Anything else you can think of? Anything that was at all different."

Lilly started to shake her head again, then stopped. "Sandy gave me money at the table, not up front at the register like usual. I don't remember seeing the girls leave."

Rebecca's eyes narrowed. "Back door?"

"Maybe," Lilly agreed. "The fire door is back by the restrooms. They could have left that way."

"Thanks," Rebecca said. "Sorry to wake you."

"It's okay," Lilly called after them.

As they hurried down the sidewalk, Rebecca said, "There's an alley that runs behind this row of storefronts. Let's check it out."

"Okay. Right." Mitchell spun away, only to be jerked to a halt by Rebecca's hand on her shoulder again.

"Take it easy. There's probably no one still around, even if he did follow them out the back. But keep your head on straight." Rebecca waited, watching, knowing that now was the moment that would define Mitchell's future.

Mitchell took a deep breath and thought back to the months and years of training that had been part of a career she had tried hard to forget. This was the war and these streets the battlefield that she had spent a lifetime preparing for. Her mission was now, and nothing would ever matter more. The roaring in her head grew still. Her heart rate slowed, her vision cleared. The faint trembling in her hands dissipated. She turned and met her lieutenant's eyes. "Yes, ma'am. I'm fine."

"Good. You approach from the north, and I'll come in from the south. We'll check the alley directly behind Chen's first, and if there's nothing there, we'll follow their most likely path."

"Understood."

Five minutes later they met again beside the unmarked brown metal door that was only identifiable as Chen's service entrance by the crates of moldering vegetable remains stacked by the nearby dumpster.

"Nothing," Rebecca said flatly. "Where would they likely head for?"

"Jesus," Mitchell muttered, rubbing her face. "If they were done talking, Sandy would either check out the strip or come home."

"If she thought they were being followed, she'd want to shake him pretty fast," Rebecca mused. She turned, orienting herself in the narrow, dank alley, trying to put herself in the place of two frightened girls. "At 2:30 in the morning, the only activity around here is on South Street. It's the only place they might be able to blend in with other people on the street." She pointed west. "And if they were trying to make it to the strip, they'd go that way. I'll take this direction, you head toward the river. Just in case I'm wrong."

"What about backup?" Mitchell asked.

"No point yet. You have your cell?"

"Yes."

"I'll check in with you every five minutes. Call me sooner if you find something."

"Yes, ma'am."

Rebecca walked quickly, eyes scanning both sides of the narrow thoroughfare. All of the business establishments were closed, and it was too early for deliveries, so she was alone. City smells accosted her: gasoline, garbage, and an occasional hint of someone's breakfast. It was fall, and the morning was cold. She left her jacket open for easy access to her weapon. She didn't think about Catherine. She didn't think about Sandy. She thought about where a young girl running for her life might go. Her cell phone rang. It was three minutes before the next check-in time with Mitchell. She looked at the number on the readout as she pulled the phone from her belt. Her hand never wavered, but her stomach tightened painfully.

"Frye."

Mitchell's voice came through clear, surprisingly steady, surprisingly normal, except for the absolute absence of inflection.

"I've got a body."

Don't touch anything, the lieutenant had said. *Secure the scene*, she had said.

Mitchell moved mechanically, instructing one of the uniforms who had arrived within minutes to cordon off each end of the alley with yellow crime scene tape, advising the other to start canvassing for witnesses. It was the first time she'd officially acted as a detective, and she didn't feel a thing. No pride, no arrogance, no nerves. Nothing. She didn't feel anything.

"Mitchell."

"Ma'am," Mitchell said reflexively, turning toward the sound of Rebecca's voice. Funny, how just that little bit of movement made her dizzy. The lieutenant had an odd expression on her face—a searching, almost tender look.

"What do you have?"

"Female…" Mitchell's voice died and she frowned. Coughed. Tried again. Odd, how much her throat hurt all of a sudden. "Female victim. Behind the dumpster. Down the alley."

"Show me." Rebecca ducked under the tape and put her hand in the center of Mitchell's back. The muscles beneath her fingers were as hard as stone. Rivulets of sweat ran from beneath Mitchell's hair, soaking the collar of her leather jacket. "Are you certain she's dead?"

"Has to be." Mitchell moved forward in measured steps, stiff legged and disjointed, far from her usual fluid stride. "So much blood."

"Did you touch her?" Rebecca's question was soft, her tone nearly gentle.

"No, ma'am. I saw…I saw an arm. The jacket." Mitchell laughed, a short, broken sound. "That stupid jacket. I told her it wasn't warm enough. She never listens." She stopped abruptly fifteen feet from a green commercial dumpster. "There was blood everywhere. He shot her. He shot her in the head." She shivered violently. "Oh Christ."

From where she stood, Rebecca could see only part of the body. A pale, open-fingered hand extended from the sleeve of a bright red vinyl jacket. A shoe, its strap torn loose from the cheap plastic sole, lay abandoned close by. Part of a leg in shiny black satin. A thick spreading puddle that could only be blood. She'd seen it before. Hundreds of times. Smelled the scent of death, felt the hopelessness and despair. This time, rage rode hard through her. Even as her fury mounted, her mind grew ever clearer, her heart colder.

"I want someone knocking on every door on both sides of this street for three blocks in every direction. Someone heard the shot—I want their name. No one interviews them but me. No one comes down this alley until the crime scene techs have cleared it. I want Flanagan. No one else." She angled her body between the victim and Mitchell. "I want you out of here. Go to Sloan's. Wait for me there."

"I want to see her." Mitchell's eyes were bleak, barren wounded things. "I didn't…earlier. I saw the jacket. The blood. I can't leave her here."

"No. You go now. Do you understand?"

"Please. Please, Lieutenant."

Rebecca hesitated, considered what she would need to do if it were…the pain struck so swiftly she gasped. Jesus. She gripped Mitchell's arm and stepped close enough to her so that no one from the street could see them. This was Mitchell's private hell, and there would be no witnesses.

"Come on."

Together, they moved within three feet of the body and squatted down. With practiced, cool efficiency, Rebecca surveyed the scene. The victim lay on her stomach, face turned away. She'd almost certainly been running and he'd caught her from behind, spun her around, and put the gun in her face. The exit wound told Rebecca that. There was so much blood even her hair color was obscured. A purse lay not far away, partially open, the clasp probably having been sprung from the force of the fall. Rebecca considered going through it, and then decided that Flanagan would shred her skin from her bones if she did. Beside her, Mitchell moaned.

"All right," Rebecca said sharply, starting to rise. "That's it. You're out of here."

"No. No no no," Mitchell intoned.

"Detective, I said—"

"There's a tattoo on her ankle."

"What?" Rebecca looked back down at the body, at the small rose tattoo just behind her ankle bone.

Mitchell stood swiftly, every drop of color bleached from her skin. "That's not Sandy."

Without another word, Mitchell pivoted sharply, marched directly to the end of the alley, and ducked under the crime scene tape. She made it another ten feet down the street before she leaned against a lamp post and vomited into the street. A dozen cops saw her. No one laughed.

Chapter Twenty-Four

"Here you go, kid. Drink some of this."

Mitchell leaned against the lamppost, eyes still closed, laboring to get her system under control. She still felt dizzy, her stomach rolled dangerously, and her heart skittered crazily in her chest. She inclined her head in Watts's direction but did not yet open her eyes. "In a minute."

"Sure. Sure. Just take your time."

"What are *you* doing here?" Mitchell finally rasped, taking the can of soda he offered. "Thanks."

"The Loo called and said we had a situation. I pulled up just as you were…uh…well."

"Yeah. Nice show for all the uniforms," Mitchell said bitterly.

"Fuck them," Watts said emphatically. "And you owe me two bucks. I used my last quarter in the machine over there getting that soda for you."

"I'll buy you a six-pack."

"Fair enough." Watts hunched his shoulders in his shapeless sports coat. "Fucking freezing out here. So…I guess the scene's pretty rough, huh?"

Mitchell took a mouthful of the tasteless but heavily carbonated liquid, rinsed her mouth, and spit it out into the gutter. Then she drained the rest of the can in one long swallow. "Yeah. You could say that."

"What's the story?"

"Looks like someone got Trudy."

"Fuck." Watts stiffened as if someone had poked him with a sharp stick. "Where's Sandy?"

"I don't know," Mitchell said hoarsely. "At first I thought it was her…down there."

Watts extended a hand and touched her arm tentatively. "You've got nothing to be ashamed of, kid. Everyone loses their lunch sooner or later."

Mitchell gave him a grateful smile. "Well, I'm glad I'm running true to form." She shoved her hands into the pockets of her leather jacket and looked past him toward the crime scene van that had just pulled up. "Flanagan's here."

"Well, I better give the Loo a hand. Why don't you take a brea—"

"No, I'm fine." To prove it, Mitchell took a tentative step, glad to discover that her still-shaking legs were functional. "There's a lot of work still to do, and—"

A commotion at the end of the block caught her attention, and she heard, "Let me through! I need to get through."

Then a deep male voice gave a shout of surprise, a splash of pale pink amidst the dark blue uniforms flashed into view, and Mitchell took off running.

"Lemme *go*!" Sandy yanked her arm from the viselike grip of the officer who tried to restrain her and rocketed down the sidewalk.

"Sandy!" Mitchell caught her around the waist and engulfed her in a near-suffocating embrace. "Jesus. Sandy. Sandy. God."

"Whoa, rookie." Sandy tried to squirm free, but failed. Then something about the vehemence of Mitchell's reaction penetrated her haze of anger and fear, and she stopped struggling. Instead, she slipped a hand around the back of Mitchell's neck and caressed her. "Take it easy, baby. What's the matter? Dell? You're shaking all over."

Mitchell buried her face in Sandy's neck, afraid for anyone to see her face.

Shocked, Sandy rocked back. In a low, gentle voice, she asked, "Baby, what? Why are you crying?"

"She's wearing your jacket." With one arm around Sandy's shoulder, Mitchell turned her back to the group of curious cops and swiped her sleeve across her face. "Come on," she said, walking Sandy further down the sidewalk out of earshot. "Are you hurt? Did he touch you?"

"Who? No. Trudy never came back, and I...What about my jacket?" Sandy's eyes widened. "Trudy has my jacket. I went straight to the diner from Chen's, but she said she had something to do first. It was so cold, and she didn't have a coat. I waited an extra hour, but she never came."

"You split up?"

Sandy nodded. "Trudy was supposed to meet someone. Some private deal, she said, but she wanted to talk after that. I said I'd wait for her at the diner." Sandy searched Mitchell's face, her own a mask of apprehension. "What about my jacket, Dell?"

Mitchell stroked Sandy's cheek with her free hand, still holding her too tightly, still unable to believe she was real. "Trudy's dead, honey."

Sandy sucked in air as if she'd been punched in the stomach and clutched Mitchell's hand. "How?"

"Shot. Did you see someone following you last night?"

"No, but Trudy got hinky in the restaurant and wanted to leave right away. I knew something was wrong, but she wouldn't tell me what." Sandy stared at the yellow crime scene tape at the mouth of the alley. "Is that where she is?"

"Yeah."

"Oh, baby." Sandy turned into Mitchell and clutched the front of her jacket with both hands. "You thought it was me. Oh, I'm sorry, baby. I'm sorry."

Mitchell shook her head and kissed Sandy's forehead. "It's okay. You're all right." Taking several deep breaths, Mitchell forced what she hoped was a reassuring smile. "I gotta go back to work, honey. But I think the lieutenant will need to talk to you as soon as possible."

"Okay. Sure." Stunned, Sandy still clung to Mitchell.

"Here," Mitchell said, slipping out of her jacket and carefully placing it around Sandy's shoulders. "It's freezing out here and you're…well, you're not wearing enough."

Reflexively, Sandy slid her arms into the sleeves and then pulled the too-large garment closed with both hands. "Where should I go?"

"Take a cab to Sloan's," Mitchell said immediately, pulling her wallet from her back pocket and extracting some bills. "Stay with Michael until I come for you, okay?"

Fisting the cash, Sandy nodded, glancing toward the alley. "Are you sure it's her?"

Tenderly, Mitchell kissed Sandy's forehead again. "Yes. I'm sorry, honey."

"Be careful, rookie. You be real careful." Sandy placed her open palm against Mitchell's chest and fanned her fingers back and forth slowly. "I love you."

Mitchell covered Sandy's small hand with hers and squeezed gently. "I love you too."

❖

Catherine arrived twenty minutes after Sandy. When she stepped off the elevator into the loft living room, Michael was waiting. Catherine leaned forward and kissed Michael's cheek. "Hello. How are you?"

Michael smiled. "Much better. Thank you." She extended a hand to take Catherine's coat. "Sandy's in the kitchen."

"Is there anything I can do for *you*?"

"No," Michael said with a careful shake of her head. "I'm fine. Sloan is downstairs with Jason already, waiting for Rebecca and the others to return. Thanks for coming. I thought…" She stopped, smiling faintly. "Is it all right that I called?"

"Perfectly," Catherine said reassuringly, slipping her arm through Michael's. "There's been altogether too much violence for everyone lately. Let's go talk."

Sandy sat at the breakfast bar, her hands laced around a white porcelain mug from which steam tendriled into the air. She glanced up at the sound of Catherine and Michael's approach, but said nothing.

"Hello," Catherine murmured as she passed behind Sandy to take the stool on her far side. "Michael told me what happened. I'm so very sorry."

"I think it might be my fault," Sandy said in a voice so low Catherine almost couldn't hear.

"Why do you think that?" Catherine nodded her thanks to Michael, who set a matching mug in front of her. The smell of jasmine and oranges drifted to her on a plume of steam.

"Someone probably got suspicious after the bust last week, and Trudy is the one who brought me there. Whenever the *cops* show up, they always blame us."

Catherine thought of the fact that both her lover and Sandy's were cops. At the moment, however, Sandy was viewing everyone in law enforcement as being on the opposite side of whatever divide had existed in her life, and her allegiance to the other young women who shared her desperate struggle was clear. "Do you think there's a possibility that Trudy's death could be unrelated to what happened at the film studio?"

Sandy shrugged and pushed her mug back and forth in a slow semicircle on the gleaming granite countertop. "I suppose. There are always plenty of people who might want to make a point by coming down on one of us. Pimps, dealers, johns. You name it." She made a deprecating sound. "And nothing makes a statement quite like a body."

"What about Trudy?" Catherine might not have questioned Sandy, except for the fact that the girl appeared to be ready to shoulder so much of the blame for Trudy's death. Even without knowing all the circumstances, Catherine doubted it could be as simple as that. And she cared for both Sandy and Mitchell too much to let Sandy accept the burden of guilt all by herself. She tried not to think about the fact that her own lover was very likely going through the same agony of self-recrimination at that moment. "Was she in trouble with anyone that you know of?"

"I don't know. Maybe. She was weird about something."

"I can imagine how it must feel to you right now," Catherine said gently, patting Sandy briefly on the back. "But try to remember that the guilty person here is the depraved individual who killed her. No one else."

Sandy angled her body slightly and finally met Catherine's eyes. "Frye will make them pay."

"Yes, she will," Catherine said with certainty. "She'll see that justice is done."

"Let's go over it again," Rebecca prompted gently.

The entire team was seated around the conference table, everyone in their usual seats, except this time, Catherine and Sandy joined them as well. Mitchell, at Rebecca's direction, moved to the far end of the table, out of Sandy's line of vision. Mitchell had hesitated only a second before tossing Sandy an encouraging smile and changing chairs. Catherine sat beside Sandy, a comforting presence.

Sandy drew a breath and repeated what she had already said numerous times. "We met at Chen's a little after two. We'd just gotten our food when Trudy started acting…fidgety, like something was wrong. I asked her, but she just said 'nothing.'"

"What did you tell her was the reason you were meeting?" Rebecca asked.

"I didn't have a chance to tell her anything. We set up the meeting through the phone tree, so I could only leave her a vague message. I didn't know who else might get it before it got to her. I said I wanted to talk to her about the extra work." She shrugged. "I figured she'd know I was talking about the porn shoot, because that's the only thing we ever did together."

"Did she say if she told anyone about the meeting?" Watts inquired.

"No, and I don't think she would. She's been pretty careful about keeping her location quiet—that's why we were using the message tree. She was freaked by what happened."

"And you didn't see anything unusual in the restaurant?"

"It was crowded. At that time of night, down there, there's always a lot of weirdos around. I didn't notice anyone who was more creepy than usual."

"So maybe," Watts said, turning his attention to Rebecca, "Trudy recognized the guy from somewhere else. From one of the video shoots or maybe the clubs where she danced."

"That might explain why she wanted to leave so quickly, and also why he followed her and not Sandy," Rebecca agreed.

"Trudy was the target," Mitchell said quietly.

Rebecca nodded. "I'd say so."

"Then why not take her out on the way to the restaurant before anyone had a chance to see him? Why risk someone remembering his face?" Sloan put out to the group at large.

"Because maybe," Watts offered, "he wanted to see who she was meeting."

Sandy stiffened and Mitchell cursed.

"That's possible," Rebecca said quietly. "It's also possible that this was the first time she'd come out of hiding since the raid last weekend, and he was finally able to pick her up. It might have been coincidence that she was with Sandy."

Watts grunted. Every cop in the room knew that there were no coincidences.

"So the question is," Rebecca continued, "what did Trudy know that was important enough to get her killed?" She stood abruptly and looked around the table at each person. "We're missing the key, and we've been missing it since the beginning. What did Trudy know that someone was afraid she would tell us? Sandy?"

Frowning in concentration, Sandy stared at the tabletop, her words coming slowly. "Well, she knew about the sex shoots, but she already told us that."

"She knew the guy who set up the shoots," Mitchell offered.

Rebecca shook her head. "No good. The feds have him in custody, and the porn ring is already compromised. There wouldn't be any point to eliminating her now if that's all she knew."

"Payback," Sandy said flatly.

Rebecca's expression didn't change. "Maybe. What else?"

"She knew the location of the film studio," Watts noted. For a moment he looked pleased, and then his grin faded. "Except it's the same deal. We already know that too."

"All right," Rebecca said. "Let's look at what we know—everything revolves around Trudy and those films. If it's not who, and it's not where, then what else is there?"

The room was silent until Catherine said quietly, "When?"

Rebecca narrowed her eyes. Watts hummed under his breath. Mitchell shifted forward in her seat. Both Jason and Sloan reached for pads of paper and began jotting notes.

"Let's assume that's it," Rebecca eventually said. "Let's say *when* the porn films were made is important. We know that Trudy got other girls to do some of them." She focused on Sandy again. "What did she say about those times?"

"She said…she said sometimes the regular girls couldn't do them, and then this guy would ask around for some of us."

"'Us' meaning prostitutes?"

Sandy's chin came up. "Yes."

"And who exactly are the *regular* girls?"

"I'm not really sure," Sandy said. "There've been a lot of new girls in places like Ziggie's in the last year or so. Dancers. Prostitutes. Both."

"All right. Let's put that aside for the moment and just say that the regular girls were busy. Busy doing *what*?" Rebecca made an impatient sound when no one answered. "Come on, people. Give me something here." She'd just spent the last two hours looking at the brutalized body of a dead girl, a dead girl she'd help to put in that alley, and for a few minutes, she'd thought it had been Sandy. The shock of that had rocked her, and the frustration and pain had her strung tight as piano wire.

"Sex party?" Watts suggested.

"Could be. I wouldn't think anyone would worry about hiding that information, unless there were high-profile clients. Judges. DAs. Cops."

"We haven't found anything suggestive of that in Beecher's records," Jason interjected. "And it seems that that would be the kind of thing he'd be into. Nothing in his calendar stands out."

"Keep looking," Rebecca instructed. "Some kind of drug transfer, perhaps. Maybe the girls were muling and weren't available to do the videos those particular nights." She made a note in her small black notepad. "Sloan? Can you run a computer check on the narcotics busts for the last twelve months—cross-reference with organized crime, prostitution, anything that might tie this together."

"On it."

"Jason," Rebecca continued, suddenly energized. "Comb through Beecher's computer and the computers confiscated during the raid. Find out the dates of all the live video broadcasts. Let's look for some kind of pattern there." Then she focused on Sandy. "What exactly did Trudy say about the nights that she filled in for the video shoots?"

"Just what I said earlier," Sandy said, weariness and stress edging her voice with impatience. "Every few months, is what she told me. I didn't ask for dates."

"I need specific dates."

"I'll ask arou—"

"No," Mitchell said forcefully. "Whoever shot Trudy saw you with her. You've been made. It's not safe."

"I'll be careful."

This time, it was Rebecca who spoke. "No. Mitchell's right. I want you off the streets."

"Wait a minute," Sandy protested. "You can't—"

"I've got an idea," Jason interrupted. "I can pull the videos from the confiscated computers, at least all the ones that were downloaded and saved. And these guys save *everything*. Sandy can screen them for me. She ought to be able to tell the ones that have street girls in them."

"Perfect," Rebecca said with satisfaction. "In the meantime, I want Mitch back in Ziggie's tonight. Watts, you and I will be backup."

Watts snorted. "Great. I get to watch the door again while *he* gets the T&A."

Chapter Twenty-Five

Saturday Afternoon

"How are you holding up, Detective?" Catherine asked as Mitchell slumped into the chair opposite her desk with a sigh.

"Not bad." Mitchell resisted the strong urge to lean her head back and close her eyes. She'd slept very little the night before, especially after awakening at three and realizing that Sandy had not returned to the apartment. She'd paced until daybreak, when she'd finally given in and called Rebecca for help.

Catherine regarded her with a compassionate smile. "Sure?"

"I'll make it. I need to be sure that all my paperwork is in order."

"It *is* Saturday, and—"

Uncharacteristically, Mitchell interrupted. "I know, but the lieutenant is a stickler about these kinds of…" She trailed off, casting Catherine an apologetic look.

"And?" Catherine prodded with the barest of smiles.

"And as long as I tell *her* I'm cleared for duty, she won't care about getting the forms filed."

"This is so you can work tonight? The surveillance Lieutenant Frye was talking about this morning?"

"Yes," Mitchell said, her voice gaining strength as she sat up straighter. "I'm ready."

"You've had a rather momentous few days."

Mitchell huffed out a laugh. "Yeah. Actually, it's been a really momentous *week*. I get stabbed, my sister shows up unexpectedly after two years, and *then* I find a body I think is my girlfriend."

"And despite all of that, you want to undertake this assignment tonight?"

"Of course." Mitchell looked confused. "This is it. This is when it all starts coming together, and after this morning…" Her voice caught unexpectedly, and she blinked in surprise.

"Tell me about this morning," Catherine urged.

For a moment, Mitchell remained silent, her eyes distant, remembering. Then she twitched as if awakening from a dream and focused on Catherine's face. "It was the worst thing I've ever experienced in my life."

Catherine nodded wordlessly.

"She's got this stupid short, red, fake-leather jacket." Mitchell laughed, the sound undercut with pain. "She looks really hot in it, but the damn thing is worthless as far as keeping her warm is concerned." Mitchell stared at her lap, her hands curled over the tops of her knees. "Trudy was wearing it, but I didn't know that. I saw the body, the blood, the red jacket."

Mitchell fell silent again, the agony of the memory written across her face. Catherine had a sudden flash of Rebecca lying in a pool of blood, her skin white, her chest unmoving. She experienced the terror again, the empty desolation. Her heart aching for the young woman across from her, she murmured, "You thought it was Sandy."

"Yeah," Mitchell said, her voice hoarse, her fingers white. "I thought she was dead, and I felt something inside of me…freeze. Like all the life was leaving my body and there was nothing left behind." She shook her head, then met Catherine's eyes, her own bleak. "It hurt so much."

"I know," Catherine said softly. "Does it still hurt?"

Mitchell took a shaky breath and nodded. "Some. I mean, I know she's all right. But I still…feel it."

"Your head knows she's all right, but your heart will take a little while longer to believe it."

"I *almost* didn't come this afternoon because I didn't want to let her out of my sight." Mitchell smiled crookedly. "She's starting to complain that she's suffocating."

Catherine laughed. "Do you think she means it?"

"Probably a little. She's pretty independent."

"I noticed. How do you feel about that?"

"Most of the time I think it's pretty great," Mitchell conceded. "But when she insists on getting in the middle of things where she might get hurt, I'm not too keen on it."

"And have you talked about it?"

Mitchell grinned. "Uh…maybe more like shouted about it."

"But you're handling it?"

"We're okay. I drive her crazy, but she knows I'm doing it because I love her."

"Good." Catherine regarded Mitchell intently for moment. "Is there some *other* reason, besides not wanting to leave Sandy, that you didn't want to come today?"

Mitchell looked down at her heavy black motorcycle boots, considering, then shrugged one shoulder. "I thought you might tell me I can't go back to work."

"Why did you think I would say that?"

"Because of this morning. I didn't handle it so well."

"Oh? I didn't notice that anything was wrong at the conference." *Other than the fact that you looked like you'd been through the wringer.* "Was there some kind of procedural problem in the field?"

Swiftly, Mitchell shook her head in denial. "Not *that* kind of screwup. I mean, I think I handled everything okay. Followed protocol. But…"

"But?"

Mitchell sighed heavily. "I pretty much fell apart when I thought it was Sandy. I kind of couldn't think. Then…well, then I heaved in the gutter." She grimaced, remembering, still chagrined. "Jesus. I can't believe I did that."

"Don't you think it's natural for someone to have an extreme reaction when they believe someone they love has been killed?"

"I'm a cop," Mitchell said immediately. "I'm supposed to be able to handle it."

"Handle that kind of loss? How?"

"By doing the job. By just…doing what has to be done."

Catherine struggled to be objective. Mitchell sounded eerily like Rebecca, so certain of what must be done and so very certain she could trade her humanity for her duty over and over without slowly dying. *God, what makes them do this?*

Wishing desperately that she understood, Catherine knew with a sinking heart that she might never find the answer to what made her lover who she was, what made this young woman believe that it was possible to bury that much pain for the good of a…a job. Not *a* job. *The* job. Suddenly, she realized that she had never asked the right question. The answer wasn't to be found in understanding why they did what they did. It was all about how the work was an extension of who they were. "What does being a cop mean to you?"

Mitchell's brows drew down sharply at the unexpected question. Taking her time, she formed her answer. "It means taking all the things that are important to me, about who I am and what I believe, and bringing them together in one place. When I'm a cop I'm *me,* more than any other time in my life except…" She smiled. "Except when Sandy and I are making love."

"When you're being a cop and when you're with the woman you love," Catherine said quietly. "That's when you're you?"

"Yes," Mitchell replied solemnly.

Catherine considered the idea, considered all she knew of her lover, all she had learned from Dellon and from other police officers over the years. She believed it. She still didn't entirely understand it, but she accepted that the essence of their being, their self-definition, was intimately shaped by their responsibility, dedication, and pride in being police officers. *Her* responsibility at the moment was determining if this one police officer could safely function, regardless of how critical it might be to Mitchell to fulfill her role on the team.

"You seem to like being undercover. Is it stressful?"

"No," Mitchell admitted. "Not when I'm Mitch. Mitch is…" Struggling, she met Catherine's eyes and found only acceptance. "Mitch is me. Part of me, anyways. I just let that part come to the surface, and it's not work."

"I've wondered," Catherine said. "Do you have to think about behaving like a man, or…how does that happen for you?"

Mitchell grinned. "It comes pretty easy. It's not just clothes or the co—other stuff. When I'm Mitch, and people relate to me like I'm a guy, it's easy to stay in character. Sure, it helps to look the part, to have the right equipment in my jeans, but a lot of it is about how other people see me. Sandy helps a lot."

"How?" Catherine watched Mitchell's face come to life, saw the energy return to her eyes, saw her body straighten with renewed strength. She wasn't entirely certain whether it was the mention of Sandy or Mitch, but something had infused Mitchell with excitement and purpose.

"She digs Mitch. She makes it work for me. She never lets me forget who I am when I'm him." Mitchell made a wry face, considering her words. "Did that just make any sense?"

Catherine laughed. "I think so. Having Sandy believe in Mitch, and relate to him with consistency and sincerity, makes it easier for you to project his personality."

"Yes." Mitchell grinned. "Having her have the hots for Mitch helps me be him."

"I think that's what I just said," Catherine murmured, and Mitchell laughed.

"I can see that the undercover portion of the assignment is not a problem for you. What about the rest of it?" Catherine asked, suddenly serious. "Are you concerned about the danger?"

"Concerned?" Mitchell pondered the idea. "No. It takes some getting used to, never knowing exactly what's going to happen, but I feel prepared. Being a cop is just like being a soldier. You train, you know you're ready, and whatever happens, you deal with it."

"Speaking of soldiers," Catherine remarked evenly, "Erica was a bit of a surprise."

"Yeah, well, she hasn't been part of my life for quite a while, so I never thought to mention her."

Catherine made a sound of assent, watching Mitchell's face.

"Okay," Mitchell conceded. "I don't like to talk about her."

After a moment, Catherine asked, "Has seeing her yesterday changed how you feel at all?"

"I don't know. Maybe. It's going to be a lot harder to put her out of my mind now."

"It must take a lot of work to keep your twin out of your mind."

For the merest instant, Mitchell closed her eyes. Then with a sigh, she said, "It's impossible. Most of the time I don't think about her, but then at odd moments, I remember something we did or something she said, or I'll want to tell her something…and she's not there." She took a deep breath and sighed again. "Then it's really tough."

"Now…with all that's going on with this investigation, is probably not the best time to explore your feelings concerning the estrangement with your sister, but at some point, I think you should."

Slowly, Mitchell nodded. "So…you and I, we could do that?"

"Yes, we could."

"Okay," Mitchell said as if that settled the matter. Then she leaned forward, her gaze intent. "So, will you clear me to get back to work?"

Catherine didn't hesitate. "Yes."

Mitch sat on the edge of the bed, leaning forward to pull on his right motorcycle boot. Sandy scooted around behind him and threaded her arms around his neck, running her hands back and forth over his chest.

"Remember, Ali said you couldn't ride the bike." Sandy kissed the back of his neck.

"I won't," he replied, reaching for the other boot. His leg ached when he stood too long or stretched too far. But basically, it didn't bother him. The stitches hadn't yet been removed, but the incision was healing fine, and he rarely thought about it. "Jasmine will pick me up in her car."

"I could come with you to the Troc," Sandy suggested. "I *am* supposed to be your girlfriend, you know."

"You *are* my girlfriend."

"So, I'll come."

"I'm going to Ziggie's after the Kings finish their show."

"I know. I'll catch a ride home with someone."

Mitch angled around on the bed until he could see Sandy's face. He grinned. "Uh-huh. Anybody who sees us together will *really* believe that I'm going to leave you to go out clubbing with the guys."

Sandy ran her fingertips along his jaw. "You look good. The shading is just right. Clubbing with the guys, huh. That's what you call it? Watching a bunch of girls dance naked?"

"I'm not watching the girls. You know that."

"Oh yeah, sure. I bet you keep your eyes closed the whole time you're in Ziggie's. I've seen the way those tables are placed. You're practically at eye level with their—"

"Come on, San," Mitch protested, snaking an arm around her waist and pulling her sideways into his lap. Her arms automatically came around his neck, and he nuzzled her throat. "I'll be working, and even if I wasn't, the only girl I ever think about is you." He kissed her neck, then rubbed his cheek against her breast. "All the time. I think about this all the time."

Sandy smoothed her fingers over the short hair at the back of his neck before guiding his mouth to the peak of her breast, murmuring her pleasure when he took her nipple into his mouth. The thin material of her camisole molded to her breast from the moisture of his lips, heightening the sensation as it tightened around her flesh. "I know how you get," she whispered, shifting her hips against his crotch, "when you're geared up like this."

Mitch groaned. "How? How do I get, huh, honey?"

"Horny." Sandy leaned back, caught the bottom of her camisole in her fingers, and lifted it to expose her breasts. Watching Mitch's face, she cupped one small, firm breast and flicked the nipple with her finger. "Just remember, I'll be waiting…" She lost her breath as Mitch's mouth closed firmly on her again.

Back arched, both hands clasped behind Mitch's neck, Sandy rocked in his lap while he moved from one breast to the other, torturing her nipples with kisses interspersed with tiny bites. Within minutes, they were both gasping.

"You know what you're doing to me, right?" Mitch groaned, both hands circling her breasts, squeezing rhythmically. He lifted his hips to meet Sandy's as she ground down against him. "You know how bad I need you right now, right?"

"Uh-huh," Sandy gasped, her head thrown back, eyes closed, her hips rolling over the prominence between his thighs.

"You trying to make me come in my jeans?"

A slow smile curved over Sandy's face as she opened her eyes partway, her expression dreamy and soft. "Can you?"

"Keep riding me like that, you'll find out," Mitch growled.

Sandy shifted with one fluid movement, reseating herself so that she faced him, her legs wrapped behind his hips as she sat in his lap. The thin barrier of her silk panties rested over the bulge in his crotch. Breath coming fast, she rubbed herself on him in short, fast circles, bearing down harder with each rotation. "I might...beat you to it, baby."

Captivated by the flickering images of pleasure racing across her face, Mitch cradled her hips in his palms and pulled her to him, increasing the friction between them. "Do it, honey. Let me see you come on me."

"I'm going to," she said in wonder, clutching his shoulders, rocking now in sharp, erratic jerks.

His own need forgotten, he tore his gaze away from her face long enough to look down, his stomach tightening at the sight of her passion soaking the denim stretched over his cock. The sight was enough to make him come, but he held back, concentrating on her—timing his thrusts to the lift and fall of her hips. "That's it, honey," he whispered. "That's it."

She gave one startled cry and stiffened in his embrace, pressing down so hard against him he thought he'd burst. Then she collapsed into his arms, soft and warm, making small, broken sounds of contentment.

"Oh yeah," Mitch muttered, pressing his face to her damp hair. "I'm gonna look at some other girl after this."

"Okay," Sandy replied drowsily. "But no touching."

"Not 'til I get home," Mitch promised. "But then, I'm gonna do a *lot* of touching."

Chapter Twenty-Six

Sunday, Early Hours

You doing okay?" Jasmine asked as she sidled close to Mitch in the semicircular booth that faced the stage.

"Great." He tried not to stare at the performers, young women Sandy's age, most of them built like her—firm and sleek and limber—and barely postadolescent. He couldn't think about Sandy and the years she had been available for the titillation and arousal of strangers, not and do the job he had to do. Between him and the bodies gyrating a few feet away, the air hung in a blue-gray cloud of smoke and dust flecks that drifted in desultory waves, stirred by the motion of the dancers. Two dozen rapt voyeurs were gathered around at tables or booths, their faces cast in deathly pallor by slanting beams of light from the recessed spots focused in three glaring columns on the raised central platform. Generic strip music blared, and Mitch had to lean close to make himself heard. Jasmine smelled of some exotic spice and a hint of something darker. Despite the dim lighting, her slender form, made sleeker by painted-on black slacks and a plunging vee-neck top, was infinitely more alluring than the naked bodies on display. "*You* see anyone interesting?"

In the last week, they'd assembled photos of dozens of suspected midlevel Mob members from police files and surveillance images—the crew captains, their lieutenants, and the street soldiers who did the dirty work—but Mitch hadn't seen anyone he recognized.

"No," Jasmine said. "They're here, somewhere. Probably in a back office. Chances are the lieutenants are all keeping a low profile because of the arrests last week. They usually send their soldiers to do the real work anyhow."

Ken Dewar slid into the black leather-covered booth next to Mitch and handed out bottles of beer.

"Thanks," Mitch said. "Find anybody worth checking out on your travels?"

"Not yet, but the night is young," Ken replied, sipping his beer. "It's the usual crowd—same bartender as last week too. I don't recognize the dancers tonight, but in this kind of work, they turn over pretty fast. Some john beats them up, they get sick, they get addicted. They don't last long."

Mitch's stomach twisted as he remembered the bright promise in Sandy's eyes and the sleek, smooth lines of her body. He swore to himself that she was never coming back to this life. "Have you ever…dated any of these girls?"

"For more than one night?"

From the other side of the table, Phil snickered.

"Doesn't matter," Mitch answered. "I was wondering if you ever went home with one of them."

Ken, bulkier than Mitch in his chest and shoulders, the barest suggestion of a beard darkening his angular jaw, shook his head. "They don't take you home. They do you in the back hall or the john. These girls don't date."

"They *don't* date or you don't ask them out?"

"Why would we?" Ken asked with no suggestion of censure in his voice. "They're all working girls. If that's your pleasure, a fifty will get you anything you want."

A muscle on the edge of Mitch's jaw twitched, and he carefully kept his voice even. This wasn't about Sandy. It wasn't about him. This was about the job. "I don't know—you guys don't strike me as the hit-and-run types, and it wouldn't be the first time some guy tried to rescue one of them."

He intentionally took a swallow of his beer and let his gaze drift over the woman who danced closest to them. She was nude, bathed in an unforgiving light that revealed the faint sheen of sweat covering her body, which was slightly thinner than was healthy, but attractive nonetheless. Her breasts were high and firm, her belly long and sensuous, her legs suggestively sinuous. As the music pulsed, she squatted with her hands on her knees—legs spread, hips rolling—opening herself for their inspection. He wasn't aroused, but he couldn't help but look at her. When he did, she smiled and extended a hand with a come-hither motion. He feigned interest, letting his eyes follow her hand as it dropped down between her thighs. "*She's* hot."

"Yeah," Ken said dismissively, "but she's not going to have your babies. These girls don't settle down. It's too late for that."

"So you don't know where they live, who they really are?"

"Never thought about it," Ken acknowledged. "Besides, like I said, they're not here that long."

They're not here that long.

There've been a lot of new girls in the clubs the last eighteen months.

"How long?"

"Huh?" Ken asked, angling his body and craning his neck as he followed the particularly acrobatic maneuverings of a tall blond working out on a pole.

"How long are they usually here?"

Ken seemed to pick up on the urgency in Mitch's voice and finally gave him his full attention. "Somebody catch your eye?"

"Maybe."

"With that little hottie you have at home?" Ken's tone was incredulous.

"I didn't give her a ring yet."

Ken looked skeptical, and Mitch figured the Kings' leader wasn't buying his story. He wouldn't either, not after getting one look at Sandy. "I'm…looking for someone I saw last week. Maybe she'll be back."

"It's not like I actually counted," Ken said.

"But you noticed." *And if you noticed, there must be a pattern.*

"Yeah," Ken agreed thoughtfully, turning to the other members of his troupe. "Hey, guys, listen up."

Mitch waited impatiently while the other guys talked.

"What's going on?" Jasmine asked.

"Remember what the lieutenant has always said—it has to do with the girls?"

"Yes, why? You have an idea?"

"Maybe."

Ken turned back. "Okay, we think two months, no more than three."

What exactly did Trudy say about the nights that she filled in for the video shoots? Lieutenant Frye had asked Sandy.

Every few months, is what she told me.

"I need to hit the head," Mitch said abruptly. He looked around the table at the other kings and Jasmine. "Anybody need a beer or anything?"

As the group chorused no, he slipped from the booth and headed back to the bar.

"Back again, huh?" the bartender from the previous weekend asked in a bored tone as he wiped down the bar.

"Best show in town," Mitch replied. He pulled a folded twenty from his front pocket and slid it across the bar. "Let me have a Bud."

The bartender took his time squeezing out the rag and folding it carefully before reaching into the cooler under the bar and extracting a dripping bottle of beer. As he took the bill and turned toward the register on the narrow counter underneath the mirror opposite the bar, Mitch said, "Keep the change."

After ringing up the sale, extracting the change from the cash drawer, and whisking it into his pocket, he swung back around to face Mitch. "Something you want?"

"Irina," Mitch said. "She here tonight?"

The bartender smirked. "Setting your sights pretty high, aren't you, stud?"

Mitch lifted a shoulder. "She liked it pretty well the other night."

"You'd have better luck with one of her girls."

"She's like, what, their keeper or something?"

The bartender's face hardened. "You ask a lot of questions." He leaned his elbows on the bar and peered over it, his gaze sliding down to Mitch's crotch. "I can think of one or two who might go for what you got in there."

"How much?" Mitch asked, his heart pounding but his voice steady.

"Depends on what you're after."

"Just some company."

The bartender laughed. "Yeah, and my dick don't get hard watching those girls up there either. You gotta spell it out, or no deal."

"All right, I want to fuck, but not back there in some corner. I want to take my time."

"It's here or nowhere."

"I'll pay for a room. There's plenty of rent-by-the-hour places around here."

"No deal. The girls don't leave this place."

Mitch watched the guy's eyes, trying to judge how far to push. "Five hundred for an hour."

The bartender shook his head. "You get a room in the back. Take it or leave it."

"I want Irina." Mitch hadn't seen her so far that night, but somehow he sensed that she was the key. She was the constant. He was praying that she would remember him and still be interested.

"You must have a lot in those jeans, boy."

"It's not how much you got, it's how much you do with it."

The bartender stared at Mitch impassively for a long moment, then cracked a smile and finally laughed out loud. "Yeah, and you got the balls too. I'll see what I can do, but it's not gonna be tonight." He tilted his chin toward the stage. "Those are new girls. Irina always keeps close tabs on them when they first start working. She won't hang around tonight."

"Let me talk to her. Maybe tomorrow night."

"You must have a hard-on that won't quit." The bartender laughed again. "But then, yours never does, does it."

Surprisingly, he sounded just a bit jealous.

"Working around here, I'm surprised yours ever lets up either," Mitch said.

"Ah, you get used to it after a while." He sighed. "Look, I'll see what I can do, okay? But you're gonna have to keep it in your pants for tonight."

Mitch dropped his hand between his thighs and squeezed. "It'll be a challenge."

"Big balls, boy, big balls," the bartender muttered as he walked away.

Mitch stopped with the bottle halfway to his lips as a hand came around his middle from behind and dropped into his crotch. He registered the unmistakable press of breasts against his back and the brush of warm lips over his right ear. Unprepared for the sudden onslaught of sensation, he forced himself not to shudder.

"Greg said you wanted to talk to me," the silky, accented voice he remembered murmured.

"Not just talk," Mitch replied, covering the hand that cupped him and squeezing her fingers around the fullness in his jeans. The first time she'd touched him like this, he'd been just as unprepared and far less used to the sensation of packing. She'd made him hot, made him hard, and he'd been frightened by his inability to control his arousal. This time, he was aware of the undeniable pleasure of the pressure, but it was manageable. "Did Greg tell you about *that*?"

She kissed his neck, twining her other arm around his middle, keeping up the subtle rhythmic, rocking motion of her hand between his legs. "He mentioned you might have something for me."

"You know I do," Mitch said, shifting her hand away and spinning on the stool until he faced her. He spread his legs, cupped her rear in his hands, and pulled her into the vee of his crotch. Her pelvis bumped against his cock, and his stomach tightened. He ignored the thrum of pleasure in his belly. "Hi."

"What is it that you want, new boy?"

Mitch shook his head. "It's all about what *you* want."

She curled one arm around his neck, her breasts against his chest. "That is not how men treat sex."

"I'm an unusual guy."

She smiled, a smile of true pleasure, and trailed her fingers over his jaw. "You are not like the others. I like that."

He judged her to be in her early twenties, dark-haired, blue-eyed, pale pale skin. Eastern European, Russian perhaps. Her accent placed her somewhere there. Her body was lush where Sandy's was slender, her breasts fuller and heavier beneath a strapless top that came to just above her nipples. Her buttocks tightened beneath his palms as she rubbed herself back and forth over him.

"But you are still a guy." She laughed. "I can tell."

"Can we go somewhere?" he asked, surprised to hear himself sound breathless.

"You are ready so soon?" Smiling, she looked down at his jeans and pressed her hand over the bulge in his crotch. "But you're always ready, no?"

"Sometimes a lot more than others." He grinned and edged back as subtly as he could, because the stimulation was starting to cloud his mind. "Right now would be one of those times. Please, can we go somewhere…private?"

She appeared thoughtful, as if considering his words, then surprised him by leaning forward and kissing him softly on the lips. “Anyone else, I would make them wait. Perhaps forever. You let me decide, and I like that too. I think I might like to see just how different you are.” She kissed him again, a slow slide of lips, her fingers stroking his neck. “But not tonight.”

“When?” Mitch knew he sounded eager, and he didn’t mind. He wanted her to think he couldn’t wait.

“Tomorrow. Come tomorrow, and we’ll see.”

She started to move away, and Mitch caught her hand. He turned her back into him, not forcefully, but hard enough that she ended up pressed to his groin again. He circled his hand in the hollow at the base of her spine, moving her against him. “Let me take you somewhere alone. You shouldn’t be doing guys up against a wall in the dark. I want to see your face when you come.”

Her lips parted in surprise, and he saw her nipples harden beneath the skintight top. He held his breath as she ran her fingertip over his mouth.

“What makes you think you can make me come?”

Mitch smiled. “I see what you need in your eyes.”

“We’ll see, new boy,” she murmured, stepping free of his embrace. “We’ll see.”

“Do you want to tell me what that was about?” Jasmine hissed as Mitch settled beside her.

“I think I’m onto something.”

“I thought *she* was going to be *onto* something in a second. Are you crazy? The guys who run these girls aren’t going to like you fooling around with their merchandise.”

“She’s not merchandise,” Mitch said in a low, fierce whisper. “She’s their caretaker.”

“What do you mean?”

“She’s in charge of all these girls, and I think there’s a lot more to it than just what tricks they might turn.”

“Where are you going with this?”

“I think I know how it all ties together.”

Chapter Twenty-Seven

Sunday, Dawn

Sandy, honey," Mitch whispered, sliding under the thin blanket and curving an arm around his sleeping girlfriend's waist as he settled behind her in bed. He was still dressed, having kicked off his boots and shed his motorcycle jacket at the door. She just looked so soft and warm, her arms curled around the pillow, her face so innocent, that he couldn't resist holding her for a second. "Gotta wake up, San."

"Mmm," Sandy sighed, scooting her butt back into the curve of Mitch's groin.

"Honey, there's going to be a meeting at seven. Wake up, honey." Mitch nuzzled the back of her neck and kissed the smooth skin along the angle of her shoulder. She smelled of sleep and cinnamon, a distinctly Sandy smell that always turned him on. Without even thinking, he slipped his hand beneath the camisole she'd worn to bed and fingered the silver stud in her navel, twisting and tugging it lightly.

This time, Sandy's sigh ended on a moan.

Mitch abandoned her belly for her breast, fondling her softly. He felt her breathing escalate and knew she was awakening. "Hi, honey."

"Hi, baby." Sandy reached behind her and wrapped an arm around Mitch's hips, pulling him closer as she backed harder against his body.

The sudden pressure against the hardness in his jeans made Mitch's head light.

"Oh man, you feel so good," Mitch muttered, his voice as thick and tight as the growing weight in his belly. He'd been a little bit hard, a little bit wet, all night. He'd kept the lid firmly on his arousal, even when Irina had played with him, but he had no defenses against Sandy. Any time she looked at him, any time she touched him, he was gone. He smoothed his hand down her belly and beneath the flimsy material between her thighs, cupping her sex as he rubbed his cock against her slowly undulating ass.

"You need something, baby?" Sandy whispered, her voice sounding as urgent as Mitch's.

"Oh yeah." She was wet beneath his fingertips, and he slicked her arousal back and forth over her clitoris, the stroke of his hand matching the slow thrust of his hips. He wasn't going to be able to take too much more of the constant friction on the screaming nerve endings between his thighs. His stomach was so tight it threatened to cramp, and his legs trembled as the muscles twitched and spasmed. He closed his eyes and rubbed his face against Sandy's hair, his mouth hot against her ear. "I wanna come so bad."

"Mmm, I know you do," Sandy panted, writhing in his arms as he worked her faster. "Stop that, baby. You'll make me come." She covered his hand, pressing his palm onto her clitoris and his fingertips just inside her. Holding him there, she ordered breathlessly, "Take your cock out, baby. Let me feel it between my legs."

Mitch ripped at his jeans with his free hand, the blood roaring through his head, his nerve endings on fire. He dragged the cock out of his pants, catching the length of it in his fly, jerking it free. Groaning desperately as the manipulation threatened to send him over the edge. He'd never felt anything like it in his life. "Fuck, I think I'm gonna come."

Sandy laughed wildly, rocking on his palm. "Just take a breath. Just hold on, baby. It gets better."

"Trying," Mitch nearly whimpered. He pressed his forehead to her shoulder and concentrated on his breathing and not on that terrible sweet ache between his thighs.

"You okay, baby?" Sandy stroked his arm as it lay across her belly.

"Better. Yeah, I'm okay. Okay."

She turned partway away, drawing one leg up to open herself. "Let me feel you, Dell."

"I don't know what to do," Mitchell confessed, quivering against Sandy's back. "I'm afraid I'll hurt you."

"Just ease it between my legs," Sandy murmured. "You won't hurt me. I want you, Dell."

Mitchell fisted her cock and eased the head along the cleft between Sandy's thighs. Suddenly, everything was about Sandy, and the urgency in Mitchell's depths subsided even as excitement pierced her core like the shaft of an arrow. She felt Sandy reach beneath her body and back between her thighs, guiding Mitchell's cock against her clitoris.

"Oh yeah," Sandy crooned. "Just right there, Dell. Just rock it there, baby."

"Turn all the way over," Mitchell said hoarsely. As Sandy complied, she got onto her knees behind her and guided Sandy's hips back against her crotch, her cock coming to rest once more between Sandy's thighs. "Is it good? Can you feel me?"

Sandy clutched the sheets and pushed her hips back and forth along the length of Mitchell's cock. "I'm so wet. Oh, baby, you feel so good."

Mitchell held Sandy's hips to steady her while Sandy rode her cock, knowing that Sandy was rubbing her clitoris against the firm head at the end of each stroke.

Feeling Sandy tremble, hearing her soft moans, all the while looking down to see the length of her cock moving in and out between Sandy's thighs, Mitchell sensed her own orgasm rebuilding. Groaning, she picked up speed, unable to stop the escalating tendrils of release slipping down her thighs. "Sandy, honey, I'm not gonna last."

Breathless, Sandy pulled away and turned onto her back. Her face was flushed, her belly heaving. "Do you boys carry safes?"

"Oh Jesus," Mitchell groaned, stricken. She was so close to exploding, she could hardly think. "Do I need one?"

"No, but you might like it." Sandy laughed and reached for the bedside dresser, fumbled inside, and came up with a foil package. Rising on her knees, she extracted the condom. "Hold still."

Through hazy eyes, Mitchell watched her roll the thin latex over the head of her cock. Sandy's hand curled around the shaft while she guided the condom, the faint motion rocking the base dangerously over her clitoris. "Sandy. Sandy…be careful…I'm really close to losing it."

Sandy glanced up, her expression hungry. "You'd better wait to come inside of me."

Then there was no thought, no worry, no uncertainty, because with one arm around Mitchell's waist and the other hand on her cock, Sandy guided her down and inside of her. Sandy cried out and Mitchell followed with a hoarse shout, and then they were rising and falling, entering and receiving, giving and taking—hands clasped, fingers entwined, eyes locked.

"Hold on, hold on..." Sandy urged, her hips pistoning, taking Mitchell deeper with each stroke. "Almost, baby, almost. Oh, there I'm there..."

"You're making me come," Mitchell cried, and then there was no holding back. Her clitoris burst against the base of the cock at the same instant as Sandy arched her back and screamed with the first pulse of release.

Mitchell managed to keep most of her weight off Sandy as she collapsed with the force of her orgasm, curled over Sandy's body, shuddering. Sandy's fingers dug into her buttocks, holding her inside as she too shivered with aftershocks.

"Just stay there, baby," Sandy gasped when Mitchell started to withdraw. "Just stay still."

Regaining some of her strength, Mitchell braced herself with her elbows on either side of Sandy's slender chest and lowered her face to Sandy's breast, finding the nipple beneath the thin silk with her mouth. She could feel Sandy slowly circling her hips beneath her, stimulating herself on Mitchell's cock.

"Is it good?" Mitchell whispered.

"Such a guy." Sandy laughed shakily, running one hand up Mitchell's back into her hair. She was breathless, trembling again. She whimpered softly. "I'm gonna come again, baby."

That did it. Groaning, Mitchell pumped once and came. When she next opened her eyes, she was lying on her side with Sandy facing her, her features soft with satisfaction.

"I think having that cock makes me as useless as a guy," Mitchell muttered. "I fell asleep, didn't I?" Her eyes widened and she stiffened. "Oh fuck, the meeting—"

"It's okay, baby," Sandy said immediately. "You've only been out a couple of minutes. And you've only been home about fifteen."

"Jeez, I didn't mean to climb all over you like that when you were still asleep."

"Didn't you?" Sandy stroked her face. "I've been wondering when you were gonna do something with all that action in your pants."

Mitchell grinned. "Did you like?"

Sandy lifted a shoulder. "Not bad, rookie. Not bad at all."

"Did you like it better than when I—"

Sandy stopped Mitchell's words with her mouth, sliding her

tongue inside, kissing her deeply. Then she drew back and scraped her fingernails lightly down the center of Mitchell's stomach until she reached the cock, still in the harness inside Mitchell's jeans, which were halfway down her hips. She gave it a gentle shake.

"I like it. I liked feeling you inside me that way when I came." She slipped her hand beneath the leather, against Mitchell's still-swollen flesh, and squeezed. "But this, I *love.*"

Mitchell thought her eyes were going to roll back into her skull. Her clitoris sprang to attention, and every nerve ending from her toes to the top of her head vibrated. "You gotta stop. I'm so wasted already, and we have to get to Sloan's."

"What's happening?" Sandy asked as she carefully withdrew her hand and worked the straps free of the buckles holding the harness.

"I think I might have figured something out," Mitchell answered as she lifted her hips and helped Sandy remove her pants and gear. "We should shower and get dressed."

"Why do you need me?"

"We have to go through the videos, and you know the regular girls."

"Hours of looking at fat guys getting blow jobs?" Sandy gave a look of distaste. "Great."

Mitchell shook her head. "I don't think it will take that long. If I'm right, we'll only need to look at a dozen or so."

"You picked up on something at Ziggie's, didn't you?"

"Maybe. I hope so, because that's what I told the lieutenant. That's why she called the meeting."

"Let's get ready, then, and get this meeting over with." Sandy swung a leg over Dell's body and shifted on top of her. "Because I think I want to spend the rest of the day right here."

Mitchell sat up and wrapped her arms around Sandy's body, answering her with a kiss. Even as she held her, she had the feeling they wouldn't be coming back for a lot longer than either of them would like.

"This better be good, kid," Watts grunted, cradling a coffee mug in his huge hands. "I've been up all night, sitting in a bucket seat too small for a midget, freezing my balls off. And the Loo wouldn't let me smoke."

"Leave her alone," Sandy said sharply on her way to the small refrigerator tucked under the counter. She pulled out a Black & Tan when she noticed Mitchell's look of surprise. "What? This is dinnertime for me."

"What's got your panties in a twist?" Watts asked.

"Maybe I'd like to be doing something else right now too," Sandy grumped and put the beer back, exchanging it for a soda.

Watts looked from Sandy to Mitchell, who blushed furiously, and slowly grinned. "Well ain't you the lucky one."

Mitchell shoved her hands into her jeans. "Yeah."

Watts clapped Mitchell on a shoulder. "You break this case, kid, and that gold shield of yours is really gonna shine."

Before Mitchell could protest that she didn't expect to break the case, Rebecca walked in with Sloan and Jason. Immediately, everyone sobered up and hurriedly took their usual places at the conference table.

"Okay, Mitchell," Rebecca said. "Let's hear it."

"I think Jason and Sandy should go through the porn downloads and chart the dates when the girls that Sandy knows were doing the shoots."

Rebecca frowned. "That's on the agenda. We'll be doing that over the next couple of days. We've got months' worth of videos to screen."

Mitchell shook her head. "No. I think we can narrow it down to a couple of days."

Everyone's attention was riveted on her, and Mitchell felt a trickle of sweat between her shoulder blades. If she was wrong, she'd look like an idiot. Worse, she'd disappoint Rebecca Frye, which was the last thing she ever wanted to do. After Sandy, there was no one whose opinion of her mattered more. She kept her hands on her thighs under the table so that nobody could see them shaking. Out of the corner of her eye, she caught Sandy's smile. And more important than her smile was the encouragement and faith in her eyes.

"I think we should look at the videos that were shot right around the time those ships came in—the ones that Jimmy Hogan was checking out with Port Authority."

There was a moment of silence, and then everyone began to speak at once.

Chapter Twenty-Eight

Sunday, Midmorning

Wait a minute—"

"Why do you think—"

"Who would've—"

"How do—"

"All right—keep it down." Rebecca's voice rang out. As the din subsided, she motioned to Mitchell. "Go ahead. Lay it out for us, Detective."

Mitchell cleared her throat. "Okay, I need to start at the beginning—at least I think it's the beginning."

"Take your time, kid," Watts said in a surprisingly quiet tone. "We ain't in a hurry. My buns are just getting warm anyhow."

"I think it all starts with Clark," Mitchell said.

Sloan snarled an oath.

"What I mean," Mitchell clarified, "is I think it starts with Justice and Jimmy Hogan. The feds were interested enough in something going on in this city to put a federal agent undercover." She looked toward Rebecca, who gave her a barely perceptible nod. "I don't think that an Internet pornography ring or garden-variety prostitution is really big enough to register on Justice's radar. Sure, they've got people working on those kinds of investigations, but usually they leave them to the locals. And they sure don't spare undercover agents. So I'm thinking something bigger than the usual Mob activity."

"The feds have run some pretty big pornography stings," Sloan pointed out. "I hate to say it, but Clark's being here *could* have just been part of a broader interstate operation, especially considering the Internet angle. Just like he said."

"True," Rebecca interjected, "but it doesn't really explain why Jimmy Hogan was undercover. Clark was up-front with us—well, as up-front as the feds ever are—about his interest in the pornography operation. He wouldn't have needed someone undercover if he were going to investigate it through channels." Rebecca turned her attention back to Mitchell. "Keep talking—give us your theory."

"With Jimmy undercover as an *undercover* narco detective, Jimmy—and by extension Clark—had access to any files that came through the police department. He could keep an eye out for the kind of activity he was *really* interested in. At the same time, he was assigned to do exactly what he came here to do, which was infiltrate the underworld organization. He was working all the angles and probably passing everything right back to Clark."

The others at the table nodded and made sounds of agreement.

"Where does Jeff fit in?" Rebecca asked solemnly.

"I think while Jimmy was investigating his real interest, occasionally he'd come across illegal activity that he didn't have time to do anything about, so he'd tip off you and Cruz." Mitchell shrugged. "He *was* a cop, after all."

"Like the kiddie prostitution circuit he clued us into last year," Rebecca said. "Okay. So far, so good. And *then*, he got close to what he was really after, and someone found out." Her face went hard, her voice cold. "And took out him and Jeff, who probably just happened to be in the wrong place at the wrong time."

Mitchell nodded. "Yes, ma'am. That's what I think happened."

Watts shifted in his seat. "Okay. Time to end the suspense, kid. What the hell was Hogan interested in?"

"Smuggling."

Watts looked blank.

"That's usually a U.S. Customs gig," Jason observed neutrally. "Not Justice."

"I know," Mitchell said emphatically, "and that's why I didn't think of it at first. Why *none* of us thought of it."

"You think Hogan got wind of something they were bringing in on those ships—the ones he had Carla looking into, right?" Watts leaned forward, drumming his fingers on the tabletop, his eyes narrowed and intent. "That's why he was trying to track the cargo."

"Yeah, I think he was trying to get a line on who picked up the cargo *and* where it was going."

"I've been over those cargo manifests, kid," Watts said, shaking his head. "I didn't see any similarities between the stuff those ships were bringing in. Usually, if you're smuggling something, you use the same carrier vehicle each time. Bags of cocaine stuffed inside coffee barrels, diamonds packed inside fake objects of art, heroin sewn into the lining of clothes from Asia. There was nothing like that. I looked."

Mitchell shook her head. "All the ships originated from ports in the same region of the world, right?"

"Yeah, but that could just be a coincidence."

"I don't think so. They came from the same region because they were carrying the same smuggled cargo."

"*What?*" Watts asked impatiently.

"*The girls.* The ships were bringing in the girls."

There were a few seconds of silence, and then Watts muttered, "Shit."

"What's the common denominator between the sex videos, the clubs, the prostitution…all of it," Rebecca said. "The girls. None of it works without them."

"And," Sloan mused, "if those girls are your business, think how good it would be to have an inside person at the DA's office. Someone who would hear about any local investigation that started getting close. Beecher."

"Not to mention," Jason said, "using him to hack into law enforcement's entire computer network. All bases covered." He turned in his seat and looked at Sloan. "What do you want to bet that the Port Authority computer system is compromised too. This organization is sophisticated, and they're going to want to monitor everything they can. If they can find an assistant district attorney to squeeze, they can find somebody at the port."

Sloan nodded, her eyes shining. "We'll need to get at that system."

"The problem with that," Rebecca said, "is if we go for warrants now, we'll have to bring Clark into it."

"No fucking way," Watts snapped. "The last time we did that, he stole the case out from under us."

"Then let's find some other way to break this open," Rebecca said, her voice like flint. She looked at Mitchell. "How did Jimmy trip to those ships? Watts couldn't find a connection between them. Different captains, different crews, different cargos."

"The timing," Mitchell said.

"No way," Watts objected. "I looked at that with Captain Reiser. Different days of the week, different weeks of the month. There wasn't a pattern."

"But they *were* at about the same intervals, right?" Mitchell knew that everything hung on this, and sweat broke out between her shoulder blades and trickled down her back. She didn't have a damn bit of proof. Only a feeling. *I must be crazy.* She took a breath. "Every two to three months."

"Yeah," Watts said warily, as if he expected a trap. Still, he eyed her with lively curiosity. "So?"

"Those are the same intervals when the regular girls weren't available to do the sex videos. That's when Trudy and her friends filled in. *Trudy* knew those dates. The *exact* dates."

"And if we got those dates from her," Rebecca said pensively, "we'd eventually match them to those ships. That could have worried someone enough to eliminate Trudy, especially with her right in the middle of that bust last week on the film set."

It ate at Rebecca to know that the sting operation she'd set up had inadvertently led to a young woman's death. No matter that she couldn't have foreseen the risk to Trudy, who just happened to know more than anyone realized at the time. Hindsight didn't change the fact that Trudy was dead. Rebecca swallowed back the bitter bile of self-recrimination and forced herself to focus. "We need to nail down those dates."

"All we have to do is check the videos right around the times those ships arrived and see if we find Trudy or any of her friends in them," Jason said, looking at Sandy. "You'd recognize most of Trudy's crowd, right?"

Sandy nodded. "I'd for sure be able to tell the working girls from the pole dancers."

Sloan looked up from the tablet where she had been jotting notes and turned to Mitchell. "According to your theory, the girls who were smuggled into the country on those ships were the regular girls—the ones who usually performed in the sex videos, right?"

"Yes. And probably danced in the clubs, were hired out to sex parties, and eventually ended up being sold off as sex slaves." Mitchell's tone dripped with revulsion. "A sweet little pipeline in human flesh direct to the marketplace. Bastards."

"What's your explanation for why the girls weren't available around the time the ships came in to do the sex videos? Why was it then that Trudy and her friends had to fill in?"

Rebecca spoke before Mitchell could answer. "Because they were being rotated. New girls were arriving, the old ones had to be moved. Probably sent out to other cities. I bet there's a network all across the country merchandising in these girls. And the new girls would need to be broken in before they could be trusted to perform in the films."

"It hangs together," Watts said with an approving glance at Mitchell. "Nice."

"We've got to fill in all the blanks," Rebecca said. She stood abruptly and paced. "Jason, how far back do you have the video downloads?"

"I've got a couple of computers from guys who stored everything. At least a year, maybe more."

"Sandy," Rebecca said, spinning in her direction. "You work with Jason and map out the timelines. I want all the dates where it looks like local girls were filling in."

"Okay," Sandy said, with no hint of her previous distaste at the task.

"Watts, you'll need to get with Captain Reiser as soon as Sandy and Jason narrow down those dates. Try to isolate those ships. The network supplying these girls has to be relatively close-knit, so I'm betting you'll find that all of them originated in one or two ports. We'll need to nail them down." She frowned, looked around the table. "What else?"

"Presumably the girls are coming into port in containers," Sloan said. "Someone has to know which ships, which containers, and where they go on the docks. Otherwise it would be impossible to free the girls and secret them out of the port."

"Unless the container got loaded directly onto a truck and went out that way," Watts offered.

"Maybe," Sloan said. "But if they're staying local—and we are hypothesizing that they are, at least for a while—all they need is a couple of vans to move them from the port to their stash houses. That's a lot less complicated than arranging for a semi."

Watts nodded in agreement. "They've got to have an inside man at the port, maybe even a couple. Don't they track all those containers by computer or something?"

Sloan's grin spread. "They do indeed. Give me some dates, and I'll tell you which container they arrived in."

"This is all very pretty," Rebecca reminded the group. "But we don't have any proof." She looked at Mitchell. "We need the girls. In operations like these, the girls are supervised twenty-four hours a day. They don't go outside the house. They don't talk to anyone. They don't move from one location to another without guards. We need to know where they're being kept."

"I might have a way of finding out."

The room became very still.

"There's a girl…a woman…at Ziggie's. Her name is Irina." Mitchell was aware of Sandy going very still beside her. "I think she's some kind of keeper. I think she watches out for them, supervises them maybe."

"That fits," Rebecca said. "It's easier to use women to indoctrinate the girls—less threatening. These supervisors teach them how to behave. Teach them how to turn tricks. Teach them that if they try to run, they'll be caught and deported."

"And you think this Irina is gonna tell you where she lives?" Watts asked disbelievingly.

"No," Mitchell said quietly. "But I think she might take me there."

"Why?"

Mitchell was careful to keep her expression neutral and her voice bland. She was also very careful not to look at Sandy. "We've talked a few times. We sort of…hit it off."

Watts stared, his brows knit. Remarkably, he said nothing.

"The girls at Ziggie's have always been friendly with the kings," Jason said, jumping into the breach. "Since Mitch is new, it makes sense that he would get noticed."

"When are you seeing her again?" Rebecca asked calmly.

"Maybe tonight," Mitchell answered.

"That doesn't give us much time to set up." Rebecca glanced at Watts. "Two-car tail? Put a wire on Mitchell?"

Watts grunted and drummed his fingers again. "We're going to need more help. Crap. That means Clark, because the second we go to Henry with this, he's going to cover his ass and call the feds."

"I can ride backup with Rebecca and monitor the wire," Sloan said quickly.

"I'll be inside Ziggie's with Mitch," Jason said. "If he's going to leave with Irina, he can give me a sign, and I'll leave first." He looked at Watts. "I can ride with you."

"You're gonna ride backup in a dress and those come-fuck-me shoes again?"

Jason smiled, a soft, sensuous smile that flickered and was gone. "As I recall, you liked those shoes."

Watts blushed beet red and muttered under his breath, "Fuck me."

"It sounds like we can coordinate the tail *and* the bust, if we need to," Sloan asserted.

Rebecca shook her head. "Uh-uh. It's too soon. We need to tie this up a little neater before we put Mitchell inside the operation. I want as much corroboration as we can get before we go for the warrant—I want enough to make the arrests stick. That means the timeline, the ships, analyzing the computer system at Port Authority, identifying the inside people moving the containers. We need video surveillance on the docks. We need a few more days." She looked at Mitchell. "You're going to have to string her along."

Mitchell nodded. "I think it will take some doing to get her to take me home anyhow." She hesitated. "That's not the way they usually do things."

"What do you mean?" Sloan asked.

"What she *means*," Sandy said brittlely, "is they usually fuck their johns in a dark corner in the back." She angled in her seat until she could see Mitchell's face. "They don't usually take their tricks home. Not unless there's something *special* going on."

Mitchell didn't know what to say in front of everyone else. She didn't know what to say, period. There wasn't anything special going on; there wasn't anything going on at all. Except, of course, the fact that Irina expected Mitch to fuck her, and Mitchell wasn't exactly sure how to avoid that without blowing Mitch's cover. From the sound of Sandy's voice and the hot, hard fury in her eyes, Mitchell knew she was in trouble. Remembering Irina's mouth, the full, lush curves of her body, the practiced touch of her hand, she realized that so was Mitch.

Chapter Twenty-Nine

Sunday, Evening

At the sound of the front door opening, Catherine looked up from the couch where she sat reading the Sunday papers. Rebecca walked in, wearing the same clothes she'd left the house in nearly twenty-four hours before. Always pale, her skin now appeared nearly translucent, with a faint tinge of bluish gray shadowing her high cheekbones and deep-set eyes. Catherine had seen her fatigued many times before. She'd seen her fight for life in a hospital bed. She knew what her lover looked like when she was nearing the end of her reserves, but this time, in addition to weariness, there was something else in Rebecca's eyes. Some pain that Catherine was surprised Rebecca allowed to surface within sight of anyone else. She patted the sofa next to her.

"Come sit down. You look tired."

Grimacing, Rebecca shrugged out of her blazer and dropped it on a nearby chair. With one hand she released the buckle on the strap beneath her right arm that secured her holstered weapon beneath her left breast. This, too, she shed with a practiced motion and let it settle atop the rumpled jacket. With a sigh, she sank down beside Catherine, where she leaned her head back and stretched her long legs out in front of her. With one hand, she groped for Catherine's, and finding it, closed her fingers around her lover's. "Hi."

"Hello." Catherine angled her body and drew Rebecca's head down against her shoulder. "Are you in for the night?"

"I wish," Rebecca mumbled, closing her eyes.

Catherine stroked Rebecca's hair, then the back of her neck, eliciting a soft groan. These were the moments that were hardest for her, when what she wanted most was to hold Rebecca for hours, keeping her close, restoring them both as only this quiet connection could. Instead, she needed to prepare herself for Rebecca leaving once again on the most dangerous kind of assignment she could undertake. Undercover operations, as Catherine had come to learn, were notoriously unpredictable. The last one had ended with Dellon nearly bleeding to death from a stab wound. And now another night loomed when she would not know where her lover was, what danger she might be in, or what harm might already have befallen her. The ringing of the phone in the middle of those dark, lonely nights was like a death knell. She tightened her hold on Rebecca and rested her cheek against the top of the blond head.

"What's wrong?" Rebecca murmured.

For an instant, Catherine hesitated, then realized that she could not expect Rebecca to share her uncertainties if she herself did not. "Missing you, a little bit."

"I'm sorry," Rebecca said immediately, starting to straighten.

"No." Catherine held her fast. "I don't want you to be sorry. It's not something for you to fix, darling. It's just the way I feel." She looked down to see Rebecca searching her face with worried eyes. She slanted her mouth across Rebecca's, kissing her hard. She felt the instant when Rebecca's tired body came to life, the faint tightening of her limbs, the sudden quivering of the muscles beneath her hands. Easing away from the kiss, she laughed softly. "That wasn't *exactly* what I meant I was missing, but that's part of it."

"I've got six or seven hours, at least," Rebecca responded, her voice already rough with desire.

"When you should be sleeping."

"It's not sleep I need. It's just you. Just you."

Catherine's lips parted in soft surprise as her heart melted. "Why, when I *know* that you love me, does hearing you say it always make me weak with wanting?"

Rebecca grinned, her eyes alive again. "I pick my moments."

"Your timing always *has* been excellent," Catherine murmured. There were things she wanted to say, things she wanted to ask, but those things could wait until they both took what they needed from one another. She smoothed her hand down the front of Rebecca's shirt until she reached the slender belt that encircled her waist. As she found Rebecca's mouth again, she slipped the thin leather through the small silver buckle and then moved on to the clasp and zipper beneath. As she licked her way into Rebecca's mouth, her hand followed a similar path into the secret pleasures between Rebecca's thighs. Rebecca moaned and sucked on her tongue, the unexpected sensation igniting the inferno that lay in wait deep inside. Waiting only for this one woman's touch.

"Oh God," Catherine breathed, breaking the kiss. "Here. Right here. Right now. Take your clothes off, darling."

Rebecca leapt to her feet, already pulling loose the buttons on her shirt as Catherine wrenched off her own top, exposing her bare breasts. Trousers followed shirt, underwear fell into the heap, and in another second, Rebecca lay between Catherine's legs. She brought her mouth down hard on Catherine's, sliding inside, slicking her way through the heat, probing deeply before she pushed herself up on her arms and stared desperately into Catherine's eyes. "Don't tell me you want to go slow. Please."

Catherine braced both hands on Rebecca's shoulders and pushed downward. "No. No. Hurry."

Then Rebecca was between her thighs and Catherine arched as hot mouth met hot flesh and she felt herself drawn into the cauldron of Rebecca's desire. Blindly, she sought an anchor, finding Rebecca's shoulder and digging her fingers into muscles tight as steel when teeth closed around the stiff, aching prominence of her clitoris. Her eyes went blind and her throat closed on a scream as passion erupted deep inside. She fought against the first wave of orgasm, wanting the urgency to build, delirious with the exquisite pleasure. When Rebecca's tongue swept the length of her, then beat against her clitoris with a steady insistent rhythm, she lost the battle. Her breasts swelled, her belly spasmed, and sweet release eclipsed will. She found the back of Rebecca's head with one hand and held Rebecca's mouth against her as the climax poured forth.

"Don't make yourself come," Catherine gasped, still coming herself. "I want you in my mouth."

Rebecca shuddered, desperate to come, but loath to separate from Catherine's still-pulsing sex. She held off another few seconds until need overpowered all else, and then she reared up to straddle Catherine's body. She gave a hoarse cry as Catherine's hands clenched on her buttocks and Catherine's mouth drove against her clitoris. Too close to orgasm to control her muscles, she fell forward and barely managed to brace herself with one arm against the sofa. Still, Catherine's mouth never left her, sucking and tugging on her, driving her mad.

"Oh Jesus, you're going to make me come," Rebecca groaned. Nearly deaf with the roar of blood in her head, she barely registered Catherine's exultant cries. She was coming, bucking and thrusting and shouting out her infinite gratitude. Then she was falling, helpless and weak, and Catherine was there to catch her.

"I love you, oh, I love you," Catherine murmured over and over, curled around Rebecca's trembling form. "You're in my blood, right down to the heart of me."

"Love you too," Rebecca muttered, struggling for breath.

Catherine laughed softly, searching on the back of the sofa for the light throw she kept there for when the evenings turned cool. She pulled it down over them and settled more comfortably on her back with Rebecca's head nestled against her shoulder. It wasn't their usual position, and she liked being the one to offer shelter. "Okay?"

"Oh yeah," Rebecca sighed. "Definitely okay."

After waiting another few moments for Rebecca's heartbeat to slowly settle, Catherine asked quietly, "Why do you have to go out later?"

"Mitchell's going back to Ziggie's. Watts and I will back up again."

Remembering the haunted look in Rebecca's eyes when she'd first returned home, Catherine knew there was more. "You've learned something."

Rebecca shifted slightly and opened her eyes to stare up at the ceiling. "Mitchell did, really. She thinks, and I agree with her, that most of the girls involved in the sex videos—and probably working a fair number of the strip clubs in the city—have been smuggled in on ships from Russia."

"Oh my God." Catherine turned on her side so that she was facing Rebecca, wanting to see her face. "Is that what this is all about?"

Rebecca nodded and gave her a quick summary of Mitchell's theories. As Rebecca spoke, Catherine listened and watched. She saw the faint flicker of Rebecca's pupils when she talked about Trudy, heard the barest deepening of her voice that only hinted at the depth of her pain. *Oh, you are so very good at hiding your sorrow.*

She waited until Rebecca fell silent, until the story had been told. Then she pressed her fingertips to Rebecca's mouth, brushing over her lips, cupping her jaw. "I'm so very sorry about Trudy, darling."

"Out of all of that," Rebecca said quietly, "that's the thing you found to talk about."

Catherine smiled gently. "That's the thing that hurts you most."

Rebecca rested her forehead against Catherine's and closed her eyes. "If she hadn't taken Sandy to that meeting, if she hadn't gone to that building to shoot that film, if she hadn't been unknowingly part of *my* operation, she'd still be alive."

"I'm not telling you not to care, darling. I'm not even telling you not to accept responsibility, although I don't believe it's all yours to bear." Catherine stroked down Rebecca's arm and clasped her fingers. "But you made the best decision you could with what you knew at the time, and you never would've put Sandy *or* Trudy in lethal danger if you'd thought that was likely. You cannot carry all the burden, Rebecca, or it will destroy you."

Rebecca's eyes flickered opened. "And us?"

"No," Catherine answered immediately. "I will fight you on this before I will let that happen. I will stand in front of that door over there and prevent you from going out if I have to. I will *not* let this job take you from me."

"You sound pretty set on that."

"I am." Catherine leaned forward and kissed Rebecca lightly. "Still ready to move in?"

"Oh yeah." Rebecca curved an arm around Catherine's back and pulled her tight against the length of her body. She kissed her, hard and deep. "Consider me moved in."

Catherine laughed shakily. "I'd forgotten how quickly cops make decisions."

"You'll get used to it."

"I don't think there's anything about loving you that I'll ever get used to," Catherine whispered, pillowing her cheek against Rebecca's chest. "And that's just fine."

"I don't expect anything to happen tonight. You don't have to worry."

Catherine saw no need to tell her that whenever she worked, Catherine would worry. It was part of their life now, and it could not be changed. "Do you really think these girls were ferried across the ocean in huge metal containers?"

"I do. It all fits." Rebecca's voice had taken on a grim tone.

"And this kind of thing is really happening on a large scale?" Catherine could only imagine the horror of girls being crowded together in a dark, poorly ventilated twenty-by-thirty-foot space for days, even weeks. How much these young women must long for their dream of America to endure such torture, only to find another kind of hell at the end of their nightmare journey. "God, it's inhuman."

"We're just beginning to get an idea of exactly how big this business is. The recent reports I've read say there are dozens of active stash houses in all of the major metropolitan cities—way stations where these underage girls and young women from dozens of countries are held captive and eventually trafficked."

"They're just—merchandise."

Rebecca nodded. "In the worst-case scenario, they may be rented out for sex for as little as fifteen minutes at a time, dozens of times a day. It doesn't take much to figure out that each girl could bring in thousands every week. Christ, the CIA estimates that every year there are twenty thousand new sex slaves imported into this country alone."

Catherine had seen and heard the worst of human behavior in her line of work, but this blatant trade in human misery was almost too horrific for her to absorb. The words were out before she even realized what they meant. "You have to stop them."

"I will."

"Rebecca," Catherine sighed softly, her cheek to Rebecca's heart. "Loving you is the hardest thing I've ever done."

Rebecca's swift intake of breath cut through the silence in the room.

"I don't want you in danger," Catherine went on, lifting her head and holding Rebecca's gaze. "I don't want to lose you, not even the tiniest part of you, to this work—this crusade—that you've undertaken. I couldn't bear for you to die doing this."

"Catherine," Rebecca protested.

"No, listen," Catherine said softly. "And as much as I fear those things happening, I *want* you to end this horror. I trust you to do it. I'm proud beyond description that you can." She laughed unsteadily. "And *that*, my darling, is one hell of a conundrum."

"Is there something I should do to make it better?" Rebecca asked seriously.

"Oh yes."

"What?" Rebecca carried Catherine's hand to her lips and kissed her palm. "What?"

"Promise me to always come home."

Rebecca never hesitated. "I promise."

Catherine closed her eyes and settled her head back against Rebecca's breast, as comforted as it was possible for her to be. Because Rebecca Frye always kept her promises.

Mitchell found Sandy in the conference room viewing video clips with Jason. They each had a lined yellow notepad covered with dates and diagrams in front of them. "Hey, how's it going?"

"Slow," Jason admitted, rubbing his eyes. "But we've got two for sure from almost a year ago."

Sandy did not look away from the monitor, and Mitchell followed her gaze. The sound was off, making the image of a naked young woman rocking furiously astride the hips of a much older man, who lay on his back, seem nearly surreal.

"Can I talk to you for a minute, San?" Mitchell asked quietly.

"Kinda busy right now."

Jason stood. "I could use a break. Let's call it a night. I need to go home and catch a few hours' sleep before we go out again." He glanced toward Mitchell. "I'll pick you up again, say midnight?"

Silently, Mitchell nodded, her eyes still on Sandy's glacial countenance. She waited until Jason was gone, then rested her hand on Sandy's shoulder. "Honey."

Sandy swiveled on her chair and looked up, her face closed, her eyes shielded. "Did you kiss her?"

Fuck. Mitchell took a breath. "Is there a difference between me kissing her and her kissing me?"

"Not even a little."

"Is there any room to talk about the job, and how I needed to convince her I was for real?"

Sandy folded her arms beneath her breasts, her jaws clenched tight. Mitchell's stomach tied itself into a knot. What she hated more than the anger in Sandy's eyes was the glimmer of hurt she couldn't hide. That was far, far worse.

"It didn't mean anything," Mitchell whispered. "It was a couple of kisses. That's all."

"Did she touch you?"

"Sandy, come on," Mitchell pleaded.

"*Did* she?"

"Not in any way that mattered." Mitchell's voice was steady, solid. "Nobody does except you."

Mitchell waited for the eruption, expecting to be scalded, *willing* to be, if it would put them right. What she didn't expect were the tears, and the sight literally brought her to her knees. "Oh fuck." Kneeling in front of the chair, she put her arms around Sandy and pulled her against her chest. She stroked her back, kissed her forehead, brushed at the tears on her damp cheeks. "Honey, come on. Honey, don't cry. You're killing me."

Sandy twisted the back of Mitchell's T-shirt in her hands, pressing her face hard to Mitchell's shoulder, struggling to stop the wash of emotion pouring through her. "You're mine," she whispered in a voice so quiet Mitchell struggled to hear. "You're the only thing I've ever had that was mine."

"Oh jeez," Mitchell choked, lifting Sandy's face, swiping her thumbs across Sandy's cheeks. She kissed her mouth, her eyes, her cheeks. "I've never wanted to belong to anybody the way I belong to you. I *am* yours."

Sandy was quiet for a long moment, her bruised blue eyes boring into Mitchell's. Mitchell looked back, letting her search, hiding nothing.

"Yeah?" Sandy asked tremulously.

"Yeah."

"I know about sex for money, Dell. I know about sex to stay alive. I know about feeling nothing when somebody touches you."

"That's never gonna happen to you again," Mitchell said fiercely.

Sandy smiled and touched Mitchell's cheek. "And I know *you*, Dell. You don't turn off so easy."

"It's just a job, honey. I'm just doing what I need to do for the job. It's an act."

"Mitch is no act."

Mitchell couldn't argue. It was true. "Mitch knows the difference between sex and love. So do I."

"I don't want you getting hurt. I don't give a *fuck* about Frye's operation, but I don't want your cover getting blown and you getting hurt again."

"Sandy, I'm not gonna get—"

"So you can fuck her if you have to," Sandy said quietly. "I don't even care if she gets off on it."

"Oh jeez, honey—"

"But if she makes you come, I'll kill her."

Mitchell couldn't be entirely certain, but she thought Sandy just might be serious. "That won't happen. I swear."

Sandy brushed her palm back and forth across Mitchell's chest. "You're so sexy, Dell. I love how hot you are. I love how sexy you make me feel." She caught Mitchell's bottom lip in her teeth and tugged, then licked her way inside Mitchell's mouth and kissed her until Mitchell couldn't breathe. "I can't help it if I want you all to myself."

"You got me, honey," Mitchell gasped, too stunned by the onslaught of sensation to make much sense of anything. Whenever she expected one thing from Sandy, she got just the opposite, and she couldn't keep up. That was one of the things that she loved most about her. That, and her raw honesty. "I love you so much…it's like this constant hunger needing to be fed."

"Well, you don't have to worry, rookie." Sandy moved her hand from the center of Mitchell's chest to her breast and teased her nipple into erection. "I don't intend to ever let you go hungry."

Mitchell knew if they stayed there much longer she'd be too turned on to walk. She was already so swollen and hard she ached. "We gotta get out of here. You're making me crazy."

"I know just what you need, baby." Sandy smiled a slow, satisfied smile and dropped her hand between Mitchell's thighs, squeezing gently until Mitchell's eyes blurred and she moaned quietly. "Let's go home and I'll show you."

Chapter Thirty

Sunday, 11:00 p.m.

Michael stood in the doorway of the spare bedroom and watched Sloan remove a small walnut chest from the top shelf of the closet. The expression on her lover's face as she keyed the lock was one that Michael did not think she had ever seen before. Fierce concentration, which was not at all unusual, was underlain with what appeared to be grim determination. That hardness in Sloan's rigid profile produced a sinking feeling in the pit of her stomach. Sloan looked dangerous, and cold.

Remaining silent, she saw Sloan remove first a soft, brown leather holster and then an enormous automatic handgun. At least to Michael the gun appeared enormous, because of what it signified.

"Sloan?" Michael asked quietly.

Turning, the weapon in her hand, Sloan met Michael's inquiring gaze. "It's okay."

"I don't see how it *can* be, if you're doing something that requires that."

"It's just a precaution. I'm going to ride backup with Rebecca later tonight, and I ought to be armed. I won't be much use to her in an emergency if I'm not." Sloan smiled and clipped the holster to the back of her belt, then slipped the automatic into it and out of sight. "I'm licensed to carry it." She slipped a slim leather folder from her rear pocket and flipped it open to display the laminated photo ID badge that Clark had provided her when she'd first agreed to investigate the Internet pornography ring. "And I've got my federal credentials to prove it. Just procedure. Nothing to worry about."

The logic was faultless, as Sloan's logic always was, but Michael knew that beneath that unassailable rationality seethed a host of volatile emotions that had yet to be assuaged. She could feel the cold hand of

Sloan's icy fury from across the room. "If he *is* there somewhere, you have to promise me you won't do anything. Nothing at all."

There was no need to define who *he* was, because they both knew. Sloan had related some of the smuggling story to Michael, and it seemed only reasonable to her that the man who had nearly killed her in the misdirected murder attempt on Sloan might be one of the bodyguards who ferried the young smuggling victims from destination to destination. And if that were the case, Sloan was likely to come across him in the course of the surveillance or subsequent arrests.

Michael did not want her lover anywhere near that man when she was carrying a gun.

"Not a problem," Sloan assured smoothly. But the hard edge in her eyes remained.

Shaking her head, Michael crossed the room and settled her arms around Sloan's neck. She was close enough to kiss her, but she did not. Instead, she studied the depths of Sloan's violet eyes, assessing their ever-changing emotional landscape. "Even if you were able to get away with taking revenge on whoever's responsible for putting me in the hospital, you're not that kind of person at heart. It would take something from you. Destroy something in you." As Sloan began to protest, Michael shook her head again. "I need all of you. I *need* you."

Sloan made a strangled sound in her throat and buried her face in Michael's hair, holding her close, swaying as she stood with Michael in her arms. "If you knew how it felt when I thought I'd lost you…oh Jesus…"

"You didn't and you *won't*." Michael thrust her hands into Sloan's hair and tilted her head back, forcing Sloan to accept the truth in her eyes. "I love you and I will not leave you. You have to promise me the same. You have to take care of yourself." She touched her fingertips to a spot above Sloan's breast, over her heart. "*Here.* Here where I need you so."

"I promise," Sloan said, her voice hoarse. "I promised you before, and I'll keep my promise. I won't do anything to hurt you."

"Be sure that you don't let anyone else hurt you either," Michael whispered, her fingers still buried in Sloan's hair. She brought her mouth down on her lover's, tasting her, taking her time and kissing her thoroughly until she was sure that she was all Sloan could feel. Then, reluctantly, she relinquished Sloan's mouth. "I love you."

Sloan closed her eyes and rested her cheek against Michael's. The anger had dulled, muted by the much more powerful force of what they shared. "Don't worry. I won't let anything touch what we have."

"Nothing ever could, darling," Michael murmured, and kissed her again. "Take good care of yourself tonight. I'll see you when you come home."

❖

Sandy answered the knock at the door and opened it wide to admit Rebecca.

"Hiya, Sandy," Rebecca said, casting a quick glance around the small studio apartment. It was as neat as she remembered it from the one time she had been there before. The small sofa bed, closed and covered with colorful throw pillows, the slightly scratched coffee table in front of it, and the sparkling clean kitchenette off to one side.

"Hi," Sandy replied with no hint of warmth.

"Mitchell ready?"

Sandy crossed her arms over her chest and tilted her head toward the bathroom. "Just about."

Rebecca walked to the coffee table and deposited the small canvas gym bag she carried in one hand. Squatting, she unzipped it and removed the contents, lining up the equipment she would need in a neat row. She looked up to the sound of the bathroom door opening. Mitchell—Mitch—approached in tight, faded blue jeans and a torso-hugging black T-shirt. His chest was flat, his face long and square jawed, his crotch obviously but not ostentatiously full. Had she not known differently, Rebecca would've thought him to be a young man of twenty. "The transmitter's about the size of a deck of playing cards, a little bit thinner. Do you have room for it anywhere?"

"Where's the best spot?" Mitch inquired, sliding his hands into his front pockets.

"Most guys will wear it down the back of their pants, maybe on their back, or occasionally in their crotch."

Mitch's lips twitched, and he unconsciously brushed the bulge beneath his fly. "No room there."

"I gathered," Rebecca said dryly. She stood, the transmitter in her right hand with the attached wires dangling. "Where's Irina least likely to touch you?"

"Uh…" Mitch sidled a glance at Sandy, who remained motionless, her face set and her eyes firmly on his face. "Probably my back."

Sandy snorted. Rebecca seemed not to notice.

"Okay, then, pull your shirt out and turn around," Rebecca instructed. When Mitch hiked up his T-shirt, Rebecca saw the thin wrap encircling his torso. "I think if I tape it under the lower edge of the chest wrap, that'll camouflage the shape enough to hide it, especially with the T-shirt over it."

"Okay," Mitch said, holding still as Rebecca worked. "What'll I do if she wants to take me back to her place tonight?"

"Stall her."

"What if I can't?"

"You'll have to figure out a way. We're not prepared for a takedown tonight, and I don't want you getting into a situation where I can't extract you quickly."

"Yeah, but…"

"If she keeps after you," Sandy said quietly, "make her come right there in the bar, but don't fuck her. Tell her you're saving that for special."

Mitch blushed, and sweat broke out over his entire body.

"Jesus," Rebecca complained. "I can't get the tape to stick to you like this." She turned to Sandy. "Can you get me a towel?"

"Sure."

"She's going to kill me before this is over," Mitch said when Sandy disappeared into the bathroom.

"She'll be okay," Rebecca replied. "Just remember who you are and why you're there. Do what you need to do, and then you leave it there."

Sandy held out the towel, giving no indication that she'd heard Rebecca's words, but her angry expression had softened. "It would be kinda nice if you all made sure that Mitch's ass doesn't get hung out to dry."

"Sandy—" Mitch started to protest.

"He'll be fine. We'll be monitoring everything that happens from now on." Rebecca pressed the last strip of adhesive into place and rearranged the chest wrap over it, smoothing out the wrinkles with her hand. "Tuck your shirt in." She waited until Mitch complied and then walked around him, eyeing his back critically. "In dim lighting, that's not going to show. Just make sure she doesn't get her hands back there."

"That's not where she's going to be putting her hands," Sandy commented.

Mitch groaned softly and gave Sandy a beseeching look.

A flicker of amusement passed over Rebecca's face as she clapped Mitch on the shoulder. "Sloan's downstairs in the car. I'm going down to test the audio feed with her. It's a one-way transmission, so you're not going to know that we're on the line. But we'll be there."

"Yes, ma'am," Mitch said with absolute certainty. "By the way, I'm wearing an ankle holster."

Rebecca nodded as she repacked the duffel bag. "Good. That's something a guy like Mitch might do, so if anyone notices it at all, just say you've had some trouble and want to be prepared."

At the door, she added, "If I don't call up, it means we're reading you with no problem. Remember, all we want tonight is for you to reestablish contact with Irina and convince her that you want to spend time alone with her where she lives. Following her to the stash house won't be enough—we need you inside to give us some idea of the occupancy, the layout, and the number and position of the guards. We definitely don't need a hostage situation when we get ready to take the place, so we're going to want to go for the guards first." She fixed Mitch with a firm stare. "Your job is intelligence. You're our eyes, okay?"

"Yes, ma'am."

Mitch had the sense that someone was watching him. He set his bottle on the bar top and eased off the stool. Taking his time, he made his way to the back hallway that led to the restrooms and whatever else lay hidden in the bowels of the building. She was there, in the shadows.

"Hi," Mitch said, leaning a shoulder against the wall. At the far end of the corridor he could see a flickering neon sign that said Exit. He knew there were other rooms opening onto the hallway, but for the moment, they seemed to be alone.

"Hello, new boy," Irina purred, placing her palm in the center of his chest as she leaned close to kiss him lightly on the mouth. "Back again."

Mitch slipped one arm around her waist and drew her against him. Tonight she wore some kind of dark red satiny slacks that hugged her voluptuous figure and a blouse that was more of a hint than a reality. It was so sheer he could see the lace of the flimsy cups that barely contained her breasts and the dark hue of nipple beneath. As she moved into him, she parted her thighs and settled into his crotch with his denim-encased cock neatly nestled between her legs. This time, he was prepared for the sudden surge of pressure, and when he bumped his pelvis into her, it was Irina who gasped. "I told you I would be here. I was afraid *you* weren't."

She stroked a fingertip along his jaw. "I am always here."

For a second, Mitch considered questioning her, trying to get some information about the girls, but then he realized she would be on the lookout for that kind of questioning, no matter how subtle. He couldn't afford to make her suspicious of him now. Instead, he nuzzled her neck and brushed his mouth over her ear. "You must go home sometime."

Laughing, she tilted her head back and allowed him her neck. "Not until all the little boys have gone home happy."

While he sucked the pale flesh of her throat, Mitch dropped his hand from her waist to her buttocks and kneaded the firm flesh. He circled his crotch against hers and moved his mouth back to her ear. "What about the big boys?"

"You are very…smooth, new boy." She was breathing a little faster as she kissed him again, teasing her tongue along the inner surface of his lips, darting into his mouth and out again. Just as she drew away she nipped at his lower lip. "Mitch. You taste good, Mitch."

"You *feel* good." As they spoke, Mitch was aware of the transmitter on his back and tried not to think about his lieutenant and Sloan listening to this conversation. He had a fleeting instant of gratitude that it wasn't Watts monitoring the wire. "I want to make you feel a whole lot better."

"I don't know why," Irina mused as she edged a hand between them and cupped the swelling tucked in Mitch's jeans. "But I believe you."

"Maybe," Mitch said, ignoring the practiced stimulation that she so effortlessly delivered, "because the other guys are just thinking about getting off." He lightly teased an erect nipple through the flimsy layers of material, flicking it with a fingertip as he kept his eyes on her face. When he saw her lids flutter, he caught the hard peak in his fingers and squeezed. She moaned, and he squeezed again. "But remember what I said last night. I want to make *you* come."

"Do the other one," she whispered, her voice tight and urgent. Her eyes were nearly closed, her hips rolling rhythmically against him. When he started on her other nipple, working them both to the same rhythm, she forced her lids open and gazed at him through a haze of pleasure. "Did you make yourself come last night, thinking of me?"

Despite the icy control he kept over his own physical responses, he tightened deep inside at the words. Beneath the cock, his hard sex ached. Hoarsely, he said, "Oh yeah. All night long."

"I imagined you fucking me, new boy." Irina smiled, her lips swollen and moist. "Until I came, screaming."

Mitch kissed her, one hand on her ass, the other tangled in her hair. He held her head while he plundered her mouth, until she was shaking in his arms and he knew she was his for the taking. He pulled his head away, breathing hard. "I want to fuck you 'til you scream. But not here. Take me home."

She shook her head.

He spun her to the wall and pinned both of her arms against it with his hands around her wrists. He pushed his cock hard between her thighs, his lean hips between her spread legs, and he pumped into her while he took her mouth again. He worked his cock against her until she whimpered and writhed beneath him, then he pulled back, his own chest heaving. "Take me home so I can give you what you want. What *I* want."

"I…" Her eyes were glazed, her mouth bruised, her breasts swollen—hard nipples exposed beneath the see-through material. "I…" She took a long shuddering breath and her eyes finally focused. "There are others there. I cannot."

"Then I'll take you somewhere else. A hotel."

"No. I must stay there. I…cannot leave."

He jerked one of her hands down the wall and thrust it between his legs, squeezing her fingers around his cock. "Feel me. You know you want this." He dropped his forehead to hers, shivering as she automatically started to jack him off. "Please, Irina. Please. Please."

"After," she whispered urgently. "You come after they are asleep."

"When? Where?" Mitch knew he sounded desperate, because he was. He had to get her hands off him, because there was only so much stimulation he could take.

"I will tell you when." Then she pushed him abruptly away. "You just be here, new boy."

Mitch sagged against the wall and watched her disappear into the darkness at the end of the hall. Tilting his head back, he closed his eyes and worked on quieting the storm she had stirred. When he thought he could walk without stumbling, he returned to the bar and signaled to Jasmine that he was leaving.

Five minutes later, Jasmine met him at the car, and they drove six blocks in silence before pulling to the curb. A dark Ford Escort pulled in behind them, and Rebecca walked up to the driver's side. She peered through the open window at Jasmine and Mitch.

"Everything okay?" Rebecca asked, her gaze fixed on Mitch.

Mitch nodded wordlessly.

"All right. Good job." To Jasmine, Rebecca said, "Take him home."

Mitch let himself into the apartment, made his way carefully in the dark to the bathroom, and closed the door behind him before turning on the light. He stripped and tossed his clothes into a pile, then removed the chest wrap and his drag gear, laying everything on top of the toilet tank. With one arm, he reached awkwardly behind his back and jerked the tape from his skin, mindless of the quick rush of pain.

Then Mitchell stepped into the shower and turned both dials on full. The first blast to hit her was icy cold, but she never flinched. Eyes closed, she washed the smell of smoke and beer and dark secrets from her skin. Eventually she felt clean, at least on the outside. She toweled off, brushed her teeth, and turned out the light before opening the door. Moving by memory, she made her way to the sofa bed, carefully lifted the sheet, and slid in. Then she lay on her back, her eyes on the ceiling, wide awake. She could feel the heat of Sandy's body only inches away, but she did not touch her. She lay there, remembering the stroke of Irina's tongue inside her mouth, the crush of Irina's breasts against her chest, the tease of Irina's sure hand between her thighs, making her swell and ache and long for more. She thought of the lies and wondered what part was real and what had only been an act. Her mind and body were alive with confusion and, worse, simmering desire, but she dared not touch Sandy. Not now. It would be wrong.

She didn't notice the tears until Sandy's fingertips brushed over her cheeks.

"C'mere, baby," Sandy said softly as she drew Mitchell's head down to her breast.

"Sandy, honey, I…" Mitchell had no idea what she should say. "Tonight—"

"Shh. It's okay." Sandy kissed her forehead. "I don't need to know what you did. You're here. That's what matters."

Mitchell turned on her side and wrapped her arms around Sandy, drawing up one thigh onto Sandy's, trying to get as close as she could. She closed her eyes and held on tightly. "I love you."

"I know, baby. I know."

CHAPTER THIRTY-ONE

Monday, 7:20 a.m., Sloan Security Offices

Rebecca handed Mitchell a cup of coffee. "You did good work last night, Detective."

They were alone in the conference room, waiting for Jason and Sloan to gather the preliminary data from Sandy's review of the videotapes. Mitchell rested her hips against the counter and stared into her coffee.

"Thank you, Lieutenant."

"Undercover work is one of the most difficult things a police officer can do," Rebecca said conversationally as she leaned next to Mitchell. She sipped her coffee and gazed through the windows opposite them at the crisp blue sky. "A good undercover officer is an invaluable asset to a team like this."

"I'll do my best."

"Never doubted it." Rebecca angled her body and studied Mitchell's face. "Mitch is unique. He gets us in places that no one else could. I also appreciate that his assignments, especially this one, put added pressure on you."

"It's all so new," Mitchell admitted quietly. "Mitch, the work, how it all fits together. Me and Sandy."

Rebecca nodded. "It's a lot to handle, and you're doing just fine. I wouldn't put you out there if I didn't trust you to deal with whatever comes up. No arrest is worth one of my people."

"I just don't want to let you down."

"You won't. Not if you keep your head on straight." Rebecca took a sip of coffee. "How's Sandy doing?"

Mitchell colored. "She's good. Okay." She turned the coffee cup in her hands and finally tasted the contents. It was hot, and that was about all she could tell. "I think she understands what I'm doing. On the job, I mean."

"Then you're luckier than you know."

"No," Mitchell said softly. "I know how lucky I am."

"You have a problem—on the job, at home—you come to me. We'll work it out."

"Yes, ma'am. Thank you, Lieutenant."

Rebecca straightened as Sloan and Jason came in. "Okay. Let's get to work." She took her seat and the others followed suit. "Tell me you have something for me."

Jason passed copies of a printout to both Rebecca and Mitchell. "Not everything, not yet. But we've got a start."

Rebecca perused the list of dates, mentally counting off the intervals between them. "It's a loose pattern, but it's a pattern." She looked from Jason to Sloan. "Can we get the rest of this today?"

"Sandy's on her way," Jason affirmed. "I think we'll have the rest of the dates for you in a couple of hours."

"I want to get a look at the central computers at Port Authority," Sloan said.

"I'll make some calls," Rebecca replied. "The captain down there is a good officer. I think she'll be willing to let us work outside channels a little bit. Watts is meeting with her this morning, so the two of you can coordinate at that end."

Sloan nodded.

"When are we going to bring Captain Henry in on this?" Mitchell inquired.

Rebecca shrugged. "When I can bring him a solid package of evidence and enough of a plan to convince him that we don't need the feds to run this operation."

"Fucking-A," Sloan muttered.

"At some point," Rebecca advised, her eyes on Sloan, "Clark is going to get involved. The international human smuggling, trafficking these girls across state lines, the Internet angle—it's all federal. But before they grab up the perps like they did last time, I want the guy who did Hogan and Cruz. And I know he's part of this."

"Got to be," Mitchell said. "He's probably the enforcer for this arm of the organized crime network. I'm willing to bet he oversees the transfer of the girls from the port to the stash houses and probably runs all the guys who guard them too. That means he's got rank in the organization."

"I agree." Rebecca appeared pleased with Mitchell's assessment. "Which means he's just the kind of guy that Clark is going to want to try to turn—someone high enough up in the organization to name names. And I want him first for the murder of two cops, a bent ADA, and an innocent young girl."

"Then let's move fast," Sloan said, eyes gleaming. "I need to stop by Police Plaza to see how my new guys are doing with the work on retooling the computer system. Then I'll head down to Port Authority."

"I expect that Irina will move on Mitch tonight," Rebecca said. "We've got fifteen hours to put this together."

Sloan grinned. "Plenty of time."

Monday, 8:45 a.m., Port of Philadelphia

Captain Carla Reiser passed Watts a pastry on a paper plate as she sat down next to him on the worn plaid sofa in one corner of her office. She gestured with her coffee cup to the stack of printouts in front of him. "These are the most likely ships to fit the profile and dates you've given me so far."

Watts rifled through the stack, softly humming a refrain that approximated "We're in the money." "Can we get duty rosters for the shifts when these ships came into port and also for the time they were being off-loaded?"

"I've already got the computers working on that."

"That so?" Watts gave her an appreciative glance as he took a huge bite from the cheese Danish. He chewed, swallowed, and shook his head approvingly. "It's nice you're not busting my balls over sharing this info."

Carla took a healthy bite of her own Danish and regarded him thoughtfully. "Why should I?"

Watts lifted one beefy shoulder. "Interagency cooperation is more of a pipe dream than a reality."

"This is a big port, Detective. Tons of merchandise move through here annually. I could tell you that no one could keep track of it all, and that would be the truth." She lifted the stack of papers and let it fall to the table in front of them with a thump. "If there's evidence in here that large-scale—no, scratch that—if *any* kind of smuggling is going on at this port under my watch, I want to know about it. And if it *is,* it's not happening without inside help." Her chocolate eyes grew even darker with fury. "I want to see the son of a bitch who's been using my turf like his own personal playground strung up by *his* balls."

"Now that's my kind of police," Watts said with a happy smile.

"The shift lists will need to be cross-referenced, drivers checked, a lot of background info run—Lieutenant Frye says she's sending over a computer expert to sort through it and nail down how the transfers are being made."

"That would be Sloan," Watts said. "If anyone can put it together, she can. She'll need a secure place to work because we don't want to tip our hand."

"She can use my office." Carla stood. "Let me take a quick tour around the docks before she arrives. Assuming we get a chance for lunch, I'm buying."

"Nah, let me get it." Watts cleared his throat. "I, uh…like working with you."

"Good. Same here." As she reached the door, she looked back. "But lunch is off the clock. And on me this time."

Watts stared after her, grinning, and was still grinning when Sloan walked in a few minutes later.

"Please tell me what there is to be happy about," Sloan said by way of greeting.

"I finally ran into a woman on this job who likes guys with *real* dicks."

"Yeah?" Sloan's attention was already riveted on the computer on Reiser's desk, and she headed for it. As she settled into the captain's swivel chair, she muttered offhandedly, "Rumor has it there's one or two of them still left around."

Watts picked up the shipping manifests and schedules, his smile still in place. "It only takes one."

Thinking of Michael, Sloan nodded, her fingers already racing over the keyboard. "As long as it's the right one."

Monday, 1:00 p.m., Sloan Security Offices

Mitchell rested her hands lightly on Sandy's shoulders and bent down to kiss her cheek. "How's it going?"

Sandy tilted her head back and sighed. "We're almost done."

"We picked up the first one that Trudy did," Jason informed her. "You should take a look at the one right before it."

"Why?"

Wordlessly, Jason scanned the disk and, finding the file he wanted, played the image. Mitchell hunkered down next to Sandy, resting her hand on her girlfriend's knee as she stared at the monitor. The setting was generic—a nondescript bedroom, very little in the way of decoration, harsh studio lighting. Two naked women and a man lay tangled together on rumpled sheets. As she watched, Mitchell saw the two women get to their knees and then straddle the man. While facing each other, one lowered herself onto his erect penis and the other settled over his face. Then, they leaned toward one another and kissed. The woman who rocked rhythmically above his mouth was Irina.

"Fuck," Mitchell said.

"Looks like she came up through the ranks," Jason remarked. "Probably supervising the girls looks like a lot better job to her than this did."

"Is that her?" Sandy asked quietly. She looked at Mitchell. "The one you're hooked up with?"

Mitchell didn't see any point in correcting her terminology. "Yeah. That's her."

Sandy narrowed her eyes and studied the images. "Nice body."

"Turn it off, Jason, will you," Mitchell said curtly. She took a breath, struggling to clear her head, but the anger kept pushing back. "Can we use this somehow?"

"I don't know," Jason said. "Maybe. It's more circumstantial evidence to tie the girls at Ziggie's to the porn ring. By itself, it probably doesn't mean much. But it's one more piece of the puzzle."

"Yeah." Mitchell stood and tried to shake the tension from her shoulders. "What about the ones Trudy and her friends did? Do they fall out at the times Hogan was investigating those ships?"

"Yep. Right on target."

"You think this will be enough for the lieutenant to go to Captain Henry?"

"If Watts and Sloan come up with something for us at Port Authority, I think so."

A muscle in Mitchell's jaw jumped. "Good. 'Cause I'm ready to end this." She turned and stalked the length of the building to the windows that overlooked the river. She braced both hands against the steel frame and stared out, but she wasn't seeing the water or the ships or the arch of bridge that dwarfed it all. She was remembering the vacant look on the women's faces as the cameras captured their pantomime of passion. She barely moved when she felt Sandy's arms come around her from behind. She knew her lover's touch so well that no words of recognition were necessary.

"What you thinkin'?" Sandy asked, resting her cheek between Mitchell's shoulder blades.

"I was thinking that I'm no better than that guy in the video. Just using her—only because I'm doing it in the name of justice, it's somehow supposed to be better." Her tone was bitter, her body stiff and unyielding.

"Somehow I don't see *that* guy feeling guilty about getting off," Sandy said. She stood on her tiptoes and kissed the back of Mitchell's neck, her arms crossed around Mitchell's middle. "And because he never gave it a thought and you're standing here feeling bad about giving her what I'm willing to bet she *wants*, that shoots your argument full of holes, rookie."

"The lieutenant said this morning that it takes somebody special to be undercover." Mitchell's voice wavered. "I don't think I can do it."

Sandy angled her hips and spun Mitchell around to face her, then planted her palms flat against Mitchell's chest. "Let's just get clear on what's really going on, okay? Do you feel bad because you're lying to Irina or lying to yourself?"

Mitchell frowned. "What do you mean?"

"What do you feel worse about?" Sandy said slowly, as if speaking to a child. "That Irina doesn't know you're a cop, or because deep down inside, you really want to fuck her?"

"What I feel bad about," Mitchell said quietly, "is that deep down inside, I really don't."

Sandy cupped her fingers around the edge of Mitchell's jaw and kissed her sweetly on the mouth. "I knew it had to be something twisted like that, because only you could get yourself all worked up over *not* wanting something."

Despite herself, Mitchell grinned. "You think you've got me all figured out, don't you."

Solemnly, Sandy shook her head. "Uh-uh." She moved her hand over Mitchell's heart. "The only thing I know for sure is that you're good. *Really* good, inside. I love that about you."

Mitchell swept her up into a hug, lifting her off her feet with the force of the embrace. She kissed her, holding her off the ground, lost inside her. Only Sandy's fist in her hair tugging her head back brought her back to awareness.

"Jesus, baby, cut it out," Sandy ordered. "We're supposed to be working here."

Chest heaving, Mitchell set her down but kept her arms loosely around Sandy's waist. "I love you. You make everything inside of me feel right."

Sandy smiled. "Ditto, rookie. Ditto."

Monday, 5:20 p.m., Police Plaza

"You think we'll be able to get this by Clark?" Watts asked as he and Rebecca stepped off the elevators.

"Not indefinitely, but maybe just long enough."

"You think maybe we should wait on telling Henry, then?"

Rebecca shook her head as they approached the Vice Squad room. "We need to put Mitch back in Ziggie's tonight, or else Irina will wonder why he's not there. And I don't think she's going to wait another night to get him alone somewhere. We have to alert Henry that we may need backup if the bust goes down. We can't risk Mitch out there by himself."

"When are you going to let me listen to that tape from last night?" Watts asked for the tenth time.

"You're starting to piss me off, Watts," Rebecca warned.

"If *I'd* been with you instead of riding hind tit in the second car on the surveillance last night, *I* woulda got to hear Mitch in action instead of Sloan." His tone turned wistful. "I bet that boy is smooth."

Rebecca stopped short just outside Henry's office. "Watts, are you trying to tell me you think you can learn something from Mitchell about the ladies?"

"Have you happened to see the way Sandy looks at her? Like she's been starving for a month, and Mitchell's USDA prime."

"We're not going there." Rebecca shook her head and knocked on Captain Henry's door. "End of conversation."

"All the same," Watts muttered as he followed her inside. "I shoulda been listening."

Then the rumble of Henry's deep voice commanded their attention as the door swung closed behind them. *Showtime.*

Chapter Thirty-Two

Monday, 6:40 p.m., University Hospital

"Well," Catherine said, slowing as she approached Rebecca, who leaned against a column in the hospital lobby. "*This* is a nice surprise."

Rebecca pushed away from the column and kissed Catherine's cheek. "Done for the day?"

Catherine hooked her arm through Rebecca's as they both turned toward the lobby exit. "I am. And I don't have any patients scheduled tonight. How about you?"

"I've got work later." Rebecca went on quickly, "I thought we could grab a bite to eat, unless you want to have something at home?"

"Let's do something easy, and you can tell me what prompted you to come pick me up."

"It's not enough that I missed you and wanted to see you?"

Catherine smiled softly. "Oh, it most certainly is. Anything whatsoever that brings you here unexpectedly is perfect." She squeezed Rebecca's arm. "However, with you, there's always a reason."

Rebecca let out a sigh. "I don't know how it happened that you know me better than I know myself."

On the sidewalk in front of the hospital, Catherine turned to face her lover and kissed her quickly but affirmatively on the lips. "Oh, darling. That's what happens when you love someone."

"I don't feel like I'm doing a very good job in that department, then." Rebecca's voice held real worry. "I have no idea half the time how to show you how much I love you."

"You don't have to worry about it, darling. You do it without even knowing it."

"Lucky for me," Rebecca muttered.

"*But*," Catherine said, making Rebecca's brow furrow in concern, "if you really, really love me, you'll take me to the diner and we'll have something sinful like ribs and French fries."

"Now that," Rebecca said with surety, "is something I can do."

Fifteen minutes later they sat with a mound of nachos supreme between them, a beer for Catherine and coffee for Rebecca on the table, making small talk. Catherine munched a chip and studied her lover. "What's happening tonight?"

"We're heading back to Ziggie's again," Rebecca said after a few seconds' hesitation. "There's a good chance that Mitch will get invited back to the stash house tonight. If he does, we'll probably take it down."

"That's what you've been wanting, isn't it?" Catherine's heart raced with sudden anxiety. She knew without needing to be told that a place holding illegal immigrants—for all practical purposes, sex slaves—would be heavily guarded by men who would think nothing of shooting police officers.

"Yes, but there's more to the picture than just where the girls are held and who's running them. Once we move on this house, we'll have exposed our hand. Everyone involved in the smuggling operation will run for cover, including the dockworkers who were in on the transfer of the girls from the ships."

"I see. You need to coordinate all those arrests."

Rebecca sighed. "Unfortunately, we need to coordinate it with the feds. It's the only way to make sure we get the Port Authority guys rounded up."

"And that means Clark."

"Yeah."

"Does he know yet?"

"No, but Henry has called a command meeting for nine. With Clark." She sipped her coffee and grimaced. "He didn't give me any room on this. I'm just waiting for Sloan to give me the names of the inside men at the PA. She's been pulling stuff together all day down at the docks. I talked to her right before I met you, and she says she's close."

Catherine reached across the table and covered Rebecca's hand with hers. "I know how much it means to you to put an end to the abuse of these young girls. And to catch the man who killed Jeff."

Rebecca threaded her fingers through Catherine's. "It's my job. It's what I'm paid to do." She blew out a breath. "And yeah, it's personal this time." She gave Catherine a long look. "But I won't let my feelings for Jeff cloud my judgment. I won't risk Mitchell. She's my priority tonight."

Catherine said nothing, waiting.

"And I won't be a hero," Rebecca conceded. She lifted Catherine's hand and skimmed her lips over Catherine's knuckles. "I won't let you down. I promise."

"There, you see?" Catherine said softly. "You *do* know just what I need."

Monday, 7:45 p.m., Sloan and Lassiter Residence

The elevator doors slid open soundlessly, and Michael stepped into the loft. She started down the hall toward her office alcove and stopped short when she saw Sloan stretched out on one of the sofas. It was such an unusual sight that she simply stood and stared. There was no question—Sloan was asleep. Carefully, Michael set down her briefcase and tiptoed into the living area. She knelt by the side of the couch and brushed back the dark hair from Sloan's forehead. Then she leaned over and kissed her softly on the lips.

"Mmm, nice," Sloan murmured, eyes still closed, as she stretched, then cupped her fingers behind Michael's head. She returned the kiss lingeringly before opening her eyes. "Hi."

"Hi," Michael said softly. She rested her elbow on the sofa and propped her chin in her palm, stroking Sloan's cheek with her free hand. "Why didn't you call me and let me know you were coming home? I would've left the office earlier."

"I don't think you're supposed to be working yet," Sloan observed.

"I feel much better, and I didn't drive. I didn't even spend that much time on the computer. I just met with the various division heads to make certain our current projects were on schedule."

"Uh-huh. I know what those meetings are like. It couldn't have been an easy day."

Michael rose, indicated for Sloan to sit up, and then settled behind her on the sofa, guiding Sloan's head back into her lap. She ran her fingers through Sloan's hair and replied, "It was fine, really. I know not to overdo. Believe me, I don't want to end up back in bed." She laughed softly. "Well, at least not because I have a headache."

Sloan grinned and rubbed her cheek against Michael's breast. "If I had a little more time, I'd take you up on that not-so-subtle suggestion."

"Darling, you can be sure I'll never be subtle about wanting to make love with you." She brushed her fingers down the center of Sloan's chest and edged her fingers beneath the waistband of Sloan's trousers.

Sloan groaned. "I have to work tonight. No teasing."

Michael grew still. "The surveillance again?"

"Yeah. Plus a meeting at Police Plaza in an hour. I just wanted to see you for a few minutes." She grinned. "I didn't intend to fall asleep."

"No," Michael murmured, keeping her hand against Sloan's stomach. "That's very unusual for you. Are you all right?"

"I'm okay. Don't worry."

"Don't ask me to do the impossible," Michael said with a gentle smile. She leaned down and kissed Sloan again. "Did you get what you were after today?"

Sloan's fatigue dropped away and her eyes brightened. "Oh yeah. These guys were playing a pretty nifty shell game, moving containers from one spot to another and conveniently forgetting to log in the secondary locations. They bypassed the initial Customs inspection that way. Once the girls were picked up and transported from the docks, they moved the container back to the original location and altered the documentation stored in the computer."

"And no one noticed the discrepancies?"

Sloan shook her head. "There's no reason to review those records as long as all of the merchandise contracted for is eventually received. Since the containers carrying the girls held no legitimate merchandise, there was no reason to track their contents. And you'd never find that out unless you followed individual containers from point of origin to final destination, *and* coming off those specific ships. These guys were counting on the fact that no one would. And no one did—until today."

"It sounds too simple to work."

"Exactly," Sloan said with a hint of respect. "The simpler the scam, the more likely it is to go unnoticed."

"So—is tonight going to end it?"

Sloan's eyes darkened and her expression hardened. "One way or the other."

Michael drew Sloan's face closer to her breasts, holding her tightly. Everything that needed to be said had already been said. Sloan had made her promise, and Michael trusted her to keep it.

Monday, 9:00 p.m., One Police Plaza

Rebecca leaned with one shoulder against the wall, her arms folded across her chest, taking stock of the others present as she waited for the meeting to begin. Avery Clark stood with his back to the room, his hands loosely clasped at the base of his spine, his legs slightly spread—a position that suggested military training somewhere in his background. He appeared oblivious to the low hum of conversation in the room, but Rebecca had no doubt that he was completely aware of everything that was transpiring. Sloan sat at the small conference table, her laptop open, apparently engrossed in whatever program she was running. Rebecca had no doubt that Sloan, too, knew exactly where everyone was positioned and precisely what was happening. Mitchell occupied another chair at the table and, with her legs stretched out in front of her and her hands tucked into the pockets of her jeans, appeared genuinely calm. Watts, looking bored, drummed his fingers on the tabletop.

The door opened and Henry walked in, looking neither right nor left but walking directly to the head of the table. He did not sit, but leaned with his broad hands braced on the tabletop. "Lieutenant, bring us up to speed."

Rebecca straightened. She was aware of Clark turning from the window to face her, but she kept her eyes on her captain as she gave a succinct rundown of the evidence they had gathered, stopping at one point for Sloan to update the group on the results of her computer searches at Port Authority. She ended by saying, "We believe that our undercover operatives will have the location of at least one stash house tonight. I'm sure there are others, but we should be able to get more information on that from the suspects we bring in."

"And if you can't," Clark said mildly, "then all you'll have done is apprehend a few midlevel enforcers while alerting the entire organization to how much we know. Or don't know."

"Between the inside men on the docks, the bodyguards, and the girls themselves, we'll find someone who wants to deal," Rebecca said with confidence.

"The longer we wait," Henry interjected, "the more chance that they'll move the girls permanently or that someone may get wind of our investigation." He grimaced. "God knows, *this* place leaks like a sieve."

"Working on that, Captain," Sloan said jauntily.

Henry just grunted.

"Since the moment we infiltrated the Internet pornography ring," Rebecca said, "the organization has to have known we might get wind of the bigger picture. We can't chance waiting until they move this arm of their operation somewhere else. I recommend that we go now."

"I concur," Henry said. "I'll make the calls."

"That won't be necessary," Clark said. "Since we have jurisdiction, we'll handle that."

"You might have jurisdiction," Rebecca countered smoothly, in a surprisingly calm tone, "over *some* aspects of the investigation, but you won't have anything at all if we don't find the stash house."

"Meaning?"

Rebecca lifted her shoulder. "*Meaning,* it's our show. If you want your team to pick up the dockworkers and the inside men at Port Authority, be my guest." She turned to Henry. "But it's my people undercover, and I'm the one who will be leading the takedown team."

"Seems fair," Henry said. "Lieutenant, why don't you and Clark coordinate the details of the joint strikes. We'll have an assault team standing by in case you think it's necessary. You'll lead the assault on the stash house, Lieutenant."

"Yes, sir," Rebecca said, careful to keep the triumph from her voice. She waited until Henry left to make his calls and secure the necessary warrants before turning her attention fully to Clark. "Just how much of this did you already know when you put Jimmy Hogan undercover?"

"We didn't *know* anything," Clark replied. "We've known for some time that trafficking in girls from Eastern Europe and Mexico was picking up, but we didn't know their points of entry and, more importantly, their destinations once they were over the border. Now and then we'd get intelligence from girls who'd been arrested or who'd run away from abusive *owners*, and we'd get some hint of how big this had become. Hogan never had a chance to get close."

"That you know of."

Clark nodded. "I suspect he was closer than he realized, and that's what led them to take him out."

"If you'd told us," Sloan said through clenched jaws, "we might have found the connections a lot faster."

"If I'd known where to point you," he rejoined, "I would have. Only a team like yours has the street intelligence to make this kind of case."

"Yeah," Watts grunted. "And then when we do, you can take the credit."

Clark smiled. "I don't want the credit, Detective. I just want a good source of information."

"Well, this time," Rebecca said flatly, "you're going to have to get in line."

Monday, 11:30 p.m., Seventh and Fitzpatrick

"It's gonna happen tonight, isn't it," Sandy said as she watched Mitchell strap the ankle holster just above the bottom of her jeans.

"Probably."

Sandy drew her legs up onto the sofa, wrapped her arms around them, and rested her chin on her knees. "You think the guy who killed Trudy will be there?"

"The lieutenant does." Mitchell settled beside Sandy on the couch and draped an arm around her shoulder. "I think so too. He has to be a ground-level part of the operation, because every step we've made, he's been right behind us. This guy knows who we are."

"Do you think he knows Mitch?"

Mitchell tightened her hold and kissed Sandy's cheek. "I don't know, honey. I don't think so."

"You're gonna be inside that house alone with her, Dell."

"Sandy, I'm not…"

"I don't *care* what you do with her," Sandy said vehemently, turning to press against Mitchell's side. She kissed Mitchell's neck, then her mouth. "Just don't get your ass shot up."

"Wouldn't think of it," Mitchell murmured, stroking Sandy's cheek before kissing her again.

Finally Sandy drew away and took a long shuddering breath. She stood, extending her hand. "Come on, then. Let's get Mitch ready to roll."

Chapter Thirty-Three

Tuesday, 1:40 a.m., Tenth and Arch

Static filled the interior of the Ford Taurus.

"Jesus, can't you clean that up?"

Sloan heard the uncharacteristic edge of anxiety in Rebecca's voice as she made some adjustments to the receiver. "Mitch is probably standing behind some kind of barrier—a concrete column maybe, or a steel door."

"I thought you could get through anything with that. I've got to know what's happening every second. Christ." Rebecca looked out the driver's window at the blacked-out windows of the long, low-slung building. There was very little traffic, and the street was eerily dark. Even the streetlights had been knocked out by gangs using them for target practice. What little illumination there was came from the flickering red fluorescent sign that announced Ziggie's. The place looked like a black hole, and she had two of her people inside. She flicked a glance in the rearview mirror and checked on Watts, moderately comforted to see him sitting in a similar nondescript department-issue vehicle on the opposite side of the street.

"Don't worry, this kind of interference is usually temp—"

> "Hello, new boy. You are late."
>
> "Oh yeah? Have you been missing me?"
>
> Low throaty laughter. "Give me your hand. Mmm, you feel? What do you think?"
>
> "I think your nipples are hard because you've been imagining my mouth on them." Mitch's voice came through the small speakers sounding rough and urgent. "I bet you're wet too."
>
> "Maybe. But maybe not for you."
>
> "Oh no. It's for me. You're on fire."

"You think you know what I want, Mitch?"

"Give me your hand. Now feel that." A quick gasp, a deep groan. "Oh yeah, just like that."

"You've been thinking about me too, new boy." More laughter, sharp and triumphant. "Yesss. I can feel what you brought me, so big and hard already."

"Uh-huh, that's what I thought you wanted. Jesus, go slow."

"Why? You want to come now, I can tell. Come in my hand—do it. Come all over that big cock of yours."

"Not here. Not like this." The sound of quick, panting breaths. "Irina, don't jack me off here. Come on, baby. You know how much I need to come inside you."

"I have a room back there. I want you to fuck me now, new boy."

"No. No. I want to touch all of you. I wanna take my time." A rustle of fabric, a low keening sound of pleasure verging on pain. "You're so wet, baby. I wanna make you come all night long." Another whimper. "Take me home where I can make love to you, Irina. Please."

In the hallway, Irina arched beneath Mitch's hands, her head back, her eyes closed, her fingers clamped around his wrist—pushing his fingers deeper between her thighs. Mitch felt her clitoris lengthen and harden, and knowing she was about to come, lifted his fingers and eased the dangerous pressure.

"Please," she moaned. "Mitch, Mitch…"

"I'll make you come, baby," Mitch murmured, his mouth against her neck. "I promise. I'll make you come until you scream. Just take me home with you."

Eyes glazed, breasts heaving, she dug her fingernails into his arm. "Let me come now."

He moved his fingers from between her legs and cupped her breast, rubbing his thumb gently over her nipple. "Wait, baby. Wait. It will be so much better when I can do you right."

Irina's eyes flared with anger and need. She twisted her fingers in his hair and kissed him, her teeth closing on his lip until he groaned.

❖

"Come on, come on," Rebecca muttered, staring at the rectangular metal box propped on the console between the front seats. Her fists were closed tightly on her thighs, and she had to fight the urge to jump from the car and storm into the building. "Give us a fucking address."

"He's almost got her," Sloan said quietly, intently. Every few seconds she made minute adjustments to the dials, modulating the sound and damping the background static.

> "Bastard!"
>
> "Oh, come on, baby, just think about me inside you, how good it will be."
>
> "I don't know— "
>
> "They'll be closing here in twenty minutes. I'll just follow you home."
>
> "No." Firm and sharp. "No, they will be watching for that."
>
> "Who? Who will be watching?"
>
> "It is not important. You come in an hour."
>
> "An hour's a long time to wait when I'm this hard."
>
> Laughter, light and relaxed. "Then you'll be sure to come, no?"
>
> "Oh yeah, baby. I'm going to come all right. And so are you."

Five minutes later, Jasmine exited the club and walked at a leisurely pace down the street. No one followed, and after one quick scan of the street, she crossed directly to Watts's vehicle and got in the passenger side. Ten minutes later, Mitch came out the door and strode directly to the car that he and Jasmine had arrived in.

"He's got the address," Sloan said with satisfaction.

Mitch's voice came through the speaker clearly. "I'm supposed to park in an alley behind the 500 block of Levick in North Philly. She's going to let me in the back door in an hour. She didn't give me the exact address but said she'd flick the light over the door twice when she was ready to open it. She's careful."

"Too careful to be taking a stranger into the stash house," Rebecca said with a frown, frustrated by the lack of two-way communication. "And that's what's worried me the whole time about this setup. Why the hell would she risk it?"

"Mitch isn't exactly a stranger. He came with the regulars, and that made him part of the scene. And let's face it. He's got her hooked so bad, she's not thinking straight." Sloan laughed softly. "Jesus, he's dangerous."

"Still, I wish I could talk to him."

"Mitch knows the plan. He'll be fine, because we'll be right behind him."

"Let's make sure we are." Rebecca checked her watch. "We'll wait another twenty minutes to make sure Irina and the girls are gone. Then we'll drive ahead and set up a perimeter around that block."

"Black-and-whites?"

"I don't see any reason for an assault team at this point. They'll just—"

Mitch's voice cut in. "I'm going to drive around for a while, because I don't want anyone who might be looking to see me hanging out here." There was a beat of silence. "See you when it's over."

Rebecca watched Mitch's car pull away, then reached for her two-way. "This is Detective Lieutenant Rebecca Frye, requesting backup at the following location."

Her mind was clear, her focus sharp. It had begun.

Tuesday, 2:46 a.m., North Philadelphia

Mitchell sat in the car in the dark in the narrow alley that ran behind a series of opposing row houses identical to those that lined every block in North Philadelphia like so many Monopoly houses arranged on a board. Every fourth or fifth building showed a light burning somewhere, but less than a handful had the single lamp adjacent to the rear door lit. Ground-floor garages opened onto the alley with narrow second-floor decks jutting out over them. The back door was tucked beneath the overhang adjacent to the garage. She guessed that the door opened into a room or hallway that led to the stairs to the rest of the house. With luck, the rear entrance wouldn't be guarded, at least not on the basement level. She could only assume that was the case, since Irina apparently planned to let her into the building that way.

She checked her watch and peered into the gloom at the far end of the alley. She wondered where the lieutenant would set up the perimeter. She was out there, she was confident of that. She couldn't see her, or hear her, but she knew that the lieutenant and the rest of the team were behind her. She waited another minute, then got out of the car and carefully closed it as soundlessly as possible. She started slowly down the alley, scanning the rear of the buildings ahead. One light flickered twice in rapid succession, and, after counting down the row from the corner to identify which one it was, she whispered the location. Then she hurried toward it.

"Shh. You must be very quiet. The others are asleep."
"Jesus, it's dark down here."
"Here. Take my hand."
"Are you sure we won't wake everyone up?"
"They are all upstairs. My room is on the first floor."

"This is Frye," Rebecca said into her radio. "Hold your positions until I give the word." Then she switched channels. "Watts? You set?"

"I'm in the middle of the block facing the fronts of the buildings with two uniforms. Nothing happening. You?"

"Mitchell's inside, eighth house from the corner. You go on my order."

"Roger. Watch your ass."

"Thanks. You too." She clicked off her radio and turned to Sloan. "I want to get closer to the building. I'll take the receiver now."

"Bullshit. I'm coming. You need your hands *and* your eyes clear. I'll monitor Mitchell's transmissions."

"You can come down the alley, but you stay back when we go inside."

"I've got a vest on. I can use a weapon." Sloan's voice held a challenge.

"And you're a civilian—"

"I've got federal credentials," Sloan said flatly as she eased her car door open. "And you can use me. Let's go."

"All right," Rebecca conceded, because Sloan was right. She wanted people she trusted to go in first. Any screwups could cost Mitchell. "But stay the hell behind me when we go through the door."

Sloan grinned. "Yes, ma'am."

> "How do you know they're all asleep?"
>
> "They are. Don't worry."
>
> "So we're finally going to be alone? God, I want to feel your skin against me, all over me."
>
> "Mitch, there is someone else here. A man—"
>
> "Christ, a boyfriend? Husband?"
>
> "No, no Mitch. It is not like that."
>
> "What, then?"
>
> "He…works here."
>
> "Where is he?"

"Come on," Rebecca murmured, her eyes on the rear of the building. "Lay it out for us, Irina. Tell us where he is."

"Is this going to be enough for probable cause?" Sloan asked.

"All she's gotta do is give some indication that those girls are being detained against their will or that they're here illegally. Either one will do it for us."

"And if she doesn't?"

Rebecca met Sloan's eyes head-on. "Mitchell's inside. I'm not leaving her in there, so if we run into reception problems and I can't tell what's going on, I'm going to have to take the door. Whether you come along is up to you."

"Let me know when you're having trouble with the receiver, because I'll be going in with you."

"He is upstairs. My room is down here, in the back… come, Mitch, we are almost there."

"Is he asleep?"

"No. He is watching."

"Watching? Irina, watching who?"

"Don't you know, new boy?"

"No. Irina, what—"

"Us. He watches us. So we stay."

"That's good enough. Let's put Clark to work rounding up the Port Authority suspects, then we go." Rebecca thumbed her radio. "This is red team. Blue team, go." She switched channels yet again. "Watts, there's one guard, upper floor. The girls are up there too. We'll go in silent from the rear, and once we're in position, you'll take the door. Wait for my signal."

"What about Mitchell?"

"Bedroom, first floor. Make sure she's secure. Protect her cover if you can."

"Okay, Loo."

Rebecca glanced at Sloan. "Any good with locks?"

Sloan nodded, her eyes glinting in the moonlight. "Spycraft 101."

"Let's see just how slick you feds really are."

Sloan picked the lock in under sixty seconds. She held the door open, and Rebecca led the way inside, weapon in hand, stepping carefully in the dark.

"Stairs," Rebecca whispered.

A sliver of light at the top of the stairwell gave them direction as they moved stealthily upward. The house was dark and still, so still it was hard to believe that anyone inhabited it. Rebecca's skin tingled, but her pulse was steady and slow. At the top of the stairs she stopped and edged her shoulder to the corner. "Take left."

Without waiting for a response, Rebecca spun into the hallway, her gun arm extended. She had the sense of Sloan moving in tandem with her, facing the opposite direction. The rooms opposite them, their doorways little more than dark yawning mouths, appeared unoccupied. Rebecca pointed with her left hand down the hallway where a staircase ascended to the second floor. Sloan nodded.

Rebecca saw no indication of motion sensors on the walls or ceiling, no cameras, no light beams crossing the hallways that might trigger an alarm if interrupted. Obviously, no one was expecting visitors. In all likelihood, the guard was there more for intimidation of the occupants than for security. Nevertheless, she approached the stairs carefully, her back to the wall, leading with her weapon as she carefully climbed upward. Two steps below the top, she stopped and pressed her radio to her mouth. "Watts, go."

Silently, she counted to ten and then inched around the corner and into the upper hallway. A light shone from an open doorway halfway down, and the muted sound of a television drifted to her. She hand-motioned Sloan to stay behind and cover her. She had just reached the open door to the room when she heard the crack of the front door exploding open. With both arms extended, she swung into the open doorway and swept the room. She caught the blur of motion from the corner of her eye and pivoted in that direction, shouting simultaneously, "*Police!* On the floor."

She heard what sounded like a string of firecrackers on the Fourth of July at the same time as the first bullet struck. The impact knocked her back and she bounced off the opposite wall, lost her footing, and went down. She tried to raise her gun, but her right arm was numb. He was coming, the submachine gun pointed at her head.

Catherine, I'm sorry.

She heard the next shots too, but she didn't feel a thing.

Chapter Thirty-Four

Tuesday, 3:23 a.m.

The staccato sounds thundering in the air shook the walls and trembled through the floorboards.

"What is it?" Irina's voice rose in terror.

The roar was replaced by ominous silence.

"Stay here," Mitchell said sharply as she spun toward the closed bedroom door. Just as she reached it, she heard shouts, the words indecipherable above the crack of splintering wood from somewhere close by. She debated drawing her weapon, but instinct warned her to wait. Only the immediate team members knew she was an undercover cop, and getting shot in a case of mistaken identity would be just plain dumb. She pulled open the door and stepped out into the hall, her hands at shoulder level.

A chorus of voices screamed.

"On the floor! On the floor! Hands above your head. Police."

When Mitchell caught sight of a uniformed officer swinging a weapon toward her chest, she dropped facedown, her arms spread-eagled at her sides. "Irina, get *down*," she yelled toward the bedroom as someone roughly jerked her arms behind her back and cuffed them.

"Got a gun here," a female officer yelled, adrenaline making her voice sharp and brittle.

"Give it here," Watts said as the uniform pulled the revolver from Mitchell's ankle holster.

"Civilian in the bedroom," a male voice called simultaneously.

"You two! Get the civilian out of the building and call for more backup. Leave this one here for now." As the two officers half dragged Irina out the front door, Watts knelt by Mitchell's side. "You okay, kid?"

"Yeah, but all hell's breaking loose upstairs. Jesus." Mitchell jerked her arms. "Get these off."

He keyed the cuffs and they both got to their feet. He handed Mitchell her weapon.

"Here. Clear the downstairs." He hesitated. "And get your badge on before some eager uniform plugs you full of holes."

"I'm coming up with you," she insisted, digging deep into her front pocket for her badge.

"You ain't wearing a vest, and the Loo said to protect your cover. You stay down here for now."

"You might need me."

"I need you, I'll holler." He was already halfway to the stairs and didn't look back.

The hall was filled with the stench of cordite, the pungent smell of blood, and the screams of petrified girls. Watts saw the body on the floor, and the air gushed out of his lungs as if he'd been punched in the gut. *Oh, fuck me, I'm* not *seeing that.*

Sloan pivoted toward him, gun extended, and he yelled, "Police, police. Sloan, it's Watts. Jesus."

"I can tell who the hell it is, for Christ's sake." Sloan's eyes were hard dark stones. "Clear downstairs?"

"Mitchell's sweeping it." Watts wasn't looking at her, but at Rebecca slumped against the wall. "Jesus Christ."

"Call for the ambulance and a coroner." Sloan holstered her weapon and spoke in Russian to the group of young women huddled together at the far end of the hall. Most were garbed only in flimsy sleepwear or T-shirts, all were barefoot, and all were clearly terrified. "They say there's no one else up here," she called back to Watts, "but I'll do a room-to-room. You stay with Rebecca."

"Loo?" Watts knelt by Rebecca's side. Her eyes were open but glazed. Blood shimmered down her face and neck. "Take it easy, Lieutenant. The ambulance will be here in a minute."

He waited, holding his breath, but no answer came.

Catherine opened her eyes to darkness, her heart racing. The bedside clock read 4:26 a.m. She listened for the sound of the key in the lock, but there was only silence. She sat up and reached for her robe. The feeling of foreboding was oppressive and heavy, a weight in her chest that squeezed the air from her lungs and turned her limbs to stone. She forced herself from the bed and, after pulling the robe around her naked body, walked into the living room. When the knock came at the door she was not surprised. For seconds that felt like eternity, she did not move. In that instant she understood the true power of denial. If she did not open the door, she would not suffer the loss. If she did not hear the words, she would not experience the anguish. If she did not accept, it would not be true.

The quiet knock repeated.

Catherine steeled herself and opened the door. She hadn't meant to speak, but when she saw Sloan's face, she whispered an agonized *no*.

"She's hurt, but she's alive. She's at University ER. Ali Torveau's with her."

"I'll just be a minute," Catherine said evenly, but when she turned, her legs were unsteady. She didn't draw away when Sloan's arm came around her waist.

"It's going to be all right," Sloan murmured as she walked beside Catherine back to the bedroom.

"Tell me what happened."

Sloan averted her gaze as Catherine, apparently oblivious to Sloan's presence, removed her robe and stood naked in front of the closet. "We took the stash house. The guard was armed."

"Oh God." Catherine closed her eyes and braced her hand against the closet door.

"She was wearing a vest, Catherine," Sloan hurried on. "I couldn't tell for sure, but I don't think she took a body shot."

"She would have called me if she could have. What aren't you telling me?"

"There's a head wound. I'm not sure how serious."

Catherine gave a small cry before fighting back the terror that threatened to immobilize her. Blanking her mind, she slipped into a blouse and slacks, heedless of the fact that she wore no underwear. She stepped barefoot into low-heeled boots and pulled a blazer off the rack.

She walked determinedly toward the front door with Sloan in her wake. "How could this happen? Who was with her?"

"I was."

Catherine finally looked directly at Sloan. "Are you all right?"

"Yeah."

"And the…person who shot her?"

"Dead." Sloan pointed. "My car's over here."

"You killed him?"

"Yeah." Sloan keyed the remote and opened the passenger door for Catherine.

"Are you sure you're all right?"

Sloan handed Catherine into the car, pulled the seat belt across Catherine's chest, and hooked it. "I'm just fine."

Catherine remembered nothing of the brief, rapid journey to the hospital. She was out of the car nearly before Sloan was able to halt the Porsche in front of the emergency room entrance. She rushed through the automatic double doors into the familiar chaos of the trauma admitting area. Tonight the waiting room was awash with a sea of blue. Tonight, the PPD had turned out en masse in support of one of their fallen brethren. That realization passed quickly through Catherine's mind as she grasped the arm of the first passing nurse. "Lieutenant Frye. Wounded police officer. Where is she?"

"Trauma One, I think."

"Thank you."

Sloan caught up to Catherine before she was halfway down an adjacent hallway that sported curtained exam rooms along both sides. "Maybe you should wait until I find Ali and get an update."

"No. I want to see her now."

"Okay," Sloan relented. "I'll see what I can find out."

Before she could turn back to the crowded waiting room in hopes of finding someone who would be willing to give her information, she heard the deep rumble of a familiar voice.

"Dr. Rawlings," Captain Henry said in a surprisingly soothing tone of voice. "I'm sorry to see you again under these circumstances. Can I get you anything?"

"Where is she?" Catherine asked immediately.

"Radiology, at least the last I heard." He slid an arm beneath Catherine's elbow. "No one is telling us very much, but the doctors listed her in critical, but stable, condition. Why don't you come sit down in the family waiting room."

"She's not in the operating room?"

Henry looked perplexed. "No. No, they said something about a CAT scan."

Some of the terrible pressure around Catherine's heart eased. If they hadn't taken her directly to the operating room, then she couldn't be in grave danger. She might be hurt, but she wasn't dying. *Please, let that be true.*

"I'm going down to radiology," Catherine said.

"Of course," Henry replied.

"You want me to come with you?" Sloan asked.

Catherine shook her head. "No, I'm all right." She smiled at Sloan. "Thank you for coming to get me. You should call Michael. She'll be worried." Suddenly, her expression changed to one of concern. "Everyone else is all right? Dellon? Watts?"

Sloan nodded. "All okay."

"Good. Good. I have to go."

The first thing she saw when she exited the stairwell was Watts pacing in a tight circle with an unlit cigarette dangling from his lips. Then she saw Mitchell, arms crossed, face pale, leaning with one shoulder against the wall next to the entrance to the radiology suite. Still in her tight black jeans and motorcycle jacket, with the curves of her face shadowed and dark, she looked like a dangerous young animal. But her eyes, when they met Catherine's, were drenched with pain.

When he saw her, Watts hurried forward. "I woulda come to get you, but Sloan wanted to."

"It's all right," Catherine said gently. "It's good that you're here watching over her." Her gaze moved to the closed doors. "Is she still in there?"

"Yeah, and they won't tell us a goddamn thing."

"Well, they'll tell me." And then she pushed her way through the doors.

She saw Ali Torveau immediately, leaning over the shoulder of an X-ray technician who was scrolling through a series of images on a computer screen.

"Let me see the cranial cuts again," the trauma surgeon instructed.

"Ali," Catherine said, "how is she?"

Ali Torveau spun around in surprise. "Catherine. Lucky, I think. We're not done with the head CT. When she came in, she was unconscious, but I'm not seeing anything other than some occipital swelling."

"Where was she…shot?" Catherine found it almost impossible to get the words out, but she forced herself. As she asked the questions that were so hard to even conceive, she glanced through the viewing window into the room where the huge machine even now shrouded her lover's body.

"The vest took the brunt of it," Ali said. "We haven't scanned her chest, and there was considerable bruising over the mid-thorax. She may have a fractured sternum, but my main concern is her head. She's got a deep temporal scalp laceration that looks to be from a bullet wound."

For a few seconds, Catherine's vision wavered and she pressed her fingertips to the countertop to steady herself. "Can I see her?"

Ali pulled over a rolling chair and guided Catherine into it. "As soon as the scans are done. I need this information, Catherine."

"But she's going to be all right?"

"Let me finish my evaluation, and then we'll talk, okay?" Ali's tone was gentle but firm, and her attention was once again on the monitor. "Peter, run that series again, will you?"

Hand in hand, Michael and Sandy pushed through the crowd of police.

"There!" Michael pointed, having caught sight of Sloan and Jasmine standing off to one side in the hallway by the elevators.

Sloan looked in their direction at the sound of Michael's voice, and some of the tension drained from her face. Both she and Jasmine hurried to meet them.

"Hey," Sloan murmured, kissing Michael quickly.

Michael rested her palm on Sloan's chest, her eyes roving over her lover's body. "You're all right?"

"Yeah, fine."

Threading an arm around Sloan's waist, Michael turned to Jasmine. "Sarah will be here any minute. I called her on the way over. She's bringing a change of clothes in case you want them."

"At the moment, no one is paying any attention to me," Jasmine replied. Gesturing to her skintight red dress and stiletto heels, she added, "But it won't be long before they do. I think tonight I could do without the attention."

As if on cue, Sarah emerged from the elevator, a canvas tote under one arm. When she saw the group, she approached with her usual composed expression. "Here you go," she said as she kissed Jasmine briefly on the mouth. "How's Rebecca?"

"No word yet." Jasmine squeezed Sarah's hand. "I'll be right back. I just need to find a phone booth."

"Where's Dell?" Sandy asked sharply. Michael had come by to pick her up after Sloan called. When the phone had rung, she hadn't been asleep. She'd been waiting. Waiting and trying not to think about where her girlfriend was or what she might be doing. She'd been entertaining visions of hunting down Irina and tearing her limb from limb. Now all she wanted was to see for herself that Dell was all right. She couldn't have cared less what she might have done with Irina.

"She's downstairs with Watts…where they took Rebecca."

"Okay, thanks." Sandy did a quick 360, spied the stairwell on the far side of the elevators, and headed for it. When she pushed through the fire door on the basement level, she saw Dell immediately. The rush of relief made her weak. That was nothing, though, compared to the way the look on Dell's face made her feel when their eyes met. Warm and shaky and strong all at once. She took three steps forward just as Dell moved to her, and they ended up in the center of the hall with their arms wrapped around one another in a fierce embrace.

"You okay, baby?" Sandy whispered, running her hands up and down Mitchell's back.

"Rebecca's shot," Mitchell said, her face in the curve of Sandy's neck. "God, Sandy. God."

The tremor in her lover's voice almost broke Sandy's heart. "She's gonna be okay, rookie. She's always okay."

"I'm so glad you came." With effort, Mitchell straightened up. "It's like…everything is coming apart."

"Look, rookie," Sandy said, her voice firm. "Frye will be okay. She'll be okay because…" She shrugged. "Because she's what holds all you guys together, and that's not gonna change. You need her, and she knows it, and she won't let anything screw that up."

"You think?" Mitchell whispered, needing desperately to believe.

Sandy smiled and stroked Mitchell's cheek. "I *know.*"

From a few feet away, Watts heard the words and whispered a silent prayer that Sandy was right.

Gunfire echoed in Rebecca's head. The smell of adrenaline and fear and hot metal permeated her consciousness. And somewhere, *somewhere,* struggling for dominance over all the other sensations, was the urgent need to reach Catherine. Catherine. She had to see her. Touch her. Tell her not to worry.

"Catherine," she murmured.

"I'm here. Rebecca, darling, I'm here." Catherine caressed trembling fingers over Rebecca's forehead, gripping Rebecca's hand hard with her free hand. "You're all right, darling."

"Sorry." Rebecca forced her eyes open, then blinked, even though the lights in the intensive care room were dim. After a few seconds of trying, she was able to focus on Catherine's face. There was so much anguish in her eyes, Rebecca shuddered. "Sorry. Didn't mean to frighten you."

"I know." Catherine lifted Rebecca's hand and kissed her knuckles one by one. "I know that. Don't worry, just rest."

"Sloan…Mitchell…my team…hurt?"

"No, darling. All okay." Catherine kissed her gently. *Only you. Will it always be you here like this?*

Rebecca frowned. There were things she couldn't remember. She saw the dark, narrow alley and the back door of the row house, saw herself climbing the pitch-black stairwell and inching down the hallway, saw herself crouching in the doorway and the flash of movement from her right. She jerked slightly, hearing the gunfire again.

"What is it?" Catherine exclaimed as the heart rate readout on the screen over Rebecca's bed jumped twenty points and alarm bells rang. "Are you in pain?"

"He must've been sitting there watching TV with the automatic in his hand." Rebecca grimaced. "Careful bastard."

Catherine didn't want to think about someone lying in wait, ready and willing to kill her lover. But she knew that for Rebecca, talking it out, *working* it out, was the best way to heal. "You couldn't have known."

"I went down, and he kept coming." Speaking slowly, still vague, still in pain, Rebecca moved her eyes back to Catherine's. "I was afraid he would kill me and you would be the one left hurting."

Catherine caught her lower lip between her teeth, but it was too late to stop the tears. "I love you. I love you so much."

"Catherine—love. I'm so sorry."

"I couldn't bear to lose you." Catherine brushed away tears.

"I don't want that to happen. I don't want you hurt—ever." Rebecca squinted against the sudden rush of pain. "Christ, my head is exploding."

"You have a concussion. A substantial one." As she spoke, Catherine scanned the monitors rapidly. Everything seemed stable, and she looked back to her lover. "Your head is going to hurt for a while. Your memory might be a little fuzzy."

"I got hit. I remember that now." Rebecca brought a hand to her chest and pressed lightly, then winced. "Couple of places, it feels like."

"Yes." Catherine closed her eyes against the images that came unbidden. Of Rebecca lying on the warehouse floor, a river of blood pouring from her chest. Rebecca lying pale and motionless in the intensive care unit. Closed her mind to the nightmare of losing her…the empty bed, the silent house, the barren life. She attempted a smile. "Ali says you'll be out of here in a few days."

"Good."

Rebecca closed her eyes for so long that Catherine thought she was asleep. However, when she tried to withdraw her hand, Rebecca's grip on her fingers tightened.

With her eyes still closed, Rebecca said, "I'd quit if I could, so that you would never have to go through this again. But I can't."

"I know." Catherine leaned down, kissed Rebecca's lips. "It's enough that you would if you could."

Chapter Thirty-Five

Tuesday

I killed a man last night."

Sloan said the words so quietly that it took a few seconds for them to register. When Michael understood the significance of what her lover had just said, she tightened her hold on the woman in her arms. Sloan lay with her head on Michael's shoulder, one arm loosely around her waist. Michael rested her cheek against the top of Sloan's head and slowly caressed her back.

"Is that what the detectives were talking to you about for so long at the hospital?"

"Yeah, they were taking my statement." Sloan spoke with her eyes closed, savoring the warmth and scent of Michael's skin. "Took my weapon too. Until the investigation is completed."

"Are you in trouble?"

"I don't think so. I shot the guy that shot Rebecca. No one is going to look too hard at the circumstances."

Michael searched beneath the cool, even tone for what Sloan might not be saying. "This man…is he the one?"

Sloan was quiet for a long moment. "I don't know. He could be." She shrugged. "I think there's a fair chance we'll never know."

"And if we don't? Can you live with that? Can you let it go?"

"Yes." Sloan tilted her head back and opened her eyes. She smiled softly at Michael. "The only thing that matters to me is that you're all right and that we're together."

Michael smiled and kissed Sloan softly. When she drew away, her expression became serious. "Have you ever shot anyone before?"

"No."

"Are you all right with it?"

"He was going to kill Rebecca. Then he was going to come after the rest of us." Sloan's eyes never wavered; her voice remained steady and calm. "I didn't enjoy it, but I'd do it again. If it was the guy that hurt you, I'm glad. Either way, I'm not sorry he's dead."

Michael nodded. "I think I'd rather you do your investigating with the computer from now on."

Sloan grinned. "I think I agree with you."

❖

"Hey," Watts said. "I thought you'd be long gone by now."

Carla Reiser smiled up from her desk. "Fat chance. I've got about seven hundred more forms to fill out."

"That all?" Watts ambled in and sagged into one corner of the sofa. "The feds gone?"

"From your mouth to God's ears," Carla said fervently.

Watts chuckled. "I guess you liked spending the night with Clark about as much as I would have."

"Officious, condescending men are not my favorite types."

"If I was half as slick as most of the women I work with, I'd say something smart to that." Watts shrugged. "I can't think of anything."

Carla smiled. "I don't require that you be real smooth."

"Good thing." Watts felt around in his jacket pockets for his cigarettes, then gave up. "How did it go?"

"Like clockwork. One thing I'll say for the federal boys, they've got plenty of manpower and neat toys. Once Sloan gave us the names, we had audio and video surveillance up and running on the suspects here and at their homes within hours." Carla stood and walked to the counter where a full pot of coffee steamed. As she poured a cup, she said, "As soon as we got the green light from Lieutenant Frye, we took everyone at once. Only one of the suspects was on shift here last night, and we just walked him out to a car and put him in it. No muss, no fuss. Clark had secondary teams who picked up the other guys at home."

"Is Clark doing the interrogations?"

"That's my understanding." Carla lifted the pot and an inquiring eyebrow in his direction. At his nod, she filled another cup and handed it to him as she sat beside him on the sofa. "Clark made it crystal clear that the smuggling operation was his jurisdiction and we weren't getting any piece of the arrests."

"Any way you look at it, though," Watts said as he sipped gratefully at the coffee, "the organized crime organization in this city just took a big hit. Personally, I don't think Clark is going to get anyone to flip on Zamora, but the feds will bag a nice number of midlevel guys. Enough to make the papers."

"That's fine with me," Carla said. "As long as my docks are clean again, I don't care who gets the glory."

Watts nodded appreciatively. "I'm with you."

"Yes, I noticed. It's kind of nice."

Watts blushed and tried desperately to think of a comeback. He still couldn't.

Sandy curled on one side beneath the covers and watched Mitchell pace, a cell phone to her ear.

"Look, all I want to know is what's going to happen to them." Mitchell blew out a frustrated breath. "Okay, fine. Your best guess, then." She paced a few more steps. "Thanks. Yeah. I'll check again later." She flipped the phone closed, tossed it on a chair, and stripped. Naked, she slid into bed beside Sandy.

"Roll over on your stomach," Sandy said.

"Huh?"

"You're totally wired, Dell. Roll over."

Mitchell flipped onto her stomach and cradled her head in her folded arms. A second later, Sandy settled astride her butt. Her heart and a few other places lurched at the sensation of heat and wet against her skin. She groaned softly.

Sandy pressed the heels of both hands into the center of Mitchell's back and kneaded the tight muscles. "So what did they say?"

"Doesn't matter," Mitchell mumbled, her eyes closed.

"Don't be a jerk. What's going to happen to them?" Sandy shifted lower on Mitchell's rear to get her thumbs into the small dip at the base of Mitchell's spine. She dug them in, circled and stroked, and Mitchell moaned again.

"INS has them…Immigration and Naturalization Services." Mitchell lifted her hips and felt Sandy push back, the start of a slow, steady thrust-and-press that was going to make her awfully hot, awfully fast.

"So they'll do what? Send them back to wherever they came from?" Sandy turned her hand around and slid her fingers lightly down the cleft between Mitchell's legs, barely touching her. A feather-light caress.

"Jesus." Mitchell caught her breath, struggled to focus. "I don't know. They're here illegally, but they're victims too."

"Even Irina?" Sandy asked, her tone casual. She stilled her movements but kept her fingers resting against Mitchell's sex.

"Yeah, I think so. I can't see her having set up any part of that operation." Mitchell rolled her hips and turned onto her back, unseating Sandy in the same motion. She caught Sandy as she started to topple onto the mattress and pulled her down on top of her body.

"What'd you do that for?"

"I gotta see your face if we're gonna talk about this stuff." Mitchell opened her thighs and settled Sandy's hips between them. She kept an arm curved around Sandy's small waist. "And you know what you were doing was gonna make me crazy."

"Maybe," Sandy said with a small smile. "But it relaxes you too. And then you don't notice when you're talking about stuff you don't want to talk about."

Mitchell raised her head and caught Sandy's mouth in a hungry kiss that definitely made her forget what she'd been talking about. When she dropped her head back to the pillow, her body was buzzing. "Pretty smart."

"Is she under your skin?" Sandy asked quietly.

"Not the way you think." Mitchell looked directly into Sandy's eyes. "I don't want her. I don't love her. But I feel…sorta responsible for what's happening to her."

Sandy rolled her eyes. "Jeez, rookie. You didn't put her on that ship or force her to shoot those videos or make her train those girls, or whatever she did with them."

"I know. But…I connected with her. And I used her."

"Most cops wouldn't care about that."

"Rebecca would."

"Yeah yeah." Sandy stretched out full-length on Mitchell's body and nuzzled her neck. "And so do you." She caressed Mitchell's chest, her abdomen, the tops of her thighs with slow, soothing strokes. "So you're going to keep asking around, and I suppose you're probably gonna go see her."

"I don't know. I'm sure the feds will keep them here until they find out everything they can about the smuggling operation. The girls probably know something about the local organized crime operation too." Mitchell caught Sandy's hand and pressed it between her thighs, keeping her fingers over Sandy's. "There's probably nothing I can do to help them."

Sandy eased a finger on either side of Mitchell's firm clitoris. "But you're going to try."

"Yeah," Mitchell said, a hitch in her voice. She squeezed Sandy's fingers hard around her. "Probably."

"Okay."

"Okay?" Mitchell's belly was on fire.

"I know you gotta." Sandy slicked her tongue over Mitchell's lips, darted inside her mouth, and teased at her with quick flicks. She matched the movements with her fingertips between Mitchell's legs. She watched Mitchell's eyes glaze over and her eyelids flutter nearly closed. "And I know you're mine."

Then she proved it.

Rebecca turned her head toward the door as a shaft of bright light cut across the room. "I thought you were going to go home and get some sleep."

"I was. I did." Catherine crossed to the bed, leaned down, and kissed Rebecca. "I couldn't sleep." She stroked Rebecca's cheek with the back of her fingers. "How are you feeling?"

"Better." Carefully, Rebecca inched toward the opposite side of the bed and patted the space beside her with the hand that did not have the intravenous line attached. "Want to stretch out?"

Catherine kicked off her shoes, then unbuttoned her suit jacket and draped it over a nearby chair. She'd showered and changed when she'd gotten home. At the moment, a few wrinkles were the least of her worries. Taking care not to jostle the bed, knowing that Rebecca's headache must still be brutal, she eased down beside her lover. She grasped Rebecca's hand, entwined their fingers, and leaned her cheek lightly against Rebecca's shoulder. "I always have a hard time falling asleep when you're not beside me."

Rebecca brushed her lips over Catherine's hair. "I know. I'll try to get home earlier from now on."

"Now *there's* something to look forward to." Catherine closed her eyes and sighed. "Is this investigation over?"

"Our part of it. For now," Rebecca answered quietly. "We've exposed the human smuggling operation, crippled the Internet pornography ring, and freed some of the victims. We've taken a respectable chunk out of organized crime, but it takes more than this to break its back. We'll gain ourselves a few well-positioned informants within Zamora's organization, and that will help us in the future."

"Just one chapter in the book," Catherine murmured.

"Yeah," Rebecca agreed. "That's what police work is all about. The story never really ends."

Rebecca closed her eyes, and together, they slept.

About the Author

Radclyffe is the author of numerous lesbian romances (*Safe Harbor* and its sequels *Beyond the Breakwater* and *Distant Shores, Silent Thunder*; *Innocent Hearts*, *Love's Melody Lost*, *Love's Tender Warriors*, *Tomorrow's Promise*, *Passion's Bright Fury*, *Love's Masquerade*, *shadowland*, and *Fated Love*), as well as two romance/intrigue series: the Honor series (*Above All, Honor*; *Honor Bound*, *Love & Honor*, *Honor Guards*) and the Justice series (*Shield of Justice*, the prequel *A Matter of Trust*, *In Pursuit of Justice*, and *Justice in the Shadows*).

A 2003/2004 recipient of the Alice B. award for her body of work as well as a member of the Golden Crown Literary Society, Pink Ink, and the Romance Writers of America, she lives with her partner, Lee, in Philadelphia, PA, where she both writes and heads Bold Strokes Books, a lesbian publishing company. She states, "As an author, I know how much more it takes to 'make a book' than just adding a cover to a manuscript. Done with respect and love for the craft, creating a book is a never-ending joy. As a publisher, my mission is to provide that experience to every author at Bold Strokes Books."

Her upcoming works include selections in *Stolen Moments: Erotic Interludes 2* from Bold Strokes Books, *After Dark* from Bella Books, *Hot Lesbian Erotica* from Cleis, the next novel in the Honor series, *Honor Reclaimed* (Dec. 2005), and the romance *Turn Back Time* (Feb. 2006).

Look for information about these works at www.boldstrokesbooks.com.

Other Books Available From Bold Strokes Books

Course of Action by Gun Brooke. Actress Carolyn Black desperately wants the starring role in an upcoming film produced by Annelie Peterson, a wealthy publisher with a mysterious past. How far is Carolyn prepared to go for the dream part of a lifetime? And just how far will Annelie bend her principles in the name of desire? (1-933110-22-8)

Justice Served by Radclyffe. The hunt for an informant in the ranks draws Lieutenant Rebecca Frye, her lover Dr. Catherine Rawlings, and Officer Dellon Mitchell into a deadly game of hide-and-seek with an underworld kingpin who traffics in human souls. (1-933110-15-5)

Rangers at Roadsend by Jane Fletcher. After nine years in the Rangers, dealing with thugs and wild predators, Sergeant Chip Coppelli has learned to spot trouble coming, and that is exactly what she sees in her new recruit, Katryn Nagata. But even so, Chip was not expecting murder. The Celaeno series. (1-933110-28-7)

Distant Shores, Silent Thunder by Radclyffe. Ex-lovers, would-be lovers, and old rivals find their paths unwillingly entwined when Drs. KT O'Bannon and Tory King—and the women who love them—are forced to examine the boundaries of love, friendship, and the ties that transcend time. (1-933110-08-2)

Hunter's Pursuit by Kim Baldwin. A raging blizzard, a remote mountain hideaway, and more than one killer for hire set a scene for disaster—or desire—when reluctant assassin Katarzyna Demetrious rescues a stranger and unwittingly exposes her heart.
(1-933110-09-0)

The Walls of Westernfort by Jane Fletcher. All Temple Guard Natasha Ionadis wants is to serve the Goddess, and she volunteers eagerly for a dangerous mission to infiltrate a band of rebels. But once she is away from the temple, the issues are no longer so simple, especially in light of her attraction to one of the rebels. Is it too late to work out what she really wants from life? (1-933110-24-4)

Change Of Pace: *Erotic Interludes* by Radclyffe. Twenty-five hot-wired encounters guaranteed to spark more than just your imagination. Erotica as you've always dreamed of it.
(1-933110-07-4)

Fated Love by Radclyffe. Amidst the chaos and drama of a busy emergency room, two women must contend not only with the fragile nature of life, but also with the mysteries of the heart and the irresistible forces of fate. (1-933110-05-8)

Justice in the Shadows by Radclyffe. In a shadow world of secrets, lies, and hidden agendas, Detective Sergeant Rebecca Frye and her lover, Dr. Catherine Rawlings, join forces once again in the elusive search for justice. (1-933110-03-1)

shadowland by Radclyffe. In a world on the far edge of desire, two women are drawn together by power, passion, and dark pleasures. An erotic romance. (1-933110-11-2)

Love's Masquerade by Radclyffe. Plunged into the often indistinguishable realms of fiction, fantasy, and hidden desires, Auden Frost discovers a shifting landscape that will force her to question everything she has believed to be true about herself and the nature of love. (1-933110-14-7)

Beyond the Breakwater by Radclyffe. One Provincetown summer three women learn the true meaning of love, friendship, and family. Second in the Provincetown Tales. (1-933110-06-6)

Tomorrow's Promise by Radclyffe. One timeless summer, two very different women discover the power of passion to heal and the promise of hope that only love can bestow. (1-933110-12-0)

Love's Tender Warriors by Radclyffe. Two women who have accepted loneliness as a way of life learn that love is worth fighting for and a battle they cannot afford to lose. (1-933110-02-3)

Love's Melody Lost by Radclyffe. A secretive artist with a haunted past and a young woman escaping a life that proved to be a lie find their destinies entwined. (1-933110-00-7)

Safe Harbor by Radclyffe. A mysterious newcomer, a reclusive doctor, and a troubled gay teenager learn about love, friendship, and trust during one tumultuous summer in Provincetown. First in the Provincetown Tales. (1-933110-13-9)

Above All, Honor by Radclyffe. The first in the Honor series introduces single-minded Secret Service Agent Cameron Roberts and the woman she is sworn to protect—Blair Powell, the daughter of the president of the United States. First in the Honor series.
(1-933110-04-X)

Love & Honor by Radclyffe. The president's daughter and her security chief are faced with difficult choices as they battle a tangled web of Washington intrigue for...love and honor. Third in the Honor series. (1-933110-10-4)

Honor Guards by Radclyffe. In a journey that begins on the streets of Paris's Left Bank and culminates in a wild flight for their lives, the president's daughter and those who are sworn to protect her wage a desperate struggle for survival. Fourth in the Honor series.
(1-933110-01-5)

BOLD
STROKES
BOOKS